THE WATCH

THE WATCH

A Novel

CARLO LEVI

STEERFORTH ITALIA

AN IMPRINT OF STEERFORTH PRESS · SOUTH ROYALTON, VERMONT

Copyright © 1999, 1951 by Carlo Levi

First published in 1951 by Farrar, Straus & Young.

ALL RIGHTS RESERVED

For information about permission to
reproduce selections from this book, write to:
Steerforth Press, P.O. Box 70,
South Royalton, Vermont 05068

Library of Congress Cataloging-in-Publication Data

Levi, Carlo, 1902–1975
  [Orologio. English]
  The watch : a novel / Carlo Levi.
    p. cm.
  Originally published: New York : Farrar, Strauss & Young, 1951.
  ISBN 1–883642–81–7 (alk. paper)
  I. Title.
PQ4827.E930713 1999
853'.917—dc21   99–15665
                                           CIP

Manufactured in the United States of America

FIRST PRINTING

I

*A*T NIGHT IN ROME ONE SEEMS to hear lions roaring. The breathing of the city is an indistinct murmur among its dark domes and faraway hills in the darkness sparkling here and there with lights; and once in a while there is the hoarse noise of foghorns, as if the sea were nearby and ships were leaving port for unknown horizons. And then that sound, at the same time vague and wild, cruel but not without a strange sweetness, the roaring of lions in the night desert of houses.

I've never understood what causes that noise. Perhaps invisible factories or automobiles on the slope? Or perhaps the sound comes not from the present but rather from the depth of memory when wild animals roamed between the Tiber and the woods along the solitary hills, and wolves still nursed abandoned children?

I bent over to listen intently and peered into the dark over the roofs and towers, into that world crowded with shadows, and the sound penetrated me like an image from childhood, terrifying, moving, and mysterious, bound to a distant time. Even if born of machines, it was an animal sound that seemed to issue from hidden bowels or from throats open to search in vain for an impossible word. It isn't the metallic sound of the streetcars at night on the curves, the long and exciting rasp of the Turin streetcars, the sorrowful but confident cry of those nights when we were at work in the cold and empty air. It is a sound full of apathy, a bestial yawn, vague and terrible.

One can hear this roaring from all parts of the city. I'd listened to it the first time years ago coming through the grating of a cell in the Regina Coeli prison, along with the shouts of the sick and insane in the prison infirmary and the distant clang of iron bars. It seemed to me then like the very breath of that mysterious freedom that must still exist outside. Now I was listening to it a few months after the liberation of Rome from a room high above the Via Gregoriana, an ephemeral and temporary port in those times of change, as a providential destiny led us here and there.

This room was ephemeral and temporary indeed, like the hundreds of others where I'd slept, hidden, and worked, ever since a tempestuous wind had started to blow over the bitter lands of Europe and had carried men like leaves stripped from the trees along white, unknown roads. Now, after seven years of pain and slaughter, the wind had fallen, but the old leaves still could not return to their branches and the cities looked like naked woods, waiting under a modest sun for the haphazard flowering of new buds. Yes, the cities had somehow gone back to wilderness since men had abandoned their familiar walls, and behind every street corner danger was hiding and green uniforms ran like lizards on the asphalt. Death could be anywhere and black and obscene blood was spreading over the pavements. Now, in the forest of Rome, the hue and cry and gunfire of the manhunt were finished, exuberant sap burst through the trees; but how difficult it still was to fine a refuge!

The difficulty of finding a refuge wasn't due so much to material reasons, like the shortage of housing because of the sudden arrival of big crowds of people, but rather to a shifting in motive, a deeper crisis, a desecration of a world poor and petty, yet accustomed to permanence.

For a year now houses hadn't been places to live in, to stay in permanently, closed and private, but hideouts, transient refuges, likely to be violated at any moment. Behind the blinds girls no longer peeked out, but there were men with their ears strained for the noise of hobnailed steps, their minds on the hidden exits and pathways over the roofs. Actual and cruel intrigues were substituted for the intimate feminine intrigues of the forgotten days of peace, when searching for a room was a small journey of adventure into a world miserable yet filled with an antiquated candor of its own, an underworld of expedience, scheming, and privation, certain of the expedience, scheming, and privation of tomorrow.

Many years before, around 1930, I'd lived in the furnished rooms of Rome and I knew them. In those almost prehistoric days, I used to work near the Porta San Giovanni. I'd wanted to live down there rather than in a hotel in the center of town to save time and avoid the boredom of travel. So I set out with a friend to search for a lodging in the petty bourgeois neighborhood around the basilica. There was no front door without a FOR RENT sign on it. Renting rooms is in a way a form of prostitution, if only mild and symbolic, a giving of part of oneself for money. The whole quarter seemed agreed on that vocation. We climbed the dark stairs of great palaces in that part of Rome whose architecture was inspired by the Piedmontese. We rang doorbells, stepped over wet rags and pails of dirty water in the halls, and were led by enormous matrons to admire Turkish divans, parlors filled with dolls, and bathrooms smelling of chlorine and strung across with laundry. From the coatracks hung officer's capes, sabers, and caps. We caught glimpses of unmade beds, stockings, old slippers, and skirts. We heard laughter and whispers, and through a half-open door the mean, black look of a girl appraised us from under her dark, untidy hair.

We fled from these horrors and went down the stairs, only to climb up another identical flight and everywhere the same world of officers, Sicilian noblemen, petty clerks, *commendatori*, girls, chlorine, stuffed dolls, Turkish beds, buckets of dirty water, rags, furtively revealed thighs and armpits, arid greed, petty avarice, monthly bills, magic numbers (where 27, symbolical of payday, was sacred and mysterious), clothes hung up to dry, caps of the Blackshirts, obtuse continuous whispering intrigue, glorious inferiority complexes, and genuine poverty.

Finally we resigned ourselves to living in the apartment of a railway porter, perhaps hoping that this kind of work might make him and his family different from the average government employees and their wives and daughters. His house had looked to us more bearable than hundreds of others we'd seen, just because it was simpler. But we soon realized that it wasn't so different after all. Here too were black-and-white tiles on the floor, Pierrots painted on the sofa cushions, dolls, and chlorine in the bathtub used for people and clothes. I could never make out when the porter actually went to work, for I saw him wandering around naked at all hours (it was summer and very hot) hunting flies with a napkin. It looked as though this were his only occupation. He relaxed every now and then by shouting, mooing like a cow, or indulging in naps with his mouth wide open. That was the way he spent his days. He was big, fat, and pink, his skin shiny and hairless.

Later toward evening when the west wind came up, he dressed, went downstairs, and sat at a table in a nearby tavern below his house on one of the desolate streets that cross the Via Appia Nuova. Here his wife would join him. She too was big, fat, and a do-nothing. They'd sit together for hours without talking, and then come back and snore all night across the partition. Their daughter, a little girl twelve years old with a crooked face, a thin little body, and straight hair raining over her eyes, had to take care of everything in the house. She fended for the porter, for her mother, and for the signori.

At last we tired of the boredom and the noises, and of little Rosalia's worn-out face, and took a room with an aged widow who lived alone. "Alone," she told us, but we found out the very day of our arrival that she had an idiot son of some fifteen years. His mother used to tell us endlessly of her troubles while the boy spent his time at the balcony spitting on the heads of the passersby. The bathroom door didn't close and no sooner were we naked under the shower than the idiot boy would come in, look at us sneeringly, point his finger, and shout, "Whoo! Whoo!"

Finally we fled the whole neighborhood and settled for a classic roominghouse keeper in the Via del Babuino. Here the staircase was older and the rooms larger, but none of the things we'd tried to avoid before were lacking: caps of the Fascist Blackshirts, sabers, raven locks, brassieres, Sicilian barons drinking coffee in bed, and the mistress of the house! Oh! — The mistress of the house was a widow from Bologna with gold teeth and completely gold hair, who used to wink at us and would have liked us not to sleep alone.

How far away now were those naive horrors, that small world of boredom and permanence of the Fascist "Empire" years, those widows, those porters! They too had been swept away by the wind of adventure, which like a storm on the mountains had penetrated even the smallest cracks, through the doors and locked windows. Those easy mysteries of life were gone forever, people had different faces. We slept where we could, but by now we were accustomed to chance.

I'd come to Rome a few months before, after the liberation. The main hotels were taken over by the Allies. I'd lived here and there, sometimes with friends in the prosperous Prati section, where cockroaches ran over the marble kitchen floors at night, sometimes in luxurious hotels, and sometimes in small shady ones with enormous repulsive beds and gray comforters impregnated by the erotic dreams of traveling salesmen and transient Albanians. Now, I'd come up to this room on the Via Gregoriana, but I wouldn't be able to stay here for long either.

It was a spacious, dark room in a fashionable house with a huge flowered marble stairway from the beginning of the century, the kind that was built in such numbers all over Italy, and doesn't seem to be tied to any ground, to any particular life. The abstract character of that room, the sensation of not being in any particular place was accentuated by the furniture; old Florentine furniture of no special value, but in dignified contradiction to the "Liberty" style of the house, with an entirely different and discordant history. Where was I then, and where was I going? The air was cold. I stood at the window, looking at the night and listening to the faraway indistinct roaring of the lions. The room was dark and it seemed to me that there was nothing but emptiness behind me, and that I was leaning out from a great height over a mysterious forest.

—◌ **2** ◌—

I was looking for the last time from up there at that nocturnal forest. The very next day I was going away again without turning back. I would leave the Florentine furniture and the flowered stairway for a real studio on the top of an old palace, where I hoped finally to be able to stop after so many years of error. Was this, then, the last halt before reaching port? Could this abstract room without roots be my Phaeacian Islands?

I hadn't found a Nausicaä there, princess or washerwoman, nor the shining gold vases of King Alcinous. Yet nonetheless in that cold red-tiled chamber, in that unpleasant, out-of-place mixture of Florentine and "Liberty," there was something attractive that had filled me with bliss: a high, wide, marvelously soft bed, such as one seldom finds, between whose cool sheets, warm blankets, and light comforters I could drown in delight. Who could have carried up this wonderful structure so propitious to dreams? I undressed in a hurry and plunged in, driven by a pleasant fury, like Narcissus into the mirror of waters. And I waited for sleep, looking at the stains and cracks on the ceiling.

How often in my life that is now so long, in how many different beds, had I stayed like this, motionless on my back, contemplating, completely empty of thought, how many different ceilings! The painted and colored ones are the most stimulating and changeable, but even in white ones there is always a mark, a line, a shadow. The ceiling of a prison cell was the only one denied me. A small malignant bulb, screwed in the center as an insult, forbade the images. But even lying on the ground in a forest one sees a far distant heaven through the black leaves. In the twilight of memory and fancy, while going to sleep or waking up, those hollows and ridges, those insignificant traces of time, change their aspect and at first take on the shape of fantastic figures, faces, monsters, landscapes. As long as these shapes still have a name and a definite form, this is no more than an illusory game, an idle improvisation like the spots on Leonardo's walls. Later, they flatten into something airy and vague that leaves space and time and belongs to another world, far away and escaping until in deep sleep or in waking they are erased. Alas, they now seem either colorless or too true! But what is the longing, the hunger, that calls them back and then regrets their disappearance? What is that power of theirs to move us? What is that search for something else beyond them, as changeable as fire?

When I was a small child, in the very first years of my life, my greatest pleasure was to get into my mother's bed. I slept there sometimes, but only when my father was on a journey. More often I would go in the early morning to play with those immense pillows, then fall asleep again, hardly realizing it. This was a pleasure full of glory. That bed was a true bed in a true world, not a cradle or the crib of a child.

It was an endless bed, almost without confines. It was a large, calm sea where, by only moving a foot, waves and tempests were born. It was a large plain covered by snow where over the folded knees big wide mountains took shape by magic. The linen sheets were so heavy that they crushed me, but if I covered my head I was under the earth in an infernal and marvelous grotto.

On the ceiling was painted a naked cherub with the tiny wings of a butterfly, holding a great bouquet of wild flowers in his hand. This bouquet spread out over the whole ceiling in a great parabola of stems, leaves, grass, and flowers. The winged cherub looked at me and smiled with its small half-open mouth full of little white teeth like those of a doll. And I spent hours watching it and following the curve of the leaves, the flowers, and the stems. One day (how can I say when? That moment seems to me the remotest of infancy, the root itself of memory), one day my wandering eye fixed by chance on a point in the great arc of flowers a yard above the child's rosy arm, and there it stopped. There was nothing remarkable about this point, only a bunch of curved almost parallel stems, but looking at it a feeling of terrible power entered me. It was something absolutely ineffable. How then could I possibly describe it? It was not a figure, nor an image, nor a perfume, nor music, nor anything pertaining to a sense or having a sense, but perhaps the sense of senses itself; like a rhythm without sound, an immaterial, swinging wave, the beat of invisible blood, filled with infinite attraction and infinite anguish. It was like an enormous, shapeless pendulum moving outside of space, and its continuous, curved motion had an irregularity, a sudden missing, an indeterminable suspension. And it seemed to me that this very suspension was at the same time sanctifying and blessed. Sanctifying, more than anything in the world; blessed, more than anything in the world; an absolute and mysterious power.

This sensation lasted perhaps a minute that seemed to me eternal, then it disappeared of a sudden and left me filled with both terror and longing. I looked back with hope and anxiety to that point in the bunch of flowers, and lo! the dark rhythm returned and filled me again like a delicious tempest.

To create it, I had always to look intently at this special point in the parabola and it would then come when it chose; heaven knows from where, with its infinite violence. Later I learned how to evoke it by only thinking of that point. But with the passage of years it became rarer. And when I grew up only the memory of it was left, and the emotion.

This ineffable sensation was perhaps pure power, gathered in an immaterial point, and perhaps now it has scattered and been transfigured into things hidden in phrases, in gestures, in the interrupted curve of paintings. I feel that I have always understood what it was without being able to explain it, and what I think and feel about it now is still what I felt instinctively as a child of three. That irregular and infinite rhythm was a pure image of an eternal flowing of eternal power. It was time itself, the true time before times. And what was that anguished suspense, what could it have been? Who can say? But there is a terrible significance in the relationship to time of things being born.

3

I was thinking and reminiscing thus as I started to undress. The childhood memory rose unconsciously in me while I was listening to the noise of the city and the occasional roaring of the lions, and it seemed to me as if the entire darkness, like a fluid and sonorous mass, were oscillating in the vague emptiness of memory. The fire was burning in the fireplace and the intermittent light of the flames moved along the walls like a fugitive recollection.

I undressed in a hurry. With my usual every-night gesture I took my watch out of my pocket. I kept it in my hand a little while and held it to my ear before putting it down on the table beside my bed. I could hear its regular ticking and thought that the time of a watch is the exact opposite of the real time inside and around me. A watch has a time without hesitation, a mathematical time, continuous material motion without rest and without anxiety; it does not flow, but jerks in a series of successive actions, always alike and monotonous.

The watch was now on the marble of the night table, balanced obliquely on its open case, quiet, yet animated by an internal motion, like a big, shiny horsefly ready for flight. It was a very beautiful watch with a double case of the best make; an Omega chronometer that did not miss a second. It had been given to me by my father years and years ago on graduation day, as is the custom.

These pocket watches are huge, heavy, somehow solemn and slightly antiquated, but mine had (besides the hands for counting hours and minutes, and the smaller one for seconds) the long thin hand, stopping or starting when commanded by a slight pressure, a modern element in this ancient machine of time. All such watches have a story of their own, a family and paternal history. One rarely buys them for one's own use. They are almost always a gift, and an important gift, from father, grandfather, or uncle on an important occasion at the most decisive moment of life, when a young man enters the world, acquires his autonomy, detaches himself from his past, from the uncertain security of the tepid family clan to start walking through his own personal time. It is then that we receive from our father the watch that will follow us always, that will follow all our hours, attached to a robust gold chain so that it does not stray, so that it is not lost.

Bound like a servant, it will start its life in the smooth obscurity of the pocket, flattened and hidden in the darkness like the heart of an insect, a heart beating without pause, and pitiless, not pumping warm blood into the veins but still pulsing like an intellectual, bodiless essence, tyrannically trying to drag along our own heart with it.

Our heart does not notice at first and goes on unaware; later it resists and defends itself; then little by little allows itself to be seduced and corrupted by that even ticking. It is so hard not to fall into step! Here are the soldiers marching behind the merry band: One! Two! One! Two! Our feet seem to move by themselves, and before we know it we are following. But the cadence, the military march quickens, and our heart follows it, not knowing how to get away from it anymore. And the time runs and flies, and today in an instant has already become yesterday and joins, without being able to contemplate or know itself anymore, the time that is already lost. Thus the gold chain that once tied down the innocent watch becomes the chain that binds us and drags us. And it is this small pocket machine that by now masterfully holds the end of the firmly tied chain, and faster and faster leads us by the bit like bulls to be slaughtered, who knows where.

How long, how endless were the days of childhood! An hour was a universe; an entire epoch could be filled by a mere game, as if it were ten dynasties. History was motionless, stagnating in that eternal game, perhaps the same game that I saw a Chinese boy playing on the sidewalks of downtown New York, drawing with chalk on the ground and hopping on one foot. Sunsets lasted for hours, as if the day refused to end and the childish sun, already half hidden among the blue mountains, was all too comfortable up in the sky. They were exceedingly slow sunsets, filled with the most wonderful colors, where the red of fire changed to orange and yellow, and to a strange sea green full of enchantment, and to purple of flowers as clear as the violets in spring and then more and more dark and nocturnal. These colors came down from the clouds, moving as gently as a woman coming out of sleep, filled the air, and seemed to make it as dense as transparent water. Suddenly bats appeared in this visible air and flew silently in uncertain circles, as black and as close as the night, and as far away. Vague sounds made their way among these wavering flights like lights from paradise, and seemed to navigate, boats filled with sails in that heavenly water.

The world was there, opened out beneath my balcony, and would never end, like some interminable ceremony. The eyes that saw all this needed to be large. The sudden music of trumpets came from the river's bank, like a last color full of golden sparks. It was the retreat of the Third Alpine Regiment. It started at the end of the bridge under the municipal clock on the house at the corner. From there the soldiers left for their barracks, followed by the boys of the quarter. The music moved farther away, and became dimmer and vaguer like the sky. Then, a little later, when shadow already covered the houses, a long moving note sounded taps. The window closed and everything was over.

— 4 —

That time was indeed long, stood still, and was filled with things, with everything in the world, and was somehow almost eternal, as it was in the Garden of Eden, a myth of both childhood and eternity. Later, time shortens, slowly at first in the years of youth, and then faster and faster once we pass the promontory of thirty, which encloses the vast boundless ocean of maturity. Actions crowd in, days fly one after another, and there is hardly time to look at them, to count them, to see them even, before they are gone, leaving us a handful of ashes. Who has driven us from the Garden? What sin, what angel? Who has made us run this way without rest, like the busy passersby on a Manhattan sidewalk? Is it only positive time itself that, following a mathematical curve, shortens progressively until it reduces itself to nothing on the day of death?

"Maybe Martino's right," I thought, as I carefully covered myself with the comforter and stretched my legs between the cool sheets, shivering pleasantly. Martino is an old schoolmate of mine with a long, long head, an interminable, rocky forehead and chin, a big shapeless nose that looks like a stone, and two eyes, sweet and full of tenderness in that mountainous desert of a face, slanting down eyes of a beautiful hazel like those of a dog. He is an excellent doctor who doesn't despise fantasy and likes to stop me whenever I meet him to present his biological interpretations of whatever topic arises. I'd mentioned to him a few days before my feeling about the progressive shortening of time, and Martino had immediately built a theory on it.

"That time should get shorter," he had told me, "is natural. You've only got to think that time is but the measure of our vital processes, of the rhythm of our metabolism, of the quantity of work accomplished by our body cells. The number of things that happen in an hour, the amount of nutrition, secretion, excretion, and cellular division; that is the real time in which we live, our internal measure of which we have, somehow, an intuition or a sensation.

"Now this number, very large during the early part of life and during adolescence, from then on keeps decreasing. As you know, the heart of a baby before birth in its mother's belly beats twice as fast as our heart, and all its organs, tissues, and cells are in a continuous and intense process of formation. Every one of the child's moments is so full, every hour of its time contains such a vast number of new creations that it may be said to be living in eternity. After birth these processes slow down, but still go very fast. In a few months, in a few years, one grows an incredible amount and learns an infinity of things. One learns everything: to look, to walk, to think, to talk. An hour can hold so many things! We're no longer in absolute eternity, but we're still very close to it. We get away from it later, as we become grown men, grown men where nothing much more can grow. The body's complete and so is the soul (if you want to talk of soul). The biological processes slow down. In an hour only a few things happen; only a few cells divide and reproduce, only a few changes take place in this machine of ours, functioning now in a monotonous fashion, without novelty, mechanically.

"Thus, as we have become slow, we begin to feel that time has become fast, and look back with nostalgia. Then old age comes and decay: the body's almost unable to move anymore, sclerosis immobilizes us, and it takes us ten minutes shaking and leaning on a cane to cross the room. The senses are blunted, we're shut up within ourselves, slow, lazy, awkward, and impotent. And then time slips from our hand and it seems to us as if it were running away like a wild horse, and we lose even the hope of being able to follow it with our eyes. Until, when we stop completely and death comes, time becomes so infinitely quick that it stands still again, and we return to another eternity, perhaps the same from which we had started, perhaps nothingness."

"Maybe Martino's right," I thought, more and more vaguely, as sleep came over me like something indistinct from the pitch-dark corners of the room. "As long as time is full, it's very long, and when it's emptied, it shortens and ends. Or is it that at a certain point we cease to resist it?"

I remembered a picture (in an old book of travels or was it maybe in an illustrated dictionary, the kind that delights children) where a canoe carved out of the trunk of an exotic tree was in the midst of the tempestuous current, in the rapids of a large river a few yards above a waterfall ending in an abyss. Some half-naked Negroes in the canoe were battling with rough paddles to resist the fury of the water and avoid being dragged into the vortex, while a white man, a hunter with a colonial helmet, watched far away from the shore. The scene was only a drawing, yet I knew what was about to happen. As long as the Negroes were fresh and strong they would succeed in keeping in the middle of the river, but eventually they would tire and start to move, almost imperceptibly, then faster and faster toward the waterfall, until their arms would give way, the paddles would fall from their hands, and the canoe, turning on itself, would run crazily toward the abyss only to stop as it smashed on the rocks below. The hunter would keep on looking at the inevitable tragedy, and the beasts of the forest along with him.

Should one then stay on the bank because there is a shore full of green trees and sweet sleep, and not be seduced into boarding canoes whose paddles beat the water fatefully regular like the hand of a metronome? But you may be chased way even from there, like Orestes by the Furies, or like Orpheus by the Bacchantes. I saw a picture, a picture I would like to paint (and maybe I shall paint it), in which I myself appeared in the guise of Orpheus, and the unleashed Bacchantes longing to tear me to pieces were armed not with thyrsi but with timepieces of all shapes: sundials, pendulums, alarm clocks, hourglasses. Sand ran in the hourglasses, making a thin rustle like that of light seashells blown by the wind. And to this rustle I fell asleep.

How warm the bed was, while outside the season was sharply turning to winter. In that dark warmth I was sailing toward morning. This is the hour of dreams, the invisible hour when we know that the world is unwinding and working and other people live and the sunshine is already shining on the houses and the smoking chimneys. Fanfares sound in the barrack courtyards, sirens call workmen to their daily tasks and boredom, and you look at yourself in the mirror maybe for the first time. It's the time when in prisons noises start, and bells and the monotonous falling of hours. The watches still register the hours, the bells ring, and the hour hands turn slowly on their towers, but we in this hour of dreams are on a secure shore, in a soft bed, outside of time and watches and bells, and we see things that do not happen.

I was in Turin, not in the small villa where I'd lived for so many years, but in a house I'd never seen before. I was in an ordinary apartment on the top floor of one of those Piedmontese houses of the eighteenth century, its large courtyard paved with stones from the bed of the river, with grass growing between them. (Paved like country streets in the olden time for the passage of carts when nights were filled with the noise of wheels on the stones, while a reddish light hung waving from the back of the cart and the dog behind barked, trying unsuccessfully to wake up the sleeping driver.)

The courtyard, far back under the long wooden balconies, was closed in by low buildings. Perhaps a house on the Piazza San Carlo, as it was before bombs and fire reduced it to a line of murky skeletons, the one where Vittorio Alfieri used to climb the staircase with his horse, or was it rather the other house where, in the back of the courtyard, lived Bourlot, dealer in old books, where I went as a boy, full of trepidation, to spend my savings. The little house of the bookseller had just one floor, dark, its lights on even during the day. In front, in the courtyard, there were two tall trees with large, tender green leaves; what kind of trees I never knew.

Now, however, I was up on the top floor sitting in a half-empty room I'd never seen. All at once I realized that I no longer had my watch, the one my father had given me. I made no effort to look for it because I already knew with certainty that it had been taken from me (*taken* was the word I was sure of, not *stolen*) some time before, in another house of mine on the hill of Alassia, where an exhibition of objects of art (furniture, paintings, ornaments, and pieces of sculpture) had been held. Many beautiful women, splendidly dressed and with veils on their hats, had come to look at the exhibition and one of them had *taken* the watch at the time without my even knowing it. She had later sold it or given it away. The watch had passed through who knows how many hands nor was it possible to say where it was by now. But I knew that at this very moment a tribunal was deciding the fate of my watch, and that the tribunal was in this very house, not in my apartment but in the little low building in the courtyard beneath. I must go there at once without losing time. I leaned out of the window, saw the roof of the building where my fate was being decided, and flung myself down the stairs. They seemed much longer than the four floors of the house, yet in a second I was at the bottom under the main door. I opened the small gate, crossed the yard, and entered the courtroom.

It was much larger than I'd imagined when I looked at it from the outside, a big, bare hall filled with all sorts of people who walked, talked, and screamed in a deafening noise. It didn't really look like a courtroom but rather like a Turkish bath or a covered market. There were no benches, seats, stools, or platforms, only a long table at one side, covered with a green baize cloth. All the people there were judges, both those behind the tables and those more numerous who were walking around the room, screaming and gesticulating. Only a few, though, were dressed as judges, with the black togas and caps and white starched bibs, and even those wore their insignia sloppily. In the main, they were ordinary people, most of them young men dressed in gray unpretentious suits with anonymous, inexpressive faces. A crowd of women of every kind was there, some tall, blond, slender, very elegant — aristocrats. Others were vulgar and common, modestly covered by scarves or wearing loud blouses and skirts, their faces tired and heavily made-up like sidewalk prostitutes. The president of this noisy variegated tribunal was a small old man with skin covered by tiny scales like those of a fish, who sat behind the green table. I looked at him as soon as I came in. I recognized him and felt better, and how could I have helped rejoicing? It was Benedetto Croce, the Virgil of Naples: honor, light, lord and master, teacher of my contemporaries.

I tried to approach him but we were separated by the men and women who walked to and fro, pushing themselves between me and the table, so that I couldn't get close to him or make him listen to me. Nobody at all listened to me, or seemed to notice me. Everyone was supporting loudly the most opposite points of view and my own voice was lost in the din. I did manage to understand, though, that the tribunal had to decide to whom, according to law, the watch belonged, the watch that had passed through so many hands and whose whereabouts nobody knew. The legal question was endless, but the judges, both men and women, seemed to be talking of something else and I was unable to follow their arguments in the general confusion. All I knew was that no one was looking for me and that nobody was taking care of my interests and my rights. It was just as if I were not there. I therefore had to take care of my own defense, but my efforts were useless. No matter what I did, I was neither seen nor heard.

While I was struggling fruitlessly, the tribunal decided to confer privately in a small committee room next to the big hall. I was quick to run to the door and slip inside along with the few who were to be the judges. I found myself in a small, bare room like the waiting room of a police station, with a small table covered by dirty oilcloth, and a few wooden chairs. The tribunal had shrunk to a few judges: Benedetto Croce, the president, was there, three young men in togas, three in plain gray, three tall beautiful and elegant women, and three small ugly and vulgar ones. These were the ones who were to decide on what was so close to my heart.

Here too, at first, no one wanted to listen to me, and it looked as though in making a decision about my watch, the judges would ignore my rights and my presence. But just when things seemed to be taking a bad turn and I was beginning to despair, I started my speech and the tribunal listened to me.

I told the story of my watch, of how it had been mine for so many years and how it had been *taken* from me. I made a long speech with much involved eloquence and I affirmed my indisputable ownership of that object, but I didn't mention at first that the watch was my father's gift. I knew I should have told them so but I was self-conscious about it. My father was dead and it didn't seem right to mix his name and memory with a question of property.

I don't know exactly how I came to make up my mind at one point. Perhaps I'd be able to move them, or would they think that I was trying to move them and consider it unfair, as it really would be? Still, it's impossible to finish a speech without an appeal to emotion. I was blushing and smiling inside while I used this technique in the most brazen fashion, though, after all, what I was saying was only the truth.

"This is a memento, the only memento of my father I have left. How can you deprive me of it?" While I was saying these words, I noticed with shame that they were having an influence on the judges. In fact, the tribunal decided then and there that the watch was mine, and nobody else's. The case was won.

But where was the watch?

To be proclaimed its rightful owner was meager consolation if one didn't know where it was or who had it. Once the legal side of the matter had been taken care of, the judges appeared to have lost all interest, and I felt completely helpless. How would I find it again? Who knows how many complicated tours it had made, into the hands of how many strange men and women it had fallen, in unknown, faraway houses and villages. I would never be able to re-cover it, deprived as I was of a guiding thread in my search.

Then I saw an alarm clock on the table between myself and the judges; a clock I hadn't noticed before, intent as I was on the discussion. It was a big alarm clock of white pressed metal, with a bell on top and Arabic numerals on its rough dial, one of those cheap alarm clocks, loud-ticking, sharp-ringing, that one finds sitting on the maid's night table on a white cover with hemstitching and fringes.

Following a sudden impulse, I seized it greedily and began rapidly to unscrew the dial and the case. They were indeed screwed together and not soldered in the usual fashion. Yes, that rough primitive alarm clock hid my precious watch, the dial and case of which had been taken off and replaced by those of the alarm clock. My watch was there, attached to the alarm clock, and I turned the fake dial until I had unscrewed it completely and at last held it in my hands. And I finally held what was my own. The dial and case, all the front part of the watch, were missing — who knows where they had been thrown? But the mechanism was still intact and working and I held it in my hands, feeling slightly clumsy because the crystal was gone. However, I was filled with great joy, and in this joy, I woke up.

A clear and violent light came in through the shutters I'd forgotten to close in the evening. The sun must already be high in the sky. Usually I wake up slowly, with effort, as if my body and my senses had trouble in coming out of the paralysis that bound them through the night; and I cannot say I'm completely awake and alive until a long time after. But the feeling of pleasure coming to me from the happy ending of my dream made me cross that dubious interregnum in a hurry. Without delay I jumped out of bed and ran into the bathroom, at the end of a long hall bordered by locked attic rooms. There was no hot water these days. The cold air and the frozen water I used for washing woke me up completely. I went back to my room and dressed in a hurry. When I'd finished dressing, I went over to the bedside table and picked up my watch to put it in my pocket. For some years I haven't had my chain, my old gold chain. I sold it in France when I was hard up during the German invasion of 1940. It's a very simple thing, therefore, to put the watch in my pocket, because it isn't necessary to fasten it to anything, nor to snap the cover, but only to let it slip in like this! So I took the watch and had it firm on my palm when, rather than falling, it jumped like a frog into water, and splashed to the ground in the middle of the room on the carpet, its face forward. When I bent over, puzzled, to pick it up, I saw that it hadn't stopped but was working as usual. The mechanism was intact, but the crystal was broken, the dial cracked, the hands bent, and the gold case flattened on one side. It was all as in the dream. The watch I had just picked up was like the one I'd found inside the alarm clock, from which crystal, dial, and case were missing, and I felt uncomfortable as I had in the dream because the crystal was lacking as I held that fragile, unprotected object. And it seemed to me that the dream was not an ordinary dream, but that it had a meaning that escaped me; that it was, somehow, an omen.

I wrapped the watch carefully in a sheet of tissue paper and hurried out through the streets of Rome in search of someone who would know how to fix it.

2

*I*T WAS A CHANGEABLE DAY. The sun shone occasionally in midsky and then was veiled behind light clouds that ran rapidly in the wind. It had rained now and then in the early morning. The stones in the street were still wet. As I walked rapidly down the sidewalk everything was clear, warm, and bright. The signs on the shops sparkled and the red and green packages of cigarettes on the corner stands looked from far away like bunches of flowers. Then suddenly the light seemed to go behind the torn hem of a cloud and everything turned gray and cold, but then came alive and bright again, as I were walking under a huge linking electric sign or a continually winking eye.

The sky of Rome is not so high as that of the cities in the north; as the blue-gray sky of Paris that seems to stretch for thousands of miles over our heads, or as high as the strangely colored sky of London or those exotic and tempestuous skies of America. This Roman sky is rich, dense, crowded with baroque clouds full of changing curves that rest on homes, churches, and palaces like a fantastic dome the wind wraps up and turns around. It wanders here and there, following in an airy geometry a changeable rhythm of its own as capriciously as a dog follows a trail. Under the nervous rhythm of alternate light and shadow, of heat and cold, of spring and autumn, I quickened my step, pushed by the first northern wind at my back, looking at the shops to find the right one.

A huge Omega watch hung from a sign over a window full of clocks, gold bracelets, and silver vases. I went in. The watchmaker was fairly young with a small, blond mustache and the short-sighted apologetic air of those accustomed to looking with only one eye, the one stuck to the lens. He gave me an obsequious little smile, took my parcel, unwrapped it, held the open watch to his ear, listened to it, searched with the magnifying glass, touched the split hands with a small pair of pincers, tried in vain to fit a new crystal in place of the broken one, and finally handed it back to me with a gesture of desolation.

"The case is dented," he said. "It needs to be fixed before I can put back the crystal and the dial. That's a job I can't do. Go to a casemaker and then come back to me for the rest. There used to be a good man in the Via dei Prefetti, but I don't think he's there anymore. Why don't you try to find him? That's all I can tell you. Try somebody else, if you want to."

This annoyed me. I've always resented petty inconveniences. But it didn't surprise me. In fact, it seemed almost natural, a logical consequence of the event that had determined it and had struck me by its strangeness. I was still under the influence of the dream, of the waking up; almost, in a way, enthusiastic about what had happened. And I felt a strong impulse to talk about it. So I told the watchmaker briefly that the watch had fallen out of my hands a little while before, just after I'd dreamed about it, and I asked him whether the episode didn't seem strange to him.

"Watches are quixotic," he answered. "Sometimes they seem to have a will of their own. My poor father, for instance, was a watchmaker before me. He had this shop many years ago, and kept in the window — right there — a splendid gold Swiss watch — a unique piece. He had only one specimen of that make. It was very dear for those times and so for years it hadn't sold. One day a foreigner came into the shop, an occasional customer passing through town. He'd seen the watch in the window. He liked it and wanted it. He didn't discuss the price, which had frightened so many people. My father was already rejoicing at this unexpected sale. But when he had wound it up and was going to hand it over he noticed it wasn't running. He opened it, looked inside, and saw that the flywheel was upside down. A trifle, but it had to be taken apart. He wouldn't have the watch ready until the next morning. The stranger said he was leaving the same night and must not delay. He was sorry but he couldn't buy it.

"He had scarcely left the door, though, when my father picked up the watch again and shook it. He was very angry at having lost the sale. And now the watch was working perfectly, with the flywheel in proper position. My father immediately ran out to call the customer back, but the man had already disappeared and there was no way of finding him.

"The watch had refused to leave with the gentleman. It had not wanted to go. It had played a trick. They do it often, watches."

I said it would be interesting to know why that stubborn watch had shown such obstinacy. Had they ever found out who the stranger was?

"We never knew anything for certain," he answered. "But that same night a foreigner, a wealthy Hollander, was murdered. There was a great to-do about it. It was a mystery. People gossiped about spying, documents, diamonds, and women. My father always said he felt certain that the murdered man was his lost customer. Many years later the watch was sold to a Roman surgeon."

I picked up my parcel again and hurried out. How could I find a casemaker if someone in the trade couldn't tell me of one. Perhaps I'd better try some other shops. I went into the ones I found on my way, but everywhere without success. At last I was told of a watch shop that specialized in repairs. It was a huge room, somewhat reminiscent of an early nineteenth-century workshop, with black iron tables all around and spiral stairways of darkly painted metal leading to the upper floors. A great number of employees and workmen were intently examining watches, balances, and other precision instruments. One had to procure a check with a number on it, handed out from a sort of iron pulpit in the center of the room, and then, timid and impressed, approach the man who matched the number.

This man took my watch in silence, with the casualness of one who handles thousands, gave it a quick look, shook it, and immediately without a word began fingering through a small box of crystals by his hand and testing them one after the other, pushing them with a kind of violence to fit them into position. He tried one. He tried another. He tried a third. None would go in. After all these futile attempts, he finally noticed the dent in one side of the case and looked at me severely, with the hurt look of the employee who thinks you do not take him seriously. Alas, not even in this temple of mechanics, in this solemn artisans' clinic for operations of the most difficult kind, could my watch be repaired. I did at least get the name and address of a casemaker; but he lived far away and it was late by now. I had to go up to the newspaper I was editing, for the usual work. I had no choice but to wait until afternoon, so I put the frail tissue-paper package back in my pocket.

The wind blew sharply in the street with a taste of winter. It seemed to bring a feeling of snow from invisible mountains, so that one looked up expecting yellow and brown leaves to be flying on the air. Teresa the cigarette woman was at her usual corner, a dozen steps away from the door of the newspaper.

"Cigars, cigarettes, American tobacco?" she asked. She was still a young woman, thin and dry, with a pointed nose and chin, painted lips and cheeks, and a burning, excited look in her dark eyes. She sat on a folding chair behind a white wooden box on which she kept her wares. Her brown hair, cut short, came out in mussy fringes from under a little dark felt hat. She wore a light coat with a worn rabbit collar. An American blanket was wrapped around her legs and another one thrown over her shoulders. She looked up at me, taking off a huge pair of glasses that gave her the look of an intellectual, and pulled the blanket over her chest.

"Do you feel it — the wind? On this corner it blows from every side. Now the wind has come, and the cold, then we'll have winter, many months of winter and the rain and the snow! It's terrible out here in the street! The police come too. They came the other day and took away my cigarettes — twenty-seven thousand liras of cigarettes, a whole year's earnings. It's terrible."

In her eyes a black fire of enthusiasm and delight burned as she looked up and told me these troubles in a high, metallic, tense voice. "I was a lady. My husband, that rat, is a lawyer. He was a Fascist — a Fascist *Republichino!* He turned in his own brother, who was also a lawyer, an anti-Fascist who was shot. My husband went north with another woman and left me alone. . . . I'm sick. I have a tumor. . . . And now the police have been here and winter is coming."

I looked at her in astonishment. Her voice rang out monotonously, as if she were reciting a litany or speaking of other people's affairs, but her eyes sparkled with pleasure, with a true irrepressible pleasure, languid and at the same time fierce. How alive she felt herself to be! Poverty, desertion, sickness, military police, winter — how many enemies to fight! Where were the olden times, the boring everyday life with a husband, a house, and nothing close to her heart! Now one must wage one's own war alone in a hostile world filled with ambush and terror. All plans had fallen apart, all the ties and inhibitions and the leaden blanket of deadly daily habit. For the first time, at last, Signora Teresa felt she was alive, alive yet destitute, thrown into the great world in a whirlpool of dark and marvelous forces that surround all things and move them and drag them along. She was no longer asleep on the shore but in the rush of the stream, in the full flow of its water and whirlpools. She was awake and she shivered with the happiness that sparkled in her great eyes.

A few steps farther on, the same look, mixed with irony and almost victorious scorn, filtered through the drooping eyelids of a face on the ground surrounded by a grayish bush of hair, eyebrows, mustache, and beard. Rather than a face, it was a shapeless combination of flesh and hair, a nose, a forehead, cheeks that seemed brought together by chance on the purplish countenance of an old man. He was not so much lying on the sidewalk as thrown there like a discarded object, like a piece of garbage. He lay on his back blocking the whole passage. That monstrous face of his, the rheumy eyes and the mouth shaped to a continuous moan, was attached to a half-naked body, its bare chest a wilderness of white hair. A few rags, thrown here and there, scarcely covered his belly and his thighs. One leg was stretched out, the other bent up under him almost as if to simulate a stump. His feet, naked and swollen from dirt and cold, looked like large pieces of rotten fruit grown by some chance on the twisted trunk. He was motionless. A kind of uninterrupted grunting came out of his mouth. In this muddle of limbs, in this perfect image of horror, an opaque look came through the slit of the eyelids, a look full of irony, of a sense of superiority, of aesthetic satisfaction and of mad beatitude that betrayed an incomprehensible, ambiguous existence, a willful theatrical pose, a weighty judgment.

Under the weight of his look, I started to step over him (he was there crossways, like a frightful spectacle, so that everyone would be forced to step over him, to be filled with horror and throw him a coin) when I heard Teresa behind my back screaming in a huge voice that someone had robbed her. They had stolen a package of her cigarettes. This, it seems, was a frequent happening. Two young men who pretended not to know each other came to her stand. While one looked absentmindedly at her wares, the other asked to buy a single cigarette, made her open up various packages, sniffed them, discussed their quality, said that this or that tobacco was fake, then lighted the cigarette and paid with a hundred-lira note. When Teresa, confused, put on her glasses and bent down to look under the stand for change, the first young man, quick as lightning, pocketed a whole package of cigarettes and vanished.

As the woman screamed, the boys who were wandering around the place ran up and shouted. In this confusion, who could find the thief? The black marketeer sitting on the opposite corner, a fat young woman with a gray apron and a shawl on her head, mocked Teresa in Roman dialect, and Teresa, who had a notion that this rival and competitor was the instigator of the thefts, poured back a stream of insults and profanity. A crowd of children, girls, old women, idlers, hunchbacks, soldiers, and prostitutes immediately gathered, listened to the insults, picked them up, and flung them back with laughter and a great racket. Fleeing the noise, I stepped over the monstrous old man and without looking back entered the dark doorway of the newspaper.

—ᴗ **2** ᴗ—

At the entrance there is one step. Often in Rome a step (a mythological step) divides one world from another. As the song goes:

> *Inside Regina Coeli there is a step.*
> *Whoever has not climbed it*
> *Is no true Roman.*

One then enters a dark and dirty hall, among metal and black-glass plates with the names of the lawyers and dentists of the house on them. The newspaper's was the most modest, a big piece of paper, already half torn, with our name on it glued to the wall in the least visible spot.

The editorial offices were on the fourth floor and because elevators were in those days still a luxury of the past, we had to climb all the stairs, black as a well at any time of day. True, the elevator was still there, encumbering the shaft of the stairway with its mass of iron doors and gates. There'd even been some attempt to start running it. But by one of those extraordinary expedients of stinginess, always so fertile in devices and so alive to technical progress, the elevator wouldn't go unless a token was dropped into a little box, a special token that only the porter could supply. The porter, a little, obsequious old man, wavering in his walk, was not to be found most of the time, maybe by secret agreement with the landlord, and when one met him by chance the current was sure to be off. There was nothing to do but walk by that useless machine and climb up, cursing the ingenuity of misers!

There exist in the world an irritating number of instruments and gadgets in the service of this insane passion: coin telephones, perfect meters, doors revolving in jerks, time clocks and factory apparatus of every kind to enforce uninterrupted work, to render the postures of rest uncomfortable and impossible and to block sleep. In an old studio of mine in Florence the tenants only, and not visitors or strangers, could (because of the cunning of the landlord, a greedy dwarf later strangled by thieves) turn on the light on the stairs by means of a portable plug that one had to search for in one's pocket in the dark and then, fumbling, fit into the socket on the wall.

So I had to climb up to the newspaper office; and because it's difficult for me to climb stairs slowly (maybe it's a leftover from the gait of my adolescence), I run up taking two steps at a time without stopping, and always reach the top panting.

I'd run up these stairs for the first time a few months before, not because of this old habit of mine but out of enthusiasm and happiness. It was at the end of August, 1945. I'd come straight from Florence, carrying my traveling bag in my hand. A few hours before I'd left behind that town where everyone still lived in the stimulating atmosphere of the Resistance and one didn't believe there was a difference between politicians and ordinary people; where everyone did what he did naturally, in a world independent and without closed compartments, in the factories, on the job, or on the local committee of liberation. This active and creative freedom, like all miracles, lasted for only a short time, but at the moment it was real and one could touch it with one's own hands and see it written on the faces of men.

In Florence too I had worked on a newspaper, a paper that, because of a lack of technical facilities, of money, of news, had to be created by immediate and spontaneous collaboration, clarity of ideas, and community of will. Everything went marvelously and without difficulty in the natural course. The circulation was high and still growing. The editors' work was pleasant to them; we had a popular following. When I was called to the capitol everyone thought it was fine, that I'd find a larger field of influence in Rome for the cause that interested all of us, and they hugged me when I left with wishes full of naive hope. Carried on the crest of this enthusiastic wave, I'd arrived in Rome that afternoon. I was hesitant and didn't feel up to my task. I knew nothing of the mysterious forest of politics in government and of the newly born political parties, already so involved with a sacred and conventional language of their own, their symbolic and incomprehensible ritual, and I knew nothing of their habits so well hidden from the layman. But I hoped to be able to penetrate those secrets soon with the help of those who already knew them and practiced them. That day I ran up the dark unknown stairs with joyous anticipation. At the top I found myself in a bare apartment. The door was ajar. I pushed it open and walked into a dark hall. Outside, the August sun blistered the pavement, cutting it into neat strips of burning light and shadow. I couldn't adjust my eyes quickly to the darkness and I stood there blinking like an owl at noon. In the hall there was nobody, no messenger boy, no secretary.

"Anybody there?" I shouted. The perfect silence of the summer afternoon remained unbroken except for the muffled noises of the automobiles from the street below.

"Anybody there?" I decided to push open one of the several doors off the hall. I saw a half-dark room crowded with untidy desks and full of papers (the shutters were closed on account of the heat and only the reflection from the houses opposite filtered through in burning threads). I went into another room, smaller and equally deserted, then into another like the first. As I crossed I saw, pasted on the wallpaper, drawings and caricatures: women, faces of politicians, and especially many Mussolinis and King Victors in ridiculous postures. Old larvae we had long ago forgotten, even if the king was still formally on his throne, as one forgets when grown up the monsters and terrifying tales of childhood. These scrawls were hung there with a kind of teasing respect, like portraits of the hated teacher scribbled surreptitiously on the classroom blackboard at recess. This room was certainly the editorial office if one could judge from clippings, proofs scattered here and there, old newspapers piled up, and desks covered with papers. Here too disorder reigned, silence, and an unpleasant atmosphere of abandonment and decay.

At the far side of the huge room there was a glass partition and on the door a handwritten sign, EDITOR-IN-CHIEF. And I entered the room that was to be mine. It too was dark and disorderly, and because there was no one here either I looked around with curiosity. Across from the partition I had just come through was an identical room, the glass covered by frowsy, yellowed curtains. The third wall had a door opening on the entrance hall, and the fourth a window through which the noises of the street came deafeningly. Beyond the partition was a small, empty room and beyond that, a terrace.

On the editor-in-chief's desk, in a corner by the window, reposed a little bundle of printed sheets with the letterhead of the "Young Fascists' Political Education Center," and in big letters the heading "Expense Account," then after many rows with blank spaces for figures, at the bottom of the page in block type, "For signature, the Commander." I couldn't imagine why these forms were on my desk and it was only later that I found out they were used for the sake of economy as writing paper. All the best prose of the newspaper was created on them and from now on I myself would have to graft my thoughts onto "Expense Accounts of the Political Education Center."

Nobody came and I decided to wait. Aside from the desk, the room had no other furniture but a glassed-in bookshelf in imitation walnut, locked, but entirely empty, with lion's-paw legs and a Renaissance edging, and some solemn high black chairs with wooden arms and worn leather backs. I tried one but it was rickety and lame in one leg. I got up and started to walk up and down, smoking my cigar. I felt uneasy in the silence, the squalor, the emptiness of the room at an hour when everybody on a newspaper usually works, and when news, telephone calls, visitors, contributors, and readers keep coming in.

I had now toured the whole editorial office. I'd seen everything about the rooms that were to be the place of my everyday life for months to come. But could I really stay here? Who would I have at my side in this unknown town? With whom would I carry out all the plans I had in mind? Or was my present loneliness to last forever?

I was tired of these doubts and of walking among the broken-down chairs, and I went to the window and opened the shutters. A gust of hot air came up from the street, bringing with it a smell of earth and asphalt and the rusty, panting grind of faraway motors. I leaned on my elbows on the windowsill and looked out. The sun, already low, still came straight down the street and made it shine with a white, blinding fire. At the crossroads the shadow of the opposite house cut this light violently and looked like a hollow, black abyss. On the line between light and shadow it was as if red and green ribbons of air were wavering vaguely, alternating before my eyes until they disappeared.

For a moment the street, divided in white and black like a coat of arms, was completely empty. Then a man wearing dark glasses appeared from the left, walking slowly, and another man in a gray suit came from the opposite side. They passed one another nonchalantly. Where had I seen this meeting before?

It was a little over a year ago. I was in Florence one day in July, one of the last weeks of the German occupation. Fascists and Germans were looking for me and I spent most of the day in a secret house with false papers and a false name; I was writing, sitting at a small desk near a window. In front of me was the Piazza Pitti, its rustic slope like an inclined wall meeting at an unexpected and exciting angle the bare facade of the palace with its uninterrupted geometrical stonework, broken only by even rows of windows like an enchanted prison closing from sight the hidden gardens of Alcina.

This square, all propped up, similar to a picture with its imaginary perspective, steep as a mountainside meadow and harmonious as an intellectual fantasy, had been filled until a few minutes before with a crowd of children and youths dressed in the strangest way. That morning they had looted a military supply depot at the Costa San Giorgia and had come back dressed in green coats and draped in patchwork camouflage material of every color. On their heads they had real helmets, heavy steel-gray military helmets. They played at war, imitating with their voices the fire of rifle and machine gun that accompanied the night hours of the city, deserted because of the curfew. They charged against each other and beat each other on the helmets with wooden sticks for swords, then they separated again and went on fighting and firing.

When a patrol of the Fascist militia went by the boys quickly scattered along the alleys. The square was empty under the sun. Only up high some old women in black and some little girls, small because of the distance, were sitting on the ground in the shade of the cornice. I had stopped writing for a moment; the noon silence was too deep and brought almost a feeling of anguish. I looked idly out the window at the white stones and the motionless sun.

A man in a dark suit appeared from the left, his eyes covered by sunglasses; another, dressed in gray, came from the opposite side, walking slowly. As they passed each other nonchalantly, right under my window, a single revolver shot echoed dry and clear in the silence. I looked down. The man in black was on the ground and blood was coming out of his mouth. The man dressed in gray went on walking quietly, without quickening his pace. He covered the few yards to the neck of the alley and without turning back, noiselessly disappeared. The other lay on his back in full sunshine. He was not yet dead. Blood broadened around his face, around his hair and his red mustache. The black glasses had fallen and were next to his left hand on the stones. He was making continuous spasmodic gestures with his hand to recover them, but those few inches were unspannable. His eyes were wide open without defense, and he did not see the sun as it entered them. The blood came out of the mouth ever slower and blacker and the contracting of his fingers brushing the glasses became more and more convulsive until suddenly they were still.

At the sound of the shot my hostess, Maria, had run in from her room and leaned out of the window beside me. She was very upset and she was screaming, and because she was a kindly woman, wanted to run out and help without thinking of the danger.

"Let's go down, quick!" she said.

"The partisan has aimed well," I answered. "It's too late."

"Let's throw him a pillow at least; his head's on the ground!" she shouted. Taking a yellow silk cushion from the sofa she hurled it out of the window and it fell there, shining like a big golden coin next to the dead man. Not a single window in any of the houses around was being opened, and those already open were hastily closed, but behind every shutter there were eyes peering and tense.

A few people went by, but as soon as they saw the dead man they turned away with gestures of disgust, satisfaction, or terror. It might mean arrest and execution to be found near the body, and there was danger of a house-to-house search. Only a few children came closer and they were immediately called back by women's voices from half-shut front doors. A truckload of Germans went by quickly, looked down at the man, and speeded on their way. The old women in the shadow of the palace did not dare move but made themselves smaller, almost hidden in the ground. After half an hour a young priest passed, a young priest with straggling hair and a cassock white with dust, holding his hat in his hand because of the heat. He bent down and mumbled something distractedly, as if this were an everyday spectacle, made an elaborate sign of the cross and looked around. He beckoned to the women and some idlers to approach but no one moved. He signaled a car full of German soldiers with a motion of his hand, but after a moment's hesitation they went on. Much later, an ambulance of the Misericordia Brotherhood came. Two men got out, took the body by the arms and legs, threw it on a stretcher, slid the stretcher into the car, and left. The priest left too, without losing a minute. On the pavement under the sun was a pool of black blood and the golden pillow.

The dead man, we heard later, had been a butcher, an informer.

⁀ 3 ⁀

The moment of solitude in the street below the newspaper office
was over. Suddenly, at every crossroad, jeeps driven by Negroes and
small battered CITA trucks had appeared like streaks of lightning;
and a noisy variegated crowd filled the streets. I thought I heard
sounds in the hall. I left the window and turned around. I went to
the door, nobody was there. How long would I have to wait in this
deserted office? I closed the shutters, sat down on what seemed the
best of the high chairs behind the desk and opened some of the
drawers at random. They were full of old papers, letters, and caricatures of the kind I'd seen pasted on the wall in the editorial room.
On the walls were some sketches showing a particularly unpleasant, tiny king and a few long-nosed politicians. The desk
drawers hadn't been opened for a long time. They were so dusty
that no sooner had I touched the papers than my fingers were
black. I hastily shut them and put my dirty hand on the arm of the
chair, but as soon as I moved, the arm, only there for show, fell to
the ground, uncovering the white wood of the support. I picked it
up, feeling the natural and absurd sense of guilt one has at such
times, and tried, with my hand covered with dust, to put it back in
place. While I was busy at this useless job, the door in the partition
opened and the editor, the man I was supposed to succeed, came
forward with arms stretched out to embrace me. I was still holding
the arm of the chair.

"Never mind," he said, "it's always broken." I gave him my
chair, as it was still his, and remained standing before him. We had
been friends for many years, but I hadn't seen him for a long time,
a time crowded with extraordinary events. And the difference in
our ages, his long political experience, the mysterious work he was
rumored to have done in various countries of Europe and America,
his recent past as a government official, the important role he had
played in the events of our country, his reputation as a great newspaper man and speaker, his absolute integrity, his kindness — all

this combined to temper my feeling of friendship with respect and a touch of awe as I stood before him.

He was a man of about sixty, but didn't look it, of medium height, rotund but not fat, elegant, but elegant in an old-fashioned if faultless manner. He hadn't taken off his jacket in spite of the heat (I realized then that I was in my shirtsleeves). He wore a dark jacket with a silk handkerchief in the pocket. His hair, once blond, was combed with extreme care and precision in a straight part on one side. His fleshy face carried with pride a short, aquiline nose, making him look vaguely like a bird of prey; a martin, though, rather than an eagle.

He wished me luck with my future work on the newspaper, in kind, sophisticated, and somewhat oratorical words. Then he spoke of the political situation with nobility and fine scorn, praised the organization and the editorial staff, and confessed with proud reserve to all the difficulties with which he had had to cope. I listened. At one point I put the arm of the chair I'd been holding in my hand all this time on the desk. When his eyes fell on it, the flow of his eloquence was interrupted and his thoughts and words turned in another direction.

"You don't know," he said in an entirely different tone of voice, "how many humiliations there are in this place! Nothing can be done. The paper has no money, you'll see. There isn't a cent. I myself have come to the point where I have to fight for a few hundred liras. . . . And I have a wife and a family. . . . How humiliating!"

I was touched to hear this famous man talking like this, in a sorrowful voice, his eyes filled with tears. I felt a great impulse to go away, to give up the post and go back as soon as possible. But a heavy step in the hall sounded, the door was thrown loudly open and an old man I didn't know and had never seen before came toward me, gave me a big pat on the back, and shouted gruffly and loudly, in a strong Sicilian accent, "Carlo, you here? Good! Very good! Have you a place to sleep? . . . I'll find you a room right away in the house of some of our comrades. It won't be expensive. Let me take care of it. Everything will be all right. . . . The editors are lazybones, they never do a thing. See! At this hour nobody's here yet! One's worse than the other. They keep complaining. . . .

They'd like money, but what do they do? Nothing. . . . They are a bunch of misfits. You have to keep them in line and not listen to them when they ask for cash. . . . We have to work for an ideal. You'll be very happy. . . . I'll take care of everything. Don't worry. Be comfortable. . . . I'll be right back." And before I could say a word, he turned around in the same agitated and fantastic manner he had used to jump on me and disappeared.

"It's Canio, our business manager." My friend barely had time to whisper this in a frightened voice from behind his desk when the old man was back again with a great banging of doors. I looked at him more closely this time. He seemed like a dry stone or a bare tree. He was a peasant with white hair, his walk rude and awkward. He had a healthy appearance, a thick and rough skin, but his eyes were filled with the hallucination of a dominant passion, single, violent, and irresistible. In this hand he was holding a bunch of blanks with the heading "Young Fascists' Political Education Center," exactly like those I had already seen on the desk.

"I've brought you some paper. I'll give you some more later. . . . You can start writing whenever you feel like it, naturally. . . . I'll give you some envelopes, too. . . . You'll like it here, Carlo. Now the whole advisory committee will be coming. At your convenience, at your convenience." And he left.

The sun had nearly gone down and the darkness in the room became thicker. A shy sound of steps and whispers from the other side of the partition told me that the editors were arriving. I wanted to meet them, to see the men with whom I was to work. One by one they came in to greet me, respectful and scared but with a certain light of hope in their eyes. They were all young, most of them thin and worn with the look of those who do not have enough to eat and who live in constant terror. To my questions about their schedule and their habits of work and the reason for their coming so late to the office they answered that they had to keep up other jobs because the management didn't pay their wages. Besides, they added, there was very little to do at this time of day. Subscriptions to news agencies didn't exist, nor did we get other papers or articles by correspondents, so that except for the editorials the work amounted to putting together the few news stories of the night.

The reporters looked like skeletons just out of a concentration camp. They had to walk all day long through hospitals and police stations, and this was very good for them, said Canio, because they were learning the trade. They hardly dared to complain and yet they didn't know what else to do but complain; they looked like poor fellahs from Egypt, forced to carry heavy burdens and work in the water for a handful of unsalted rice. In the growing darkness, listening to their plaintive talk, I expected to see a flight of ravens rise from the dark dusty corners, blackbirds in a fantastic house of Poe.

I had intended to get them together to explain my plans, but decided to put it off to the following day. I wanted to understand first the meaning of the dark-circled, sorrowful eyes and pale skin of one of them, the Jewish melancholy of another, the black beard of a third, and the mustache, shrill voice, quarrelsome complaint, and fashionable volubility of a fourth, and so on. Only one of them was fat and strong; an oxlike uncomplaining fellow. He came to work after everybody else, when his day's work in a shoe shop was over.

Meanwhile several friends had arrived for what I learned was the time-honored custom of evening conversation. Among them were a future cabinet minister, diplomats, and several writers. They all congratulated me ironically and offered me their condolences. "You'll have fun!" said the first one, a young man full of intelligence and frank defenseless ambition, who gave a funny grunt between one word and another and constantly blinked. "We've all had a try at it. It's impossible. However, you may as well try, too."

Perhaps my face looked incredulous or overconfident for he said: "Don't have illusions. It's as I tell you." And he launched on a lengthy explanation of all the difficulties that lay ahead in the technical management of the newspaper; on the interference of politicians divided into opposite parties, each of them trying to offset the words and the attitudes of the colleagues on the opposite side.

Grunting in his friendly way, he told me in detail of these abstruse subtleties, of these abstract rivalries, of these metaphysical attitudes. Since he realized I wasn't too frightened by all this, but inclined to imagine that I could dispose of it with a shrug, he started to talk of the practical difficulties, worn-out type, lack of paper, poor distribution, and other grave problems.

"Back of all this," he said, "is Canio, the great Canio. You've seen him, but you can't imagine without knowing him well what he really is. Start in with his name. They say it's the name of a saint of his village, a half-saint not recognized by the church, a Carthaginian warrior or something, whom the local peasants worship with possessive obstinacy in spite of everyone. He's not without strength of character, you know. That's why people like him. And also because his honesty's proverbial. He's the most honest man in Rome, maybe the most honest in all Italy. He'd give everything he owns for his political ideals, and even though he has a hand in some pretty big business deals I'm sure he'll go on living like a poor peasant, wearing old clothes and keeping a modest house. He's a jewel of a man, but he has a devouring passion that ruins everything. Did you see his eyes? Did you read the stinginess in them? You can't possibly imagine to what extraordinary and storybook extremes it reaches, so very extraordinary as to become almost beautiful, and to create a sort of admiration and respect. Did you notice the paper he makes you write on? Just think! In order to economize he keeps an employee — whom he pays very little but to whom he still must give something — for nothing else than taking the envelopes that come in the mail and turning them inside out like gloves. With these inside-out envelopes one is supposed to do the correspondence of the newspaper. When we have to put up signs or posters on the walls to announce an article or to advertise the newspaper, if it's really impossible for him to oppose it, he has them printed, but leaves them in the press room to get out of paying boys for putting them up.

"It's a whole series of marvelous devices inspired by the most resourceful stinginess. When I think of it I always remember my grandmother. She lived to be over ninety and in her old age became madly stingy. She spent her days wandering through the house turning off the gas and the electricity and supervising the maids, haunted by the idea of saving. We children were here terror. 'Wastrels!' she'd shout at us all the time; for each candy, each colored pencil, each sheet of paper. She took all our toys away from us because she said we would spoil and break them, and locked them up in a big black closet of hers. 'I'll give them back to you when you grow up,' she used to say. That black closet comes back every time I look at Canio's face and at this newspaper office. You'll see, yourself, and you'll enjoy it."

I was thus coached by my friends with jokes and smiles.

Later the members of the advisory committee came in: an ambassador with a skin smooth and fresh and very soft; a Tuscan lawyer with a pointed face; an Apulian lawyer with a shapeless face; an Umbrian lawyer with a face like a shriveled apple or one of those Incan heads shrunk to the size of a fist; a Turinese lawyer with a chin elongated by legal subtleties; and finally, mysteriously feared and worshiped by all of them, Canio, the bizarre old Sicilian peasant.

It was evening now and we were sitting on the balcony. From the street came a ceaseless buzzing, and the golden purple shadow covered us like a mysterious mantle.

I talked to them of my plans, of the way I thought the paper should be edited and managed. I talked of editions, correspondents, of a general reform in the direction we would take. I was saying things I had meditated about for a long time, things that seemed important to me, and were really necessary and important. But I felt that my voice was falling into empty space, and that this group of men, all of great value, who only a few months ago had shown such illustrious qualities of courage, disinterestedness, and true freedom, were now making a show of listening to me but were thinking of something else. I realized that my being chosen for this position was, without my knowledge, due largely to a compromise between two opposing factions, and that whether I did one thing or another didn't really interest anybody. Perhaps most of them, indeed, for reasons unknown to me as well as to the others, hoped I'd do nothing, that everything would be indefinitely postponed; and I realized that these men were bound by ties I could not understand. I had fallen into a stagnant pool of interests and intrigues, into a closed and impenetrable world I would never be able to understand. We were sitting talking on the wall of the terrace in the growing shadows, and underneath us was the hollow of the street and the obscure murmur of the city. It seemed to me as though I had come back to a village of Lucania and was listening to the signori talking of their eternal hatred and eternal boredom, sitting on the little wall of the square over the ravine in front of stretches of red clay covered by shadow.

3

I HURRIED UP THE STAIRS in the darkness, cursing misers, as I'd done every day for months since the first naive and enthusiastic time of my arrival. Electric current was rationed to different sections of the city on a rotating schedule. The darkness was thicker and blacker for those coming from the glare of the street, so that the climb seemed each time an underground interlude or a small nighttime adventure. The people one met on the way brushed by unrecognizable, close in the darkness, and you didn't know whether they were friends or enemies and waited for a voice to reveal them when you turned to follow their vague shapes or the red point of a lighted cigarette. Along those four endless flights I never could find out whether the people passing were my editors or patients from the dentists on the floor below ours or somebody else. They always had a little of the mysterious and hostile air of masked figures or of strangers met at night along a solitary street.

Now too, somebody was climbing up slowly ahead of me. I could hear his step on the stairs. As I was about to pass him on the third floor, the stranger stopped and lighted a match and I saw in that light the curved outline of a hunched back, the shabby suit, the white shirt youthfully open at the neck, the long face of a boy grown old, and the actions of a hurried bird hopping from one branch to another, as if pushed by who knows what impatience — my friend Martino the doctor!

"How are you?" I asked, climbing along beside him, and I already knew his answer.

"Wonderful, wonderful!" he said in a rush, as I'd expected, with an anxious emphasis on the words coming out of his mouth, like violent incantations intended to ward off by will power and magic all the evils of the world. "Wonderful, wonderful! . . . Very well, really well. . . . Now things go really well." I knew the statement was false, and sprang from one of Martino's thousand psychological rules. His life, lacking any chance for real ties, had become interwoven with yoga, psychoanalysis, astrology, chiromancy, symbolism, and a good dose of sharp wits. His optimistic exclamations were his personal version of the formula for healing (advising the sick to repeat, "I'm well . . . I'm well . . . I'm well.") that can actually work only on someone willing to renounce both the act of suffering and of being alive. The underlined and explosive intonation he used meant, therefore, simply that the evils against which he was trying to defend himself and which were overwhelming him were not small evils.

I didn't know the everyday events of his private life, events that he usually kept hidden; but I knew or could guess the fundamental weakness at the root of his life, otherwise so brilliant with talent and varied with interests. It was a fundamental weakness common to so many men, an inability to live, a lack of compatibility with the life around him, a horror of blood, an impotence that isolates many men in an empty despair and drives the best of them along the streets of symbols, the involved patterns of escape, quests, religion, and heroism. As for Martino, he took refuge in intellectuality, in strange and infallible erudition, concerned in large part with a world symbolic and arcane, still the best substitute for simple knowledge. Like many other men, he was incurably deaf to the direct voice of things, to a sense of color, form, sound, and sentiment, and did not accept this deafness but restlessly fought to get out of it, always looking beyond for what was bound to elude him forever.

No phase of human activity escaped the eager interests of Martino, from psychology to politics, from the most abstruse science to the smallest private love affairs of his acquaintances, particularly if they were women. He knew all about each one, yet he did not accept them for what they were but saw them as clues to something else, a hidden truth one couldn't know but only try to interpret. Yes, Martino was the interpreter of a nonexistent world, an interpreter (a priest) enthusiastic and desperate. The despair and the enthusiasm of his speech, so rich in superlatives, in implications and originality, always touched me because of its desolate poverty as, for the same reason, do the paintings of Picasso and the poems of Montale and T. S. Eliot. But Martino, alas, is neither poet nor painter; he doesn't have a crumb of the poet or the painter in him; he cannot create even idols or monsters but only fleeting speeches, carried away by the wind. Superior to them in his own way, he observes and interprets, nothing more. Or perhaps there is something more, since every man must in some way act. Martino's action is the only one the dry perfection of his nature allows: he is one who plays the accompaniment to souls of others, a Hermes with hazel eyes.

With great patience and gracefulness he takes them willingly to a symbolic limbo of his own. Their souls are most of them feminine souls. Martino is attracted by women (and women by him) more than anything else. Not to touch them, to admire them, to bask in their warmth, for these are denied him — but because women are the most natural and mysterious beings in the world, for whom at the same time his deafness is deeper, and to whom he looks for healing and salvation. They are the simplest and the most difficult to interpret.

Only women could with a breath overturn the marvelous magic castle where he lives alone. But that breath, so fervently expected, will never come. As a compensation, his secret desire for power finds an outlet in persuading them, bewitching them, in interfering with their lives from the outside, in accompanying their souls to limbo. Yet these feminine souls have bodies, real bodies with weights and appetites of their own, possessed by husbands and lovers. And sometimes they feel ill at ease in that limbo, and complications, family problems, and sentimental tragedies result. But Martino, the desperate missionary, like an expert spider, dauntlessly starts reweaving his web every day in the impossible hope of not getting caught in it. To defend himself from this spiderweb he went on saying, as if it were a prayer, his "Wonderful! Wonderful!" hurriedly, almost panting, as we went together up the last dark steps and through the lighted glass door of the newspaper office.

The appearance of the office, the disorderly rooms, the tables, the imitation furniture had not changed from what I had first seen during these months. The arms of the chairs had not been glued and I was fooled again every time I happened to take hold of them. The drawers I'd never opened were still full of dust and old, useless papers. The Fascist forms still waited to be covered with the prose of daily editorials. The inside-out envelopes were still used for correspondence, and the old Sicilian peasant ran up and down the rooms to make sure that no one had left a light on.

Some of the caricatures on the walls had been removed by my orders; not all of them because some were pasted on and a shadow of respect for the artist had kept us from destroying them. But even if the place was the same (it is my nature to accept things as I find them and I rarely remove a piece of furniture or a chair or have the wallpaper changed in places where I've happened to live, for they seem to me like people we meet and with whom we must become acquainted and cannot hope they'll change their dress and the color of their hair for us), even if the desks, the curtains, the papers, the drawings, and the stingy boss had stayed the same, the atmosphere of the office, the rhythm of its life, the tone of the conversation, the mood, surrounding us like impalpable air, were completely altered.

There were new editors; some of the old ones were missing, and those who were still around did not seem the same anymore.

They had, almost all of them, lost the humiliated sadness of slaves; and if they were not much better fed than before, they were less depressed and languid, hung around less, and were putting into their badly paid work all possible good will. The newcomers were two young men full of inspiration and drive who seemed to get great fun from whatever they did and lived in an exciting wine of youth, splashing happily in an artificial sea of paradoxes, irony, ideas, and contempt for anything conventional.

To look at them, Casorin and Moneta seemed totally different, and indeed they were. Though they were old friends, I cannot say they were really fond of one another. The opposing trajectories of their lives had reached a point where they touched; but it would not last long. They started from points far from each other and would soon drift off again, going farther and farther in opposite directions, one here, one there. For the time being they were together and enjoyed it.

Casorin was a tall, slender Tuscan with a sharp, asymmetrical face, close-set eyes, and an irregular, conical head covered with short, reddish-blond hair. His hollow cheeks had the color of copper because of his ill-shaved beard, heavy or light according to his mood, which changed often with his alternating periods of excitement and complete depression. His most striking features were his ears, attached to his head at different levels. They were extremely white at times and bright red at others, almost spies of his inner thoughts. It would have been difficult to imagine ears shaped as they were, almost without lobes and with intricate insides like two small, hard, braided rolls.

Moneta, on the other hand, was short, round, and fat. He came from a town in the South and he carried its cadence and accent along with him. His hair and eyes were black and his skin was rosy white, thin, velvety, tender as that of a petal or a nursing baby. Casorin was languidly elegant in his movements, affected a bored manner and light sport clothes, while Moneta stuck to the dark suits and buttoned collars of the bourgeoisie of his native town. In spite of the pleasant fatness that made him look like a ball, he moved about with the rapidity and liveliness of a child.

These two stars, Casorin and Moneta, moved in opposite trajectories, as I have said. In the sky of their lives, one might say Casorin came from the north and was going south and west, whereas Moneta from his astral home in the south was pushing his smooth sphere north and east. Casorin had become a Communist during the Fascist regime. Later, always an enemy of the present, dissatisfied and inclined by nature to changes, he had become a Socialist. Still later, he'd made another change and joined the Action party. It was easy to foretell that he wouldn't stop there, but would continue to change without altering anything in himself.

As for Moneta, he came from the Fascist Youth, and later had been a Liberal and a disciple of Croce. Then he too had joined the Action party. Momentarily, indeed, the paths of these two stars were in conjunction, but soon they'd be separating again. When Casorin had become a Liberal or a Christian Democrat, or his changeable political activity had melted into nothing, as an iridescent soap bubble shifts in form and aspect, fades, and suddenly disappears, Moneta would be asking to join the Communist party. So whatever direction they took, their sum would always be the same, like two complementary colors brought close together, shining with one identical light, a splendid white light.

Their interests and abilities were complementary, too. Casorin thought he was a philosopher, a critic, a politician, and played the part of an extremist and sectarian, but all this was only a veneer and a game of his to hide the writer and the poet. His ideas, his verbal excesses, his logical sharpness, his boredom and indignation, his clamorous exaggeration were outlets of an essentially well-balanced nature, a comfortable warm inner fire, built of innocent images alone. Moneta, on the other hand, was a critic and a literary man by profession and imagined himself endowed with the understanding moderation and the taste for variety and tolerance of this profession at which he was very good. But his apparent control and the gentle smile on his priest-child face concealed the old sectarianism, the fanaticism, ripened for centuries under the desert sun of the South, the abstract madness of a southern humanist.

In every village on the crest of the Apennines, high above the desolate and malaria-ridden valleys, there lives a solitary Don Quixote, eternal and immortal hero of these peasant lands, tragically certain of his own truth and justice, even when time and events cause him to hide under the long black coat of an opportunist landowner. There was something of the knight in Moneta's soul, in spite of his rotund Sancho-like appearance, and something of Sancho in the tall, thin, sad figure of Casorin. This temporary pair had a great deal in them of that other timeless pair, but the roles were mixed in such a way that it was difficult to distinguish between them.

This is the way Casorin and Moneta were at that time, and whatever they may really have been like, the way I'm talking of them shows clearly, I think, that I loved them both. What I say of them here is indeed only a thousandth part of what I might say of them. Men live, their eyes shine and dampen with tears, their hearts beat without stopping, blood runs in their veins, thoughts flower or stagnate like still or running waters, a pallor, a sudden blush comes to their cheeks — and we know or suppose that all this exists; but we are cutting a slice of this infinite reality, making a partial image of it, giving it a name, Casorin or Moneta, and forcing it into our lives, our times, our standards of measurement. We know that all the rest, the things we do not say and must neglect, exist; and we can feel its existence like a regret, a perfume of things lost. It's like riding through the suburbs on a train, and seeing lights go on in the windows, and discovering for a second a mother under a lamp pouring soup into the children's bowls, or a girl leaning on the windowsill to sing, a workman sitting out on a balcony in his shirtsleeves to read the newspaper, or a child waving his hand, actual visions with whom we would like to stay. Who are they? The train carries us on and they are left behind motionless in that one pose of theirs, a woman pouring soup, a child waving.

And so involuntarily we build the plot of a novel from this endless wave of reality, from a human being who, like ourselves, identical to ourselves, has no limitations. One colored tile of a mosaic that has been designed in advance, one function in an abstract game.

~ **2** ~

"A function! A good function! A good cipher, a cog in the wheel, we have some excellent functions!" shouted Casorin, and his voice was so shrill it was impossible to tell whether he was irritated, shocked, or only amused. He laughed as I came into the office with Martino.

"Functions. . . . All of us here say elements or, if you prefer, agents. You too, Moneta, are an excellent element, in case you don't know it. I know very well where that bad habit comes from. A political party, it seems, is a machine or a radiator, so instead of having men we have elements and we play elemental politics . . . functions, agents, cogs — documents!"

Casorin was sprawled in my armchair while he shouted all this, his feet on my desk and a lighted cigarette between his fingers. He stopped his oration when he saw me come into the room.

"You'd like to sit down, wouldn't you?" he said, getting up and giving me his seat. "Sit down, tyrant!"

Moneta, active and solicitous, was holding a bunch of morning newspapers. He had already marked them, as he did every day, with long red-penciled lines along the margin beside the articles and the news he thought would interest me. He hurried to put them down in front of me, exactly where Casorin's feet had been a minute before.

I should have looked at the papers at once; these were important days. The Cabinet had dissolved, the Parri government had been overthrown and the crisis continued with its pauses, its dramatic surprises, and its maneuvers. We all knew very well (although the various party leaders seemed totally unaware of it) that these were decisive events and that they would affect the future of Italy for many years.

The question now was whether that extraordinary popular movement called the Resistance would actually develop further, remolding the shape of the country, or would be pushed back into historical memory, disavowed as active reality, be relegated, at best, to the depths of the individual conscience, like a spiritual experience without visible fruits, filled only with the promises of a distant future. In these days the movement's strength was being tested, and not only in terms of sheer impulse, motivation, numbers, and influence, but in terms of its capacity and ability. (One should always take into account the strength, capacity, and ability of one's adversary, and the vainest of habits is that of tearfully accusing the enemy of one's own defeats.)

It was one of those times when everyone's destiny hangs uncertain, when the ablest politicians assess the forces in the field and prepare clever moves in a complicated game of chess, a game they are doomed anyhow to lose, since the only way to win it would be to find a word, a true word, capable of creating new forces, of overturning the chessboard and transforming the game into a living thing. Would the word be found?

These were silent hours of expectancy in the midst of the everyday clamor. Other words with no resonance filled the air, old words, rich in nobility and memories, but abstract and so worn by time that they had lost their shape like white pebbles on the bed of a river. Their sound was sweet: democracy, socialism, freedom, power to the masses, and so on. But they held no strength. Still, the men were there, peasants on the path with the donkey and the goat, workers in factories, longshoremen on harbor docks, sailors on ships, and all the others. Here too, Teresa the cigarette vendor shivering happily at the first autumn wind, and the millions of Teresas in the fields, on the roads, and in all Italy's houses, who had left forever their former life and had learned to suffer and rejoice on their own. They were here, they were with us and we were with them. What was it that was keeping us apart — what blocked us from understanding one another and nailed us to the green tables like tired gamblers toward dawn playing a lost game? Perhaps those sweet words, smoke of incense, dark cloud of vain nostalgia.

I knew that these were the thoughts and feelings of Casorin and Moneta. But I also knew the natural restraint that kept them silent about important things so that when most fired by passion they talked warmly of trifles, of football or the hermetic school of poets.

Martino's passion, on the other hand, was to look for the passion in others, and the rays of his own sun were spent after they had searched here and there and pursued the most complicated angles reflected in the thousand mirrors of a dark room.

While I was going through the papers they were talking and I listened to them, half attentive, half absentminded.

"Functions." Casorin started in again. "Functions! When we start calling men functions, then we're through. We're fitted into a mosaic, a Byzantine mosaic. If we could at least find out whether we'll end up on Christ's forehead, or on a toenail, or even on the devil's hoof, or on the tip of the nose of the artist's patron as he looks on from one side."

"There's no difference, my friend, no difference at all, all *ad majorem Dei gloriam,*" answered Moneta sweetly, but Casorin went on with his apostrophe, pacing up and down the room, and as I listened to him I often confused his words with the ones I was reading. "A five-party government or a six-party government?" "Meeting of the Committee of National Liberation." "The Lieutenant of the Realm is not supposed to get into the question, or give out assignments or choose. He's not supposed to influence the decisions of the parties. He can only sanction the committee's choice." And so on and on.

"I hate them!" I heard Casorin shout. "I hate them. Those monsters! They really are monsters, those functions, monsters! Each of them with a wife and children, a home and family affections. That's not what makes them such hateful monstrosities. As you know, Moneta, I'm all for Catholic ethics, all for wife, family, and home, and I'm against that ridiculous, romantic Bohemianism, old-fashioned and in bad taste. But for them the family and the lampshade, the sentimentality and the faithful little wife *are* their Bohemianism, the hateful Bohemianism of the conformist revolutionary. Just imagine what complications, what ferocious and bloody experiences are necessary to get them there. Take Antonio, as an example; but there are thousands like Antonio.

"You know Antonio and his sexual mixups. He couldn't stand women and so on. Well now he has become a hero, he has killed, risked his life, married the most womanly of women, and has a child. Therefore he has now recovered, and he's happy. To accomplish things so simple he turned heaven and earth and had to go through an entire program of cruelties, ferocities, blood, death, torture and all the heroic deeds one can think of. Now he has the nerve to want us to be like him, with a faithful little woman by our side and a baby clapping his hands. Touching, isn't it? I'll write a book about it! . . . I'll use Antonio as my model. . . . A monster! It makes me vomit!"

Moneta shook his head. But the romantic conformism that so enraged Casorin didn't seem to shock his friend so much. How could one tell whether Casorin was really angry, or why he was angry? He liked to be swept along by a profusion of words, by verbal violence, truculent and out of proportion. You never knew whether it was a true target or a kind of false one at which he aimed his guns, to hit some unknown point farther away.

Moneta shook his head with that mincing little motion of his, like a sparrow looking for worms. "That's the way all novels end, Casorin. Or at least many of them. It's in the classical tradition."

"You can keep your novels and your characters, those optimists and socialists, they're monsters, worse than Antonio! Your Bezuhovs, your Levines, along with their Katyas and Natashas! After they've been conscience-stricken thousands of times, they decide in the end to get fat, to make children, work on their farms, farms of some thousands of acres, of course. It takes a war for them to achieve these happy results; Moscow in flames, Napoleon! Millions of people must go to pieces, beautiful women throw themselves under trains, all for their sake, for their final triumph. They are certainly monsters and there's no sense to them! They don't make sense as characters. They completely fall apart. Imagine them in life, when life itself imitates them. They don't have any value in the novels, nor do the novels have any value. Just caprice and falseness.

"Caprice and falseness," thundered Casorin like a fanatical preacher, like a Savonarola standing squarely in the center of the

Piazza della Signoria, unmoved by social conventions and accepted truths. Where did comedy end, where did truth begin? Moneta, however, was insensible to comedy. To him everything was serious and without subtlety. He could not listen to this fierce improvised attack on one of his most beloved authors and spiritual idols without protesting.

I was still leafing through my newspapers, and I heard him defending Tolstoy, using appropriate arguments and mature criticism, based on ideas of Croce's with a few elements of Marxian aesthetics grafted on. And these ideas of his were alive and passionate because Marx was new to him at this point in his development.

Moneta was arguing warmly, but also with the timid restraint of a man venturing out on a winter morning to skate gaily over a lake without knowing how thick the ice is; explaining Tolstoy's characters as necessary stages in the historical evolution of the middle class under the pressure of the awakening masses.

I saw Martino listening in silence, with intent eyes and the expression of a man who has just swallowed a big juicy bite of steak. He wrinkled up his nose in a grimace of greedy pleasure, looking like some strange chimera or other fabulous animal, as he always did when anything seemed to fit into his schemes or enrich him. But Casorin aggressively interrupted Moneta's calm reasoning.

"You think you can explain everything by this historicity of yours, with a few references to the bourgeoisie and the proletariat thrown in. We know all that. Everybody acts that way; they are all stages of history, Tolstoy and the hermetic poets too. From Petrarch to Gatto. Everything gets explained, and we understand nothing."

Here the discussion became confused, as in one of those moments in a sonata when several themes, previously developed by themselves, impinge on one another and seem to stagnate, moving lazily like the flowing waters of many mountain brooks that join as they reach the plain before they start off again brightly and clearly and with new impetus. Moneta tried to defend himself like a wise general who abandons one position after another, retreating without too many losses. Martino interrupted with elliptical phrases, the meaning of which he alone understood. Casorin, like a fencer on the stage, carried out a series of unnecessary lunges that drove Moneta back into the wings.

It is not only in conversation and music that we find these confused and apparently senseless interludes. They exist in the lives of all, in empty hours of boredom and apathy that the romantic poets have nonetheless sung about with such lively passion. In history too there are certain eras when terrible forces, unloosed at the four corners of the earth, neutralize one another and it seems as though nothing has happened; this causes the greatest delight among pupils in the high schools. We always find tedious places, languid and dark places, in books, in the best books. And especially in paintings, which are mythical landscapes of the soul no matter what subject they represent, and cannot be without intricate, pathless woods, without swamps, without this idle and nocturnal tedium.

I've always mistrusted paintings in which a bland style covers the whole canvas like the iridescent oil on the motionless waters of a harbor, and that are too beautiful, that do not have breaks or vacant spots. But there are critics who value this grammatical competence, this unity of style, as the highest and most to be revered quality. They stand in front of paintings like commissioners of public safety in front of the accused, saying: "This is art; this is not art." "This is law; this is crime." Their eyes shine with pleasure behind their glasses and their glasses' glasses when they discover, like some hidden crime, one of these vacant spots. Without realizing it, they have perhaps found one of the keys to the world, an invisible key that drops unused because their powerless hands are incapable of holding it.

When Moneta was tired of retreating and had been driven behind the furthermost wings of the stage, after he had abandoned one by one his historical and social and aesthetic arguments and there was nothing for him to do but leave the theater, he used his last resort, enveloping himself in a protective cloud, in the black ink of a cuttlefish, and ascending into the sky clothed in the halo of authority.

He quoted Lubbock, Grabe, Muir, Wharton, Forster (E. M. Forster), and more than anyone else Beach (Joseph Warren

Beach), and his theories on the technique of the novel. He talked about the dramatic novel, about the use of "I" in writing and its disappearance, of Carruthers, of the "well-made" novel, of three different kinds of subjectivity, and of neo-realism. He expected Casorin to become irritated by this shower of erudition or, as he had done at other times, to oppose these real authors' names with others entirely imaginary and Rabelaisian, turning the whole thing into a game. But surprisingly, Casorin wasn't irritated and didn't start to joke. Instead he went back to the very beginning of the discussion, pirouetting like a ballet dancer. Authors and theories did not matter to him. Everything can be said and everything has been said, and he left such rhetorical quips to Moneta and the old humanists and rhetoricians from the villages of the Apennines and their English and American followers and imitators. He would have preferred Capellina's handbook on elementary style or even the aesthetics of the Jesuits to these technical analyses. If he had talked of Tolstoy and his unrealized characters, it was not just to please himself by indulging in banal criticism.

Tolstoy was not a novelist. The huge machines that he used carried him who knows where, but his true value was a different one. He was like a poet writing lovely verses as he sits in the compartment of a moving train. What really counts are his poems and not the miles speeded over by the locomotive. All Tolstoy's stories rush toward a conclusion, and this is not only a loss from the human point of view but also from the artistic. In spite of the complexity of his stories, the working out of destiny, the succession of so many and such harmonious parts, there is never any true development in Tolstoy, although there may seem to be. This is because he is the poet of the unique instant, which cannot last nor repeat itself nor change. What is it that he can really tell us? He talks of everything but expresses one thing alone. He makes immediate the fullness of life, of youth, of complete happiness. Happiness, blissful youth, beauty maturing, love: actions outside of time, outside of every novel and every story, fixed and eternal. Think of Natasha singing in an empty room, and of Prince Andrei, who finds himself again overcome by happiness as spring once more renews the oak. One never has the feeling of death. These are moments of life fulfilled, without limits, without shadows, beyond storytelling. The rest does not count. All of Tolstoy is here. He's an impressionist. He's like the great impressionistic painters. And like the impressionists, he doesn't need to tell a story or paint historical pictures. All he needs to do is to catch, once and for all, an instant that will never come back, that has no before or after. He's like Renoir.

"Who wrote this?" Casorin asked. "Listen —

"*The cherries blackened on the plate with juicy brightness, our clothes were fresh and clean, the water in the jug sparkled in the sun with rainbow colors. And I felt so well! What can I do about it? I thought. What fault is it of mine that I'm happy?*'

"It's a picture by Renoir, only it was written earlier, in '59. 'What fault is it of mine that I'm happy?'" Proud of his quotation, Casorin, who knew entire pages of his authors by heart, maintained that this sentence was the most perfect definition for impressionism.

"It's true . . . you're right," Moneta answered, "but what do you prove by it? . . . *I'm* not happy, nor are you, Casorin."

"You're right, you're right!" shouted Casorin, as excited as someone who's had a sudden revelation and cannot express it clearly even to himself.

"You're not happy. We're not happy. Neither is he" — and he pointed his finger at me — "although he pretends to be. Let him pretend. . . . As though he were happy. We're not deceived by his Olympian looks. But never mind about him, he's a serpent. We're not happy, you say? We do not permit ourselves to be happy, you, I, and even he, that monster" — and he pointed his finger at me again — "and many others, there are many of us, we don't even know how many."

"Without realizing it you've given us the reason why we can't stand those novels, or novels in general. Because *they*, unlike us, really *were* happy. 'What fault is it of mine that I'm happy?'"

"The wickedness and the sorrow have disappeared. There are no shadows in impressionistic paintings; the shadows are colors like all the rest. They're not black but blue and green and pink. If those writers carried along with them all that huge machinery of the novel, they were nothing but frames for absolute happiness, old gilt frames for a modern picture. It was the same with their perspective, which still existed in memory but had vanished entirely in that atmosphere of blessed light outside of time. They were outside of time in an Earthly Paradise — and they were right.

"They could very properly say 'I' because in saying 'I' they included all things. The mistake came later, when by saying 'I' one meant nothing but one's own small self, alone in the world, divided in a thousand pieces, abstract, dead, and with nothing whatever around them. And the abstract story was written and painted in an abstract time that from beginning to end is cut off arbitrarily from the world. The individual is there; there are the masses, but there are no human relationships. Take any man, alone and barren, and divide him into different plots, make an object of him, complicate him by events, close him up in a first and an afterward, and then tell his story if you can. You still don't get out of the abstract.

"What sort of novel do you want after Auschwitz and Buchenwald? Did you see the photographs of women weeping as they buried pieces of soap made from the bodies of their husbands and their sons? That's the way the confusion ended. The individual exchanged for the whole. . . . There you are! Your *tranche de vie* — a piece of soap."

Casorin talked in this fashion, intricate, obscure, like a man searching a street in the dark, but with enormous heat, with a kind of furor that made his eyes seem darker and closer together and compelled us to believe that his disconnected phrases made sense.

"A piece of soap," he continued, without giving us a chance to interrupt him, "that we must bury with tears. A piece of soap that is the body and soul of man. That's the result of the Faustian action. That's the conclusion, the destination of your novels and of your abstract reasoning. It forces you to act, to do something in the abstract and individual time marked out on watches, where nothing is true and contemporary, and it forces you to sum up at the end of the book with a piece of soap. We, on the other hand, are rooted in an awareness of things around us. There isn't just one blade of grass in a meadow, there is not one tree but a forest where all the trees stay together, not one in front of the other but merged, big and small, along with mushrooms, bushes and rocks, dry leaves, strawberries, myrtle berries, birds, wild animals, and perhaps fairies and nymphs and boars and poachers, and wanderers who have lost their way, and who knows how many more things. . . . There is the forest."

Through the open window the lament of a siren suddenly entered the room. Casorin interrupted himself; all of us involuntarily shuddered, and for a moment our thoughts shifted.

This sound was still the voice of war, too close to have regained its familiarity and casualness. It was the harassing and intermittent howl we had heard in the gray dawns of Paris, after which followed nothing but an absurd anguish rising from that fierce modulation. Pursued by the mechanical scream, so peremptory and funereal, one went to the window and looked out over the roofs, barely visible in the leaden air of first morning. Lazy smoke came from the chimneys of the houses across the way and seemed to halt in the motionless air, terrified by the sound. One day I lifted my eyes from the still dark roofs high up into the sky. The first ray of the sun arrived, and in this ray was a luminous point shining like a star, surrounded by little white clouds. It skimmed gaily through the fresh, clear air — the first German airplane coming to announce the invasion.

In Italy the sirens did not have that intermittent, cruel, physically intolerable panting sound. They were long, continuous, and deep, but they were followed by the roar of motors and explosions.

It was another voice from those hundreds of different whistles that marked the hours in the industrial city of my childhood, when we tumbled out of bed because the whistle of Diatto had already sounded, warm and low like those on ships. And we ran to school while the high note of Fiat sounded far away and prolonged, roaring through the sky.

Mothers said: "Your milk's ready in the kitchen; the whistle has blown."

Then various whistles and sirens sounded before the bell for the end of the lessons. Others started off at sunset, all at the same time, as if they came from a cathedral organ in the city with pipes scattered through all the suburbs. They ceased one by one, first the shorter ones and then the others. This complex sound of high note and low note dissolved into its various parts, notes hoarse and shrill, whistling and strident, this musical breath of the factories, this puffing of a huge animal, patient yet rebellious, this friendly shout of a force compressed and then liberated, of steam released, until the sound of one siren only remained, the last one in the flaming sky that announced the night and the warm vapor from soup on white tables under the lamps. Where had this noisy army of benign spirits gone, affectionate companions of each hour of the day? The new sirens of the war were different. They did not follow the time but lacerated it; grotesque sounds, they made the heart beat without reason.

"There is the forest," Casorin repeated softly as the sound died away, "and there is God."

"It's noon," said Martino, raising his left wrist to check his watch.

3

I too instinctively looked for my watch to regulate it by the siren and found it enveloped in tissue paper. I put it on the table and un-wrapped it. The watch was there with its cracked dial and dented case. I showed it to my friends and told them, in brief, of my dream.

"Very interesting indeed!" Martino exclaimed before I had even reached the end, wrinkling up his nose. I was curious to hear what he might say, for with his inclination to interpret, there was nothing he explained better and with more competence and interest than dreams. They were his study and his glory; with extraordinary ease he could draw out strange revelations from his analyses. Casorin and Moneta did not follow him on this terrain. They did not like it; it made them feel uncomfortable. Moneta, already wavering in his orthodox idealism, was repulsed by the mysterious world of dreams, of the subconscious, of magic and psychoanalysis, which he accused of lacking clarity and distinctiveness of its own. To free himself from magic he used the magic wand of logical analysis, making it all disappear into something far vaster and more indeterminate, into that infinite cosmic mystery which art and philosophy continually illuminate. Casorin, on the other hand, scorned such things as being complicated and untrue.

"What do they think they've discovered?" he asked. "What's the use of analysis and its scientific pretensions? We have the confession, we have prayer, and we don't need anything else. I go to confession, I pray, and everything is much simpler, clearer, and more profound. You talk of ambivalence, of complexes — lovely inventions! I fiercely hate my enemies but I pray for them. Every evening on my knees beside my bed, before I fall asleep I pray to the Child Jesus. And I really pray to Him only for my enemies. While the war was on, during the day, as you know, I did everything I could against the Fascists to help to defeat them, and if possible to kill them. And every night I prayed for them. I got down on my knees and prayed for Mussolini, for Koch, for Carita, and for all those wretched, miserable, poor, and absurd assassins. There is really no need for Freud; he is false, snobbish, useless."

Nonetheless, my dream interested them and in spite of their preconceived opinions I noticed that they too were curious to know what Martino would say. Whatever technique of interpreting dreams is adopted, from the most common and popular to the most refined, whether wrapped in the mystery of a sacred rite, or reduced to a graceful society game, or vulgarized into a mere conspiracy for discovering winning lottery numbers, it is too much a part of the memory of the world for anyone to escape its enchantment. Alas, Martino assumed that I knew a great deal more than I did, and thought it unnecessary and perhaps offensive to offer simple and detailed explanations. Therefore he confined himself to vague hints and generalities. My dream was interesting,

very interesting indeed, and to explain it completely he would
have to study it at length, which he would do gladly later on. But I
should not stop (as he supposed I knew) with elementary Freudian
interpretations and sexual significance. All that was superseded
now. It was not a question of symbols, but of principles. Sexuality
was, in itself, a symbol, but Freud had not noticed it. Reality was
made up of an infinite number of layers put one on top of another
endlessly, as though composed of fowls, of fowls speared on a
roasting spit. But why should he tell me such obvious things? I
certainly knew the most recent theories, later than those of Jung
and the others.

As for the watch, it might symbolize many things. First of all, it
was a curved, round, closed object like an Indian *Mandala*, and
what's more, it was an astrological object divided into twelve parts,
like the twelve signs of the zodiac. He added, parenthetically, that
the number thirteen, which does not appear on a watch and is
considered an ill omen, actually brings bad luck (as he supposed I
knew) only in countries inhabited by people who will never develop. Furthermore, a watch is a jewel, a precious object, and the
watch, in essence, had now established itself scientifically, securely, and without any possibility of doubt. It was *Unity*, or rather
the *Selbst*, namely the point where the conscious "I" meets the
subconscious "I," except that now of course they are no longer
what they were. Internal *Time*, true and absolute time or in other
words the real "I," is the profound nature of the individual. To lose
a watch means to be outside of one's own true time, to lose oneself. I had lost mine in my dream, and then I found it again, but
inside another timepiece, an alarm clock. Also, it was broken.
One must analyze all the details. For example, the alarm clock
was another *Selbst*, but coarser, commoner. Perhaps my social experiences, my populist sympathies, and my political activities
were hiding me from myself and were destined to fail, or perhaps
it was all just the opposite. We didn't have enough data. We must
reflect patiently. If I could keep in mind all the symbolic meanings of a watch, I would myself realize the complete significance
of the dream, the most exact and private and hidden ones.

"And what about all those women? Those little women, those tiny women?" Casorin asked, jokingly. "What was their significance in your dream, I'd like to know?"

Then Fede and Roselli came in, hurried and excited, as if they were being pushed by an invisible wind of their own. They didn't look as though they had the time or desire for dreams or nonsense. How could they be interested in dreams, in the dreams of others, when they were living in a dream of their own?

These two were the youngest leaders of the party. Their faces shone with capability and noble willpower. The confidence they had in themselves and in the rest of the world made them seem even younger than their years. They hadn't yet had time to spoil, to let themselves be caught by the gears or to close themselves up, as the best politicians usually do. Both of them had spent most of their youth in prison and had been freed at a time when the country was outside the usual law in full civil war. They fought, talked and thought, and found themselves guiding and directing other men before they had ever had time to observe men, to touch solid things, to turn around. They were still filled with that strange holiness of prison, a thing dehumanized and rarefied like air in high altitudes. They were free in a way that one can only be free within the four walls of a cell, free in a glorious, cerebral sky, an invigorating and clear sky that they thought of and talked of as politics, and under which, millions of miles below, stretched the lazy, foggy earth. They knew everything about this sky: the colors at different hours and different seasons, in all possible altitudes, when it was calm and when it was tempestuous, its myriad cloud formations and their names, the bizarre shapes of the cirrus, the breaking up of the cumulus, the degree of humidity, the pressure, the electricity, the cosmic rays that go through the clouds like a knife into butter, and the way from time to time an overload of potential is discharged with frightening relief in a flash of lightning.

They had had so much time to look at that sky from behind iron bars and deep, heavily shuttered windows like the mouths of wolves, and to imagine it, hour by hour, minute by minute, for years and years without end, in darkness. It had no secrets for them. When the bars had fallen and the mouths of the wolves opened wide, they had been carried on the wings of the wind that had passed over all Europe high up to the very center of that sky, and had found, in the blue, intoxicating transparencies, the same reality that had been with them all that endless time in prison. Flying drunk with motion like solitary eagles among those currents, among the winds of the north and the south that seemed geographically defined to them, they thought themselves inside the heart of the world, in the center of the only true reality. They were realists.

There were, however, differences in the degree of their realism. Roselli was the bigger and heavier of the two; his wings were smaller and his torso was more massive, and the laws of gravity, therefore, compelled him to fly a little bit lower. He was, as a matter of fact, very, very large and very heavy and, to top it off, in the middle of his round, ruddy face he had an enormous mustache of a glossy, barbaric blackness. It hung down so far that instead of a dark silk tie, one imagined he was wearing necklaces and golden chains around the strong column of his neck. His head was round, large, gigantic, his forehead high under close-cropped hair, his eyes big, dark, and fiery, his voice strong and willful, dry and without resonance. The towering bulk of his great body moved with speed and agility. He seemed like a Hun general in civilian clothes who had dismounted from his horse for a moment to deploy his hordes in battle array.

Fede, on the other hand, was short, slender, and delicate, with a long transparent face shining with the brightness of his glasses. His pointed nose, exactly in the middle of his pale cheeks, was like a sentinel on guard in a field covered with snow. A small mouth opened underneath with arched, fleshy lips, the chin strong and divided by a cleft. He had a concentrated, careful air, like someone handling a loaded pistol; and when he was silent, he seemed not to listen or rest, but to keep an eye on the trigger so that it would not go off involuntarily. The weapon was actually there, and dangerous, because when he spoke it was not a pistol shot but the burst of a machine gun, or rather multiple crossing and arching shots fired from some unknown point.

It was this ability and the cunning of his mind that made him hide his arguments, to pull them out suddenly at the most unexpected time with the violence that was natural to him, to turn his concepts around, twisting them into skeins and balls and releasing them all at once, like a trout fisherman who patiently winds his line on the reel with a nonchalant, monotonous movement and then casts it far out.

But Fede's nature was reinforced by his will. In his meditations on the sky of politics where he now roamed, he thought he had discovered immutable, eternal laws, hard Machiavellian laws that he accepted like a Stendhal hero with enthusiastic assurance.

Fede was even more like Julien Sorel when he had to give his attention briefly to something other than his political sky. Like a man who has lived very little, has been kept under a glass bell and has been deprived of his best years, he had an irresistible urge to live, to live in a hurry to make up for lost time, to grow older, to reach his own age, like a soldier left behind on a march who runs along beside the regiment to find his place in the line again. His very haste and his eagerness for experience prevented him from seeing things and from being able really to touch them. He was like a hungry man who gulps down all the different kinds of food on a huge table at the same time, without being able to taste any of them. He would have liked to have loved all women, or perhaps to have had them love him. Who knows? He didn't know himself. He attacked them all with a fire, a violence, and such excessive passion, at the same time hurried and inexpert, that he frightened and offended them, and although they recognized other merits in him, they all repulsed him. He responded to his first rejection by doubling his error, planning the most elaborate tactics, showing his impatience too openly, employing exaggerated and unexpected gifts, gigantic bouquets of flowers; and from all this he expected the most marvelous and certain results. When even greater alarm and amazement brought about stronger refusals, he was driven by his eagerness for life and his horror at the time he had lost to abandon one battlefield and then quickly make new attempts on others, with the same impatience and even greater furor. As far as I know he went

from defeat to defeat, but he found refuge in politics where he had
no dealings with such strange beings as women, but only with
people like himself, and with eternal ideas.

————————————————

F ede and Roselli had arrived to explain the latest news of the
crisis. They had just come from a meeting of the committee.
Before that they had been to party headquarters and had seen, privately, delegates from the other parties. They had many things to
tell me and they dragged me immediately into the small room off
the terrace, leaving Martino, Casorin, and Moneta in my office.
The things they told me were so confidential that I shall not repeat
them. Besides, whom would they interest after so many years? The
memory of great events or what seemed like great events is so
short! Everyone has forgotten them. They explained their projects,
the steps they had taken, the maneuvers that must be opposed, the
hidden intentions of the other party leaders, and the special interests concealed under the maneuvers. All this seemed to be taking
place up in that sky filled with strange birds battling one another
in the solitary atmosphere where I too sometimes fancied I was.

As different from one another as we were, all of us were up there.
Some flew awkwardly like old ravens, thinking only of food and
their prey, ready to pounce on the innocent dove; others lingered
wheeling in wide majestic circles, waiting for who knows how long
a time for who knows what faraway prey. Fede and Roselli were not
looking for anything or wanting anything but the pleasure of flight,
the joy of huge aerial arches, the turns, the unfolding of wings, the
complicated evolutions, the feeling of great height. From that great
height neither they nor the others could see the earth except as distant smoke, and how could they distinguish in that smoke and at
that distance the faces of the men and women who moved in the
cities, hoed the fields, worked in offices and factories, disputed over
money, eating and making love. How could they see from up there
the face of Teresa behind her box on the street corner, and the
chilblains on her hands at the first cold of winter? No matter how
sharp their birdlike eyes were, they could not distinguish them.

The Premier, however, the fallen Premier whom they wanted either to support or replace, did not fly in the sky nor did he even turn to look at it. He walked over a small earth, and did not want to know and see anything but Teresa's chilblains, Teresa's face, and the faces and hands of all those he met on his way. He stopped to talk with them, forgetting everything else, and he wept for their tears. What could one do? How could one associate such incongruous things as the birds, the Premier, and Teresa? What chance was there to resolve the crisis that was much more than a change of government, involving as it did events with no intercommunication, and times diverse and incomprehensible to one another? I was reminded of my first primary school arithmetic book, which stated (a statement that never completely convinced me when I was a child, or later) that one cannot add together sum totals of different kinds of things — that one should not say, for example: "Five loaves of bread plus three roses make what?" They don't make anything if you follow the book.

There had been a time when men felt close to one another and to the world, when they had seen death and lived and breathed the same air. That time was not yet ended, it was still alive in those who had learned to live among terrors and sorrows, who had searched the rubble, who were conscious that they existed and had learned to do without the things they had lost. Six months before, in the days of liberation, I remembered crossing the Plain of the Po. Huge bonfires of rejoicing rose in the night from every village and above the serene chant of crickets in the countryside; and the gay rattle of firecrackers came from all parts of the horizon. As we entered Reggio our car broke down and at that hour there was no one to fix it. The town was dark, the streets deserted, the hotels crowded. A waiter from a tavern, an old partisan, came along with me on the difficult hunt for a place to sleep. As we walked a long time through the cobbled streets, a continuous murmur came from behind the cracks of the doors, as if they were filled to bursting with people all talking at the same time, saying the same words, whispering of happiness. In the window casements, faintly illuminated by the wavering reddish light of candles and oil lamps, shadows of men and women appeared, moving with gentle mystery, and now and then from the distant suburbs came the sound of a shot. We continued to walk, turning into dark alleys, surrounded by vague whispering. At last we reached a house where we knocked at the door, and an old woman dressed in black came to open it. She had a room for me if I'd be content with it.

I was left alone in a room that was both room and hallway. There was a table covered with stockings to be mended, cards from an interrupted game of solitaire, a sewing machine near the windows, a fireplace, and on the walls old popular prints that I could barely make out by the dim light of a yellowish candle. While I was trying to decipher, in this semi-obscurity, the details of one of the prints, showing a large crowd forming a procession in the wake of a holy image, a door opened at my shoulder and I heard a woman's voice inviting me, if I liked, to go to my room. It wasn't the old woman, but a lovely young girl, holding a flashlight, who was wearing a flowered silk wrapper over her nightgown. She was tall and shapely, with big, languid eyes, a round, rosy face on a long, white neck, bizarrely marked by the shadows. She wore a strange kind of turban on her head, made from a big white handkerchief that covered her from her forehead to the nape of her neck and gave her a kind of oriental look. She had a laughing air but she shuddered as the sound of shots came occasionally from the distance. She asked me if I was sleepy, if I was tired from the trip, if I wanted to eat something first or would rather go to sleep immediately. While she showed me to my room with the light, she told me she was the old woman's daughter, that she was called Rosetta, and that they lived alone.

I saw her again the next morning when she came to wake me up and bring me coffee. She was wearing a bright, short little dress, but as on the evening before, her head was completely swathed in the turban. I was astonished to see her still wearing such an exotic headdress at that hour, and I stared at her. Rosetta noticed this. She hesitated a moment as she looked at me, as though deciding whether or not she could talk freely to me.

"They shaved me," she said, and left the room.

Rosetta had been shaved two days before in the square because she had been seen during the winter months with German soldiers. The old woman told me about it at length, defending her daughter and her virtue, while I was saying good-bye before I left. Everything in those days seemed so natural, everything fitted together for a unity of all things; the old woman and the shaven Rosetta and her oriental turban.

Presently our automobile, driven by an enthusiastic partisan at a reckless speed, was rushing over the roads across the plain. We met farmers on wagons, armed partisans with great beards and long hair falling on their shoulders, priests on bicycles, their cassocks tucked up, and everyone greeted us and we exchanged quick glances of friendship with everyone. We had to stop to change a tire by a grove of trees whose leaves, swelling with sap, reached toward the sun.

On a bank I saw the bushes opening, and in the crack, the face of a girl with short, ruffled hair who peered at us intently at first, and then came out. Her legs were bare, her feet dirty with mud, her breast and belly scarcely covered by a few rags. A wild and pastoral apparition. She did not speak. She looked at us, invited us with a movement of her hand, and ran off along the woods toward the edge of the brook.

When we arrived in Milan we found the city in ruins. The streets were filled with an exuberant, inquisitive, and happy crowd. They were going to meetings, to rallies, for a walk, or who knows where. They all seemed happy to see one another, to bump against one another, to breathe, to discover themselves again, to feel they were alive. The city seemed fuller of people than usual. "How many of us there are!" the people of Milan seemed to say to each other, winking at one another in agreement and wonder as they sat on the grass in the park.

Night was falling and groups of young people filled the court-yards of half-destroyed houses. In all the courtyards one danced to the music of improvised orchestras. Paper lanterns and green branches hung on ropes stretched from second-story windows. The people of Milan danced. Hours passed, the night deepened, the dancing continued without interruption as though a miraculous trance controlled the muscles of those girls who had eaten so little for so many months. The lanterns went out one by one, and the dancing still continued. Red handkerchiefs around the neck, light blouses, old summer dresses, military trousers circled and pirou-etted in harmony — not even the ugly and the old were neglected. The moon was high in the sky, its rays penetrated the holes of the broken windows and the irregular profiles of the bombed walls. In that light, in the whole city, the people of Milan danced, embraced one another trustingly, as though it were the first night of the world. When the sky turned gray before the first dawn of the new day, the tramping cadence of feet still filled the air, along with the sound of accordions and violins among the rubble.

One can't go on dancing forever," I thought vaguely, listening to the plans and political interpretations of Fede and Roselli. "Perhaps that's all over and the reality of today and tomorrow is theirs. And still . . ." A heavy step sounded in the next room, the door opened a little and Canio's face showed through the crack, looking like a statue made out of cork.

"Ah, you're here?" he said in his roaring voice. "Are you working? . . . Bravo! Bravo! Don't interrupt yourselves. Keep at it!" And he shut the door and disappeared.

As usual he had come to keep an eye on us, but at this hour there were no lights to be turned off. We could hear him from the other side of the partition, screaming at Moneta who, as a de-fender of the poor, was reproaching him because the reporters hadn't been paid their wages. Regularly every day Moneta threatened to quit because this was no way to carry on.

"You're always the same!" the old Sicilian shouted. "The same good-for-nothings! Tell the reporters to get their work done instead!" And we heard his footsteps going off, and the noise of a violently slammed door. Our window opened wide at that blast, a gust of fresh wind came into the room along with the confusing noise of the street and the distant sound of church bells. Over the terraces and the ridges of the roofs the sun now shone in the clear sky, as though it were a mirror cleaned and polished by the north wind.

The table in front of us was covered with telegrams moving around in the wind. There were hundreds of telegrams from every part of Italy, from local sections of the party, former partisans, and from all the inner committees of the workmen. They all said the same: be loyal to the government; protest against the crisis; incite to resistance. Behind each telegram must have been men with their own faces and their own passionate wills, but Fede and Roselli didn't see the faces or think of them. To their realistic minds these were words, political forces, functions, yes, functions in a great and most difficult game. It was so difficult that they had every right to smile at the ingenuousness of some of my observations, which seemed to me to be the fruit of plain common sense. I didn't realize, they said, that the present stage was not revolutionary, but would some time develop into a revolution. And then too I didn't take into account the psychological resistance of L—; the interests of G—; the ambitions of R—, who wanted a job in the ministry and whose support was absolutely essential. We must accept these small political expedients and use appropriate and flexible tactics, giving in temporarily to our opponents so as to be ready ultimately to take over the direction of public affairs, overturning the whole present political array, clipping its wings in favor of an elaborate and infallible strategic plan of their own devising.

Their plan was certainly brilliant and fascinating. I listened to them, allowing myself to be seduced by it, and it seemed to me that along with them I was in that high sky of pure politics, filled with marvelous birds.

As I cradled myself in these dreams, suddenly there came through the window the shrill sound of grinding brakes, the noise of shattering glass, and the harrowing scream of a woman. I ran out on the terrace and looked down.

The street was filled with people running in the same direction. In a moment they had all come together, like a varicolored ant hill, around a jeep and an old automobile that was crushed against the sidewalk. From the wheel of the jeep a Negro soldier gesticulated to the threatening crowd. Four enormous MPs were already making their way forward, with white gloves and white helmets shining in the sun, holding their rubber truncheons. A space formed around the jeep, and the Negro got out. Pieces of glass sparkled on the ground. Pushed by the police, the crowd moved back and the clamor was followed by a complete silence. A few yards in front of the car a light-colored form lay on the pavement. It was a woman. She was motionless on her back, her head on the sidewalk, her body on the street. Her skirt was pulled up over her stomach, leaving her thighs naked and horribly white. For a very long moment everything was motionless and silent. Then the light sharp voice of a little girl called, "Mamma," and repeated the call, "Mamma, Mamma," without stopping. I did not see her at first because she was in the middle of the crowd. She tried to move forward but someone held her back to keep her from seeing her mother; then she stayed alone on the sidewalk. She was tiny. She must have been about six years old; she wore a pink apron and a pink ribbon in her hair, and she called, "Mamma, Mamma."

I left Fede and Roselli to read all the telegrams. Crossing the room where Casorin, Moneta, and Martino leaned out of the window, I slipped into the corridor.

Canio yelled after me, "You are leaving? Are you through already?"

Without answering him, I rushed down the stairs. When I reached the street I could just see the jeep leaving. The child and the woman were gone. A crowd of women and youngsters were looking at the car on the sidewalk; one of its doors was bashed in and twisted, the headlights shattered. Farther on there was a small pool of blood on the ground.

Teresa had already gone back to her corner behind her bench, in fear of thieves, and near her the monstrous old man was raising his monotonous lament.

"She's dead," said Teresa. "Did you see what a lovely girl she was? And young, too! . . . Crossing the street with her child. . . . Those jeeps! they think they're in America. It happens every day. There isn't a day that somebody isn't run over. Who cares about us? They'll end up killing everyone. American cigarettes, American!"

Some young men stopped to buy cigarettes. They touched them, squeezed them, smelled them. "Are they real ones, or do they come from Isola Liri?"

Automobiles in long, irregular lines drove up the hill, their motors roaring, their exhausts open, and among them went pushcarts, and bicycles with their bells ringing. The street was full of people crowded elbow to elbow: summer blouses, heavy topcoats, shawls, handkerchiefs, hats, rags, Allied military tunics, sandals, boots. Shapely women, moving their hips and thighs and throwing inviting looks around them, old ladies studying the window displays, excited and dirty youngsters running to play who knows what games or to bargain, soldiers — Americans, English, Italians, Negroes — workmen in overalls, clerks through with their work in the banks and the ministries, ready to jump on the sagging trucks that had replaced buses. Everybody moved, gesticulated, looked out of black flashing eyes, thought, talked, shouted, their faces full of passion and character, intently pursuing their daily adventures. And they themselves, all in all, were an adventure, an indeterminate river made of a thousand ever new waves, running between rocky banks and flowered islands.

4

I FOLLOWED THE CURRENT DOWN the street, letting myself be carried along by the swarming movement. Beyond the
crossing, after the street had descended like a waterfall from the
highest parts of the city, there was a dark, narrow way between old,
dusty bookshops. Farther on were huge posters inviting atten-
dance at an archery contest to be held in a hall to the right, not yet
open at this hour. It offered two attractions: the betting, and the
girls who were to shoot the arrows dressed in costumes looking
something like cowboys, red Indians, and American WACs.

Here the crowd was engulfed between the high banks of the
houses, hurrying toward the wideness and the quiet of the next
square, that opened out like a lake.

This lake was shaped like an irregular hourglass, with all sorts of
inlets around it, and the river was lost among lesser currents. The
automobiles hurtled at a crazy speed, running in circles, crossing in
front of one another, slipping like acrobats through hoops into the
side streets from which other automobiles emerged. They hesitated,

looking like turtles coming out of their shells, before they launched themselves into the merry-go-round. In the midst of this confusion, horse cabs, slow and imperturbable, passed by, and bicycles skimmed around like mosquitoes. Carts and pushcarts displaying the most varied wares stood here and there like furniture in a room crowded with knickknacks.

Pedestrians pushed into all this ceaseless and riotous commotion, and flowed untidily along the edges. There was a dead corner at the left side of the entrance where no one passed by, where beggars and women loaded down with packages rested like flotsam at the sides of a stream.

I stopped for a moment to look at the golden houses, a fantasy not bound by rule, and beyond to the other dead corner at the far end, where high palm trees were swinging in the wind. No matter how hurried one is, how urgent one's business, how tormented by private sorrow, each time one passes here one cannot but stop to look, to allow oneself to be filled with that involved sense of things fixed and moving, of masonry extending and hollow, of fullness and emptiness, of lights and shadows, of the familiar and the exotic, the alive and the pressing, the ancient and the reposed. A pleasant spice is added to this complex and exciting sensation by the very name of the piazza itself, its illustrious title — one of the famous centers of the world: Picadilly, Broadway, Place de l'Opéra, Red Square, Piazza di Spagna! *Cette Reine, Cette Princesse, La Vidame!* Thus one addresses queens: before this glory, this dignity, this noble name, the simple mortal stands still and bows and enjoys the sound of the name that embraces such a great period of history, that imperturbable sense of divinity that is contained in it.

It is names, only names, that can give meaning and certainty to all things; the names of the gods make nature an open and legible book. In America our eyes rest uncertainly on those splendid landscapes where nothing has happened, and we do not see the green trees, the meadows, the houses, the nameless streets, because they are all too young, and no rustic god has had time to choose them for his dwelling. Here in Rome, however, the air is filled with words, with magic symbols so dense and heraldic that the very flies seem to be eagles.

I fell in with the tempo, and flinging myself between one automobile and another, crossed the square. I went by the column swathed in bronze embroidery that stands in the middle. On the steps under the statue three nuns, like mother hens, had gathered about them a swarm of little girls dressed in white. I reached the opposite bank in the narrowest part of the lake, and in a few steps I was at the great stairway of the Trinita dei Monti, defended by a trench of luminous flowers. On the steps behind the stalls and the umbrellas of the flower vendors, a juggler performed his tricks. Hanging down from his neck was a small table, and on it he was rapidly displaying three cards. People were crowding around him to place their bets; old cronies, women, farmers come to town to sell their lambs, clerks, youngsters, soldiers, black marketeers. Money ran quickly from hand to hand. The queen of spades appeared and disappeared like an elusive fairy. The short and sturdy dealer, his hair shining with brilliantine, moved his hands swiftly, shifting the cards, pocketing the money without a word, and giving a slanting and suspicious look now and then, ready to run off if a policeman came by. Near the players a woman sat on the steps feeding her baby at the breast, and farther on lovers were embracing. On the wider stone steps men were stretched out. Some of them seemed to be sleeping, others were watching the crowd in silence, posed on one arm like the classical sculptured figures symbolizing rivers, or else lying flat on their backs, their hands crossed behind their heads, looking at the sky.

Around them people went up the steps, paused, or came down toward the maternal hollow of the square and toward its most feminine center, the fountain. It was La Barcaccia, modeled in the form of a boat and anchored in the middle of the lake. I went with the crowd and stopped at the edge. Nothing could be more womanly than this bark with its gently chipped and ragged lips, its elongated and pointed oval and the warm dampness of the stone. But the fountain had been empty now for some time and seemed calcified, too white from the utter dryness. At the bottom a green, shining moss covered the parched stone. Inside, instead of the water, some boys were hiding, coiled up with their knees between their arms, as if they had returned, half-naked, to conceal themselves in their mothers' belly. Astonished by the metamorphosis, I looked at them, bending down as if to mirror myself in the absent waters.

The wind brought a vague smell of frying food along with the scent of the flowers, and I began to feel hungry. It was time to look for a place to eat. Since I had let myself be carried this far, I decided not to go to the usual, simple mess where I often ate at noon. I would have had to climb the steps again and walk quite a way. Laziness persuaded me to go down instead and to find a place closer by. And then, too, the mess was so forlorn! I'd been going there only because it cost so little. Just after the war, one didn't earn anything, and everyone had to watch the smallest expense. Therefore one adapted oneself to those squalid messes where, on the paper tablecloth, a single piece of bologna as thin as paper was spread out all by itself on the plate, or calcium-white mashed potatoes invaded the shriveled edges of beefsteak. Pieces of black, rationed bread came along with the juice of canned vegetables, until at the end the apple appeared — that eternal apple of college days that seemed to shiver from cold and boredom; small, tired, green, and worm-eaten.

Actually, my mess was one of the best, one of the most prosperous in the city. It was on the second floor of a lovely palace and was a so-called private mess run with much care for foreign refugees and members of the left-wing parties. My editorial staff went there, my political friends such as Fede and Roselli, and hundreds of others, union organizers, members of the *Consulta* (the pro tem parliamentary assembly), cabinet ministers, undersecretaries, an infinite number of characters known and unknown, many of whom were interesting and lively. But I knew them too well, they were always repeating the same speeches, serious or joking, and the word "politics" returned every minute like an obbligato refrain. I do not like closed societies or restricted circles, nor do I like sweet little apples, so I'd started to look for different places and different company at meals. Somehow Rome was not a

place for low-cost kitchens, which are pleasant only when privation is general and a kind of heroism is in the air. They still went
to them happily in Turin, as I had noticed when I took a trip there
a few weeks before. Everybody waited patiently in front of the cash
register for a meal ticket. Eighteen lira, or twenty-four if one
wanted to celebrate with a glass of wine. Nobody cared what they
put in their mouths; it had the exciting pleasure of collective sacrifice, of austere order. One went away light and filled with hope
into the parallel and straight streets with a vista of the blue and
transparent profile of the mountains at the end. But in Rome,
where the streets were filled with forbidden merchandise and the
shop windows crammed and bursting, and where everyone fought
a bitter war against any kind of constituted authority with all the
energy of his individual character, these messes had only a taste of
melancholy misery. Ours, the mess of the politicians, with its intellectual asceticism, seemed like an island in foreign soil, a piece
of glacial and puritanical tundra, fallen by some magic into the
midst of a virgin forest.

I left the fountain and the children behind me and, crossing the
square, hurried into a side street that went down on the left,
looking for a restaurant. I walked along between wooden stands
and rickety carts that were lined up along the walls, or stood in disorder at the corners and even in the middle of the street. They were
all loaded with black-market food. Everywhere towers and pyra-
mids of white bread rose like triumphal monuments to peace. The
bread was golden, fragrant, and of different forms, every piece
beautiful: some small, round, or elongated, others like canes or
made in a ring like cakes, or in knots, braids, and spirals, like shells
or like radiant suns. It crunched sweetly in the hands of the women
who were testing its freshness, fingering it before they thrust it into
their big, linen shopping bags. On other tables cigars were laid out,
cigarettes and little mountains of tobacco, the fruits of a patient
harvesting of cigarette butts. The white powder of sugar bulged out
from open mouths of linen sacks. Other sacks showed rice, beans,
dried peas, lentils, noodles, spaghetti, white flour and yellow —
those two keys, silver and golden, to the paradise of the kitchen.

Another gold shone green in bottles and flasks, as olive oil was carefully poured through small funnels into the customers' bottles. Besides these, there was every other kind of merchandise: toothpaste, soap, medicines, canned goods, caramel candy, salami, biscuits, meat, brushes, eyeglasses, fountain pens, chewing gum, vitamins, chickens, chocolate, and tripe — all that Italy and America had to offer for the hunger and need of the people.

The ground was covered with dirty paper, cabbage leaves, and remnants of fruit and vegetables. Children and beggars rummaged everywhere, looking for something they could use. The women vendors shouted, the women customers haggled, loiterers chatted, and in this continuous noise, like the commotion in a henhouse, the selling went on. I stopped in front of a table to look at some well-browned loaves of bread, lined up side by side like an army on a holiday ready for the parade. How wonderful were these forbidden goods, in the open, in front of everyone, in the pungent air of the streets.

Some of the customers, heightening their joy in the forbidden, would duck furtively into a doorway to hide an extra package of sugar in their basket or to weigh macaroni or oil on a hand scale. The thrill of the illicit, of sharp dealing in the marketplace — oriental and perhaps hidden in the memory — lit up every face. The woman selling bread was enormous, middle-aged, wrapped in a gray shawl, with her feet slipped into wooden shoes. Boasting of the freshness of her merchandise and the purity of her flour, she pulled out loaf after loaf from an immense sack and filled the empty places in that parade of hers. The sun beat on her dark face, on the wooden stand, and on the bread.

Suddenly there was the cry of a boy, like a whisper, "It's raining! — It's raining, it's raining!" and the voices of anxious women took it up. A murmur ran rapidly down the whole street, I didn't have time to realize what was happening. The stand with the bread on it disappeared, the tables were folded away in a great rush, the bottles hidden, the cigarettes pushed into bosoms, the sugar under skirts. The women ran into doorways, carrying their folding benches; canned goods, rolls, cigars, beans tumbled down on the ground.

Hands moved here and there, legs shot up, skirts whirled, shouts and screaming filled the sky, and the wind carried up bits of paper and spun them around in the blue air.

In a second, after the riotous confusion, dead silence followed. The black-market merchandise was out of sight, the women wrapped in their shawls were again sitting on their folding chairs along the walls, and innocent fruits and rationed canned goods had appeared on the stands in front of them. In the midst of this virtuous silence two *carabinieri* passed by. They walked slowly up the street, talking together without looking around. They had the scrubbed fresh faces of farmer boys from the south, and their eyes were doll-like and fixed. They were probably indulging in some chatter of love and their day off. Walking very slowly, arm in arm, they rounded the corner and disappeared.

It had been a false alarm. A moment later in an outburst of both relief and regret the market took shape as before, the women emerged noisily from the doorways, sugar, oil, and tobacco reappeared on the stands and it was calm again. My bread-seller had not budged after she had hidden the bread, except to take off one of her wooden shoes and brandish it in the air, ready for battle. When the *carabinieri* had rounded the corner, she screamed, "Curses on you!" shaking her wooden shoe at them. Then she put it on again, unfolded her little table and set it up, pulled out the sack she had hidden behind her against the wall and emptied its contents on the table. The bread rolled and jumped around like leaping fish. One loaf fell on the ground. She picked it up, blew on it, dusted it with her sleeve and put it back with the others. "They certainly give us a hard time," she said. Then she sighed deeply and sat down, content.

Like the *carabinieri* I too turned the corner and found myself in a street as crowded with stands and merchandise as the one I had left behind me, but also with shops, posters, and old parked automobiles, where a crowd of boys and men buzzed, looking for something to steal. At one side of the street in front of a shop stood a small Sicilian cart drawn by a tiny donkey; the sides, the body, even the hubs of the wheels painted all over with scenes from the life of Roger, the French paladin. On the other side porters were unloading barrels from an enormous truck that blocked almost the whole passage. In the middle a toothless old man was waving his cane around, quarreling with five or six women who were making fun of him. The old man was drunk and could hardly stand on his legs. He threw himself forward, swaying toward his enemies who retreated a few steps. He stood still for a moment as they advanced from all sides, then he turned to attack them furiously. Avoiding the old man and the women, I slipped behind the truck that hid the entrance and the window display of a restaurant.

I'd tried that restaurant a few days earlier and had come back several times. I often stopped to look at the window display where big pieces of red meat were framed by violet and green artichokes with long, jagged leaves. I hadn't dared to go in because the richness of the display and the music that came from inside led me to believe that the prices would be too high for the pinch of the times. But one day, perhaps because I felt richer than usual, or hungrier, or more eager for novelty, I picked up my courage, mounted the step to the entrance, pushed open the polished glass door, and went in.

In the front room sat a few customers; government clerks, vendors from the nearby market, a woman they addressed as Countess and a group of Allied soldiers. It was a rather large room with tables all around it. In the middle was a sort of glass case filled with silverware and heaps of fruit. The air was stunned by an infernal noise; music, played loudly and savagely, echoed from the ceiling and the walls, and seemed to attack me like the motor of an airplane dragging one through the sky. I heard these savage sounds but could not see the players. They were in a second room, separated from the first by two arches. One arch was open and used as a passage, the other shut off by a row of green plants. The orchestra was installed behind the plants on a kind of platform; there was a base drum, a violin, a snare drum, a saxophone, and a battery of traps. Each player was doing his best to get as much noise as possible out of his instrument. This little company was directed by the traps player, who kept time by beating the cymbals with insane fury. He was a short, dark, middle-aged, suspicious-looking fellow who liked to pass himself off (on what basis I couldn't imagine) not only as a musician but as a doctor, and boasted most loudly of the fact that he was a high-ranking police official. From the way he talked it was more likely that he was a stool pigeon. That he actually had something to do, if not with the police, with the underworld of which the police are an essential part, seemed probable to me. One night when I needed lodgings, I'd tried without success to obtain them by telephoning from the restaurant to all the hotels I knew. He noticed my dilemma, as he was listening to me between numbers.

"Just leave it to me," he said. "Anyone in the police can always find a room." He immediately telephoned in an authoritative and peremptory voice, and although it was two o'clock in the morning he easily found me a room in one of the most dubious and lurid hotels in town. It was the kind of hotel that simple people think exist only in the imaginations of writers or in shady French films. The keys do not turn in the locks, the sheets are damp, the enameled basin and pitcher stand on a shaky tripod under a dirty mirror in a corner. Sounds of quarreling rise along the damp walls and it seems as if the door is about to open in the darkness, the face of some monstrous woman or a murderer's gun with a handkerchief around it showing through the crack.

Beyond the room where the orchestra was playing, two parallel halls separated by a partition led to the big back room. I preferred it there because the music was muffled. One of the passageways served as a pantry and opened into the kitchen. The other was filled with tables and chairs, where seven or eight girls sat sadly over plates of bean and noodle soup. The same girls were there every day, and they stayed in this hall that was reserved for them like a frightened herd in a cattle pen waiting to be led out to munch grass in the field. They ate their bean and noodle soup moodily, drank water, looked at the time, got up, went to have a look in the front room, and sat down again. They were simple, plain-looking girls, family girls, with peroxide hair, dark dresses, and cork-soled shoes. They were waiting, patient and bored, for some Polish soldier to invite them to his table. They would then appear in the front or the back room laughing, talking with gestures, speaking rudimentary Italian, using only the infinitive verbs, "to go," "to love," "to eat," finally getting a real meal, with chicken, spaghetti, and wine. They were the little neighborhood prostitutes of this quarter.

The Poles were a great resource. Now that the British and Americans had moved or gone home, only the Poles were left, these men of General Anders who had no place to go, who couldn't return to their homes and would perhaps stay here forever. They were handsome men, tall and stout, with ruddy faces. Many of them wore long blond or red mustaches. Most of them were no longer young, they were bald or gray, with fat bellies, but there was something aristocratic in the way they carried themselves, like noblemen. They were good company. It was evident that they were wealthy in their own country, that they owned land and castles.

Often they didn't even ask the girls to go to bed with them, but only wanted companionship while they drank, to be reminded of family and home. Drinking they loved; they drank on for hours and hours. And music. They were not content with the restaurant music, which was already making enough noise, but called in musicians and singers from the street who played the violin close to their tables, almost touching them with their instruments as they bent over. The Poles treated the women well, let them eat whatever they wanted, held their hands, and called them "Signora." They were god-fearing and religious. They wore sacred images: medals, little saints and madonnas, crucifixes. They wore them everywhere — around their necks, around their wrists, in their wallets, and inside the linings of their hats. They always talked of family and church and of the Jewish unbelievers who must be exterminated. One could see they loved their country. They said Italy was beautiful, but their country was much more so, that their women were much taller and plumper and rosier than ours; and also the fruit. The apples and the potatoes of their country were much bigger than ours, and each of them owned boundless estates that could not be covered on foot but only on horseback. They were, indeed, rich gentlemen!

They wore many decorations and many service stripes on their sleeves. None of them could have been anything less than a major or a colonel. Yes, it was fun to be with them, hand in hand, to watch them drink and listen to music, so serious and so respectful. Then suddenly they would fall into a rage for no particular reason, shouting, quarreling, and throwing plates and glasses on the floor until some of their friends came to take them by the arm and lead them outside. When this happened the girls often did not have to go home with them, but could either spend the evening with someone else or rest.

Yes, the girls of the cattle pen were happy with Polish soldiers. They had little money, they made too many serious and moral speeches, they were not young or amusing, but they were the last resource, the daily resource of the poor, that small resource left after the fabulous wonders of the past year. The Americans had been an entirely different story. They were young and rich and gay and came out of another world, a world across the sea, from the dream country of fortune. They brought fortune along with them. They brought it here, and one had only to reach out and touch it.

Just before I left Florence I went to say good-bye to Marietta, a model who had hidden me in her room one night when I had no home and the Germans were looking for me.

Marietta was a good girl, serious, simple, and tidy, a peasant girl from Mugello who lived scantily from her work. I hadn't seen her since that time. When I went into her kitchen, I found her standing by the stove cooking her supper, and the good smell of a roast came from the pot. She seemed rejuvenated and prettier, with a new dress, a necklace, and snakeskin shoes.

"You seem very fine!" I said. "What's happened?"

She looked at me gaily. "Follow me," she said, running into her bedroom and throwing open a mirrored wardrobe. "Just see!" The wardrobe was full of clothes, and also a modest fur coat, and several pairs of shoes. While I praised the beauty of the clothes Marietta pulled out some bureau drawers and proudly and happily showed me shirts, lingerie, handkerchiefs, towels, and sheets.

"America has arrived!" she said. "They even want to marry me. Two of them, a sergeant and a private, and both want to marry me and take me with them."

Marietta's brown eyes were brimming over with joy. America had arrived, had come to her and into the dark basement of her tenement. There had been war, hunger, fear, bombs, cold, and privation, and yet they had brought America, paradise. Her peasant common sense, her practical nature had not allowed this paradise, this marvelous compensation, to escape. But she accepted it as a miracle that had happened for some unknown reason and could not last because the place for paradise is in heaven or in the mysterious lands across the sea, and, like heaven, it had better stay in her dreams.

"They want to marry me, both of them. I don't know which I'd rather have. I don't know how to decide. But I believe I'll stay here. Besides, I managed to put aside seventy thousand liras. How does it look to you? Give me your advice. You see, don't you? America has arrived."

For the girls in the restaurant, however, there were left only General Anders' Polish soldiers, that small, minor America, poor in myth and hope, with so little poetry, without the sea between, made out of red mustaches, pictures of saints, and bottles of beer. This was nevertheless a strange and unusual reality, minute and miserable, but a reality. These rootless Polish soldiers of fortune, proud and desperate, were ignorant and presumptuous. But they were foreigners, guests, men from outside with whom one could sit at a table. The girls were satisfied with them.

By now I knew all the girls by sight, but they were so gray and anonymous that it was difficult to tell them apart. Only one of them stood out with a kind of savage beauty in her round, dark face. She had strong features, thick red lips, sparkling black eyes and untidy black hair that fell down over her cheeks and forehead. She was called Elena and had only one leg that stuck out from under her skirt like a stork's leg. She moved along by hopping, supported on two long crutches slipped under her armpits. She never stayed still, she never sat down; she went around from room to room, appeared and disappeared, followed by the dry noise of the wood on the floor. One could meet her everywhere, up to the late hours of the night, at the restaurant, at the cafés, in the streets, unexpected, silent, with a questioning smile, hopping along quickly, searching for something like a bird. Now she was leaning against the wall of the passageway, looking down at her companions sitting there. As I went into the back room I passed her and she gave me a friendly nod.

Giacinto, the waiter, rushed forward obsequiously to offer me a chair at a free table. The room was almost empty and Giacinto was in a talkative mood. He had found out at other times that I would listen to him with patience and now he took advantage of it.

"These Poles," he started, as he put in front of me a plate of noodles that he thought I ought to eat even if I hadn't ordered them. "They're always hanging around here. Who knows when they'll ever go away. War's a bad business, and military life, too. But everyone gets his turn at it. I was a soldier myself for ten years."

I peered up at him with my mouth full. It would have been difficult to imagine anything that looked less military than Giacinto. Not only was there nothing warriorlike about him, but he seemed rather to be a living, deliberate and almost theatrical refutation of such virtues. He was a short, rather stout man, with a slightly puffy round face and a yellowish skin that was pale, damp, shiny, and greasy. His black hair, parted in the middle, seemed wet and fell limply over his temples. He had very lively eyes that were sly, winking, and crafty with an expression both servile and watchful.

His back was hunched, not from any natural deformity but simply from an old habit of bending over, of bowing in the face of the dangers of life, of pulling his head back between his shoulders as though he was always fearing a blow in the face. He was good at his profession, quick at serving, at guessing the tastes and habits of patrons, and at appraising with a side glance their mood and generosity. He swayed as he walked, with his feet turned out, dragging them behind, flat and tired from the many hours of his whole life he had spent standing up. he liked to brag about his infirmities, his physical miseries and weaknesses, showing them off with delight. He would tuck up a trouser leg around his knee to show his thick, varicose veins standing out in purple bunches on a pallid skin that had never taken sun. He said he didn't like women, and that he had never looked at one (and perhaps he was not lying, with his evasive eyes and beardless cheeks). He pretended to shiver at the idea. "My God, let it never happen to me! What a shock it would be! What would I do? Besides, I haven't got time, and I've got too many worries. Better do for myself!"

He liked most to glory in his own cowardice, describing it in minutest detail, feigning a modest confession of constant terror. Then he would enlarge on it, making it into something gigantic, as big as the world, inevitable; so that everyone finally shared it with him.

"I was a soldier for ten years," he told me. "I was called up before the Abyssinian war and they've always held on to me for one reason or another. They sent me all over the place, even to make war against France but fortunately only for a few days; then to Cuneo, and to Yugoslavia, as far as Udine. How scared I was! Luckily, I was always a cook or a general's orderly and never saw a bomb fall. Otherwise I'd have died on the spot just from listening to the crash. Boom!" — and he puffed up his cheeks — "who could stand it? It's enough to make you lose your hearing and also your life. Let it never happen to me. And just fancy, they wanted to send me even to Russia. Who'd ever go that far? I haven't even been to Velletri. Out there it's so cold your nose falls to the ground. And then those Russians! Oh! they're proper wild men and devils. I carried enough bags of flour and bottles of oil to persuade my colonel not to send me. To Russia? What would I have done there? It's better to stay here. They took me to Africa, though, just by sheer force. To Africa, fancy that — and on those deserts. When the order came for me to leave along with the whole regiment, I said, 'Mother of God, this is the end.' How I cried! We had to leave shore and go on the sea. I'd never seen the sea. All that water, who's ever seen that much? And if I'd gone under? What would I have done?

"They took us by train to Naples to take the boat. They put us in a barracks high up on a hill. It was a whole day before we left. I looked out the window from up there and saw all that blue, and they told me that was the sea. And I, Giacinto, would have to go on it. I'd never been on a river, let alone the sea. I cried. What was to become of me? Who would hold me up?

"A lieutenant passed by, looked at me, and said: 'Do you see that sea, Giacinto? Come along with me. It's a fine day and we'll go to Marcellina for a swim.' Marcellina? I thought, who's she? I'd never known anyone named Marcellina. The Lord stand by me! I thought it was a woman, Holy Mother! Instead, it was a beach. There was sand on the ground and wooden cabins on it, and a lot of naked people, wearing only little tights, some standing up, some lying down. And many girls, too, all undressed and staring at me.

"The lieutenant gave me some knitted tights and a key and said: 'Giacinto, run to the cabin, put these on, and hurry up.' Then he shut me in. I felt ashamed. Fancy that! I'd have to undress, and everybody would look at me — also the women. I hoped the lieutenant would forget me and go take a swim by himself. Instead he knocked at the door in five minutes. 'Aren't you ready, Giacinto? Hurry up!' I took off one shoe and held it in my hand. 'Yes, sir, yes, Signor Lieutenant, I'll come right away.' He came back after awhile. 'What's the matter, are you sick?' he asked. Then he opened the door and saw me all in harness with my shoe in my hand. He was naked.

"'Well! Aren't you undressed yet? What are you waiting for?'

"'I feel faint, Signor Lieutenant, and I don't know how to put a thing like this on.'

"He started to laugh. 'Here, I'll help you,' he said, unbuttoning my tunic and pulling down my pants.

"'But, Signor Lieutenant, also my shirt? Do I have to take my shirt off too?'

"'Yes, your shirt, too.' And he pulled it over my head.

"I was as naked as a worm, like Mamma made me, and I had to put on those tights. 'Let me stay in here, Signor Lieutenant. What'll all those ladies say if they see me? What a disgrace!'

"But I couldn't persuade him. He took me by the hand, made me get out of the cabin, and dragging me all the time, he forced me to cross the whole beach. I kept my eyes shut tight because I was sure everyone was looking at me. The lieutenant pulled me to the edge of the water.

"'The sea's as calm as oil,' he said. 'Get into the water, Giacinto, and stay where you can touch bottom. Happy swim!' And he left me.

"I opened my eyes. The lieutenant had made a big plunge and was leaping like a fish. I stood there naked, as white as a silkworm, and all the girls were looking at me, and I had to get into the sea. My God! I tried the water with one foot, and it was cold! Brrr! Finally I put my other foot forward, very slowly, pushed it down, and immediately felt a stinging under the sole. God alone knows what a pain that was! Perhaps it was only a little stone, but I thought: the sea's full of crabs, and one of them has pinched me. Oh, Mother! I was so scared that I began to shout and I fell into the water. It was deep, I shouted some more and the water got into my mouth and I thought: this time I'm really dead. How bitter it was! Like poison. I started to cough and drank and drank who knows how many quarts. Finally I couldn't breathe anymore and drowned. Luckily the people on the beach ran and hauled me in, laid me on the beach, started to pull my arms and legs, squeezed my stomach, pounded me until I spit the water out again. Otherwise I'd have died. The lieutenant came and pulled my arms too, and made me sit on the ground.

"'What happened, Giacinto?'

"'I was faint, Signor Lieutenant, and I fell.'

"'And how are you now?'

"'Now I feel better.'

"'Take it easy for a minute and then we'll go over to that cliff and take a nice picture. I'll swim and you can take the camera and walk over that little bridge there.' He pointed it out with his hand.

"A fine bridge that was, just a shaky running board without any railing. He ran off to the cabin, came back with his camera, hung it around my neck, called out, '*Marsch!*' and dove back into the sea. A minute later he had made it and was signaling to me from the cliff to hurry. I was standing on the board, not daring to look around. Under me was the water. What if I fell? I had a cold sweat, felt death upon me, and was shaking all over. What a time to take a picture! I crossed myself, and with God's help I got there. It was only a few yards. The lieutenant was already standing on the cliff with one hand on his hip. I had to take his picture that way, then he took one of me. Then he asked a young lady lying nearby to take a picture of both of us. She was almost naked and wearing black glasses. I still have that picture at home. But all the time I was thinking of how I'd have to go back over that damned board. The lieutenant noticed it and said: 'I'll swim underneath and catch you if you fall in.' What a sigh I heaved when I was back on dry land again!"

"And what did you do on the ship after you embarked!" I asked him.

"Don't talk to me about it. My hair stands up if I only think of it. They lined us up on the bridge and the Crown Prince came to inspect us. He was very pretty, saluting left and right and shaking the officer's hands, and raising his arm here and there in the Fascist salute and smiling just as if he weren't standing on a ship. But then after all he didn't have to come with us to the middle of the sea.

"I didn't want to see us leave. As soon as I could I went down to my bunk and started to cry. I put my head under the blanket and thought: Where have you ended up, Giacinto? How much better it would have been if you'd become a Jesuit! You wouldn't be here now. Because I was to become a Jesuit, you know. I'll tell you about that later. They're calling me now. Here I am. . . ." And he ran off.

I looked around and saw my friend Marco at the next table. He must have been there for some time, but Giacinto, absorbed in the cheap odyssey of his cowardice, had cut him off from my sight. Marco was an old childhood friend, though I hardly recognized him. When I'd last seen him, a few months before, he was clean-shaven. Now he had an enormous black beard that fell to his chest. It was shiny and it curled. A big mustache, long and drooping, lost itself in the beard, leaving the scarlet island of his lips isolated in the middle of it. Marco had a way of changing his appearance all the time. One might meet him with his hair shaved to zero and his head as round as a ball, or again, with a rich mane of jet-black hair like a woman's, with blue reflected in it. Sometimes he wore Spanish sideburns and felt like a *hidalgo* or a toreador: sometimes he wore a mustache like an old professor's, accompanied by pince-nez on the tip of his nose and hair parted accurately on one side; sometimes a clerk's mustache and a silk handkerchief around his neck to defend himself from hypothetical drafts, or an arrogant, twisted-up mustache, as he put on a military air. All these changes did not occur for any practical reason or necessity. They resulted, partly, from a natural taste for mystification and his natural theatrical talent, but they were first of all a compensation and a defense. This is what happens to women who change their clothes and hairdress and spend hours in front of a mirror when they feel neglected by their lovers. By changing themselves they find consolation for not being able to change their lovers. Having made the change by lifting a lock of hair, or by varying the color of their lips or lashes, sorrows do not touch them anymore or are more easily forgotten. The end of a love affair demands a new dress; how could one otherwise bear the sorrow? This is how savages, too, disguise themselves and change their names to escape the spirits and the vendettas of the dead.

Marco often metamorphozed himself, escaping into always new incarnations. But this time his beard was so long and solemn that I thought something serious and important had happened to him. In the midst of the dark, hairy ocean his long thin face was like wax, with a yellow and transparent paleness that made his sharp, black eyes deeper and gloomier, his long, sensitive nose thinner, his forehead wider and marked by a straight furrow. He had tossed himself on a chair and his tall, dry body, thin arms, and long legs looked like a bundle of branches. He was resting his head on his hand, with a profoundly desolate expression, and he sighed. I called him to my table, invited him to sit with me, and asked him what was wrong.

"Well," he answered in a low and deliberately melancholy voice, "she's gone. Not to be found. You wouldn't understand it. . . . Troubles."

That was all he said. His face took on a grimace of patient sorrow, and lowering his eyes and pushing out his underlip, he started to stroke his beard.

Giacinto, having got rid of his other clients, was bringing the plates for Marco. He picked up the thread of his story. He took such delight in his cowardly role that it would have been not only cruel but impossible to interrupt him. After all, it's difficult to save yourself from the chatter of barbers, waiters, and so many others whose vain words spread out in the air of the city like the buzzing of insects in the woods. They are but harmless elements of time, parts of nature.

"As I was telling you, I was supposed to become a Jesuit before the army took me," he commenced. "I was a boy then, and had studied with the priests. Afterward I worked in a shop, but the world didn't appeal to me. I felt a certain urge to retire. I'd find peace and there would be nothing to do, I thought. I knew many sleek and important monsignors. One of them, a friend of my uncle, sent me to talk with the head of the Jesuits, the general of the Mother House himself. You should see the riches, the gold. I looked around, opened my eyes, and thought: Giacinto, this is the place for you. They took me into the general's personal study and left me alone to wait for him. Just imagine! There were three telephones on the desk and so many bells I could have lost myself among them. They can call up any place in the world from there, as though there was nothing to it, and besides that they have a direct line up to the pope and talk to him as if he were one of them.

"That's enough of that! Well . . . then the general came in with four or five other big priests who questioned me through and through. They wanted to know everything; whether I had a vocation, whether I had money, whether I was willing to study and work. Work? I thought to myself. If I'd wanted to work I wouldn't have come here. Or were they supposed to work even here? He told me I'd have to hoe the vegetable garden and chop wood and that I should think it over. Fancy that one! I didn't know what to say and as soon as I could, I ran away and never showed up again.

"So I didn't become a Jesuit, but had to be a soldier and go to Africa. Right to Tripoli, in Libya, but luckily there was nothing to fight. They put us in barracks in the middle of the desert, about five miles outside of Tripoli. Every morning at dawn I had to go to the market in the city to buy food. I took a bus that stopped right in front of the barracks. One morning I was only a minute late but I missed the bus and had to start walking down the road. It was still night, in the middle of all that sand. I'd gone about half a mile when I saw two Arabs with faces like the end of the world, and a donkey. They were coming slowly toward me. There won't be much to joke about with them, I told myself. If they get hold of you, they'll do certain things. . . .

"I stopped and looked around, but there was nothing but sand. Where could I hide? I'm dead, I thought, I'm worse than dead. The two blacks advanced steadily with their donkey until they were only a few steps away. What could I do? I turned around and started to run without looking back. Use your legs, Giacinto! I'd never run that much in all my life. Those two ugly muzzles didn't stir, but I felt as if they were right at my shoulder and I didn't stop to take a breath. My heart thumped as though it would burst. When I was finally inside the barracks I fell on the ground because my legs wouldn't carry me any farther. But I was safe."

During this long chatter of Giacinto's, Marco ate. He was distracted and annoyed and between one mouthful and the next he stroked his beard. The waiter's exaggerations, his vulgarity and his grimaces, failed to turn Marco from his concentrated sorrow. This was rare for Marco, since he usually became interested in anything that had any sort of character. Had it been another time, Marco would have encouraged Giacinto in his eloquence — although that wasn't necessary — and would have answered him back and led him on who knows where. Or he would at least have noticed and pointed out to me the art of this little Roman, who knew how to defend himself against the world and against the powerful of this earth of ours, not only with the patience and the desperate resignation of the poor, but, like a character in Belli's sonnets, with the inner amusement he got from his continuous improvisations on the theme of cowardice.

Because Marco was interested in everything, even the smallest things, extremely receptive and susceptible to words, atmosphere, colors, and the most insignificant detail, he assimilated everything in a kind of endless process of rapid and insatiable digestion. This fundamental trait of his ws in direct contradiction to his profession, which was that of a composer. Aside from Marco and a few other exceptions, I have always found that musicians, of all artists, are the most shut off, really as deaf as bells to any other interests except their own. The music Marco composed was ingenious and substantially simple, corresponding very little to his nature; and I felt that although it was lovely music he had gone the wrong way, that he would have found more precise expression if he had been a realistic writer, an actor, or a man of politics.

Now he presented a perfect picture of sorrow, so perfect that it was not altogether convincing. He was sad and at the same time he played at being sad, and found consolation by doing so. And he pretended so well he was convinced it was genuine. He was, therefore, sincere, like a great actor, if a variation of Diderot's paradox is allowed, who must not become one with the character he plays, who laughs, cries, and suffers; but who must believe that he is one with him, and believe with all his heart that he is suffering, laughing, and crying.

—◌ **2** ◌—

"Who can't be found?" I ventured to ask, to break the silence
when Giacinto, called away to his work, had left us. It was not an
indiscreet question because I was an intimate friend of Marco's
and I knew, because he had told me, many of his vicissitudes and
sentimental tragedies. I thought it concerned his wife Silvia, a
beautiful and dignified woman whom he had married when she
was very young, many years before. They had been separated and
reconciled again at least ten times. But what woman could have
lasted a long time with him? It could only have been a woman
commanding enough to dominate him or wicked enough to know
how to make him suffer every moment. Marco accepted everything in the world, assimilated and understood everything, and
drank up the life outside like milk. To accomplish this he had to
be accompanied by sadness, a sense of inferiority, discomfort,
blows, whipping, darkness, and grinding of teeth. He really loved
his own unhappiness more than he loved things or people, and he
did not distinguish it from true experience. His friends attributed
this to his excessive love for his mother, who was dour, austere, severe, and religious, and who had brought him up to weep as he
received his food, and to love life weeping. Perhaps from her, too,
they maintained, and from the education he duly received from
the Jesuit fathers, had come his taste for make-believe (which was
not falsehood), for masquerading himself, and for escape. Be that
as it may, Silvia was too proud, too shy, and too gentle to make her
husband suffer and therefore make herself be loved by him. She
was an unprotected and noble creature who did not know how to
hate, and the complicated wickedness by which Marco unconsciously sought to make himself justly hated, despised, and ill-
treated had no effect on her. So because of her sweetness and
goodness their life together was impossible.

"Who's not to be found?" I repeated. "Silvia?"

Marco lifted his beard. "No, not Silvia. Silvia has been staying
at her mother's with the child since the war started, and we

haven't seen each other. Not Silvia. Don't you understand? It's *She.* . . . It's *She!* I found her, the Queen of Sirens. . . . Fanny; imagine her being called Fanny. I found her, and now she's lost. For three days I've looked for her all over Rome. She's disappeared."

So it had nothing to do with Silvia, who stayed in that faraway country house growing flowers, letting days, months and years go by, hurt and solitary and, alas, indulgent and compassionate. But this was instead one of those thousands of women Marco pursued, following his contradictory and unattainable mother-image, always disappointed and always on the prowl, like a thin dog in the woods.

These tentative quests of his were continuous, and he always failed in the attempt. Marco was too intelligent not to be the first to recognize their uselessness, but he gave in to the impulse, partly because of his love of experience and adventure, partly for his love of being frustrated and of giving in to the powerful attraction that bitterness and anxiety had for him. Now it was Fanny's turn, the latest link in that useless chain.

"She's a marvelous woman," he said. "It's *She.* She's enormous, completely white, soft, welcoming. And absolutely passive. She doesn't speak, she doesn't move, yet lets herself be embraced and swallows you without your even noticing it. She's a force of nature. I can imagine killing myself for her; someone else must certainly have died for her and perhaps she didn't even turn her eyes. She accepts everything, good and bad. She's like this country of ours, run over by all these armies, where all crimes are being perpetrated, where people and cities were destroyed, and life continues as always, yet livelier and more callous. Yes, Fanny is really like Italy, with a great white body filled with breasts, a tower at her head, and the unseeing eyes of the goddesses. I found her and now I've lost her."

L ook at these gloves!" interrupted a thin and insistent nasal voice. "Soft, everlasting, waterproof. They are just exactly your

size. It's your hand. Try them on. They cost hardly anything." Behind this monotonous voice that continued always on the same
note to praise his merchandise, appeared a man who looked
vaguely like Marco, but without the beard. He too was tall and
thin, dark, pale, waxen, with brown and purple spots on the skin
around his eyes. He reminded one at once of a dog, but of one of
those yellow dogs with flabby cheeks, sweet eyes, and hanging ears,
that are always on the run, with a rhythmic and elastic lope around
the corners and old walls of villages. Their noses are serious as
though they were out on important business.

It was Bracco the painter, who was amiable and full of grace in
his paintings. But loved only himself and the beauty of the boys he
pursued on the streets and in the doorways. He lied naturally with
the same innocence that he breathed and painted. He lived on the
black market by reselling to his friends the most ill-assorted articles
furnished him by his adored boys, the fruits of their tendernesses toward Allied soldiers. He was strangely rigged up, since he carried
his merchandise on him. He wore two flannel shirts, three different
colored sweaters, a windbreaker, and a military raincoat, all on top
of one another. He also showed us that he was wearing three pairs
of woolen socks. This way his customers could make a choice
without fuss. And the socks also served to fill up his huge oversize
shoes, which were American too, and which he used as samples for
clients. Other objects like fountain pens, vitamins, and sunglasses,
he kept in a leather brief case, also for sale. We were forced to listen
patiently to a minute description praising each item, along with a
complete list of "authorities," the names of the customers who rec-
ommended his wares, long digressions on the graces of his young
suppliers, on the significance of beauty, and on the absurdity and
injustice of the feminine monopoly. It was impossible to get away
from his monotonous discourse, from that tranquil and steady
chirping. His talk was the unpleasant raw material of Bracco's
sweet paintings of naked boys and small familiar objects. He threw
it at everyone with candid assurance. We must look at his goods
even if we didn't need them. He could furnish us, too, with things
he hadn't brought along. Overalls, for example, wouldn't I like

some? Cesarino had a pair and he was so fair and so slender that he looked like a flower in them. Or wouldn't Marco be interested in a waterproof hat, rubber lined and the rubber was genuine, and with earflaps attached? Or an American combination comb and clipper with which you could cut your hair or your beard by yourself. How could anyone have such a black beard? *Vir es*, my dears, as Poliziano put it. The boys like it, the boys like it very much, it affects them as a uniform affects women. Boys are so strange and natural just like wild animals. It was a shame beards aged one, or he would have worn one too. And so on and so on endlessly. Who could have stopped Bracco's speeches that came from his mouth uninterrupted like the dripping from a loose faucet? The world could have turned on its hinges and Bracco would have gone on yelping without noticing a thing.

We were listening to him with resignation and embarrassment. Fortunately a friend of ours came in, bringing with him a young woman I did not know, who looked, at first glance, very beautiful. The place had filled. All the tables were occupied. The din of conversation, of silver on plates, of chairs being pulled out, mingled with the noise of the orchestra in one prolonged sound, reechoing from the ceiling as though we were sitting in a moving train. The air was smoky and the newcomer stopped a moment in this noisy mist. He looked around, came toward us, and asked if he and his sister could share our table. Bracco had to step aside to make way for them, and in doing so, interrupted himself. He skipped off to other tables, other acquaintances, and other small sales.

Ferrari (this was the name of our new table companion) sat next to Marco, and his sister Elda sat next to me. It was by chance, he said, that he had come to this restaurant to eat. It was late. And he and his wife and child lived far away in a kind of hovel or tenement at the gates of Rome, a horrible room but even that had been hard to find. He hadn't wanted to go out that far today to eat. Then

he met his sister, who had just taken a university examination, and
he brought her along. It was an unusual adventure for her. She
never left her home or her mother and sisters, especially now, after
the war, since the Germans had killed their father in the gas
chambers. Ferrari was glad to have found us here and he introduced the girl as though he thought we would interest her. She sat
silently beside me.

From her newly washed chestnut hair, shining and loose over
her shoulders, came a sharp scent like that of cut young grass. I
looked at her profile, with its convex forehead, straight nose,
pursed mouth, and firm chin, and her round neck on her slender
body. Her light eyes of transparent green, like those of a cat,
looked at us from a frown as though instinctively defending her,
intimidated by the unusual place, the noise, the smoke, and our
presence. Marco filled her glass with wine. It was not her habit,
she never drank, but she raised it quickly to her mouth with a gesture of innocent bravado.

Ferrari was some years older than his sister, who was still almost
a child. They didn't look alike. He was small and thin, with deep-
set eyes and an open, questioning expression on his freckled face.
A slight defect in his speech, the hint of a stutter, did not impede a
certain boldness and impetuosity of expression, in fact it sometimes made it more effective, underlined and proclaimed it, like a
motor that sputters as it starts to run. He was a lecturer who had
fought in the Resistance and found himself poor at the end of the
war, having lost his father who had always provided for him and
his family. He had been obliged to accept a post in a government
ministry.

"A ministry! You don't know what a ministry's like. Nobody
knows unless he's inside. It's not even anything you can imagine.
It's a world unknown, underground and infernal. It's a miraculous
collection of all miseries, all vices, and everything that is sordid, a
pure culture bred from the disease of baseness. But listen! I have
no complaint. Personally I'm very well off there. I have absolutely
nothing to do. The salary's small but what more could I ask — it's
a sinecure. In the three months I've been there, I've had only one

assignment, to write two or three little pages on the conditions of demobilized partisans, at most one hour's work.

"When I first went there I had all sorts of illusions and sometimes asked the office manager to give me something to do. He looked at me half astonished, half offended. I realized I'd have done better to keep quiet and not to have made myself noticeable, and to wait before I took any step until I had penetrated the secret rules of that strange country. Bit by bit I'm discovering them. We've been through a war that, whether you like it or not, has been a revolution; we've seen death, we've paid for our sins and those of others, we've thrown the past over our shoulders, and also what was dear to us, the affections, the sweetness of life. We've lived like men, we've felt united, we've understood what the world means, but all this is as though it had occurred on another planet. There once was gunfire on the sidewalk across the street from us. Today workmen, women looking for jobs, and American soldiers go by, but inside the ministry a few yards away it is as if nothing at all had happened. Its walls isolate from the world a restricted caste of the petty bourgeoisie; degenerate and miserable, deaf and blind and insensible to everything but their own little needs, their guilty solidarity, their intrigues, so mean and microscopic as to appear incomprehensible.

"The ministry is a kind of temple where the most abject vices are being worshiped and perfected, the three most desolate mortal sins, sloth, avarice, and envy. They are the three vices that characterize the incompetent, petty bourgeoisie who search both for security and power, who are lazy because they cannot do anything, cannot use their hands or their brains, and every kind of work is difficult for them and therefore unpleasant, tiresome, and impossible. They are avaricious because they are poor and pretentious. They find in envy the only compensation for their own misery, in the most complete envy that has penetrated everywhere, as a poison circulates in the blood. All this is bound together by a strong caste spirit, by as close a tie as the Camorra or Mafia. There they sit with their glassy eyes for hours and hours, those creatures, on their chairs in front of their desks, doing nothing, materially nothing, not even reading the newspapers, in a kind of ecstasy of idleness, or perhaps a mystical identification with the empty concept of the state.

"You ought to see their faces; terrible, ferocious in their flatness. They are a whitewashed wall, and we all batter against it without being able to beat it down. The purge doesn't get anywhere against that passive resistance. They are still the same as the ones before, and others coming in are exactly like them. Their only activity is to see that nothing new happens. The new ministers are powerless against them. And the ushers themselves? Why the lowest usher looks down on the new ministers. Now that there's a government crisis, you ought to see that ministry, with all the third-rate clerks, copyists, and drones rubbing their hands, winking at each other, and slapping one another on the back. Each one of them feels that hour by hour he has contributed something personally to the overthrow of the government, a government with the courage or the program or the pretension or the hope of bringing about a change that touches their hidden and invisible power — not realizing what a serpent has been aroused. When they get there in the morning and spread out the newspapers on their desks, they roar with laughter as they read that the factory workers of the North and the farmers of the South have protested against the crisis and have proclaimed their solidarity.

"I assure you," Ferrari went on, "we won't succeed in saving the Resistance movement, no, unfortunately we won't save it. Those clerks are like carrion crows, somehow they read the future and are only made happy by death — and they're dancing these days up at the ministry. We have done it, they say. We'll be better off with the priests."

Ferrari's eyes sparkled with indignation, his face became redder every time he stumbled ever so slightly over a word, and driven by his indignation, he stopped with his fork in his hand without eating. Marco interrupted him absentmindedly to say that all bureaucracies in all countries had the same faults. he had seen it for himself in France. He had experienced the sadism and insanity of Corsican officials, and everyone knew the classical descriptions by the great Russian writes of bureaucracy under the Tsars; after all, every country has the bureaucracy it deserves.

"But in the midst of that mob there are a few exemplary M'sieu Travets," he said. "All virtue, love for work, spirit of sacrifice, attachment to the family, sublime and hidden heroism, devotion to duty, Christian humility, faithful servants of the state, priests of the public good — don't take a step longer than their leg — hard collars, worn pants, and hearts of gold — sacrificing themselves on the altar of the fatherland, pulling in the belt without complaining, fasting to send the children to school, holding the head high — dignity and honor — not going into debt, signing no promissory notes, bearing silently the caprices and dresses of wives, payday on the twenty-seventh of the month, and the bullying of the office manager — and honesty, always honesty, again honesty!"

Marco ws reciting this declamation more and more like a lesson or a theatrical role, with the solemn and fatuous accents of a typical clerk. He thus transformed himself into a bureaucrat of the ministry; he made himself small, pulled his head down between his shoulders, his eyes dimmed, and his features took on a ridiculously smug expression. But his overelaborate beard, and possibly thoughts of Fanny, kept the imitation from being perfect and entirely persuasive.

Ferrari repeated that Italy did not have the bureaucracy it deserved, because Italy had changed and the bureaucracy had stayed as it was before. There were, of course, some good officials who took on by themselves all the work of the other parasites, and they were the first victims of the system. It wasn't for him to talk about it; he admitted that he too was a parasite, but he was forced into it against his will, and he felt he was particularly objective about it. Like the new ministers he had tried to interfere with this machine, and had failed as they had, but he had seen immediately that it was bound to crush him.

"Just try, for instance," he said, "to give the slightest reprimand to a beadle who has been remiss in his duties. He'll look at you at first with horrified incredulity. You, a newcomer, with that kind of courage? Where do you come from? Who brought you up? Then, after a menacing silence, without replying to your reprimand, without looking at you but staring at a spot on the wall back of you, he'll say: 'I know men in this office who spend their time telephoning their mistresses. To their mistresses! And others who write their private letters on government paper. I know some, too, who go out again as soon as they've come, others who turn up only for payday, and others who read detective stories during working hours. I know many more things, if I'd start talking about them.' He won't say anything more and he won't take any notice of you, and you realize that there's no escape from that wicked machine of the common guilt.

"You come into the office in the morning. On every colleague's table there's a book, a bound book. It's the *Yearly Register,* where all the facts about employees are listed, their names, their titles, their functions, their seniority. They call it 'The Little Liar,' and it's their gospel; the gospel of sloth and envy. The rumor spreads that perhaps so-and-so will be purged, that so-and-so's at home with pneumonia. Immediately all backs curve over 'The Little Liar,' for an hour a hundred hands leaf it, hundreds of eyes consult it anxiously: if so-and-so leaves, if so-and-so dies, there will be shifts. Titus is promoted, Caius jumps a grade, and I? I'm promoted. For another hour nobody talks of anything else, you whisper, you comment, you analyze, and the analysis increases and gets more complicated and propagates in every office, is disseminated over the telephone to all the detached sections, and spreads out all over Rome.

"A too-young and too-zealous minister wants to accomplish something? His files disappear, the clerks run to tell their colleagues in the other ministries to hold them up when they come through, and everything is swallowed up in the quicksands. The ministry's an immense beehive, where with great labor the envious honey of laziness is being distilled. It's an endless labyrinth where everything gets lost, where you lose yourself physically, too, where people disappear. Many of them, the cleverest of them, disappear voluntarily, they hide under the stairs or in a dead corner, and nobody ever finds them again.

"Last month I went to the Viminale to look for a clerk, Cleonte Massilli, who's a friend of mine. Do you happen to know him? He too, like me, is a poet; and like me, an honorary and parasitic bureaucrat. Naturally I didn't go to see him on business, but to talk about literature. I often went there to visit him in Room 223. One day he wasn't in. He wasn't there any longer. Nobody could tell me where he'd been moved. I spent the whole day at the ministry, going upstairs and down to every floor, following the smallest clue. After hours and hours of searching, after I'd been sent here and there, I finally came to a room where I found a package of books tied together with a string. There was a piece of paper on the package with 'Cleonte Massilli' written on it. He'd passed that way the day before, leaving the bundle behind him, his last word, like a bottle thrown into the sea, like the ambiguous message of a Gordon Pym before he vanished into the abyss. Cleonte has vanished and I will never find him again. Still I know that he's alive, that he goes to the ministry every morning, perhaps he's in the room next door. But nobody will ever know. He's found a dead corner. In this corrupt, parasitic, degenerate, and vicious world, he caught on to the game at once. And he was fortunate."

> *I'm called Fortunato*
> *But indeed, I'm not fortunate*
> *For it was a misfortune*
> *For me to be born. . . .*

sang a high, nasal, mechanical, violent voice over my shoulder; it did not seem to come out of a human mouth but from an artificial and desperate marionette. The music in the other room had stopped. The whole room was crowded with people. I turned around and saw the singer, who had been brought in by a group of Polish soldiers. He was accompanying himself on a guitar with a drum attached to it, and on top of the drum were cymbals played by a complicated lever worked by one foot. He was dressed all in black, black jacket, black shoes, black trousers, black vest, the Sunday best of a peasant; and he had the body of a peasant, short, gnarled, and awkward; and a dark face with black fixed eyes. He played his intricate complex of instruments with the motions of an automaton, hardly opening his mouth as he sang and not stirring a muscle of his face. He moved his scalp and his ears without wrinkling his forehead, making the derby that was tipped over his disorderly black hair bob up and down to the rhythm of the music. His pale, motionless, and impassive face never changed its expression of extreme vulgarity and extreme desperation. From his white lips came his hollow voice, monotonous, penetrating, and inhuman:

> *No communist, I*
> *No socialist either!*
> *Neo-fascist?*
> *No, no!*
>
> *And who am I then?*
>
> *Oh I'm just a poor beggar,*
> *Tossed around here and there;*
> *And a mouth to eat with*
> *Is all that I own.*

It was the song of rags, of the underworld of the poor, the *Lumpenproletariat*. Everyone listened; and they were silent, sitting at the tables. Elda also looked at him, with her pretty adolescent eyes. But what was it she saw? While her brother had been talking Marco continued to pour drinks for her and ask her about her examinations. Elda blushed and answered that she'd had only a twenty-two of a possible thirty, that the professors were severe; they took out their family troubles on their pupils — the usual chatter of students. Then she continued to be quiet, closed in her own circle of inexpressible and happy thoughts. One could see that in her eyes we and her brother as well were very old people, people of another generation that could not understand her; and that this restaurant was lovely to her because of its noise; that the singer sang badly but was quaint, the people around her were animated, and nobody there could know her simple secrets.

I haven't any savings,
I haven't a thing,
A mouth to eat with
Is all that I own.

Every day I hunt work
And find nothing at all.
Only hunger's a danger
And it's always there.

He sang, motionless in the room, this funereal marionette, white and black like a ghost. The song was finished but Fortunato did not stop, did not listen to the applause, did not pass the plate for money. He strummed his guitar, beat his drum, kept time with the cymbals, and having changed the tune but not his tone or his posture, started on a long succession of political ballads. The black derby bobbed up and down on his head, his eyes and his face became stiffer and devoid of any expression, like a tragic mask carved on the trunk of a tree, and he began to sing again:

Now say the Allies —
We're your brothers.
And they send from America
Peas for your soup.

This was the sad, timeless epic of the poor who have no history and to whom history is only the passing of an hour, the always diverse way in which hunger, illness, and death confront them. Without any display of emotion he sang of their protests against history and the state, of the tricks and resourcefulness of beggars, the picaresque life of the black marketeers:

If it weren't for the black market,
They'd have fetched us to our graves.

And he went on to tell of food, of small cunning, of thefts, of swindles, and of the fortunes and disgraces of prostitutes. He talked of war and peace, of Negroes, of Moroccans, of foreigners, of madonnas and saints, and that timeless world where each event lies, one beside the other, like the dead in a graveyard.

He had finished. He lifted his derby from his forehead with the hint of a greeting, and without changing his expression went silently from table to table passing his plate.

"To play, to dance!" the Poles shouted, and with Giacinto helping them, they pushed the tables against the wall to clear a space in the center of the room. Fortunato finished his rounds. A soldier gave him a glass of beer.

"Play, dance!"

Fortunato drank his beer slowly and carefully, as peasants drink after their work in the field; he dried his mouth with the back of his hand, picked up his instruments again, and started off.

He played an old waltz. A Polish soldier grabbed the girl at his table and flung himself into the middle of the room. For a moment they were the only ones dancing, then another couple followed, then another, and still others. Now both the Poles and the Italians got up from their tables, the women hurried from their cattle pen, and there were, at once, cavaliers for all of them. And the musicians came down from their platform, led by their musical doctor-policeman, to bolster Fortunato's guitar and drum with violin, saxophone, and trumpet.

One dance followed another without pause. New tunes and old songs, languid rhythms and quick rhythms, the music grew louder, the couples turned, wavered, pirouetted. The people sitting at the tables marked time with their feet and shouted. The excitement, the trampling of feet, the noise, the motion, and the whirling increased.

Suddenly a huge, red-faced Pole with a long, blond mustache and a bald head, who had been sitting alone and melancholy in a corner, jumped to his feet as though bitten by a snake and shouted. He dashed his glass of beer on the floor, signaled for the crowd to give him room, and began to dance, squatting on his heels with his knees bent, his back straight, and his hands on his hips.

Everyone stopped to look at him. Then other soldiers left their women and threw themselves into the same dance. Other glasses were shattered against the wall, shouts crowded one on another. One of the Poles pulled off his boots and started to dance on naked feet.

The violins, trumpets, and saxophones of the orchestra were silent. Only Fortunato kept on imperturbably, monotonously beating his cymbals and his drum, accompanying the barbaric rhythm of feet, the clapping hands, the shouts. And without stopping he sang in his hollow voice:

> *I'm called Fortunato,*
> *But indeed, I'm not fortunate*
> *For it was a misfortune*
> *For me to be born.*

Elena, very tall and straight, propped up against a doorway on her crutches, watched in silence, like a doll.

"It's late," said Marco.

We got up, left the smoke-filled room, walked through the corridor and the entrance, and went out of the restaurant into the wind.

5

*A*FTER THE NOISE AND SMOKE of the restaurant, the outside air seemed clearer and lighter. It was pleasant to feel it touch our faces, enter our nostrils fresh, wrap us around, and almost carry us with its sudden gusts. Close by and far away, in the bright and mobile perspective, people moved in circles, the women clasping their shawls to their breasts as though they were propelled by the same whirling motion that was lifting paper, dry leaves, and dust and spinning them around like small windmills. The fragment of sky visible between the houses over our heads was blue and serene; gray rags of clouds, changing form every instant, were speeding along, dragged by the wind behind the dome of San Carlo at Corso. We walked a short way together and then turned into a side street. There Ferrari and his sister said good-bye and ran off.

When we were left alone Marco took my arm and said, "Don't leave me. Come along. Perhaps we'll find her."

He wanted me to go with him on his search for Fanny. He had already been everywhere in the places where he thought he might find her. He did not expect me to take an active part, but only wanted my company on this last attempt. He was convinced my presence would bring him luck. I told him that to please him I'd gladly go along, but that I was rather busy. I had to write my articles for the evening edition, take possession of my new home, move my belongings, and leave my broken watch at the casemaker. And I told him briefly about my dream.

Marco insisted. He had his jeep in a garage close by. To save time he would ride me right away to the watchmaker and later, if I wanted him to, he would carry my valise to my new home. But first of all I must have the watch fixed. My dream had impressed him, and he didn't want me to keep the broken object on me for too long. He felt that the tissue paper parcel in my pocket troubled me as though I were carrying a sick man or an invalid.

How many watches he had given to Silvia during the changing years of their difficult married life! And Silvia had always lost them. Most important was the loss of the first one, a tiny wrist watch with a black dial and a circle of diamonds around it. The loss had coincided with their first separation many years ago. When they were reconciled he gave her another watch, a Swiss Le Coultre, but that too was lost on one of their frequent journeys; then she lost still others. And then one day Silvia, during a period of separation, had bought herself one with her own money, and that watch had never been lost. Now that their separation was permanent, Silvia lived with her mother and he didn't know about the small facts of her life, but he was ready to wager she still had that autonomous watch.

"That is," he said in a low voice, "unless someone has presented her with another."

As for himself, he hadn't carried a watch for some time. It was better that way, without the control, the perpetual call to order. He looked at the sun or asked people on the street how late it was. It was fun to pass the time, especially in the winter, by approaching a heavily clad gentleman in a polite and authoritative manner and asking, "Would you be so kind as to give me the exact time?" The man wouldn't dare refuse to unbutton his overcoat in spite of the cold and the embarrassment of gloves. Or better still, on a lonely, dark street late at night, where your victim looks at you frightened, mistaking you for a robber who is using the pretext of time to attack you. Or to ask young girls who answer right away, hoping it to be the start of an adventurous conversation, and who look back after a few steps, with encouraging and disappointed glances.

"What time is it, Signorina? What time is it?" Marco repeated, in a loud voice, as the garage man brought out the jeep.

"Quarter to three," the mechanic answered, as if it was he who had been questioned.

Marco jumped behind the wheel while I hoisted my feet over the gray iron plate of this strange vehicle. Jeeps still had at that time some of the enchantment and novelty they had at the time of their startling and legendary arrival. Now they ran like crazed insects, in the hands of both military and civilian drivers, all over the roads of Italy and the streets of the towns. Only a few months before, after the last gunfire, they had first appeared, with their absurd look and lively, jumping gait, carrying in their square bodies every kind of man from the most distant lands. They remained in our fantasies linked with the sparkling teeth of a Negro or the blond hair of a GI, with the first white bread, the first poster on the wall, the first moment of peace. The jeep was an image of the vastness of the world, of the fauna of the Antipodes, iron-clad and armored creatures with long antennae. They reminded us, too, of a migration across the sea, of the pioneer, canvas-top wagons of the Far West, with curtains, sails, pots and pans, guns, above the high wheels across the prairie.

But in Marco's hands the jeep changed character. He jammed an old fur cap on his head, put on an enormous pair of glasses that covered his face up to his ears, and a big pair of yellow leather gloves. Dressed up that way, with the long, black beard down over his chest and his straight, long back rigid on the high seat, he gave his machine, too, that look of comic stateliness of the first archaic automobiles. As soon as I sat down beside him he squeezed the rubber pear of the horn twice, and with that raucous signal stepped on the starter and we went off with a big noise.

Marco was a good driver, in spite of his love of playing the co-median, which now led him to go very slowly, to honk his horn and look down from his mechanical throne at the pedestrians with something of the contemptuous and baronial mien of old-fashioned chauffeurs staring at frightened chickens in the dust of empty roads.

We forced carts, pushcarts, and the groups of idlers in the middle of the street to give way to us, turned into the Corso, and slid over the smoother asphalt that reminded us of the Barbary horse races and the masquerades of the carnival. We were between the houses and palaces whose skin had been tanned by years to the warm, soft color of old leather. It was as though we walked in a shadowy room among inlaid and highly polished furniture and walls hung with brown velvet.

We avoided looking at the offensive white bulk of the "Altar of the Fatherland," that enormous block of camphor that had not saved us from the moths. In a moment we were out under the open sky at the entrance to the Piazza Venezia, where an Allied policeman was making large gestures to direct the reluctant cars on a wide detour. The piazza had been turned into a parking lot for military vehicles, studded everywhere with pails and empty gasoline cans painted white and set here and there like curb-stones, and in the center, inside a barbed wire enclosure, was a wooden shack and all makes of automobiles under canvas covers, like a gypsy camp. As we skirted this kind of mechanical cemetery we went right under the Palazzo Venezia. My imperturbable driver lifted his eyes, threw a salute toward Mussolini's balcony. He fidgeted on his seat and started to blow his horn madly. Apparently he had thrown off his complete melancholy of a few minutes before and had put on an equally complete happiness.

"Long live liberty!" he said, and threw the car into top speed. Heedless of the curves, he reached the opposite side of the pi-azza and like a rocket went up the slope of the Via Nazionale, turned to the right, passed like a landslide before the frightened faces of some Poles coming out of their quarters, and let himself fall down a steep, dark alley in the Suburra section, then turned to his left into another small street that ended in a short flight of stairs. Just before we reached the bottom step he came to an abrupt stop with a screeching of brakes in front of the case-maker's workshop.

The shop was narrow, bowl-shaped, and completely dark. When first entering it one could see nothing at all, but once the eyes grew accustomed to the darkness one could see white circles of big clock dials hung irregularly at different heights on the walls, and in the far corner was a low table like a shoemaker's, with a green felt cover and circled by a little railing supported by small wooden columns. A lamp with a green shade stood on the table and threw a disc of dim light on the felt, and behind it sat a tiny man in the shadow, perhaps a hunchback, with a lens stuck to his left eye. He held a pair of pincers in one hand and in the other a very small watch. He bent his head to look for a moment, and then raised his eyes to the ceiling as if searching inspiration for the solution of some difficult problem. He was so absorbed in his meditation that for a minute he didn't seem to have noticed our arrival. Then he put the pincers and the small watch down on the felt cloth and asked us in a guttural voice (he was therefore cer-tainly a hunchback) what we wanted. I undid my tissue paper and showed him my watch. He looked at it, said right away I could leave it and that he would fix it, but he added that he had a large backlog of unfinished work, that the holidays were coming, and he couldn't promise to have it repaired for two or three months. How-ever, it was useless for me to try anywhere else, he pointed out, as only he specialized in that kind of work on watch cases and I wouldn't find another one in the whole city. I would simply have to resign myself to waiting. I decided to leave the watch with him. This fragile object embarrassed me and I seemed to feel freer and more at ease without it. The little hunchback wrote my name and a number in beautiful handwriting on a slip of paper and gave it to me. I was still holding the empty tissue paper in my hand. I took the receipt and left.

A crowd of boys had gathered around the jeep while we were in the shop. They were of all ages and had arrived from all sides like moths around a light. Some were barefoot, others wore men's boots and old military jackets as long as topcoats with tucked-up sleeves that showed the worn lining. One little fellow wore a green shirt covered with patches, and had a freckled face and red hair. All of them had dirty faces, lively eyes, and alert movements. They touched the radiator, the tires, and some of them had already climbed into the car and were rummaging in the glove compartment.

Marco had gone out ahead of me. I stood at the door of the shop and watched him dash for the jeep, waving his arms wide, shouting in a shrill voice and pretending to be furious. "Get out! Get out!" he shouted. "If I ever catch you . . ." The boys jumped down off the car and fled like frightened birds in every direction.

I had kept my eyes on the little redheaded boy who was the only one who ran toward the stairs, shuffling in a pair of enormous down-at-the-heel slippers. When he reached the top he stopped a moment, turned toward us, opened his mouth, and stuck out his tongue; then, as though frightened by his own boldness, he ran off to hide behind the corner of a house.

There where the child had vanished appeared a woman, tall and dark against the sky. She walked with the step of a queen, upright, supple, and proud, elegant in her long fur coat, her blond hair under a crown of feathers. She never looked my way. She was holding a boy's hand in hers, a boy who walked at her side like a page, his head covered by a white hood. I recognized that walk by the beating of my heart, that beauty, that enchanted atmosphere, but already the woman and child had covered the short space at the top of the stairs and had disappeared like an airy vision behind the house on the right. The war and the passage of years had carried that queenly step away from me into other paths. Who knows where? This is a true story, and not a story of Marco's. Why should I tell it? It is a true story, too true for me to want to talk about it, or to be able to talk about it; at least until I am so old that the words will come out of my mouth like stones.

Marco was behind the wheel waiting for me. I tossed away the piece of tissue paper I still held in my hand, and perhaps along with it the receipt for my watch. I didn't realize it at the time; but when I looked for it later in all my pockets I couldn't find it. I ran toward the jeep. I was heedless and I tripped over an iron chain that lay on the ground. Instinctively keeping my balance I managed to stay on my feet, but the chain was attached to a bicycle that leaned against a group of other bicycles resting against the wall, and the involuntary jerk I'd given it knocked over the whole lot. The noise they made in falling was echoed by a shout, or rather a roar, from inside the house. I'd reached the jeep, but before I got in I turned toward the shout and looked. Between the stairway and the watchmaker's door there was a kind of junk shop. The heap of rusty bicycles I'd pulled over were only the first of many others that formed a line on the sidewalk at either side of the shop entrance. To call it an entrance was an abuse of the word because it was entirely closed off by an impenetrable obstruction of the most varied iron objects: wheels, pipes, baby carriages, instruments, rolls of barbed wire, shovels, broken machines, pails, stoves, pots and pans, tricycles, every imaginable piece of metal, even rough and minute pieces, wedged in among the rest and scattered over the ground like a kind of pavement. This pile of junk reached to the ceiling and was held together by the complicated mass of thousands of dovetailing pieces interlaced with one another; and the whole was steadied by many long iron chains, like black snakes, that wound around and across one another and disappeared in the tangle. This virginal forest of metal not only blocked the entrance to the shop like a fantastic wall but also filled the deep interior that was lost in obscurity. It was a three-dimensional block, a huge body made of thousands of leafless branches and twigs. A small passage had been left in the middle like a path or a narrow twisting corridor, interrupted now and then by a projecting pipe or wheel. No normal-sized man could have gone along it. The impenetrable path led to a back room, also piled high with junk, but with a circular, open space in the middle that one could see beyond the interlacing iron, because there was a lamp burning there. The shouts and swearing came from the small clearing under the lamp that seemed like the house of an ogre.

A middle-aged woman dressed in gray, with a handsome, calm, and patient face, was standing near the entrance. She turned toward me, held a finger to her lips as though to ask me to keep still. Then, with a weary gesture toward her forehead, she indicated that the shouting man inside didn't know what he was doing.

"It's nothing," she cried, turning toward the interior. "A bicycle fell down. Now I'll pick it up." And slowly, like someone accustomed to humoring a child, she picked up the fallen bicycles, leaned them along the wall again, and put the chain around them. Then she came over to me and said in a low voice:

"That's my husband. This scrap iron is dearer to him than his eyes. He doesn't live for anything else. He's been buying it up for years and years and won't sell to anybody. He's crazy. He brings it here. He accumulates it. Even the gigantic cellars that could hold a whole house are so full that you can't get into them. Every now and then my children take a piece of iron and sell it to buy themselves a book. They're studying, they're getting a degree. But look out if he ever suspects anything is missing. He'd be capable of killing them, of taking to his bed in desperation."

The woman stopped talking. She walked back to the entrance with an indifferent air and once more motioned me to be quiet. Her husband had slid into the corridor. He made his way slowly, rotating on himself, bending to avoid the obstacles, crawling like a lizard. After a few minutes he reached the opening of his metal lair and emerged on the street like a mole at the mouth of its tunnel. He looked suspiciously around him. He was short and very thin, with the square face of a mechanic and greedy, furtive eyes. He held in one hand a lighted blow torch that he brandished like a gun, or like a flamethrower to defend his treasures. When he saw that everything was in good order he seemed placated. He touched one of the chains to make certain that it was secure and ran his fingers over a protruding bicycle wheel, and the wheel started to spin.

He noticed a spot of varnish on a pipe and carefully burned it off
with his blow torch. We wanted to speak to him but his wife continued to signal us to be quiet, to go away. Marco was tempted to
ask him to sell us his shop or at least one of his precious pieces of
iron, but prudence and the woman's gestures induced him to be
silent. He looked at the mechanic with admiring wonder, winked
at the woman, turned the jeep around, and drove away.

As we went on Marco felt he should explain who this Fanny was for
whom we were searching. I already understood from the way he
had talked of her before that Fanny was a prostitute, a kind of a literary creation. He had met her a few weeks ago in a brothel. He
often went there in a half-boastful, half-surreptitious manner,
drawn chiefly by the pleasure of some adolescent remembrance of
sin, something forbidden and shameful, a small residue in the
hidden fold of his soul that was enough to fill him with happy sadness and beatific disgust. He had found her all white, fat, soft, and
tender with a bored expression and the big empty eyes of a goddess,
and immediately he had made an idol of her, the Queen of Sirens,
a divinity of both land and sea, the white, immense body of Mother
Nature. He had let himself be entwined in her round, white, serpent's arms, pressed to the sweet, white mountains of her breasts,
carried, in a desired and heavenly time, within the calm, white sea
of her bosom. Fanny was the opposite of Silvia and also of Marco's
mother. She had no existence of her own, no feeling, no will, perhaps not even an individual soul. She lay there on the bed like a
docile animal, a goddess. Nevertheless, she was a maternal being,
more so than his wife or his real mother. Unlike these two, who
were so Catholic and respectable, so full of virtue and perhaps also
of sin, she had not been molded by background, custom, and religion but only by her passive, imperturbable existence. Marco had

found her and imagined her thus, and his infantile needs had been satisfied. But then, one day, Fanny had disappeared and nobody had heard of her since. Perhaps she had finished her fortnight's contract in the brothel, simply changed to another, or was touring other cities. Marco did not succeed in finding out. In the past few days he had looked for her in all the brothels of Rome. He had seen all kinds of women from every part of Italy: Viennese women, French women, girls from Tripoli, but not Fanny. Now only one last possibility was left. One day Fanny had spoken of herself, of her past and her family. She had shown him some old faded photographs, in that confused and mythological way, Marco said, in which a prostitute-goddess would talk about such things. Naturally, there was the bad stepmother, and a married elder sister with a large number of children who lived with a maimed, legless husband in a bombed out house in La Garbatella. Here Fanny had taken refuge, running away from her wicked stepmother, after having been raped by a Negro (or perhaps it might have been a German or one of the police — the story was not clear). From then on, like a white stone carried by a river, she had been driven by misery through simple and extraordinary adventures, and finally to that hospitable house and that soft bed.

"We must find the sister, perhaps we'll meet Fanny there, or get some news of her," Marco said.

"But I know we won't find her. We'll never find anything. But I want to try, you understand?" Marco went on with a look of profound discomfort, his mouth turned down as if he were tasting very bitter fruit. "Now I've lost her, and there isn't anything for me to do. Let's go and find the sister, but it won't help. I've lost her because I'm a sinner. There are things I don't know how to hold on to. Fanny's like the earth, but I looked at her as a sinner and I've lost her. Do you understand? This has nothing to do with crime and punishment, like Dostoievsky. God forbid. I can't be redeemed, I'm lost; and she doesn't need it because she is redeemed by nature, without even knowing it. Don't think that I liked her because she was a prostitute, or any reasons of that kind. However, the word sounds well — prostitute. It's something. But that's not it.

Fanny herself counts, Fanny is important just because she exists, for no other reason. Only you can understand it. But I've lost her."

I was barely listening. Marco talked, driving at random through the streets. He had only a vague idea of where to find La Garbatella, where he had never been, and he was making long and perhaps useless circles. I looked around and let my eyes wander over the houses, the ruins, the columns, and the people. The sky in the west was clear of clouds. The sun shone and a sudden smell of spring came from the avenues, the grass and the pine trees moving in the wind. Why had I let myself be carried on this idle and useless search for a person who perhaps existed only in the imagination? I sat on the iron seat like a spectator who happens to be in a theater by pure chance. We were going through a poor section, through crowded markets with vendors and merchandise sprawling over the sidewalk, through narrow, winding streets that came out into squares where the sky seemed to open out behind the porticoes of churches and palaces, and we drove past antique ruins and between stands where sweet olives were being sold.

Strange characters appear among the common people. Here was a tall and gaunt old lady, with a little black lace parasol and a black dress that came down to her feet, a slender waist, a high whale-boned collar, and shoes with Louis XV heels. Superior and proud in her walk, she was an anachronistic survival of the end of the century. A man with a huge mustache, wearing a straw hat, crossed the street waving a malacca cane; then an old fellow with painted lips and his hair falling down over his shoulders; and a juggler with a heavy torso, wearing a green-and-yellow striped jersey over a pair of long, skinny bowlegs; and two slender young priests in black cassocks gaily riding by on two white horses.

It seemed as if the autumnal sun had brought out these singular apparitions like snails coming out from under leaves after the rain and lazily crossing the road. Perhaps they had been there ever since the day of liberation, when there had suddenly appeared on all the streets and squares unbelievable and forgotten figures: old men with the obsolete clothes and beards and cravats of other times; the crippled, the lame, hunchbacks and young men with their naked torsos wrapped in rags. There were shaky steps and wild steps, knowing eyes and incredulous eyes. On the Corso, in those days, one sometimes met an old man with a white, hanging mustache and a serious, concentrated face who was clad from head to foot in fresh, green, ivy leaves sewn together like overlapping shingles to look like the coat of mail of an ancient warrior. He walked proudly along, leaning on a stick also decorated with ivy, and he was followed by a crowd of boys.

"I've waited twenty years to dress myself up like this," he said. "Now I can die happy."

They had come out to that new sun from all sides, as though for years and years they'd been hidden in the shadow of houses, invisible, or covered by the monotonous lacquer of sportive and imperial masks, a population of ghosts returned to the light, drawn forth by the common gaiety. Pale from their long sojourn in darkness, absurd and old-fashioned from their long absence, they walked on the sidewalks and mingled with the commoners and soldiers.

We were already beyond the last houses. We drove up a wide deserted road lined with cypress trees, descended rapidly toward an ancient gate, an archway between reddish walls, and were among fields covered with stubble in the silent countryside. A low hill, a hump of earth covered by houses appeared in the distance. The road led to it. This was La Garbatella.

In these past months I had often heard people talk of the suburbs of Rome, and of their sinister reputation, but I'd never had the time or opportunity to see them. The newspapers described them, publishing photographs of squalid shacks made of loose boards and corrugated iron where the poor lived in promiscuity and dirt. When it rained the earth became a slush of mud, and when the river was swollen the shacks were invaded by slimy water. There was no light in these miserable and temporary quarters. Life went on in deepest misery, enforced idleness, violence, and abandon. Here, a few miles from the center of the city, they were as unreachable as if they belonged to another world. Regularly, each day, there was suffering; and crimes were often committed.

The most obscure and mysterious events out of another time took place. The newspapers had told about a woman who lived in one of those shacks. She had given birth to a child and was nursing it. But the child scarcely grew at all, and the mother felt at the end of her strength as if the little one were sucking her life away. At night she was so tired that she would fall into a deep sleep on a mattress filled with straw and thrown on the ground, the child in her arms. She would fall asleep, too, during the day, on those heat-filled summer afternoons. She had strange dreams that filled her with sweetness and fear, from which she woke exhausted, as if she had been touched by death. One day she was dozing naked, and was immersed in that vague and pleasant terror, when the child started to cry so loudly that he roused her. The woman opened her sleep-filled eyes and turned to take her son and to quiet him by giving him her breast, and in the fog of her waking she saw something long and gray attached to her left breast. It had a small flat head with two fixed eyes that seemed to stare at her, and a slender, cold tongue that touched her nipple and sucked. It was a snake. The woman was motionless from horror. The milk came out of her breast, entered the mouth of the snake, and spread over her skin, but before she could cry out, the reptile had sensed her awakening, rapidly and silently let go, and sliding over her white belly had disappeared under the mattress. Only then did the woman faint. The doctors at the hospital said it was not a case of hallucination but of fact.

They cured the mother of exhaustion, and her dreams and languidness ended. The son grew and gained color now that the milk had returned, and he did not need to share it with his gliding brother.

They went back to the hut. A few months passed, and the snake was not seen. The shack was shared by another family and the men were manufacturing some crude fireworks there. One day the powder caught fire, the shack blew into the air and four people were killed. But the woman and her child were untouched. They did not have even the slightest scratch.

"The snake was under the mattress," Marco muttered. "It's not only in Rome things like that happen!"

"When I was in America, in New York," he went on, "one evening during a thunderstorm an airplane was taking off from La Guardia. A strong wind blew in front of the plane, but as it went down the field the wind suddenly shifted. The runway was too short, the plane couldn't take off and couldn't stop. It ran off the airfield, crossed a meadow, crashed against the side of a house, and burst into flames. All the passengers, forty of them, died in the fire. When they carried away the carbonized bodies from the wreckage, a strange object was found — the twisted frame of a bicycle.

"The next day a boy came to look for it. He told them that the evening before, after school, he'd gone on his new bicycle to hunt for snakes outside the airfield. There was a stagnant pond near the house and he noticed that the snakes used to drink water there. He'd left his bicycle on the bank and was bending over to try to catch a snake on his line and he'd seen one just about to bite at his hook when he heard a terrific noise, a crash, and saw a sudden flame. He ran terrified behind the corner of the house and hurried off without turning back. Now he had come to look for his bicycle. The newspapers reported that the airline was happy to buy him a new one."

By this time we were nearing the little hill. We drove up the short incline in a few minutes and were in an open space among some houses. We had arrived. There were no huts or shacks made of wood and corrugated iron, but rather, big, pretentious apartment houses, painted yellow and built in the indefinable style combining the baroque and the so-called "rational" that mixed columns and balconies constructed like boxes, small horizontal windows, and pointed turrets in Borromini's style. This was the architecture they used to call "Empire," but which was really colonial, made with arrogance and with scorn for a people considered inferior, so that they might spend all their poor hours in the most uncomfortable and painful way in houses adorned on the outside by the signs of power and grandeur. When such apartments are built in the old and lively central part of the city, they are somewhat absorbed by the atmosphere around them. Their bleak marble walls are soon covered by posters, shop signs, and lights, their color is blended and diluted and we end up looking at them without reaction, or at least only with aesthetic vexation. In the outskirts of town, in the recently built suburbs, they are more conspicuous and oppressive, giving a feeling of falseness to the simple habits of the market, the wine shop, the games of children on the street, and to the simple ways of family life. Where trolleys run on the rails, automobiles pass by quickly, and people go to work and to their offices, this is still the city, a forest of tiles, plaster, electric wires, running water, telephones, and sewerage, the veins, arteries, and capillaries that carry the pallid blood to those oppressive barracks. But such buildings rise absurdly in the midst of a deserted countryside, among stubble, piles of rubbish, and dried out ditches where a sheep gnaws grass at the edges, isolated in the sun and dust as the cocks crow with their late afternoon melancholy; they appear monstrous and dirty, anachronistic and sad, like an evening shirt with its stiff, immaculate front that some drunken savage slips over his black, painted body.

3

In the square in front of the church a small crowd was waiting patiently, as though they were standing in line to get a bowl of soup. They told us they were waiting for the end of a funeral service for someone who had been killed under a car. On the other side, along the houses, women were selling cigarettes, sweet olives, and pumpkin seeds. We asked them where the bombed houses were. They conferred among themselves and then all answered together:

"Go to Area 42. That's where the bombs fell. Also at 41, but 42 was the worst. Go on to the end of the street and go down the hill.

The last areas are there. Have you come from the City Administration? They're always looking, but they don't do anything."

We went down some streets with the strange names of African explorers, opposite from the way we'd come, and finally reached the last building.

The entrance was a wide stairway surmounted by a solemn colonnade, and at first there were no signs of destruction. Looking closer we saw irregular cracks on the facade; the columns, their capitals crumbled, were broken off, leaving only the twisting iron girders sticking out from the architrave. They were no longer holding anything up, but stood there crookedly like the teeth of an old man. Some of the windows of the high, yellow facade had no glass but newspapers and sheets of cardboard were stuck into the frames. The space in front of the entrance was a stretch of wasteland sown irregularly with telegraph poles and fragments of ruined wall. Small mountains of garbage were piled up in front of the building, and a few pale blades of grass grew among the stones and puddles between them. Children with unkempt hair stood around without playing, as if they were waiting for something, and on the steps in front of the distorted columns women sat with babies in their arms. On one corner of the wall a sign read: AREA 42. As soon as our jeep stopped children encircled it, looking at us in silence, and they followed us as we went over to the stairway. The women stood up as we passed, and all eyes turned toward us and followed us, questioning and mistrusting. When we reached the last step under the columns and went into the shadowy entrance hall, we were already accompanied, like kings, by a court train.

It wasn't the sort of entrance hall one would have expected from the impressiveness of the facade, but a narrow hall that ran out on both sides through the whole length of the building and was lost in the shadows. Right in the middle, behind the temple-like vestibule where a door should have been, hung a rude, burlap curtain shutting off the room beyond from the eyes and the wind. At the sound of our footsteps a snarling and quivering little mongrel dog slid out from under the curtain. The edge of the curtain was pulled aside and the disheveled head of a little girl appeared in the crack; and behind her was another taller, girl, already dressed like a woman with her face smeared with rouge. They stared out at us, half hidden by the burlap, and I could catch a glimpse of a dark room where something was shining (a kettle or an iron bed) and where many quarreling voices were suddenly raised.

Marco and I stopped, looking around uneasily. But we were already surrounded by women and children. Among them was a lively girl with a child hanging around her neck, a keen, intelligent face, a sturdy torso, and fleshy, animal-like hips hardly covered by a short skirt that revealed her solid, naked hairy legs. She addressed us. "Americans?" she said, turning to Marco, whose stature and beard made him appear the more authoritative of the two of us. "Americans? Come in, come in! See our houses — refugees — bombs." And with the hand that did not hold the child she made a sweeping gesture that seemed to indicate both the walls and the sky.

Following her gesture I looked down the long, dark hall. It was like the hall of a school or barracks, with dirty, peeling, white-washed walls and a line of doors opening on both sides. Each led to a room that lodged one or more families. On some of the doors were brass name plates or calling cards. Others were bare. Women in rags and men in shirtsleeves were walking idly along the hall as if they had nothing in particular to do, and one could hear indistinct voices from behind the closed doors.

"Americans, come, look," continued the girl, pulling at Marco's sleeve as though she wanted to lead him. I understood her mistake; they thought we were foreigners because of the jeep, the way we were dressed, and our silence. Looking at Marco I realized that we really had an exotic air. That beard of his, that automobile duster and black fur cap, and I! I too looked strange in my corduroy suit and my heavy sweater with its zipper. To be among these poor people without a good reason seemed not only absurd but actually wrong, and I wanted to leave. Perhaps Marco felt the same way but he'd already answered the girl:

"Yes, Americans . . . come to inspect . . . committee . . . relief." Perhaps he had accepted this make-believe to hide his embarrassment. Or was he taking advantage of the misunderstanding to give his search an apparently more plausible motive? Was he pretending so as not to offend these wretched people? Or rather was he indulging as usual in acting a part, and believing it, so that he could participate in the life of the world with rightness, respect, and perfect humility? One thing was certain, he was now a hundred-percent American. He pulled a notebook out of his pocket and leafed it through as if he were looking for names and addresses.

"We've had many reports," he said, "but we don't have precise data, sometimes even no last names. For instance, we are looking for a family with a lot of children . . . the father's without legs . . . he's called, he's called . . . the name isn't clear. The mother is called . . . hmmm! I believe she has a sister called Fanny. Are they here?"

"Yes, it's Rosa the Jewess," one woman said.

"No — that one doesn't have a husband; she's a widow. It's the woman of Viterbo who lives with a cripple," said another. And they began to argue and quarrel about it. Finally they did agree that the family the American was looking for belonged really to the woman from Viterbo who lived upstairs on the third floor, but first each of them wanted to take us to show us her own room. We were Americans and perhaps something unattainable had come with us.

"Come! Come and look where we live," cried the lively girl who had spoken first, and taking Marco by the arm she led him down a side hall running off at right angles from the main hall.

We found ourselves followed by the women who were now shouting and all talking at the same time, and who pushed us into a dirty bowl of a room, with an uneven floor full of holes and loose tiles and a closed door at the far end. On the right-hand wall was a small window with its glass broken. The women led us to it and told us to look out.

"Look how we live!" they exclaimed, with an accent of both complaint and strange boasting. We looked out. The window opened on what must have been a covered courtyard, a salon, or a gymnasium. One could still see a few gray cement arches that must have supported a vault or a glass roof before the bombardment. Now it was a large, open space. And all the inside windows of the apartment looked on it. One could not see the pavement or, except here and there, the ruins of the fallen roof. The whole surface was covered with a thick layer of garbage and human excrement that had become hard and gray, and was piled up in heaps separated by pools of black liquid.

"There are no sewers, no toilets, no water!" the women shouted.

For three years, everything had ended up down there in the courtyard on top of the rubble, along with the rainwater and the drainage from the gutters.

On that undulating surface, perhaps some two yards beneath us, there moved, slowly and tranquilly, hundreds of black animals. I looked: they were enormous rats. Lazy and assured, they went up and down, scratching like hens on a threshing floor, sniffing, lifting their heads, rummaging on the ground with forward jerks and sudden stops. The whole yard was swarming with this constant motion, spasmodic and silent. There were so many rats that all the ground seemed covered with them and everywhere agitated by that black, mute convulsion. An unbearable stench of putrefaction rose from the silence. The infected air was filled with millions of flies like a gray cloud of dust.

"Don't they get into the house?" Marco asked, pointing to the rats.

"God knows how many, and they even get into our beds," the women answered together. "But they fare better in the courtyard. They fatten up. There's more to eat down there."

Marco drew back from the window and started to go down the hall, surrounded by the women. I stayed another moment to watch, fascinated by the unconcerned leaping of the rats, their black crawling, their continuous yet interrupted circulating, the jerks and the upheavals of these automatic inhabitants of a desolate, fetid landscape.

The women took us to the stairs, pushed us up a flight of battered stone steps and showed us the broken railing. When we reached the second floor, they led us along the hall to a sort of covered gangplank. From there we could see the whole gray surface of the courtyard and its lazy, black rivers of putrid water; and small in the distance, the rats moved over everything, innumerable and busy, like ants around an ant hill.

Marco, as a hundred-percent American sent by the relief committee, now wanted to see everything. He inspected public toilets that weren't working because there was no water and the discharge pipes were broken. He wrote the details in his notebook. He put down the names the women gave him as they told him of their family sorrows. He went into many rooms as doors were thrown open widely before us: naked rooms, with a few old pieces of furniture and filled with children. Some of the rooms were dirty and untidy, cluttered with rags and leftovers, others were kept as tidy and clean as possible, with nursing babies asleep in wicker baskets covered with cheesecloth to protect them from the flies, and diapers hung up on strings to dry. The home of the lively girl who was acting as our guide actually had some pretense of elegance. There was a veneered double bed with a yellow rayon cover, a round mirror, and a Turkish shawl draped on the wall. On a little table were some blue liqueur glasses. An advertising calendar showing a big, full-blown laughing woman, and a few framed photographs hung on the walls or stood on the bedside table. A round embroidered lampshade with long fringes of pearl beads hung down from the ceiling in the center of the room, lower than our faces, and because there was no table under it, it looked less like a lamp than a geometrical symbol or a traffic light.

Rosa the Jewess lived a few doors farther on. She was an old woman covered with shawls and skirts, with a big ancient face, a straight nose, deep black eyes, and straight gray hair parted exactly in the middle and twisted in a knot on her neck. She had three rooms, one leading into another, or rather, one large room divided by two partitions. Rosa lived in the farthest. In the others, two families were heaped up. The first room was bare. As we went in, four children were sitting motionless on a day bed pushed against the wall. They looked at us silently as we went into the second room where a thin old woman with the bad-humored face of a witch under an enormous mop of crinkled hair muttered while she stirred some cabbage stalks around in a huge pot. Rosa the Jewess was waiting for us in the third room (the rumor of American visitors had already reached that far). She sat on a chair, her hands on her knees, like an ancient queen on a throne. She started at once to tell us of her dead: her husband, her elder son — so good-looking — who was carried away by the Germans that morning of the ghetto. She showed us photographs. She started to cry. She took off a locket with a *shaddai* inscribed on it that was hanging around her neck. It held a picture of her son. A younger daughter, also, had died; the others were married. She lived alone on the small pension she got from the Jewish community. She was forced to live alongside those *goyim* in the next room. She was waiting for death to liberate her. What was she to do now that her own were no longer there? Every day she went to the temple and spent her time praying.

The woman of Viterbo lived on the floor above. Marco managed to free himself from his female escorts, asking them to wait for him downstairs, promising to come back right after his visit. We knocked at the door and went in. A little black dog, thin and mangy, came barking at us.

It was the most miserable of all the rooms we had seen so far: one room with two paper-covered windows, split by a partition into a hallway-kitchen and a bedroom. At the entrance in a corner was a small, rusty, and empty stove. There was no coal, no pots or plates, only some tin containers on a board, two old army mess-kits, and some empty tomato cans. In the middle of the room was a single, rickety chair and at one side a three-legged table where the dog had now taken refuge and was snarling. In the other room there was an iron double bed, and a cot in front of it. The straw mattresses were covered with two badly torn army blankets, and there were no sheets. Under the bed was a chamber pot. On the wall three nails held a piece of broken mirror. In a corner was a white, wooden packing box without a cover, filled with dirty rags. In neither room was there anything else, no wardrobes, no chests, no lockers, everything was in sight and in one moment the inventory was finished.

The woman of Viterbo was still young, but she was faded and spent, she wore a colorless coat over a nightgown, and her feet were stuck into a pair of slippers. She was sick, she told us, and running a fever, so she had not dressed. She hadn't even combed herself; her reddish hair fell over her face and neck, dry and soft, as though it were covered by dust. The same dust seemed to cover her face, and under that gray dust one could see the unhealthy rosiness of fever. She had not washed; she was too worn out. Her eyes were at the same time shining and tired. When we came in she looked at us with infinite weariness in her expression. She too had already been told about our visit. She offered us the single chair that stood by itself in the middle of the room and insisted that one of us sit in it. She waved her hand toward the walls and the few poor furnishings, an automatic gesture of desolation. A ten-year-old girl came through the partition into the kitchen. She was pale with big eyes and long, earth-colored braids. She was holding a baby boy a few months old in her arms. He wore a short, knitted shirt that left his belly and legs bare. He was whimpering and his sister cradled him in her arms.

"This is my oldest," the woman said. "And he is my youngest. I have five more, but they're outside — and I'm pregnant again right now!"

The dog was snarling from under the table. The woman of Viterbo gave him a look of resigned hatred. "Quiet, Tobruk!" she said without conviction. And before we had asked any questions she started to talk. At first they hadn't been badly off. She'd married, she'd had children, but her husband was working and they were getting on. . . . Then the war. To escape being caught by the Germans, her man had jumped out a window. He had broken both legs. He couldn't be taken care of properly and he got an infection. They had to amputate. So what could he do now? Nothing. He dragged himself around, and came back home at night. Probably he begged on the sidewalks, but the woman of Viterbo did not say so. And she? What could she do? She was sick and had to look after her children. Sometimes she would go to the square to sell sweet olives. But now she couldn't even manage that small business. The children were too little; nobody worked, nobody earned. They'd sold everything, even the sheets, the towels, and pillows. We could go and look: there was no linen left. They all slept together on the bed and on the cot. That's how they kept warm. Every day they went to get soup and bread from the parish church. That's what they lived on. Each got a mess can of soup and a piece of bread. It had to last until the next day. At night they ate a chunk of leftover bread. They didn't have to light the fire. The stove was there in the corner, but who would give them the coals? And what would they have to cook? It was quite a while since they'd lit the stove. The children should have gone to school. Sometimes they went, but they had no copybooks. They spent their days on the street. She didn't feel like doing anything. And now she was expecting another child.

The woman of Viterbo told all this in a monotonous voice without rebellion or resentment, one could almost say without suffering, as though she were talking of an accepted and unavoidable reality: the impersonal description of a human condition like that of many others, a destiny that does not allow comparisons or envy or even complaint.

Marco was silent. This extreme simplicity of misery, this lack of everything, including feelings or a way to express them, kept him silent. And actually there was nothing to say. I could see that Marco did not know how to question her and that perhaps he had given up the idea of asking about Fanny. He looked at the woman and stroked his beard with embarrassed gravity. Then, as she talked on, he went over to the window, raised it a crack and looked down at the courtyard filled with rats. They he closed the window and asked:

"Isn't there anybody who could help you? No relations? A father, father-in-law, brothers?"

"Nobody can do a thing," said the woman of Viterbo. "My sister used to help me. She came to see me and always brought something, money or something to eat. But it's been a long time since I saw her and I don't know where she is. I think she must have found work outside of Rome. Perhaps she'll turn up one day. Who knows where she went? She's a lady. . . . And we stay here. . . . In awhile the children will come home. I'm sorry you haven't seen them. . . . Quiet, Tobruk!"

Marco asked no further questions nor was he insistent. He took his leave, saying he hoped the committee would do something for her. The woman of Viterbo shook hands with us and saw us to the door. We went out into the hall. Outside some women were waiting for us.

Marco gave me a look. "Stay here," he said. "I'll only be a minute." He returned to the room by himself. He came back shortly with Tobruk whining after him.

Now Marco was in a hurry to leave. "We've seen everything," he told the women. "We've seen everything. We must go! We'll be back." And he turned quickly toward the stairs. Tobruk followed us downstairs as far as the burlap curtain at the entrance where the other dog who had welcomed us on our arrival came out barking again. We went under the crooked columns, down the stairs, across the open space in front of the house, and climbed into the jeep, while the women all around us cried out that we must remember them, come again, and do something for them. And they pointed to the children they held in their arms and the ones that held on to their skirts.

The sun was low in the sky, and Rome appeared far away in a golden haze behind a dusty plain covered by telegraph poles and ruins. The women shouted: "Americans! Come back, Americans." Marco put his foot on the starter, waved his hand, looked at the columns, the stairway, the yellow facade, the women, the children, cried "Good-bye," and threw the car into gear.

Crossing the suburb, Marco drove at high speed, as if he were running away, and he was quiet, watching the road with a dark look.

He continued this way in silence until we had come back to the city. Then he turned to me and said:

"Did you notice? I've told you I'm a sinner, a lost man. And I even gave her money when I went back into the room. The money from the committee. That was really the height of abuse. I played the American who gave money from the relief. Can you understand it? The do-gooder. I've appeared as the do-gooder, the benefactor. The rats, the flies, the misery, the tuberculosis, everything! — so that I could be the do-gooder, the philanthropist. And I was looking for a whore. I, the philanthropist, among the rats. You can see now, can't you, that I'm a lost man?"

So Marco, speeding among the houses, tortured himself and enjoyed the torture. He didn't care about the women of Viterbo, the children, the dogs, that desperate squalor. He didn't even care about Fanny, whom he had not found (and who I think perhaps never existed). He cared only for himself and his own guilt. I could have told him that this and nothing else was his real sin; that therefore his problems, his searches, his anguish, his desperate anxiety and nostalgia for his lost childhood were as senseless and as absurd as his speed at this moment down the Via dell' Impero toward the center of town and my room in the Via Gregoriana.

All this seemed to me to be a disconnected dream, a commotion in an unnecessary prison, and meanwhile in another world beyond our reach the rats of Area 42 continued to move in jerks in an incredibly real stench in the bombed courtyard (as they are moving today and will continue to move tomorrow), indifferent to all Marco's sins and guilt, to his conscience and to the true or false help of all true or false relief committees. I was thinking all this while we were speeding toward my house. But I said nothing because I hate moralizing. And then I knew that Marco was well aware of it, indeed very well aware, and that to discuss it would only help him to suffer and rejoice a little more in himself, in that dull echo or imitation of a foreign world wherein he had appointed himself standard-bearer and victim.

"I'll come up with you," he said, when we arrived at the door of my house. "Then I'll take you on with your suitcase." I had to pack, but that wouldn't take me long. At that time I didn't have a suit to change into, and my linen fitted easily into a small and light valise. While I took my things out of the drawers, Marco looked curiously around the room. By the big, soft bed of dreams stood an old Florentine prayer stool that had been adapted as a chair and where I put my clothes at night. I had never thought of its original function in all the time I'd lived in the room, but Marco noticed it immediately and knelt on it. He stayed on his knees in silence until I'd finished putting all my things in my valise. I closed it and looked around to be sure I hadn't forgotten anything. As usual I was sorry to change, to leave a place I had lived in, no matter how anonymous and indifferent it was. Therefore I did not stay a moment longer than necessary, and I did not look out the window.

"Let's be going," I said, as though I were in a hurry. Only then did Marco get up from the prayer stool and follow me downstairs.

In a few minutes, without speaking, we crossed the center of the city and came to a square in front of a big palace.

"Here you are," said Marco. He helped me out and said good-bye and left me alone with my valise in my hand, in front of a very high doorway between two columns of travertine, slender and delicate against the massive facade, and worn smooth and pink by the passage of years.

6

THE COLUMNS ON THEIR WORN, stone bases jutted out over the sidewalk, forcing passersby to step aside, erect like two guards who had stood on the square for endless years. They supported a ceremonial balcony like an architrave with an iron flagstaff set in it, and a stone coat of arms covered with moons and comets. Under the balcony the figure of a woman, or better a sphinx or an angel, crouched in the keystone of the arch. She had only a head and breasts, and wings sprang out from both sides of her like enormous ears with festoons of leaves and fruits hanging down from them. The angel's eyes were half closed and she seemed to peer out through her lashes from that hiding place of bats with the sensual and foolish air of a lady of the seventeenth century. The sunlight beat obliquely across the facade, crossing it with long shadows from the windows, the cornices, and the high, overhanging roofs. The big house-door was closed. Only a small panel of its huge, black surface was ajar. I pushed this open and went in.

I found myself in a vestibule paved with great flagstones that had a double rut in them for carriage wheels. This vestibule was divided into three ample passageways by two rows of pillars with high stone seats around their bases. In the faint light I could make out at the sides under the arches a number of doors, some closed and some open, leading perhaps to storerooms or to other stairways. The vestibule opened into an arcade that circled a huge courtyard, and at the right was a second courtyard as vast as a piazza, from which came the continuous splashing of a fountain, like pouring rain.

Pausing at the entrance with my little valise, I saw against the sunlit far wall of the first courtyard a dark row of pillars, and above them, outlines of the ribs of arches disappearing among dark vaults overhead. In the midst of this architecture, directly under the central arch, on the pavement of the arcade where all things seemed to converge, stood a chair, black against the light from behind. In the chair a gigantic man stretched out. He seemed to have been cut to the same enormous measure as the palace. He wore a long, old-fashioned coat that reached to his feet. It was of heavy, dark-blue cloth and had two rows of shiny gold buttons and a gold stripe embroidered on the collar. On his head he wore an old cap with a visor. He was looking apathetically at a bunch of newspapers in his hand. When I went over to speak to him he did not seem to notice me, then he threw me an absentminded sidewise glance, turned back to his newspaper, scratched one ear, and began to move slowly, almost imperceptibly. Slowly too, he bent one knee, then he drew one of his outstretched legs closer to the chair, and then the other. And slowly he rested his hands on his knees, and using them as levers, little by little, cracking like a piece of worm-eaten furniture, he gradually straightened himself up. Only when he was completely erect, towering there in his bulk, did he deign to look my way from the height of his six and a half feet. His great body, which appeared even more enormous because of the long dark overcoat from which immense shoes stuck out, was topped by a huge head. Every feature appeared to be extraordinarily voluminous. They were all large. The nose was large

and bulging, and in his broad mouth a large, black tongue showed
between his few large teeth; the ears hung down heavily at the
sides of his large, drooping cheeks; his eyebrows bristled in thick
tufts over his large, round, watery eyes. The whole face was
wrapped up in, as though it were in fact drowned in, his thick,
yielding skin like that of an old elephant. This was Teo the
doorman.

He condescended to look at me, indifferently surveying me
from head to foot. If one could gather anything from his bored
eyes, it was that he did not look on me with favor, perhaps because
of my valise. Speaking with the same slowness with which he'd
moved, he said he had been informed of my arrival. He pointed
out the porter's lodge at the right-hand side of the vestibule, the
table where I would find the mail, the bell on the wall with which
I could call him if he was not at the door. He waved his hand toward the wide stairway I was to climb at the end of the arcade.
Then, as though he were dismissing me, he bent his knees again
and little by little sat down on the chair, stretched out his legs, unfolded the newspapers, and stared idly at them without really
reading, as he had been doing when I came in.

I followed the arcade to the stairway at the rear. I climbed some
wide stone steps and found myself in a vast, vaulted space as dark
as a cave. Its walls were crowded with antique statues. In front of
me, whitish against the gray wall, an enormous Gallic warrior fell
wounded to his knees, wrapped in the narrow pleats of his barbaric shorts. On the right two naked men faced one another on
their pedestals. One was a young *ephebus*; on the other was superimposed the bearded head of an old man, strange in its bigness on
that lithe body with its slender legs. On the left was the first flight
of steps. They were so broad that ten people holding hands could
have climbed up together, and they were so shallow that I raised
my unaccustomed foot too high like the hoof of a pawing horse,
and held it in midair feeling for the earth. At the same time the
stairs were so deep that it was impossible to take them more than
one at a time. They were princely steps cut out of ancient travers-
tine, and they demanded, whether one ascended or descended, a

slow and solemn step, a ceremonial pace, filled with regal haughtiness and regal grace. It was almost a stone-ribbed slope rather than a stairway; it turned on itself among rampant arches and lofty vaults, balustrades of slanting pillars, jutting cornices, and gigantic windows like immense opened-out shelves. Statues rose here and there, ancient inhabitants of this solemn stone hollow.

At the first turn stood two female torsos, two goddesses alongside the wide glass window that looked out on the second courtyard. I could see from here women washing clothes in the fountain and some workmen, small in the distance, filing pieces of iron outside their workshop door. Alas! Someone had colored the marble lips of the goddesses with rouge, and the pupils of their eyes with coal, and had given them a cross-eyed expression, a repulsive effect on those serene, classic faces. Farther up I met people descending, others standing around leaning over the balustrade, and an old woman sitting to one side on a step. They were all miserably dressed, the gray color of their rags and faces fused with the stones and, dwarfed by that vast space, they seemed almost invisible.

So I came to the second floor and into a kind of enormous salon with statues scattered over it. It was large enough to hold an entire house. In the middle, on a pedestal made from a fragment of a column, stood an ancient marble vase sculptured with scenes from history. The walls on all sides had huge doors in them, some false, others closed, their stone frames covered with sphinxes and other decorative monsters.

The great landing was empty except for a young woman nestled in a corner in the dress of a peasant with a handkerchief over her head and a child in her arms. On the opposite wall leaned a bicycle. This space and these walls, this feeling of an ancient and hidden place, the naturalness of the woman who had been in the corner for who knows how long a time, made me imagine this a most suitable place for a Court of Miracles. And for a moment while I rested my valise on the floor and stopped to take a breath, it seemed to me that I was surrounded by a crowd of beggars: the lame, the halt, the blind, and the paralyzed. And I asked myself why Teresa and Elena and the woman of Viterbo and the thousands of other women on the street corners had not chosen this covered and hidden place for their market, their misery, and their adventure.

As I went on up the stairs I encountered in one of the niches an enormous marble finger. Was it a finger, or was it a phallic image? I looked at it more closely. It was the little finger of a hand, splendidly modeled, with the gentle swelling of the veins under the skin, and a short, round nail at the end of the last joint. It must have been a fragment of a colossal statue much higher than the highest roofs of the house itself. Perhaps this giant was beneath the ground and perhaps on him rested the foundations of the palace; perhaps he was so big that he carried it all on his shoulders. Higher up I found a Greek grammarian, rigid on his stone seat with his scroll of wisdom on his knees.

So I arrived at the third floor, smaller and more modest than the second. It was enclosed by a wall leading to a corridor, ornamented by a trophy with two sphinxes surrounded by banners, garlands, and shields. Here the great stairway ended. On the right side of the landing it turned into a narrower stairway between whitewashed walls that led to the hall of the garret and to my lodgings. I was already on the third landing, as high as most fifth floors, but I hadn't realized it because of the grandiose proportions of every element in this spectacular architecture. For the same reason, the facade of St. Peter's appears at first glance much smaller than it is. I must have climbed for more than a hundred steps. Those I was climbing now were far steeper, narrower, and rougher. They were the steps of a normal stairway. The walls had no decoration other than the filthiness of time, and some pictures and words scribbled on them with coal by the boys. The hall at the top of the stairs was paved with rude and dusty tiles that had not been swept for a long time; there were little heaps of ashes, paper, and rags along the wall. The ceiling was made out of small uneven wooden boards, some of them hanging down loose and threatening ruin. The light from three small, high windows filtered through a layer of ancient cobwebs. Arches opened out at the sides, and farther along, hidden among the shadows of the low vaults, were small, black doors that, like cells, had a sequence of numbers painted in black on the walls beside them. Number 11, 12, 13. . . . My apartment was 18. I went on up the hall, climbed other steps, turned a corner, climbed some more, reached the last steps that had become even narrower, and finally the top — and my own door. Underneath the last steps the hall twisted around and lost itself in the dark among other mysterious arches and other numbered doors.

I rang the bell and a few minutes later a woman's harsh, rude voice called from inside: "Who's there?" For a moment I thought I must be back in Florence where most of the houses were without doormen, where the apartment bells are all at the street entrance, and every ring is answered, almost like a mechanical echo, by a feminine "who's there."

During the recent period of clandestine life this question shouted from a window was particularly indiscreet and inopportune. One either said nothing or mumbled a vague or incomprehensible reply, and the women in the houses little by little learned to hold back those two embarrassing words every time the street bell rang. This cry still irritated me because of that memory and so from habit I didn't answer it. The voice became more aggressive and repeated: "Who's there?" but right afterward the dry sound of an electric buzzer made me realize I could get in. I pushed open the door and found myself in front of another stair with some twenty linoleum-covered steps. At the top stood a girl wrapped in a half-open red silk dressing gown, as though she had just got out of bed. As I walked up I told her who I was.

"Oh, you're Signor Carlo?" she said. "Come in, come in. I've been expecting you for several hours. I am Signora Jolanda. You'll find everything in good order. I had the handyman wax the floors and also wash the windows. They'd left everything so filthy — a real pigsty. I've never seen people as dirty as they were. Let's hope you're better. I have the keys for you. Come in . . . do come in."

With these kind phrases Jolanda welcomed me at the door. She was the chambermaid left by the previous tenants to take care of the apartment. They were an American surrealist painter, elegant, refined, decadent, and sophisticated, and his wife, an English actress, who was extremely young, bizarre, and fanciful. They happened to have been in Rome just after the liberation and were now back in New York. Through the efforts of mutual friends these foreigners whom I did not know had agreed to let me have their apartment until they returned; but it was suspected, and I hope rightly, that they wouldn't come back for a long time, perhaps never. Along with the house I'd also inherited Jolanda who was, so to speak, part of it. She was a tall girl, a native of Parma, with round hips and sturdy legs. She had small breasts, wide shoulders, and her neck was long, slender, and very white. The color of her skin impressed one immediately by its delicate beauty, as did the color of her hair. Her skin, white, rosy, and transparent, was a little too shiny and taut over her cheekbones; her hair was black, a refulgent black, almost blue, with greens and violets reflected in it, and it hung loose and untidy down her back. It was a very long and thick mass of hair that almost reached her knees, a waving sea full of lights. Untidy locks and smaller curls fell over her shoulders and framed her face so that it seemed pallid and blond in the shadow of that black forest. She had light eyes like a Siamese cat's, slightly red around the rims, and with thin lashes. Her nose and mouth were small, and her ears were small, too. Her lips were painted in an exaggerated and coarse fashion. There was something incongruous between the rough, peasant quality of her body, the flowing and iridescent richness of her hair, and the delicacy of her coloring and features. Her face seemed to be planted on her torso like an artificial flower without any character. Her eyes, nose, forehead, and hair said nothing, and had nothing in common with the words that came at random from her mouth. They betrayed no feeling at all except perhaps an affected boredom or a cold and malignant indifference.

"Some people were here already today to look for you. They were two men, two friends of yours. They gave me their names but

I don't remember them. Such strange names. They were two badly dressed characters, with an extraordinarily sadistic look about them."

So spoke Jolanda with an imperturbable face. I asked her if she hadn't been frightened by their sadism.

"Why?" she asked tranquilly.

Jolanda obviously had no idea of the meaning of the term, but used it at random, probably from her habit of aping her former masters, whose artificial language must have seemed the height of elegance to her, the positive criterion of a true gentleman.

From the next room I heard someone calling, "Signora, Signora!" amid a stifled cackle of laughter.

"I'll come right away, Signora Clelia," Jolanda answered. A door swung partly open. It was paneled with mirrors in which my face appeared tremulous and distorted. Through the crack I could see the white tiles of a kitchen. I looked in. Four women were in the room, rocking back and forth, laughing and slapping their hands on their hips. One was big, fat, and middle-aged, wearing glasses and a striped apron. The second was a little brunette in a gray skirt with a small shawl around her shoulders. The other two were young, with painted faces and loose hair, and like Jolanda they wore shiny silk dressing gowns that they hastened to pull chastely over their breasts when I appeared. On one side of the kitchen a trap door was open in the floor, and from the black cave where one could see a winding staircase, rose the sound of a flute lamenting.

Jolanda made the introductions: "This is Signora Clelia, the laundress. This is Signora Irene who helps me with the house-work. And these are two friends of mine from home, Signora Violetta and Signora Bice, who have come to pay me a visit."

The brunette and the laundress who wore glasses stopped laughing and looked at me with their arms dropped at their sides. Violetta and Bice coyly pulled their dressing gowns over their bosoms with one hand, offering me the other, then lowered their eyes in a chaste and seductive gesture, attempting to put on an enchanting embarrassment. Then all five women started in to talk with short cries, exclamations, little laughs, like birds in a court-yard. From their cackling one could only distinguish "Signora! Signora!" the form of address they were using continuously to one another, and that gave them, perhaps, their only reason and their only real pleasure in talking. In the midst of the confusion the flute stopped playing, a step sounded below, and the stairs creaked.

"It's my cousin! Signor Giovanni!" Jolanda said. "He was playing a bit of music down in my room. There's nothing he can't do. You'll see." And the girls echoed her, crying all at once, "What a very handy man he is!"

From the opening of the trap door in the floor emerged a kind of blond, shiny wig. The hair seemed to be bleached and was parted on one side, perfectly straight and slicked down with brilliantine. Supporting this artistic arrangement appeared a small, oval, symmetrically shaped man's head. On it was perched an enormous pair of dark glasses. The part of his face exposed under these lanterns was white and red, almost as though the cheekbones were rouged. His features were small and regular. He had a straight, tiny nose, a thin, silky mustache, a small, red mouth half open in a foppish and fatuous smile over shiny little teeth — the perfect head of a wax doll in a hairdresser's window. Below this false head the body of a small but well-proportioned man jumped out. He had short, robust arms, the chest and hips of a gymnast; he too was wrapped in a striped silk robe over a thin, white undershirt, and he had a pair of red, leather slippers. When he had at last emerged completely and had put his slippers on the kitchen floor, he came up to me and introduced himself in military fashion:

"Colitto — Giovanni!" And he shook my hand. Then he turned authoritatively around, took off his glasses to scrutinize the women, exposing two black eyes that were as shiny as they were expressionless. His little mouth turned down with the bored and disdainful look of a man who had lived too much. His small and exceedingly black eyes looked like a pair of patent-leather shoes polished once and forever. He carefully put on his glasses again, rested his hand on the table showing off his two heavy gold rings, nonchalantly crossed his right leg over his left, and said: "That's enough of the flute for now," and he stood there still smiling, allowing himself to be admired.

I had unwittingly entered the range of interests shared by Jolanda, her dubious cousin, and the women; into their own world of abusiveness and sham. Later on I was to have almost too much time to get to know it. I told them brusquely that I wanted to look over the apartment, and broke up the gathering, leaving the young man with his female admirers.

Jolanda preceded me; she opened a door that was paneled with mirrors like the other, and we came into the studio. So I started in to make my first reconnaissance of this new setting for my life, to which I must adapt myself, and which I must also adapt to my own hours and habits. I studied everything carefully since I was seeing it for the first time.

It was a huge room with a polished yellow marble floor, a high ceiling with great supports painted with leafwork and wreaths. The light walls bore signs of old leakages and spots left by the dampness. On the side where we had come in were two doors, the one from the hall and the one to the kitchen. An inside staircase like those in Capri led up to a balcony set up as a bedroom. On the balcony, separated from the room below by ash-pink drapes, were a bed and two round mirrors. Only a faint glow came through the curtains and if one wanted to see anything one had to turn on a light enclosed in a pinkish-yellow globe, which still hardly lit the balcony and gave it the atmosphere of a fancied imitation of a fancied den of lust as it might be conceived by the reader of a popular romance. A small bathroom opened out of it, with a hip bath and a wide window with a view of Monteverde and the Janiculum. From the bedroom-balcony, if the drapes were pushed aside, one could view the whole studio with its shining pavements and its two big windows on the left wall. On the upper part of the right wall was a projecting bracket supported by arches, where there were the three mysterious panels of three small doors at the height of the ceiling. These apertures, Jolanda told me, opened onto the gutters under the roof, an excellent hiding place in times of persecution and flight.

Around the walls were white plaster bas-reliefs and mosaics of Roman scenes, war trophies, standards of the Tenth Legion, buxom women carrying children and stalks of grain in their arms, probably the remains of some art exhibit of the Fascist period. Through a large window on the north wall was a view of domes and rooftops and sky. The furnishings were few: a big table supported by metal tubing, some geometrical bookcases, a sofa, and several reclining chairs. From the ceiling hung four wooden chandeliers, either antiques or copies, with many wooden arms carrying imitation candles. Evidently the apartment was the loft or big attic of the old palace, sharing with it the great dimensions, the splendid width of the windows, the thickness of the walls, the spots of dampness, and its age and nobility. Some pretentious hand had tried to graft onto this ancient stump the mirrors, the marbles, the Capri stairway, the decorations, the veiled lights, that he thought were the necessary signs of the modern and the elegant. This had happened to the house as it had to Jolanda. She had superimposed on her peasant nature a layer of badly spread make-up, a grotesque caricature of the admired ways of gentlefolk.

Jolanda stood in the middle of the room and talked without interruption. Within a few minutes she managed to say that the apartment was uncomfortable, the rain leaked in, there was no gas, the water pressure didn't come up this far; that there was much too much work, that her former masters were dirty, untidy, and penniless, that they indulged in orgies, real orgies, actual Black Masses! How many things poor Jolanda had been forced to witness and to endure these past years! The landlord was a monster, the neighbors in the attic were filthy beggars, all the inhabitants of the palazzo were scoundrels; as for the doorman he was worse than all the rest. Whereupon she started a long confusing tale of cheating, black market operations concerned with blankets in which (I don't know why) the marvelous Signor Giovanni was involved, collaboration with the Germans, and similar accusations hurled here and there.

It appeared that Jolanda was the only virtuous and honest person in the world. Driven by the wickedness of humankind to live in a constant state of suspicion, she had good reason to hate everything and everybody with a direct and total hatred. Was this barren, passionless hatred, this absurd contempt, born in the depths of her soul? Or did Jolanda hope to participate in an imagined and superior world by adopting a pose in imitation of the manners of the gentlefolk? Anyhow, I was annoyed by her flat, coldly irritated voice, her choice of unpleasant words, and the hateful expression on her fresh, rosy face under the hair of a black angel. I sent Jolanda back to her friends and her cousin in the kitchen, and went to the window to look for the first time at what was to become my daily perspective for an indefinite period, the constant background of my changing hours.

The whole city opened before me in an infinite succession of roofs, terraces, windows, domes, in a clear expanse of airy grays, light yellows, golden pinks, and of plaster transparent with age and faint violet in the shadows. Everything was bright and distant, immersed in visible and tinted air where myriad intangible gold corpuscles seemed to circulate.

At the far left the landscape of houses was closed off by the dome of St. Peter's, blue in the distance; and at the right by the yellow bulk of the Quirinal Palace where at this very moment, under the high, square tower, the Lieutenant of the Realm was receiving the Members of the Committee of Liberation. The only violent color on the whole horizon was the great flag flying from the tower, with its red and green new and brilliant.

Back of a row of white baroque statues that were lined up along the edge of the court, the ash-gray mass of the dome of the Pantheon spread out, and behind the Pantheon the Chinese spiral of the steeple of La Sapienza twisted upward. Farther on the vista was closed by the green profile of Monte Mario that sloped down to the rooftops. Another darker green, that of the gardens of the Pincio, appeared between the masses of the Montecitorio and the Collegio Romano. The city lay enclosed in the hollow among these distant heights like a great motionless stage scene. The streets were not visible, only shadowy crevasses among the tenderly illuminated walls, empty spaces set behind dark silhouettes. No sound reached me at this great height.

On a terrace a quarter of a mile away a young man in shirt-sleeves was exercising by bending his knees. On another, a boy was bouncing a ball, and a woman was carrying her laundry up a stairway. Above the houses, towers, and churches, the clouds were tinged with the first touch of pink, the transparent pink of a woman's cheek. In the air swarms of birds flew in great arches, circles, and spirals, their trajectories interlacing to form shifting hieroglyphics that the wind seemed to assemble and then to erase. They swooped close by and at great speed like small moving spots in the distance, marking, like an oscillating wave, the deepness of the sky. I stayed there for a long while, following their silent flight, until my eye was lost, enchanted in that blue and black turmoil.

—◌ **2** ◌—

The shadows lengthened and the sky took on the green of water. That evening I was supposed to go to the Viminale palace where the Premier was to make a statement. I still had some time left and I decided to look around the palace and the grounds and stroll up to the Viminale later.

I left the flights of birds and the expanse of roofs and went out. Instead of going down by the great stairway of the princes, I went along the attic hall. It was like the street of a medieval town; between plain, dirty walls, with a floor of reddish, dusty tiles, it turned and turned again, like a labyrinth losing itself as it branched off into blind alleys. One met there a population of women in slippers, men in shirtsleeves, and children; from the half-open doors came voices and the smell of cabbage and frying food among unmade beds and overladen tables. A yellowish light came from windows dimmed by cobwebs. Old women sitting outside their doors looked at me distrustfully. In a little square where two halls came together, a crowd of girls pushed around a fountain. The thread of

water was thin; to fill a pail took a long time. They were all standing around exclaiming, chattering, and whispering, like an impatient assembly of birds.

A little farther along, at the left, I found myself at the edge of a
black gulf. It was a large, stone, spiral staircase, winding down pre-
cipitately in a splendid curve like the inside of a shell. I started to
descend slowly, careful of my steps in the darkness. The stairs
were so steep and so narrow at the inside of the curve that I felt as
though I were on a mountain path, except that I had a noble,
marble handrail to hold to. It was a servants' staircase, more beautiful perhaps than the main stairway, but of course more uncomfortable. Here it was not possible to use the ceremonial pace the
other demanded, but instead a lively and guarded step, the hurried and wary step of the servant. It seemed that the men who had
built both stairways believed beauty to be a common good for all
men, but that all men are nevertheless distinguished by a different
posture, and that to each must be given the instruments necessary
to sustain his own role, whether in damask or in rags, in a well-
ordered performance.

On the lower floors I found the doors to various offices; to an
elementary school, a high school, and private apartments. Then,
in a moment, I found myself precipitated on to the ground floor
and into the second courtyard. This too was a large square, its
packed down earth paved with pebbles from the river, with a few
tufts of grass growing among them. An old carriage stood on one
side, with its long shafts resting on the ground, abandoned there
perhaps for many years. Women busied themselves around the
fountain and an old man smoked his pipe in front of a door. Only
the gurgling water varied the silence in this great cube of shadowy
air between high, violet walls and the sky.

Under the arcade in the first courtyard stood some crossbeams
and some window blinds. A few workmen were lazily painting
them gray. In the middle of the courtyard others were emptying a
load of wood on the ground. I looked vainly for Teo the doorman
to get him to explain how to open the entrance door at night.
While I stood in front of the porter's lodge, looking around for

him, an old man who was waiting there asked me if I knew where
to find Teo.

"I'm a friend of Teo's," he said. "I haven't seen him for many
years and I'd like to say hello to him."

I showed him the bell inside the lodge, and rang it myself. We
waited a little, I rang again, nobody answered. Teo was not to be
seen. The old man, who had white hair, a face full of wrinkles,
and a leather briefcase under his arm, thanked me and said: "You
are very kind. I'm sorry Teo doesn't come, but you were so kind to
ring the bell for me! To repay you, if it won't annoy you, I'd like to
tell you a story.

"This palace," he started in, "as you certainly know, is like a
city. It has everything inside it: a bank, a school, shops, a moving
picture theater, and storerooms. Once there was an embassy, too,
and Masonic Headquarters, and many other things. Also, once the
city court of Rome. I'm talking of the days when I was still young,
forty or more years ago. I worked here then because I was Clerk of
the Court, and I still am, see? And I've come here today to deliver
a summons. At that time I was a very good friend of Teo's, but now
I haven't seen him for a long while.

"How many people and events these stairs have known! One
could write a story about it. But since you've been so kind to me,
I'd like to tell you something that might interest you.

"Well, at that time, and I speak of the beginning of the century,
an American painter lived in an apartment on the second floor.
He was a very handsome man, tall and blond, with blue eyes. He
wore his hair long, and had a large beard that fell down over his
chest. He was one of the most elegant men in town. He was on top
of everything, and was the most sought after of all for every society
function. His passion was horses. He had many of them, and all of
the finest breed. He kept a stable down here in the court: Arab
horses, English horses, trotters, gallopers, sorrels, blacks, bays,
whites, grays, piebalds. It was a pleasure to see them with their
lovely saddle blankets when I went up to court in the morning as
the grooms were exercising them in the courtyard. Princesses
came to see them, the most beautiful women in Rome. And in

those days there were beautiful women in the aristocracy. But
you're too young to remember.

"One August morning, one of those days when the sun seems to
split the stones, the American ordered a horse saddled, mounted it,
gave it the spurs, and was off at a gallop. It was midday, and there
wasn't a sign of shade. He took the road for Ostia and galloped
down the empty countryside without stopping until he got there.
Today Ostia is almost a city. Everyone goes there for swimming,
and they've built an endless number of houses there, villas and
bathing establishments, too. But at that time there wasn't even a
village. We had the malaria then, and there were only a few farmhouses and fishermen's shacks and buffaloes under the cork trees.

"The American went to a hut by the sea where a peasant lived
who also acted as a barber, and he let himself be shaved. He made
the peasant cut off everything with the clippers, the blond hair,
the golden beard that made him look like Jesus Christ; and there
he was with his naked head like a billiard ball! Then he mounted
his horse again and rode over the sandy plain. He must have been
in those parts before. At any rate, he found a snake catcher who
gave him two sacks full of live snakes. He tied the sacks to his
saddle and without stopping galloped back to Rome, entered the
palace doorway, greeted Teo, who was young then but most certainly remembers it. Without getting down from the saddle, the
American started climbing. He climbed all the way up the staircase on his horse, and when he came in front of his door, started
to knock and yell for them to let him in. The servants inside were
frightened to see him there, shouting on his horse. His mother
and sister too were watching him from a small window, one of
those oval eyes that open on the stairway, and they didn't know
what to do and didn't dare open the door. They thought the sun
had gone to his head, and called for people to help.

"In a little while the police came, and ambulance attendants.
When he saw them and realized they had come to take him away,
the American, who still hadn't gotten down from his horse, started
to laugh, and to shout even louder for the door to be opened; and
as the others closed in on him he slid his hand into one of the

sacks, grabbed a handful of snakes and started to whip their faces with them. Imagine how frightened they were. The men ran off, and the women of his family opened the door to avoid something worse happening.

"Still in the saddle, he crossed the apartment and went into the salon. Here he finally got down, tied his horse to the window handle, opened the mouths of the sacks, freeing the snakes who spread all over the house. Then he sent his servants to the cellar to bring him bottles of wine, spirits, and champagne. And he offered everybody a drink — the members of his own household, the ambulance attendants, and the policemen. The horse too got his oats in the salon, amid the gilt furniture and ancient paintings. For three whole days they stayed there carousing together."

While the old man was finishing his story, we saw beyond the door in the dark entryway under the huge, shimmering, white statue of the dying Gaul, the long figure of Teo, gesturing with his arms like a windmill. We went to meet him. The old men recognized and greeted one another with great exclamations of joy. But they did not prolong these effusions because their attention, and mine too, was attracted by a strange spectacle.

A jeep suddenly appeared on the landing at the top of the wide stairway. It descended bouncing, stair by stair, with an alternate squeaking of tires and brakes, jumping awkwardly like a web-footed animal, or an uncertainly steered rowboat having a hard time getting through the rollers near the shore. When it reached the last step and touched even ground, the jeep ran in front of us, crossed the arcade, turned into the vestibule, slid through the doorway, and disappeared. The three men in American uniform in the jeep gave us broad salutes as they passed us.

Teo grumbled with his strong accent of the province of Romagna: "And now it's a jeep! They'll ruin the whole stairway. They went clear to the top and there was no way to stop them. They wouldn't listen to reason. Once upon a time the American painter went up on a horse. But now, with an automobile — !"

Teo seemed offended by that mechanical profanation but also pleased by the repetition after so many years and in such changed circumstances of an event so far away, one that had taken place in the time of his youth and the youth of his friend, the clerk of the court. The old man's face also reflected two different emotions, but most strongly his astonishment that his avocation of the past had found so bizarre a confirmation in reality. When Teo discovered that I knew the story of the horse and the snakes, he started to tell it himself. It was the same story with small variations. According to Teo, the painter had brought along not only the sacks of snakes but live night owls, screech owls, and foxes as well, but perhaps this part was the fruit of his fantasy or referred to another episode that happened before or afterward. He said the snakes that had invaded the house had almost all been caught, but others had vanished, hidden in holes or under stones. For many years after some of them would now and then reappear.

"The painter's sister," Teo said, "married and became a princess after her brother went back to America." Many children were born to her in this palace and she got the habit of turning down the sheets to look for a hidden snake before she went to bed at night. Those animals love soft, warm beds. This habit has been passed on in the family, it's been taken over by the sons and daughters, and still goes on. Besides, snakes had always been a passion in that family, even before the episode of the American and the horse.

"When the old prince who is now dead was a child, he took snakes from the countryside, pulled out their poison fangs, and hid them under the tablecloths and plates, so as to see the fright of his family. And later, when he was a young man, in the time of King Umberto and Queen Margherita, he still had the same passion.

"One evening he played a famous joke at the Circolo della Caccia. In those days, you know, dinner tables were decorated to look like gardens and woodland bowers; the centerpieces were huge, green bushes, entire branches with leaves and flowers on them. One evening at the club the prince hid his snakes in this greenery. Imagine what happened when the snakes struck out in the midst of all the guests. The ladies ran this way, that way. They screamed, jumped up on chairs, pulled up their skirts. Really,"

Teo lowered his voice confidentially, "that wasn't the joke of a true prince. But what can you expect? Of true princes, of those who come down from ancient times, few are left. As a matter of fact, if you want to go into it, I dare say that in Rome there's only one, Prince Massimo, who descends from the Romans. And believe me I know something about princes. I'm a connoisseur of princes."

The connoisseur of princes was then silent, his big hands hung down beside his hips, his huge head took on an expression of inert, century-old boredom, and his eyes that had become animated during his resurrection of the past were now watery and vacant. He had talked too much, he had been too familiar with me, a new-comer and almost a foreigner in the palace, a chance witness of an uncommon event. Teo, therefore, assumed his usual haughtiness, and with his elongated form and the squeaking in his joints, started to talk to the old clerk of the court.

I went out to the square, and since I still had time, I started to wander aimlessly through the streets of the quarter. It was the hour of sunset; the air full of changing colors enveloped the houses be-tween light and shadow. Everything seemed to glow with a true light of its own, and threw its rays on others in an infinite and im-palpable tissue. I went through narrow streets and small squares into alleys between walls constantly varied by arches, columns, embellishments, ornaments, and by mysterious relationships of space, like a language that contains all of the past, and yet in its contemporaneousness is proof of the oneness of time; among stairs, shops, bell towers, terraces, windows inhabited by silent fig-ures, and the passage of people with their faces bright in the dusk, their eyes black, the radiant white of their flesh among the wave of voices, whispers, and calls. The last sunlight struck the tops of the facades and tinged them with a rosy color, human like that of the clouds against the green and violet of the sky.

So I went from street to street as though driven and caressed by that luminous life that seemed to bind the men with the houses, envelop the people and palaces, enter the open doors of the shops, follow the women up the stairs, and arch over our heads in a sky peopled by birds. I arrived at a square among noble old houses and

tenements. The very name of the square, Margana, reminded one
of the fairies.

In the center of the square a happy crowd was gathered. I could
hear the laughter and gay shouting of the children. A little marionette theatre was standing in the middle of the crowd, the performance going on with its buffoonery and with sticks beating loudly
on wooden heads. Now a queen entered with her crown and her
dress covered with precious stones. Men, women, old people, children, laborers in their work clothes, vendors of cigarettes, collec-
tors of cigarette butts, beggars, youngsters with shiny hair, girls
with fur jackets, toothless old women, soldiers, clerks — all
watched intently, their faces open and without secrets, lost in a
happy enchantment. I, too, in this crowd of strangers, felt myself
invaded by a sense of sudden joy. I thought that all things appeared and displayed themselves without shame: the people, the
rags, the beauty, the misery, the flash of their eyes, the impetuosity
of their gestures; this thing or that thing that lives by chance her,
in front of us; this square, these marionettes, the woman coming
toward me in the darkening air. We are content. This is our share
of things. But we feel there are endless others that we do not speak
of, there are hidden, vague sentiments, and it is these, perhaps,
that lend to the sky that rosy enchantment and to the heart this
solitary fullness.

I stayed here for a long time watching the spectacle, and it
seemed to me that I should thank someone for the gift I had received, but that it was too strong for me, made out of infinite lives,
and that this vortex of life was overwhelming, so intense that one
could not bear it.

The lights went on in the darkened square. The crowd dis-
persed, and in the sky toward the Janiculum distant fireworks rose
with a muted sound in honor of some saint.

7

NIGHT HAD FALLEN BY THE TIME I had walked down the long Via Nazionale and reached the square in front of the Ministry of the Interior. Hurrying because I was late, I almost ran up one of the curved ramps that lead to the entrance of the Palazzo Viminale. The occasion was an important one, for the resigning Premier had called together the members of the Committee of Liberation, the political leaders and the Italian and foreign journalists to make a statement before them. There was no precedent in parliamentary and governmental annals for this procedure, but then the situation itself was without precedent in a period of transition and growth in which everything was unforeseen, and no institutions either new or traditional were certain or lasting. Nothing about the square or the ministry itself betrayed the gravity and solemnity of the moment. There was no array of troops or police force, but only two *carabinieri* in everyday uniform and a plainclothesman walking up and down in front of the door, looking bored. Above their heads in the still air of the night the

Italian flag hung down limply from a balcony. I couldn't make out as I passed in a hurry whether the shield of the House of Savoy was on its white, or whether the Allied flags were displayed on either side. These were questions given great symbolic weight at that time; heraldic battles in which it was considered the maximum victory to be able to display our flag big and alone and without the royal coat of arms.

The ushers received me at the entrance and led me up wide stairs and narrow stairs and through endless corridors. They wore a strangely festive air, as if the meeting going on was a big party or a masked ball in their honor, and their faces were relaxed as if a great weight had been lifted from their hearts. They felt this was the last day these strangers without titles and with the faces and clothes of another race would penetrate that home of theirs, that it would never again be profaned; that this palace which had so calmly resisted so many storms would finally return to their possession — for them, for them alone. They would no longer have to tremble at the idea of crazy reforms, senseless changes, cruel purges, and ridiculous demands for efficiency. They would no longer need to greet superiors who didn't hesitate to humiliate them by refusing honors and who insulted them by even rejecting the title, "Your Excellency," so sweet on the lips. From now on they would not have to hide away with a feeling of guilt but would be able to enjoy again, as masters, this marvelous intricacy of corridors, of anterooms, of rooms numbered and reserved, of which they alone knew the plan and secret. This desecrated place would once more become a sanctuary, a church, as was right, and they the only priests. Let the profane be cast from the temple! This meeting today of course was one last, ingenuous protest. Then one would never mention them again.

However, these barbarians had not caused much ruin. They had only timidly threatened it. The palace remained the one it always had been, from the faraway days when it was built. The great stairway was closed, the elevators weren't running, people who had no connection with the administration came and went, cabinet ministers and their secretaries stayed in their offices until late at night to do God knows what and have sandwiches for supper, but the palace was always the same and never changed its appearance. Although it didn't look like a place to hold full-dress parades and receptions, I admit it didn't look like a factory, a police station, or a military barracks either. It was neither antique nor modern; it was huge and completely anonymous. And yet one felt that the builder, perhaps quite unconsciously, had done something that was perfect in its way, something that marvelously fulfilled an aim, that expressed in its bulk, weight, and size, in its grayness and its flat uniformity the exact conception and the meaning of its function. It was nothing but an immense poorhouse, the handsomest, cleanest, most dignified, solemnest and biggest of all existing almshouses. This was the main shelter on which all the others depended. Here was found not only refuge and security but for some people moral comfort in the use of power and in identifying themselves with the state.

Perhaps the barbarians who had come in had wanted to change its aspect and tried to press it into other uses, but they hadn't planned or dared to evacuate it. The inmates had barricaded themselves in their numberless rooms, had known how to resist, and finally, today, they had won.

The usher with his bent shoulders who was acting as my guide wore an old, frayed suit and dragged his feet along. But his face shone with a deep and malicious satisfaction. This was the day in which the Lord remembered His chosen people, in vengeance and triumph.

The Premier's speech seemed to be almost over when I came into the room. Silently nodding to my acquaintances, I could hardly make my way through the crowd. There was a kind of orchestra of important persons and journalists sitting up front, and behind them and beside them others were pushed against the walls. Among them I recognized famous faces and a large number of unknown foreigners, some of them wearing the military uniforms of war correspondents; and there were many women from the most varied countries, with blankbooks and fountain pens in hand, taking down notes.

Near the entrance Casorin was leaning up against a post talking to a tall, blond French girl. His face was flushed from shyness, and he was talking under his breath, but even so, too loudly. People nearby turned around with reproachful faces as he gabbled on. When he saw me near him he left the woman immediately, as though I'd come to his rescue. He gave me a brief résumé of what the Premier had already said.

"He's a father, he's like a father to me," he said quickly. "I'd let myself be killed for him."

Then, ashamed of his sentimental outburst, he started in with his outstretched finger to point out the most famous of the bystanders, and although I made signs to him to be quiet he kept on commenting on their expressions in his exaggerated and truculent way.

"Look over there! There's Malgero. What a filthy face, with that beard of a good old grandfather, and the big, black teeth back of his mustache. And Rinaldi? Look how he fidgets to make himself seem young. He looks like a pickled eel.

"Look the other way. There's Dandi with his head like an egg. What a beautiful brain he must have inside it! They've all been disappointed. Rattoni's nose was long enough when he got here, but now it actually reaches the ground. It's a sausage, a pudding. And Colombi's mouth? it's like a big lizard's mouth. Oh yes, I know he's a friend of yours. Nice bunch of friends you have! Guerrasio pulls his beard as though his thoughts were attached to it. It's like a lamp with a chain. If you pull it, it lights up. But in this case it must have a loose wire somewhere!"

Casorin continued with his cold and ferocious jocosity. He would often find, especially in a situation that moved him or threatened to move him, that he was like a deaf man at a concert to whom every gesture, the players manipulating their instruments, the grotesque motions of the conductor, the ecstatic or bored faces of the listeners, seemed removed and incomprehensible. In the internal silence and detachment everything seemed without reason, an absurd spectacle of madness. Casorin was affected not by ironical curiosity or simple childishness but by a feeling of suddenly being cut off from things. Everything seemed transformed, awkward, and foolish, the more so because before they had seemed pregnant with significance. He himself called his state of mind "sincerity," perhaps because he thought he was breaking a convention, an arbitrary tie with the world, a something inevitably sacred. But now there was more than his usual "sincerity," as I knew all too well. He had been exalted by the words of the Premier, he had been touched by them and believed them utterly; and then right afterward the whole thing seemed a ridiculous comedy of puppet's faces, equivocal gestures made by senseless characters, like certain singers of René Clair who open their mouths without a single sound. It seemed to him that the man who spoke was alone, that all the others were hostile to him and had abandoned him to his hopeless self-defense without listening to him. They all seemed like imitation people, material for bitterness and satire. And a part of the bitterness against that game of imitation extended to the Premier himself, who was guilty of making himself beloved and then allowing himself to be abandoned.

"Look at him!" Casorin whispered. "He's a father! A chrysanthemum. A chrysanthemum on a dunghill!" Casorin made this atrocious comparison with a bored look. It was his way of expressing an intense emotion.

Even without looking at the scene through his close-set eyes and without having lost a feeling for the conventional language that is written on the faces of men of politics, there was something strange about the assembly. Everyone was there. Aside from the foreigners, who were recognizable as foreigners at first glance, there were men whose reason for being present was difficult to understand: people of all ages, of all regions, and of all parties. They had remained united until now, obligated to this union by a force greater than themselves, a force that some believed was calculation, some hope, some destiny, and some self-interest. Today the time had come for them to separate. All of them felt this but none knew where the separation lay, and with whom he would find himself tomorrow.

A group of old men like strange, prehistoric animals were stretched out arrogantly in their chairs, wrapped in an atmosphere of coagulated respectability. They knew how to survive. As indifferent as stones to the events around them, and not really backing them up, they hinted by a nod of the head that they were going along with them, but actually they stayed perfectly still. Hiding their old faces behind bearded masks they had waited, lethargically but filled with hidden ambitions, for their hour. Now they were here with their too-worn and too-familiar faces, listening to the solemn words of the speaker as they had listened to so many others in times long past. They leaned their heads on their hands, concealing their glances behind their glasses. It was a lovely day, a day of victory for them, also. Their only problem was to make their long lives last still longer; not to die now that they were needed and when people would turn to their reputed wisdom (the fruit of such marvelously long and repeated incapacity) to bring about the salvation of the country and the state.

Beside them were young men with eyes lit up as if they were taking part in something they could not understand. They suspected injustice, and they felt caught in some trap or game that was new to them. Many of them were heroes of the partisan war who had handled guns and risked their lives. And some regretted the passing of that time of intoxicated action and wished that it might come back. Others had turned toward peace with such intensity that they would have refused to define it.

There were middle-aged men with the anonymous faces of clerks or provincial notaries, with something fanatical in the blandness of their features as they listened in silence. There were restless priests in their chairs, judges, jurists, big landowners from the South wearing long, black coats and with thick clumps of eyebrows under their wrinkled foreheads. There were just a few peasants and workers. There were a great number of lawyers. There were bald heads and curly heads, black suits and sport jackets; open faces and closed and obtuse ones; sectarians, the peaceful, and even someone who was frightened.

There were the bleary eyes and sideburns of a Sicilian politician with a big future; the rotund smile of a Calabrian, friend of everyone, with a mustache on a face like a ball; the enormous and thundering bulk of a Neapolitan who rolled one eyelid back over his finger as he listened and wore his illustrious father's name like a wide-brimmed hat; the dry, hard face of a partisan chief, with clear eyes like the face of a metallurgical worker. He has fought all the way from the plateau of Spain to the plains of the Po. There were men who had spent years in prisons and concentration camps, some who had enjoyed their lives prudently, and others who had spent their lives in prayer.

There were the languid black eyes and oriental coloring of my friend Di Leo, who knew the perspective of Leningrad and the inside of the Prison of Modelo in Madrid; the strong Jewish face with the impeccable intellectual machine behind it of Tempesti, who had once been condemned to die; the jolly and flabby mass of Don Luigi Logirone, the celebrated quick-change artist from the South, famous for his friendly backslapping, his whispering to his cronies, and his rapid vote counting; very tall Germano, who was as unstable as he was energetic; gaunt, ascetic, and wrinkled Ragazzi and paunchy Borbone, the gossiping savior of Europe. Some were here as representatives of parties, groups, forces, categories, ideas, and even what one calls the Italian people. Others represented only themselves. There was every kind of man here — the present ruling class in its entirety, and it had come here to dissolve.

A few rows in front of me Moneta, round, soft, and rosy, withdrawn on his chair, listened intently. Farther on Fede was whispering some passionate comment into Roselli's ear, and the wooden face of Canio appeared at their right. At the rear, back of a long table with a green cover, sat the members of the Committee of Liberation, most of them cabinet ministers, with their expressions, their frequently photographed faces, different from the usual for this special occasion. Some of them had a look of approval and participation while others put on airs, stroking their beards and taking their glasses off and on, and still others sat stock-still, trembling with what might have been either shock or indignation. At one end of the table, isolated, like a thirteenth apostle, sat the man who had initiated the crisis. He had a long nose and

two round, bulging eyes that looked as if they might come out of
their sockets at any moment and roll on the floor. His face was red
with repressed fury; he frowned, lifted his shoulders, snorted,
clenched his fists, then perhaps becoming aware of these involuntary motions, moved his hand over his hair, lowered his eyes, and
smiled, only to return shortly to his angry gesticulations.

The Premier stood at the center of the table as he spoke,
framed by the theological and cardinalic faces and symmet-
rical, glittering monocles of the two illustrious heads of the Right
and the Left. He did indeed look like a chrysanthemum, as
Casorin had called him, repeating the epithet used as an insult
by one of the satirical journals. Yes, he was like one of these
strange flowers with delicate petals and gray, autumnal, funereal
leaves, different from all others, exotic and courageous in the first
freezing days of the northern mists, with their almost impercep-
tible perfume, yet with a pollen that kills mosquitoes; flowers
without sensuality, steeped in the faithful tears of the hoar frost.

He was different, like a stranger. They could not see or glorify
in him their own vices and virtues shown under the footlights.
Among an exuberant people he was shy. In a country that loves
rhetoric and fine phrases he was brief and stubborn. Where
everyone admired self-acclaim, he chose the obscure way, the
modest chair. Alongside a hot-blooded race he seemed pale, and
in a land bright with sunlight, with red rooftops, green trees, and
blue skies, he was slate colored like a school blackboard covered
with the chalk marks of arithmetic problems.

Sorrow was on his face as if continuous grief, the endless grief
of others, had turned down the corners of his mouth, dulled his
eyes, and whitened his hair when he was a child. I looked at him
standing between his two companions of the Left and of the Right,
their faces all too human, shrewd, able, attentive, greedy for the
things of the present. The Premier's face seemed by contrast to be
made out of the impalpable material of memory, composed of the

pallid color of the dead, of the spectral substance of the dead, of the grieving image of the young dead, of the shot, the hanged, and the tortured, with the tears and the cold sweat of the wounded and dying, of the anguished, of the sick and the orphaned, in the cities and on the mountains. His whole body seemed made of these sufferings; they ran in his blood. His skin was the color of bones whitening in the fields. They said he was not a man of politics, that he represented no real force, that he did not know how to maneuver among entangled games of the special interests, that he was nothing but a neutral and symbolic figure. But he represented, or rather was made of something that does not enter into political schemes, something hidden and nameless, something always the same, undefined, repeated a million times in a million ways, eternally the same: the dead, cold under the earth, everyday suffering and the courage that hides it.

If to identify oneself with the griefs of the world, suffering them oneself, assuming them as one's own is sanctity, then he was fashioned from the incorporeal substance of saints. He had the deceiving appearance of a saint, as well: the humility so complete that it might seem pretense, or a kind of rhetoric in reverse. To look at him with his spare mustache, the steel-rimmed glasses raised over his narrow forehead, the dark-gray suit of a bank clerk, the well-pressed trousers, the matching gray silk tie with its accurate knot (perhaps tied by his wife's careful hand before he left home), his stiff collar, modest, old-fashioned, gold cuff links, one might very well imagine that this clerklike appearance was nothing but a disguise, a mask, purposely adopted to contrast with the false heroism and magniloquence of so many of the great men of the past. But in reality this dress was only the spontaneous, simple, and very strange truth, the natural external form of his saintliness.

Perhaps what a friend of mine who happened to be at the meeting for some reason had once written in a love poem was true. I could see him leaning against the wall at one side with his great, patriarchal head and thick, black mustache, and the verses came to my lips:

Perhaps it is true that in every saint
There's a touch of the soul of a servant
And perhaps that's the very reason
They don't grant themselves love in this world.

I said these lines (written for a woman) over to myself as I listened to the speech. There was the saintliness and the humble
servitude, there was the unshriven love that he did not allow himself, all hidden in this bureaucratic raiment and that gray voice of
his that seemed the voice of a ghost. It had no tone or timbre, but
sounded always the same; gray, dull, without inflection, and yet
clear and as cold as tears. This voice, this voice of saintliness,
would not allow itself love or tenderness or even the accent of sentiment. The Premier was apparently talking of plain, simple, elementary administrative matters, without accompanying them with
gestures. He set forth what had been accomplished in the last
months as though he were an accurate secretary reading the minutes of a previous meeting. But what he was talking about under
this conventional guise was the reality outside the rules. It was a
gentle but unforgiving accusation of those who had tried for their
own advantage to overthrow events and to break the unity of
whose tragic value he felt himself to be the custodian. It was the
language of the dead who speak the truth that no one hears. He
translated it into the style appropriate to bureaucratic practice,
like a doctor's report read hastily in the hallway of a clinic so that
the students can be instructed and the patients unaware. The di-
agnosis was exact and severe: it was the return of an old world, an
attempt to wipe out all that had been accomplished, and in short
the great statement: *coup d'état.*

Had anyone ever before spoken such serious words with such
careful discretion, and made them out of pity seem so boring and
lifeless? In this gathering of men bound to passion, ambition, and
special interests, the Premier's voice was an incomprehensible
anachronism, and therefore almost unbearably irritating. Each
one of them tried to translate that voice into their own language,
to weigh and compare it with their own political game. But some-

thing remained that did not fit into any game, that contradicted them and wore the uneasiness of an invisible presence.

He had finished and he sat modestly down sideways on his chair, pulling his trousers up at his knees so as not to spoil the crease, and lowered his glasses onto his nose. His neighbor on the left dutifully made some gestures of assent because one must applaud such goodness. But his eyes were glowing with ironical pleasure. This unprecedented and incomprehensible goodness was evidently not a very dangerous weapon; it would be easy enough to get rid of. His neighbor on the right, who had already won his point, could not conceal his state of mind or even follow the most elementary rules of strategy and control his irritation. Showing himself much more human and more sensitive to the voice of the saints than anyone would ever have supposed, he jumped to his feet in a state of much agitation, his face pale and his eyes sparkling, and to everyone's astonishment started to speak. He turned to the foreign journalists and begged them not to repeat what they had heard and not to publish it in their newspapers, to silence it. He concluded by reaffirming his own good faith and the noble intentions of his political party.

A murmur of amazement and of shock rose in the room. The foreign journalists were indignant that anyone dared instruct them as to what they should say, to impose censorship on their freedom of writing. Near me a huge American with the little red beard of a westerner under his chin threw around insults and picturesque abuse in a loud voice.

"We're starting off wrong," shouted another. "They want to bring back the Index again."

Everyone talked, commented, murmured at the same time; and as if they were released from excessive tension, they got up noisily, pushed back their chairs, interrogated their neighbors or gathered together in groups in a huge clatter. They all violently deplored this uncalled for reply, so strange and almost insane coming from an old and prudent politician, renowned for his moderation, capacity, weight, and sense of responsibility. And yet, from his own point of view this weathered old serpent was right.

More than all the others he had demonstrated, perhaps quite unconsciously, that he knew what he was doing, that he knew how to defend his own solid but limited position. Driven by holy indignation, he had been poetic in his own way. He found himself in this time of no parliaments, almost without realizing it, impelled by an innate parliamentary sense to make a speech for the opposition, that obligatory speech that asserts the privilege of the successor. Also without realizing it he had restored the old state.

More important still, he had shown that he was terrified and had suddenly become aware of inexpressibly haunting presences. He had risked his reputation by this impropriety, but he had done what he thought was his duty to exorcise ghosts and chase away angels.

Meanwhile in the general confusion the Premier, followed by his spectacled young secretaries, had gone noiselessly out through a side door and no one noticed his absence.

8

*O*UTSIDE, THE NIGHT WAS COLD. The wind had become stronger and brought clouds from all directions to cover the black sky. Here and there through a rent in the clouds a veiled star shone, and a slender piece of the moon appeared and disappeared among the mists like a boat in a storm rising from the hollows to the crests of the waves.

On the level space in front of the Palazzo Viminale small knots of men lingered to talk things over excitedly before rushing off to the headquarters of their various parties to reexamine the situation and decide what should be done. They were agitated, aggressive, and preoccupied. Their voices rang out harshly in the dark air of the square. They were like gamecocks, eager to fight and ready to shed their own blood without hesitation. Large talk and uncompromising propositions were flying about. Many praised the Premier for his courageous battle, others were perplexed and whispered in low voices or smiled contentedly over some private calculation.

Fede and Roselli went by in a sweat, obviously thoroughly aware of the importance of what was in their minds. As they strode along they were disputing loudly with an athletic young man who was making wide passionate gestures and whose face was a cross between a snake's and a young falcon's. His neck swelled with rage and he was explaining in a vibrating, jerky voice how he had tried in vain to advise the Premier against making a speech that was a political error and would now have to be straightened out. It was Latorre, who was known as one of the most acute and able of the left-wing leaders. Gesticulating and lifting his strong shoulders disdainfully, he went by between Fede and Roselli, who seemed to agree with his ideas.

Casorin and Moneta were waiting for me to decide what they would write for our paper. Moneta, as usual, was ready with obscure historical references and brilliant literary allusions and displayed them before me while Casorin boiled with indignation and sneering. We stopped a few more minutes to discuss things, then slowly descended the ramp and then they left me to hurry to their work.

A young Communist girl with corn-colored hair falling over her shoulders, a serene forehead, and light eyes filled with gay assurance, went by me almost running in a quick, springing step. She did not stop but called to me and smiled.

The square was now empty, and I walked slowly toward the Via Nazionale. It must have rained during the speech. The asphalt was wet and mirrored the reddish lights of the occasional lampposts. It was cold. I put my hands in my pockets. I was wrapped in vague thoughts that held the darkness of the street, the sad reflections of the lamps, the echo of words, of faces superimposed on one another, and the slow rhythm of my steps. I realized I was whistling some unrecognizable tune because passersby turned to look at me with astonished faces, perhaps believing from those involuntary notes that I had some particular reason for happiness.

A little way ahead of me on the wet sidewalk was an old beggar with one knee on the pavement like a warrior ready to shoot. He had the shaggy gray beard of a prophet, a big head, and long hair covered by a greasy old hat with a drooping brim, an aquiline nose, and deep eyes, hollow and close-set, filled with madness. He was dressed in rags. A full knapsack hung around his neck, and sticking out of it was the gnawed end of a loaf of bread. Over one arm he carried a long stick as though it were a musket, the branch of a tree he must have cut off recently in someone's garden, because it was freshly peeled. With this stick of his, and his ferocious face turned toward the middle of the street, he waited in ambush for automobiles to pass. When a car came by he pointed his weapon, went through the motions of loading it, closed one eye to take aim, and shot. He was not satisfied with one hit but followed his passing prey as a hunter follows with a double-barreled shotgun the flight of a bird. He aimed at the car before it drove up, aimed at its sides while it passed in front of him, and continued to follow it, still shooting as it drove away. When the slaughter was ended he lowered his branch and looked around satisfied, with the proud face of an executioner who has accomplished his task well. But now another car would come from the opposite direction, and the old man would start again to aim and to shoot. At each hit he would open his mouth, as though he were making the sound of a shot with his lips, but in complete silence. When two automobiles crossed one another he hurried with rapid gestures to hit them both at the same time. None succeeded in escaping his shots. But whenever the little open trucks filled with passengers came by he lowered his gun and spared them. Nor did he shoot at the few people who walked close to the wall on the sidewalk across the way. The pedestrians and the passengers of the little trucks were not his enemies. His enemies were only those who drove the automobiles, and for them he had no pity.

A young man in the uniform of a streetcar conductor went up to him in an excess of zeal and said in a commanding voice: "Go shoot somewhere else. Go around the corner. . . . Not here. . . . Off you go!"

The old man looked at him, worried, like someone interrupted in the middle of important work, but when he saw the visored cap that looked so much like a policeman's he lifted his knee docilely from the pavement and obeyed without speaking. He took a few steps with the wavering and uncertain gait of a man who has been kneeling for a long time and who has a numb leg, rotating at every step to balance the weight of the knapsack on his hip. At first he carried his branch as though it were a gun at his side, then he rested it on the ground and it became a simple stick. He had almost reached the corner when a car with its headlights on drove very fast toward him from the end of the street. The temptation was too great; turning around, the old man saw that his persecutor, the streetcar conductor, had moved away. He dropped quickly to his knee, aimed, and was just in time to fill the passing car with bullets. And there he stayed in silence, triumphant and obstinate, awaiting other enemies and other deeds of justice.

I had stopped to watch him when I felt myself grabbed under the arms on both sides by two men who came up behind me and dragged me forward, calling out my name and laughing.

"What are you up to here?" asked the one on my right. "We've been spying on you. You've been whistling like a blackbird. Was it the minuet from *Don Giovanni*?"

And the man on the left, who had noticed the old marksman, said: "Nine months ago we were shooting in a different fashion. But the mad also know how to express themselves."

Both of them limped. Andrea Valenti had been wounded in the leg during the fighting at the end of April and had just begun to walk again by leaning on a rubber-tipped cane. Carmine Bianco limped only on rainy days because of a foot he had broken many years before.

Caught so unexpectedly and dragged by my arms, I didn't know which to turn to, but crossed the street between them as they limped along out of step, pulling me and leaning on my shoulders. I rocked like an old clumsily driven buggy that lists from one side to the other and threatens to overturn.

Carmine was small and squarely built like a peasant. And there was something of the peasant in his face, yellow as clay and prematurely lined, in the slightly staring and patient light of his eyes, the slowness of his motions, his dark and slovenly clothes, his ostentatious use of dialect, an indeterminate dialect, a mixture

of Roman, Neapolitan, and Apulian. But on his pointed nose he
wore the spectacles of a professor, as indeed he was; an expert on
agriculture and cultivator of his own little model farm. He had
the innocence of a technologist and the enthusiasm and utopian
gusto for the practical and precise. He had also the peasant's
poetic feeling for the oneness of problems, the distrust of the
state and of everything that does not originate at the very heart
of things. He had been a Communist when he was young and
had spent several years in prison, and he'd been back in prison
recently under the Germans. He had abandoned long since
his early opinions and turned to apparently smaller and more
everyday interests; to land reforms, leases, irrigation, farming
methods, and all activities that can change the face of a piece of
earth, exerting as much passion as if he were changing the entire
surface of the earth. For it seemed to him now that the true and
varied small details of life had been sacrificed to the political
schemes of his adolescence, to their uniformity and their intellectual rigidity. Yet he was still attracted by great projects and great
visions; he wavered between two poles, that of technology and the
passion for making things over.

On one day he would follow his dream of developing things
slowly and patiently, a course that flowed naturally from the problems of field and village. The next day he would follow his dream
of the efficiency of the political battle, of parties and party organization, of new ideas, of the rising power of the masses. He was
mounted on a horse with one foot in pure politics and the other in
pure technology. This very uncertainty, however, clarified his
ideas, kept him alive and passionate, and prevented him from becoming a fossil in his mental habits.

Andrea, the other one, was a bird of high flights. He too had
been a Communist until a few years ago. But while in Carmine
this experience had gone, scarcely leaving a trace, buried under
the earth overturned by the peasant's plow, with Andrea it had left
a deep mark and an infinity of problems. It showed itself in the un-
prejudiced quality of his mind, in his capacity for bringing close
the most distant ideas, in the realistic pattern of his unrestrained

fantasies, and perhaps also in a certain nostalgia. He had gone through the most diverse trials: wars and battles, party leaderships, fights in defense of party slants and factions, emigrations, exiles, concentration camps, prisons. He had made a thorough study of philosophy, history, economics, finance, human adventures of every kind, loves and storms, and finally he had played a noble role in the partisan warfare in the North.

He was still young, so young that one wondered how he had found time to combine so many and such profound elements of life. His hair was completely g ray, yet his face kept an innocent infantile expression. He had a child's small turned-up nose, a tiny mouth, a pointed chin with a pleasant dimple, chubby cheeks, keen, light eyes, and delicate hands. The inactivity forced on him by his wounded leg had increased his weight, but the heaviness I felt as he leaned against my left shoulder added an element of authority without taking away his boyish grace. He spoke jerkily, in a metallic, nervous, and impatient voice, as if annoyed at the physical time it took him to speak a word. His imagination raced ahead of his speech, the slowness of his listeners' understanding, and their ignorance and sentimental prejudices. He could not hide this contempt for everything, much as he sometimes tried.

The last months of his convalescence had kept him far away from political adventures at the very time when he would have liked most to be in the midst of them and when his clairvoyance and fantasy could have proved themselves in action. Instead, alone and obliged to rest and abstain, he had been driven to impotence, only inadequately sharing in events, the mistakes of others, and lost opportunities. Perhaps he had suffered from this forced absence. But as he was free of personal ambitions, his excess of vitality and imagination had resulted in passionate contemplation. For a long time he had foreseen the present crisis and many other events that had taken place or would take place. Delight in his own ideas consoled him for the sadness of his prophecies and his sense of inevitable disillusionment.

The pleasure of ideas joined with the pleasure of friendship — of the presence and closeness of a friend — is a youthful joy that calls back spaces, movements, the sounds of voices. The two lame ones who held me between them were continuing a conversation they'd started as they came out of the meeting. Each of their phrases sprang out as if one were born from the other, like balls aimed by players at battledore and shuttlecock. This exchanging of thoughts while wandering down the streets is not the custom here in Rome and struck me as being something almost forgotten. This city does not lend itself to it. So intense is Rome's physical vitality, so rich are its opportunities and distractions that you are obliged to turn at every instant to look at something, and to interrupt the thread of talk for some human spectacle too marvelous to be neglected. Perhaps also because in Rome all ideas seem to have been already expressed in another age and have left their mark on a stone or a countenance.

Held between my two friends, I felt that I was somewhere else, in that old and only town of my adolescence, Turin, where ideas and friendship are exalted possessions, and the tree-lined avenues are so long and vast and deserted that words can race and scatter along them without hindrance. At all hours these avenues, these solitary streets, open themselves to the young who have important things to say to one another, things high and sharp like the white mountains in the background. At night the whole city becomes a great portico, from the eighteenth-century arcades to the bridges over the Po ornamented by flowery and matronly statues. In this youthful portico we walked up and down in those exciting times of first friendships, and our voices ran along the dark corridors of the streets until, behind the trunks of the plane trees, they met in the distance other excited and enthusiastic voices. These endless streets seemed built purposely for this peripatetic and adolescent exuberance, filled with unlimited and undirected power. Even now, every time I go up to Turin, I meet in the hours of the night groups of young people, masters of the street, among the intricate shadows of the trees in the middle of the road, and they suddenly challenge one another to race, flying like swallows for a short stretch, and then without resting pick up the interrupted conversation again, heedless of the solitary man on a bicycle who brushes silently against them, his visored cap on his bent head.

After they had crossed the street the two lame ones went on until they reached the *Traforo.* Here they let go my arms and slowed their pace until they finally stopped. The tunnel opened before us like a nameless cavern, faintly illuminated by a few lamps that lit up the white tiles on the curved walls. Filled with the smell of burned gasoline and light gray smoke, it has something aggressive and dirty about it. The city disappeared in the darkness at the two entrances. The noise of the passing cars and the voices of men who looked black against the white background boomed and were thrown back again in the vault and joined in a deafening roar like that of a huge waterfall.

In this subterranean gallery one felt as in no other place freed from the seduction of eyes, hidden to all, outside of time. Perhaps that is why my two companions sought refuge here, in a sibyl's cave, designed for words of prophecy.

The sidewalk was too narrow for the three of us. Carmine stepped down, then stood looking up at me and said:

"They don't know what they want; or perhaps they know what they want isn't worth wanting. But they believe willingness is a duty, or anyhow is good, the only good. And they're in a hurry, a tremendous hurry just to do something. Naturally success doesn't matter to them; in fact they have a liking for sacrifice and martyrdom.

"Action's the only thing they understand. But what for? Do you think they know what a tree is? Or that they've ever bothered to find out? . . . Or a goat? . . . an animal? A force of nature? . . . The earth, the power that lies in things and binds them together? . . . Of course not . . . that's unknown to them. They're always in the clouds and move hither and yon. They have to move like that — without consistency. Sometimes that's all right, when they want to be negative, you understand? Just for the sake of opposing anything, just not to give in, just to be 'anti.'

"But now the time has come to be positive, to get the feel of things, to be close to the people, the people who get up in the morning, have their work and their own thoughts; who are preoccupied with eating, with cohabiting, with hoeing, lighting fires, fixing up their broken houses, and in many other things of that kind. . . .

"In parenthesis, I believe the Premier will find himself quite alone, that nobody'll pay anymore attention to him.

"Now it's important to know what one wants: this or that or this! . . . Look at Fede. . . . You know how fond I am of him, what a fine, unselfish, intelligent fellow he is — in every way much better than I am. But what does *he* want?

"He went to prison when he was almost a boy, and I'm sure the reasons why he went didn't matter at all to him. . . . He knew perfectly well there were many other important things that counted for more. . . . At the bottom of his heart he really didn't have any faith in it all. But he thought it was his duty to get into action, so he's always been an example of extraordinary courage.

"And now it's exactly the same story. Do you imagine he believes all those lovely political formulas he invents every single day? Certainly not. He just believes that you must have some political activity, sacrifice yourself, stir around, act as if you believed. And all these things a peasant would never understand."

A streak of lightning, a puff of cold wind, the rolling crash of thunder came from the entrance of the tunnel behind us. Then the sound of a violent downpour of rain. We turned to look into the dark that lay hidden behind, like water threaded in a spiderweb, visible and silver in the lamplight. We were under cover and safe as if we were in a cave.

"The peasants wouldn't understand," Andrea said. "That's natural. How can you expect them to understand things that are based on nothing, that are nothing but conventional words, that we wouldn't understand either if we hadn't made ourselves decide one day to accept them for good?

"We're running after shadows, and you'll see that what's going to happen to us is what happens in those anguished dreams when you want to clutch at something — I don't know what — a woman or something else that's desirable . . . and your hand reaches out with a terrific desire to get hold of it, and almost touches it — when it escapes and makes off. . . . And we run after it again and it still eludes us. It runs farther, getting smaller in the distance, while we go on pursuing it with the same passion and increasing anxiety.

"We started out wanting a world revolution; later we were content with a revolution in Italy. Then later with a few reforms, then for a place in the government, and finally just not to be kicked out of it. Now we've reached the point where we're on the defensive of a party, or a group, or a smaller group; then — who knows — perhaps for our own persons, for our honor and our soul. . . . Always smaller and more distant objects, but the abstract passion remains the same.

"It's sad, but you'll find that's what's going to happen. I had time to think and to reflect in those months at Putti getting my leg cured. We've been defeated for many reasons that didn't depend on us, but it was also our own fault, because we didn't want what we ought to have wanted, and we played at being Machiavelli, pretending to reform the structure by preserving and restoring the very same structure we wanted to reform. And we fawned on and rebuilt the very bureaucracy we wanted to destroy, entrusting it with its own suppression, astonished that it didn't answer our prayer to do us a favor by committing suicide.

"Naturally the peasants didn't understand. It's exactly as if you pretended that hail makes grass grow, or you appointed mosquitoes to combat malaria. I know very well that in some circumstances you can't draw a fine line. You must take advantage of whatever's useful. One can use the industrialist's money to expropriate him, one can pick up the strangest allies and traveling companions on the way, and be ready to throw them into the ditch at the first opportunity.

"But there must be a definite road. One can be less prejudiced the more one knows what one wants and the more clear-sighted and uncompromising one is.

"To travel north to reach the south is nonsense! I don't blame your peasants for not understanding it. I don't understand it myself.

"Watch out, now! The people aren't yet aware. They're all taken up by daily problems, still thinking of fighting and winning. But we know. Our political battle is already lost. This is only the beginning. There's nothing to be done."

Carmine protested to all this, agreeing that mistakes had been made but pointing out at the same time that they weren't irreparable. Moreover, much had been accomplished, he said, and there were endless other things that could be done, in fact must be done. At the worst, while we were waiting for other developments, it was important to concentrate on a good and simple administration. After all, he explained, events do change rapidly. Even though we now found ourselves at a standstill, we'd soon be moving again. Even if we were now governed by priests, it wouldn't last long. A few months, a year at the most.

"Remember what history teaches," Andrea replied. "And don't get any illusions. After all, there's been a revolution. We've had our hand in it, everybody's had a hand in it one way or another. Now the peasants can't understand, but nine months ago, a year ago, and two years ago they understood it very well indeed.

"They all understood one another then, both in the city and out in the country. You could knock at all doors and they'd open without the use of a password. We recognized each other then by a mere glance, by a sniff. We all agreed. Everyone was at his post and felt he belonged at it, and was able to accomplish things he never imagined he could. You know all that. . . .

"But watch people's faces today. Watch their gestures and what they're doing. They haven't lost what they found then, and perhaps they won't lose it for a long time. They're alive, they're active, they're putting up their bombed walls, getting married, making love, trying in every way they can without laziness or complaints to earn a living and better themselves. They've forgotten the war with incredible speed — and all the fear, blood, servitude, moralizing, the hypocritical virtue of the state and the law, the lies and atrocities of the past years.

"The politicians, on the other hand, who should represent them, be their spokesmen and guide them, too, haven't forgotten anything. Moreover, they haven't even learned anything. They've revived old parties, old ideas, old prejudices, and old quarrels. And they fuss around and become more and more incomprehensible. It's easy to foresee what's going to happen."

We went a few steps farther into the *Traforo* and stopped again. In this cavern, while it went on raining outside, Andrea seemed possessed by his soothsaying mood and went on prophesying future divisions, collapses, decays, and splinterings of the various parties, the separation of the nation bit by bit into two factions over false issues and false line-ups, and he prophesied many more things.

Some of the things he foretold that day have now come true, and we will find out through the years whether the others will come true or not. At the time he said all this, his visions of the future seemed daring and fantastic to us. Though we listened with interest as one listens to the reader of cards, the sibyl, or the pythoness, we expressed our doubts and told him that what he said was possible, but of course many other things were just as possible. Therefore it was better to limit ourselves to things of the present and busy ourselves with what could be done now.

Andrea defended his thesis and added that before long we and many others too would come up against unacceptable dilemmas. If we refused a forced choice, we'd discover we could no longer find a single party or movement that represented all our ideas. Then we would indeed be driven to the examination of conscience and the historical analysis that Andrea, so far in advance, had been induced to make by forced inactivity.

"You too," Andrea said, "will discover yourself alone in a confused world as I have, and you won't be able to accept what's cooked and served up to you every day. You too, like Descartes when he was thinking out his *Discourse on Method*, will discover yourself some winter, with war raging outside and the country full of snow and cold, by a lighted stove in a nice warm room, wrapped in furs. And you'll start to debate all the ideas you've received and you'll reject them all until you've examined them, and you'll work your way back in that voluntary desert of reason to the origin of thought, pure reason alone.

"You'll look about you, and what will you find left of all the political structures, of theories, of ideologies, or parties? Nothing — or very little.

"You'll find that independent of you and independent of the life and needs of the country as well, there are two forces that can't be eliminated. They may increase or diminish, but certainly not by your efforts, because they're two forces that are in a certain sense eternal, tied to religion and universal interests, and indifferent to the temporal and the domestic. These you will put aside. They'll each pretend to represent the whole world, and try to exclude the other, but in reality they're partial to one another, similar, and even in their natural conflict, closely allied.

"You won't fall into scholarly and academic errors. These abstractly opposed forces are nothing but idols, names, deceptions of history. Like them were 'Papacy and Empire,' 'Reformation and Counter-Reformation,' and so on. Even in those days life sought after truer things, simpler or more difficult or perhaps smaller, and those great ideas and institutions were only intellectual diminutives, approximate symbols, worshiped each in its turn like a divinity that embraces everything in itself; images and simple names and an infinity of true and forgotten tales. Who remembers King Marcone of Calabria? Who remembers the little characters? Who remembers the truth of days, the truth of the living and the dead, or ideas that were once reflected on and true?

"Only names, institutions, and wars are left," Andrea went on, "like animals of a time that is gone whose shape we reconstruct around their fossilized skeletons with the assumed simplicity of the archeological imagination.

"Today these untouchable schemes, these symbolic forms are called 'Communism and Vatican.' They are two elements of nature, like a mountain and a river that rise in a landscape covered with snow or swollen by rain or parched in the summer. They will always be there. You'll have to reckon with them but you'll never be able to modify them, and you must exclude them from your analysis.

"Taking those two forces away, you should find the varied spectacle of human thoughts and interests that lie between those two

pillars of nature. What will you find? . . . A vague whirlwind of
dust, the disintegration of liberal and socialist ideas in all their gra-
dations. You'll see that none of them is related anymore to anything alive or real. Reality is somewhere else and doesn't seem to
know how to express itself. The field is littered with rubbish, with
old banners, with worn coats of arms, nostalgias, memories, habits,
cabals, cliques, business clients. They're all anachronistic leftovers, like old bric-a-brac that once had meaning and taste, told
a story of lives and sentiments, and ended cluttering the junk
dealer's counter.

"All this is now called — at wholesale — socialism. But aside
from a name, what is it? Have you ever thought of the slowness,
the laziness, the incredible immobility of a thought that for a hundred years has remained what it was? If today a courageous editor
were to publish — I don't say *Das Kapital*, but simply the *Mani-
festo* of 1848 — it would seem to everybody just a librarian's novelty. A century's gone by, a century full of extraordinary upheavals.
In any other epoch, a century would have been too long a time for
the fresh impact of a book to be preserved. It has nothing to do
with the book, but with those who should have read it, with their
deafness and their mental obtuseness. I certainly should be allowed to say so since I've always lived on the inside of these matters, and I know what I'm talking about!

"These people always live with their heads turned backward.
They think of rules for life and action, of congresses held sixty
years ago, as though they were things of today. Like priests of a
mysterious religion they mumble in the spirit of the Congress
Genoa, according to the principles of '92 or '98 — you never know
what they'll dig up.

"What is left of a whole century of thought, and I don't mean
among specialists or the teachers of doctrine (and they can be
counted on the fingers of one hand) but to all those who pretend to
defend these ideas, the so-called militants among men of politics?

"A few little formulas from a catechism. . . . The class struggle
for instance. . . . The class struggle? All right — but these formulas
have a vague, generic notion in them, as old as the world, a simple

expression of good common sense. Thousands of books have been written about it, and millions of people have dedicated their lives to it, and many have lost their lives for it without really understanding what it's all about. If you ask them further, if you demand that they explain what they mean by the class struggle, they'll prate on of the bourgeoisie and the proletariat, assuming a candor, a simplicity, and an assurance in their words that will disarm you. Just like Aristotle's Simplicius, they swear in good faith to the existence of things that don't exist, imaginary organizations, flames that reach to their appointed sphere and stones that fall to theirs, and they naively ignore the fact that there's a Russia and an America, and that Nazism and an infinite number of other things have dimmed and obliterated Épinal's simply and boldly colored lithographs of their preconceived black-and-white pattern of the bourgeoisie and the proletariat.

"But watch out, because all this doesn't result, or only partly results, from the inadequacy of man or his lack of culture or passion. Taken individually, men have their own reasons and interests. There are some first-class people among them; not many, but a few. But the fact is that all of them, even those who might be able to see and to think things out, are on a false road, forced there by the power of circumstance. They're like certain painters from the provinces, even in the best periods, who had natural talent but who were constrained to go on painting in the methods of an old-fashioned school that would be of no interest to anyone except professors several centuries later.

"And do you know what this false road is? I'll try to explain it to you."

After frequent pauses we had now reached, step-by-step, the middle of the tunnel. Here we could not hear the falling rain any longer, but the booming noise was louder, and although Andrea raised his voice I had a hard time following him.

"Let's accept also the lithographs of Épinal," Andrea went on, "let's set ourselves on their same level with an effort at simplicity and even naïveté. It's necessary. They say bourgeoisie and proletariat; a simple formula. Perhaps that was all right once; but what does it mean today? A commonplace . . . what's become of them? . . . Let's look around . . . we don't find them . . . or we find them mixed up with other things, scattered, and branching out into reality.

"Of course we know that there aren't just two forces, two poles, but many, a great many in such a complicated civilization as ours, and so on and so on. . . . Everybody knows that . . . and yet we really ought to try, at least in a mythological sense, if not historically and scientifically, to arrive at some kind of bipolar division of our own. The attempt to divide the world in two is not without its motive. In such matters reason plays only a small part, and everything unfolds as if it were a miracle play with angel and devil, white and black. I believe that without altering the truth but by attaining a simpler and deeper truth we can understand in dramatic and mythological terms into what two forces, classes, categories, species, or what have you Italy is divided. And then our mental panorama will change and assume significance.

"I'll give names to these two forces, groups, or, if you prefer, diverse and opposed civilizations, because they're characters in a play. But you must let me give them dramatic or mythological names that suit their nature. What I mean is, if you're not contented with a name of this sort and you say I'm being poetical in the wrong place (you know where I come from they scornfully call extravagant people 'poets,' people who have their heads in the clouds and never achieve anything serious), if you really insist, I'll translate these names into practical, historical, and political language, in fact I'll satisfy you in every way I can.

"But it won't be necessary. I hope my names, for different reasons, will persuade you both and that you'll understand them without too much explaining.

"Listen! . . . The two true parties, as they'd say in the South, that fight each other, the two civilizations that face each other, the two Italies, are the *Contadini* — the peasants — and the *Luigini*.

"Contadini and Luigini," he shouted, raising his arms in the din of the cavern. "Behold two movements, hostile and impenetrable. Behold the only two categories of our history. Contadini and Luigini, Luigini and Contadini."

We looked at him inquiringly without saying anything, a bit astonished by his poetic fervor that, as he said, was not like him. He started to laugh as he looked at our faces, and went on.

"Now I'll explain, if I must. Things have to be called by names, and I've chosen these names because they're true. There's nothing I have to add to Contadini, is there, Carmine? . . . As for the Luigini — I've used the name of an imaginary character who through no fault or merit of his own embodies them completely, in a book you certainly know" — and here he turned to me — "that Don Luigi, mayor and schoolmaster in a village of the South, as you well know, Don Carlo. Are you both beginning to see?

"Well, then . . . who are the Contadini? First of all they are the peasants, of course, those of the South and also of the North, almost all of them, with their civilization that lies outside of time and the course of history, with their closeness to living, their kinship to animals, to the forces of nature and the land, to their pagan and prepagan gods and saints, with all their patience and all their wrath. These are all things you know. It is another world, a world of magic and indistinctness, a civilization of oral tradition with a language based on the ideophonic rather than the ideogrammatic. It is the dark vital root that lies within all of us.

"It's you who have taught me all this. But the Contadini are not only the peasants. . . . Of course there are the barons, too — What? . . . Don't eye me that way! . . . This isn't a question of separating the good from the bad. . . . I'm not a preacher nor a demagogue nor a moralist. I said 'barons'; the real ones, with castles on the tops of mountains — the peasant barons. You know them, Don Carlo.

"Then there are the industrialists, the contractors, the technicians, most of them in small and medium industries but some of them in big business as well. I don't mean those who live on protection, subsidies, gambling on the stock exchange, tips from the government, theft, favoritism, tariffs, contingent shares, important rights, corporation privileges. I mean the others who know how to build up a factory, that small part of the bourgeoisie who are energetic and up-to-date, who still survive in our country anachronistic though it may seem. And also the agrarians, even the rich landowners — they belong to you, Carmine — who know how to carry on reclamation projects and restore the abandoned and degenerated land. They too are Contadini.

"And the workers too. I don't mean those who are corrupted and join with their masters in the petty affairs of their regions; the sort you don't know whether to pity because they're exploited or to despise because they themselves are the lowest kind of exploiters. But all the others, the great mass of workers who are educated in the creative rhythm of the factory, its voluntary discipline, the value that exists in it. It doesn't matter what they think or which party they belong to, they too are Contadini and not only because most of them come from the countryside but because on another level they have the substance of peasants.

"Nature for them is no longer the land but lathes, grinding mills, sledge hammers, presses, drills, furnaces, and machinery. They have direct contact with this nature of iron, and they grow things from it, including hope and despair and a mythological vision of the world. All men who make things, create them, love them, and are content with them are Contadini. Contadini, too, are artisans, doctors, mathematicians, painters, women — true women, not the imitation.

"Finally, if you'll permit me, we are Contadini. I don't mean the three of us, but those who used to be called by that odious word 'intellectuals'" — and here Andrea started to laugh again — "the 'progressive intellectuals.' In short, to use another odious word you might like better, those I call Contadini are the producers, and if you prefer that name, call them that. But as for myself, since we're not talking of economics or accomplishments or production, but of a distinction between civilizations, I prefer giving them their true name: Contadini.

"And who, then, are the Luigini? They're the others. The great, endless, formless, amoeba-like majority of the petty bourgeoisie with all its species and subspecies and variations, with all their miseries, inferiority complexes, morality and immorality, misdirected ambitions, and idolatrous fears. They're the ones who submit and command, love and hate the hierarchy, and serve and reign. They're the bureaucratic mob, employees of the state and the banks, model clerks, the military, the magistrates, lawyers, the police, college graduates, errand boys, students, and parasites. These are the Luigini.

"The priests too, of course, although I know many who believe in what they say and who are not Luigini but Contadini. Then there are the industrialists and businessmen who keep going on the multimillions of the state, and also the workers who stand by them and the landowners and peasants of the same sort. All these are Luigini.

"There are the politicians, the organizers of all sorts and shades. They are perhaps Luigini without realizing they are or wanting to be, Luigini by circumstance, although many of them would rather be Contadini. I add them all together: Communists, Socialists, Republicans, Christian Democrats, Action party, liberals, *qualunquisti*, neo-Fascists, the Right, the Left, revolutionary and conservative, whatever they are or pretend to be.

"Add at the end to complete the picture, the literary man, the eternal literary man of the eternal Arcadia, even though luckily he can neither read nor write.

"Those are the Luigini, the great luiginian party. Beware, then, because the Luigini are the majority. Democratically, vote for vote, they're the winners. There are more of them, so the statistics tell us, in this petty-bourgeois country. There are more, but not so many more, for obvious reasons.

"We, the Contadini, are the minority, but a huge minority — close to half, almost forty-nine percent — that wavers toward reaching this maximum limit and can't diminish much. Because no Luigino can live without a Contadino to suckle and nourish him, therefore he can't allow the Contadino offspring to thin out too much. If you figure things out, the Contadini will always be close to victory but can never win, although everything comes from their hands.

"The Luigini have the numbers, they have the state, the church, the parties, the political language, the army, the courts, and the press. The Contadini have none of them. They don't know that they exist, that they have any common interest. They are a mighty force that doesn't express itself, that doesn't speak. That's the whole problem. The language of the others, their state, flags, parties, do not suit the Contadini and have no meaning in their mouths. They too must speak, but in their own way. And up to now they've never been able to.

"What I'm saying is far from being a novelty or a discovery. It's been talked about a little in other terms, in all ages. Machiavelli, who was a Contadino, said it from his point of view, and so even did Guicciardini. In more recent times how many have had these ideas and tried to unite the peasant forces! Stop and think for a minute. Gramsci, Govetti, De Viti de Marco, the liberalists who were against Giolitti, Salvemini, Giustino Fortunato, Abbot Padula, Dorso and the Meridionalists, the members of the Action party, and so many other unknown and simple folk — all of them tried.

"But they were usually isolated men, or small groups of students or of men of culture. Or else they tried it in countries during violent, short-lived revolts that ended in death or prison. If they reached the point of founding a party or a large movement, it soon changed and corrupted, denying its own beliefs for something luiginistical. Gramsci was a Contadino who thought about such things before I did and thought them out better than I have. He built his own party like a peasants' party, but in a few years events made it, at least partly, into a perfect and efficient luiginian instrument. The Action party was a peasants' movement and, if you like, still is. But right from the beginning quite a bit of philosophical and nonphilosophical luiginism had filtered into it. And you'll soon find out that either it will become completely luiginerized, or to escape this miserable fate it will prefer to break up and disappear. The truth is that the formation of our party system is luiginal, the techniques of our party battles and the structure of our state are luiginal, so that if a peasant movement wants to survive, it must find a new form and organism of its own.

"Have you ever thought on what principle this state of ours is founded? Have you ever reflected on its extraordinary originality? And the true moral and civil supremacy of the Italian people?"

Andrea looked at us laughingly and questioningly.

"You don't believe me," he continued. "And still we have a supremacy that no one suspects. These people say that there are only two ways, only two principles on which one can construct a state and a society. The Russian and the American. Well, there's a third, completely different and equally important. It's the Italian way.

"The American way, they say, is that of Liberty, the Russian way that of Justice; but the Italian way's another, it's that of Charity. Do you really believe that charity, which is one of the cardinal virtues, is worth less than the others? Our state is founded on Charity, it is a state of charity. Naturally this governmental charity has a certain, special character. It is a charity that turns toward itself and considers first and only the member of the state of which it is the foundation. The state is the incarnation of charity, and its dispenser, and spreads it among its own members, its functionaries, their families, their friends, on those who live on it directly or indirectly."

"*Prima carita sincipi tabego.* Charity begins at home," Carmine said. Andrea laughed.

"You're right," Andrea went on. "A great poet, that Belli! *Prima carita sincipi tabego:* holy words! They should be written at the entrance of all public buildings. While the other states busy themselves with justice, equality, or liberty, ours is a big, charitable organization for those who are part of it, namely, in simple language, for the Luigini. Someone's got to pay the expenses for public charity, the expenses of the state. And those are the ones who don't play any part in the state: the Contadini. No one can hope to grow very fat for ours is a poor country and there are so many Luigini.

"But we must be content. The system's ancient. It's still the Bourbon one, but perfected by time, and finally, under Fascism, rendered official and completely legal.

"We thought we'd overturn it, but we didn't succeed. And now the lay charity of the Italian state is about to receive another touch, the holy oil of Christian charity. That way, the deed will be perfect and our supremacy incontestable.

"Within this state of luiginistical charity, with its rituals, its formulas, its rights and consolidated interests, imagine what could happen to socialist structures. Luiginism would expand and propagate among them like a malignant tumor. Therefore socialism can't revive, it has stayed where it was a century ago and every time it makes an effort to go farther, it looks backward with a most touching and declamatory nostalgia.

"I don't fool myself that it's easy to unite the peasant forces, and history proves it. It can't be done with parties or within the party frameworks that are luiginian by definition, less still with the luiginistical mistrust within the parties themselves. It is also difficult because of the inability of the various peasant elements to express themselves and understand each other.

"One needs to think not of what one used to call politics but of an infinity of independent organizations that concern themselves with real problems, the only true substance of politics, and are bound together by an overall organization that speaks for everyone. It's an almost impossible achievement but the day will come soon when we must attempt to do it. You'll see. All the old parties that have sprung up again after the storm have first triumphed and then one after another failed. What I'm going to tell you now will seem clear and painful.

"To win is difficult. It happened only once in the whole history of Italy, and that victory is over. We've seen it and lived it. The Resistance was a peasant revolution, the only one there's ever been.

"The Luigini have jumped on the horse's back and now think they've tamed it, but something's left even if they've given the horse a bit and a bridle. Now we're at the end and the Premier has fallen. Did you notice that the Resistance chose a peasant Premier, dressed like a Luigino? The Luigini profited even by that.

"We'll have to start again from the very beginning and this time without hurry, without illusions, day by day, without heroics but with clear ideas. After all, no pure Luigino exists, nor Contadino either. They all have a bit from the one and a bit from the other, only in different measure.

"We'll have to allow the Luigino that's in everyone to find an outlet in organizing the parties, while we prepare another role for the Contadino. It's still too early. Even if the wheel seems to stand still it has already turned to their side, and for some years we won't be able to stop it. We'll have to listen to luiginian talk. We'll see many things happen. But we'll be deaf and blind and we'll hoe the earth."

Without realizing it we had come to the far end of the *Traforo*. Outside the tunnel a few raindrops were falling on the wet asphalt. After the gasoline fumes of the tunnel, the damp air in the open seemed filled with the fresh smell of moss, leaves, and tree trunks, like a forest in autumn.

The two lame ones took me by the arms again and rolling from one side to the other dragged me in a rush toward a café.

We stopped in front of the entrance.

"Don't trust me too far," said Andrea, and he started to laugh, curling the corners of his babyish mouth. "I'm a bit of a Luigino myself, quite a lot, very much so when I choose. I know their language too well not to use it on occasion. I know there are some people who'd consider what I've told you an expression of petty-bourgeois theory, a petty-bourgeois deviation" — and he laughed again. "Now I must go use this linguistic and deviationistic virtue of mine. I have a meeting. I'll see to persuading R—, L—, and G— to agree with F—, and to hold firm in order to come to a more favorable solution later on. They're miserable creatures who don't know the ABC's of their trade. I'll have to listen to a lot of speeches, bad imitations of the ones I've been hearing for twenty years in all the capitals of Europe.

"And now that I'm back in Rome they'll draw me into their old routine. But I'll have to do it. I'll have to save the salvageable. I'll see you later at the printer's."

He turned brusquely and moved on, leaning heavily on his stick.

"I'm coming with you," Carmine shouted, leaving me to follow him. I watched them walking away, wavering like two boats in a nocturnal sea, and I went into the café.

—◌ **2** ◌—

It was a long, narrow room full of smoke, noise, and people. Along one of the walls was a zinc counter. The cash register rose at the center of the counter and behind it sat the proprietor like a schoolmaster at his desk. He was a young blond, with his hair parted at one side, and a thin little mustache. Against the rear wall stood an apparatus for playing bagatelle, and an automatic shooting range. Facing the counter between two long mirrors a huge American machine was enthroned, a wardrobe with glass panels illuminated from within by iridescent lights that changed from yellow to red to green to violet. When a token was pushed into the slot, the machine would start playing with a deafening uproar and a change of color. Many listening and admiring people stood around it, others lined up to play bagatelle. And many others crowded into the place, waiting for their drinks to be served or to pay for them, and they were all chattering together.

The evening crowds came in before the closing hour. In those days the cafés closed early, late hours were considered unhealthy, and the darkness of the streets in the center of the city encouraged frequent holdups.

The day was over. A sudden rain had chased all the vendors and the women from their corners. This was the time to make the rounds of the cafés and bistros, to warm the stomach a bit before making the last nightly beat in the Roman bushes before returning to the outskirts of town. It wasn't easy to get to the counter. In front of me was the back of an enormous man, a phenomenon for a tent show. He was a young man with a small pink face on a normal-sized neck under which broadened a body bursting with fat, that grew like a colossal spindle from his chest to his belly and his hips, then shrank into his thin legs and tiny feet. He must have weighed at least four hundred pounds. He wore striped cotton trousers held up around his abnormally huge waist by a strap. His torso was packed into a green sweater, wide as a field, and on it was woven in big white letters: "Pediconi Sweater Mills," and the address of the factory. This out-of-size trunk made a natural background for posters and publicity.

The man with the green sweater was talking to another fat man. But the first one was thin in the extremities and swollen in the middle, while his companion was made the other way around. He was tall, not much sturdier than normal, with big feet, big, red hands, and a gigantic head with a dark purple face resting on a collar of multiple double chins. He was dressed in black, with a black hat that slightly darkened his apoplectic face. Grouped around them stood other ugly, thickset, and violent men. They were holding glasses of hot punch in their hands and sipping it.

A blond little boy of seven or eight, wearing a dark-blue velvet jacket, his eyes slightly squinting and fierce, appeared and disappeared between their legs, looking up at them with hatred. He slipped behind the giant with the green sweater and launched a kick at him, then like a swimmer making for the open sea, he flayed a passage among those outsized, ugly bodies, and escaped crying toward the door while the fat man threatened him with a tiny hand. As soon as the man turned around, the boy stopped crying and came back like a fly, unobserved, his lips pressed together in fury, gave him another kick, and ran away again. While I was waiting to order my coffee, these corpulent men finished their drinks and jovially went out into the street. The child followed a few steps behind, weeping.

The space left by their departure allowed me to make my way to the counter. A short young man stood there leaning against it with one arm. His hair was smoothed down with brilliantine. He had the flat, twisted nose of a boxer, a strong jaw, and unshaven black cheeks. He was talking to the waiter with bold, vulgar gestures in the inflection and accent of pure Roman dialect. His tone was gay and swaggering, contrasting with the first words I heard, which were nothing but a list of German concentration and extermination camps: Auschwitz, Buchenwald, Mauthausen, Monowitz, Belsen: terrible names that reached me now from a voice sounding as though it were enumerating places of delight.

I leaned forward to listen and the man, who noticed I was looking at him, asked me if I too had been in some of those countries. I answered that luckily I knew them only by reputation, but that I had lost many friends in them.

"I've been to all of them," he answered. "You should have seen them. . . . What neatness! What organization! What size — like real cities!"

As I listened to his boasting and observed his satisfied face I began to suspect that he'd been in these places not as a victim but as a jailer. however, I didn't dare question him directly. The answer came by itself and astonished me.

"After they took me with the others on the sixteenth of October at Portico d'Ottavia, they made me go through them all. In Austria, in Germany, even in Poland. Real cities with streets, why the houses even had four stories, and all of them filled with us prisoners! . . . Those Germans — they do everything in a grand manner . . . what neatness. We all had numbers right here on the arm — look at mine, how long it is! . . . How little one ate! And bad food, really bad food! But there was everything else in those towns: offices, laundries, baths, gas chambers, even a hospital. And the work — Oh! how we worked! . . . Hard enough to rub us out! And the beatings they gave us — what beatings!"

His eyes shone with enthusiasm as he remembered the extraordinary violence and ferocity of those beatings. I looked more closely at him. I could never have imagined that such a strange, admiring reaction to the atrocious life and death of the camps could be possible. There was something almost bestial about him, with his low forehead, his twisted nose, and the apelike suppleness of his strong-limbed body. Perhaps he had been saved by the concentration camp law of selection in reverse.

"We even had to learn German," he winked at me and went on. "They sent us to work in the mines.

"Everything was regulated like a watch! Each of us had a lamp with a number on it and we had to give them back when we came out. Anybody who couldn't say his number in German at the entrance couldn't get a lamp, or others had taken them and you got left without one. In that case, what beatings . . . what beatings! . . .

"The very first thing was to learn my number. It took me twenty-four hours to learn it. And I still remember it: *Fünftausendsieben-hundertvier und dreisig.* But twelve hundred feet below ground in the mines we were worse off than on top. We didn't eat any better and we had to go every day. And we had to work just the same whether it rained or snowed, while my comrades, the lucky ones who worked in the open, didn't have a thing to do."

He still envied them today. I asked him how many of those privileged friends of his had escaped.

"Not even one," he answered. "Still we were worse off. Later on they sent me out into the countryside. And there too what neatness there was! What a country! How clean, how well organized . . . you wouldn't have any idea of it. . . .

"Toward the end during the last days two of us escaped. We went through the woods and ate raw potatoes we found in the fields. Those Germans certainly know how to get things done. What power! You had to see it to know. . . . And yet I managed to get away from them. And for a whole month I ate raw potatoes!"

He smoothed his hair down and walked off swaying his shoulders like an athlete.

I moved to a corner to watch the players at a pinball machine. They were pulling back the levers carefully, betting and commenting on every shot, tilting the base of the machine cleverly so as to make a bigger number of hits without cutting off the electric current and stopping the game. The little silver balls, shot out by the spring, climbed up, ran along a curve at the top, hit an elastic obstacle, bounced away, seemed to stop, started to roll again, slid into grooves, knocked against bells that started ringing, lit up tiny lamps, struck sparks, while numbers flashed on the dial — 1000, 2000, 3000 — with the clicking noise of a gear.

I watched it a long time, one game after another, fascinated by that motion, until a woman who had come in meanwhile started screaming in the middle of the room in front of the cash register.

She was old, with untidy gray hair that rained in dusty locks over her thick, yellow skin and her prominent cheekbones. Her nose was large, her chin pointed. She was extremely short, almost a dwarf, with wide, square shoulders and a short neck. Her eyes were scared and vague, and uncertain words came out of her toothless mouth where her tongue, heavy from drinking, moved clumsily. She staggered from having drunk too much wine, and she wanted to go on drinking and offered drinks to everyone. She was angry at the proprietor, who would not serve her or answer her. She shouted confusedly that she had money, lots of money that belonged to her. She was dressed in rags with several skirts put on wrong side out and one on top of another. They hung down to her feet that were covered with little brown cloth shoes. A white canvas bag hung over one arm. In a rough voice she declared she wanted to treat everyone to coffee and a liqueur for herself. She took the bag by the handle and started to swing it under the nose of the proprietor. She waved it back and forth, and her eyes lit up with daring and satisfaction from a sense of wealth and power that nobody could take away from her. It abolished all her limitations of age, ugliness, and misery, and made her mistress of everything she desired and entirely happy with herself.

"Coffee for everybody and a glass for myself. I'll pay everything—" she repeated, stammering. It was an order from both a queen and a witch.

She moved her oscillating bag closer to the proprietor's face, as if she wanted to make him smell it, as though that nonchalant movement were a major act of conquest. Then she put her right hand in and started to pull out money. The bag was bursting with paper currency, old, pre-war, thousand-lira notes with an M on a violet background, Allied military currency of all sizes, and ten-, five-, and one-lira notes, big and small, crumpled, rolled up, pushed together almost with disdain, like so much wastepaper. With a haphazard and disconnected movement of her hand, the

old woman groped in this bundle, pulling out one bill and dropping others on the floor. She almost lost her balance as she bent to
pick them up, and others spilled out of the bag. Clumsy but triumphant, with a fixed smile on her lips, she went on gesticulating,
waving her bills like flags, letting them fall, trying to catch them in
midair in painful, endless confusion.

Then a young man who had been standing behind her without
speaking came forward and quickly started to pick up the money
scattered on the floor, to put it in order and push it back into the
open bag. He was a dark-haired young man, showily dressed in
light-colored trousers and a blue jacket, a knitted pink vest, and a
big, lemon-colored silk handkerchief knotted around his neck. He
had many gold rings on his fingers. His dainty-featured face
seemed painted, with two red lips and pale cheeks that looked
powdered, blue eyelids, and long black lashes soaked in mascara
over languid eyes. He moved in a finicky and extremely effemi-
nate way. He raised his manicured hand to his face, the little
finger stretched out from the others, as though he were about to
caress himself, wriggled his hips, stirred his flanks, and pointed
one foot in front of the other like a ballerina.

After he had gathered the money in the bag he kept out one
bill and paid at the counter. Then he tried to push the woman toward the door, but although she looked at him with the sweet eyes
of a kitten, she refused to go.

The attitude of the young man and of the old woman revealed
a strange intimacy; they were certainly old acquaintances but one
couldn't make out whether he was the lover, the exploiter, the
master, or the son. He was at the same time deferential, imperious,
affectionate, protective, and servile. Perhaps he wanted to prevent
her drinking and extravagance, perhaps he was only concerned
with the money that had caught his eye. Some other young men
gathered around the couple and egged on the old woman, ironically praising her beauty, asking her to sing, telling her they were
eager to hear her. The old woman started singing in a thread of an
off-key voice, and fell into a long, incomprehensible love song,
keeping time with her precious bag and surrounded by laughter.

The young man knotted and unknotted his handkerchief with an affected gesture, now and then saying to the old woman: "That's enough now, Palmira. It's late. Let's go sleep."

But as she wouldn't listen to him and continued her refrain, leaning against the mirror beside the talkative American machine, he took her by the arm and started to push her toward the door. The old woman turned, showed us her bag, and started her off-key song in an even shriller voice. When they reached the door the young man wheeled and winked at us with vulgar innuendo.

"I'll see her home," he said. "They might take her money away." And he went out on the street with her.

I imagined that the chief danger to the old woman's money might be the protector himself, and I followed them down the dark streets. They turned around a corner and proceeded arm in arm for a few blocks. Then they stopped in front of the door of a house. I saw the young man rummage in the bag and take out a big key that had been hidden among the bills, put it in the lock and open the door. The old woman said good-bye to him, grabbed him around the neck, pulled him down to her, and kissed him on the mouth. Then she went in and shut the door behind her. The young man saw me come up and gave me a sly smile. He winked at me again, straightened his handkerchief around his throat, and said:

"Now Palmira's safe. She's a maidservant and makes lots of money with cigarettes. She lives here on the fourth floor. At night she spends her money and drinks. I have to take care of her. There are so many dishonest people around . . . I take care of her —"

He smiled at me fatuously, lit a cigarette, inhaled the first puff with exaggerated delight, and went off, tossing his waist around.

The printer's shop was not far away. I walked toward it slowly through the dark street among almost invisible people wrapped in obscure shadow.

9

THE PRINTER'S SHOP WAS underground in a succession of
great cellars without light and without air. One entered directly from the street through a little door at the corner of the alley
and went down a long, narrow staircase that led to the workrooms.
Another stair, an external one, was dug in a ditch of the alley and
a hollow of the house wall and led from outside straight to the
presses. At the bottom was an old door, half wood and half glass,
protected by an iron grating, but it was barred and I never saw it
open, not even to air the place.

It was a big cellar, divided by partitions and by the pillars that
supported the building. To the left of the staircase was a small
room reserved for making up our paper. It was almost entirely
filled by a big table. On the table among the frames for the pages
was heaped up the type for articles and news notes that had already been set up. The proofs were wet with fresh ink, and the
original manuscripts had the mysterious notations for the size of
the type. Workers' bicycles leaned against the walls. There was so

little space that moving around the table one was constantly knocking into a handlebar or a pedal. On the right of the stairs in the press room stood seventeen old linotype machines in a double row, grabbing the matrices with their long arms, in the bluish light of the little flames under the pots.

In one corner two low, glass partitions shut off a tiny space with a shaky little table on one side, a wooden stool, and a high board attached to the wall. During the day this was the cage of the manager of the printing shop. There was a telephone, almost always out of order, electric-light switches, and heaps of proofs of the various publications, satirical journals, sport sheets, magazines and leaflets. At night it was reserved for the management of the newspaper; actually, at least in theory, for me alone, so that I could write in greater tranquillity behind the partitions and a door that could be closed, instead of on a bench in the noisy passageway. The fact of the matter was that everybody came in, and while I wrote on long scraps of paper, perched on layers of old proofs, editors and visitors came at every moment, pulling themselves up by their arms to sit on the board, chatting, shouting, asking for enlightenment. Meanwhile someone would run to the telephone, turn the light switches, or look for something among the heaps of proofs. On the glass door hung a useless sign, and handwritten on it, the warning: MANAGER. NO ADMISSION.

Beyond the linotype room was a long, narrow hall where the paper cutters and routers were set up, and in the rear an old-fashioned furnace for melting the lead. Under its round bulk, wrapped around by crooked pipes, flames shot up. The hot air was filled with metallic fumes. In those cold winter days we went every now and then to warm our hands at the violence of the furnace. From here we could see through an arch the back part of the cellar where two rotary presses stood and big cylinders of paper were piled up.

It was the poorest and most antiquated printing shop in town, the one that had the oldest type, broken and unreadable. It was, perhaps, also the cheapest. Our Sicilian rustic must have chosen it for that reason, and with an insurmountable passive resistance, he refused to change. Possibly he had sentimental reasons as well.

They had worked here under the German occupation and secretly put together clandestine newspapers. Here Moneta, who had escaped being shot by a miracle, had been arrested. And besides, even if the printing was miserable, the paper bad, the work slow because of a lack of forms, the printers were doing their very best after all. They were comrades and they were friends.

This consoled us for our technical difficulties, but it wasn't enough to stop my annoyance every time I went down the stairs and saw the squalor, the narrowness and disorder of those cellars. I tried to hide my feelings, however, because I didn't want to heighten the bitterness of the editors. Down there Casorin and Moneta were the masters, and unchained they let loose their anger in a most vociferous manner. There wasn't an evening they didn't raise high lamentations, and they cursed and swore when the articles arrived set up in different type from what they'd asked for. A graceful Elzevir would turn out absolutely illegible because the type had been corroded by use, and everything went so slowly that dawn arrived before they could lock up the pages. To calm them I would describe the much more difficult circumstances when we got out a daily paper in Florence right after the liberation.

With weapons in hand we had run to occupy a splendid printing plant, rich with the latest rotary presses and every kind of modern equipment. But because of the lack of electric current all those machines that seemed ours by right of conquest were nothing but useless and paralytic pieces if iron. We came to an agreement, then, with an old publishing house famous for over a century for its fine, clear editions. And there, setting the type by hand, we composed the newspaper, printing the copies on a flat press run by an automobile motor. It was a very long job and lasted an entire day and the good part of a night. In those days of action and enthusiasm it never mattered if the news aged for a few hours. Here were printers who had for fifty years watched over the pages of books so that they might be exact, clean, and harmonious. And now they lent themselves willingly to this unfamiliar and hurried work, teaching us how to give a headline a dignified and courtly look, according to the standards of their tradition.

At night, after work was over, they were even ready patiently to remake a page when some obese English military censor, overloaded with whisky and regulations, came in and cut at random and without reason an article or a brief. And they helped us with complicity and solidarity to hide rolls of paper and to falsify our circulation figures; double what were allowed by the jealous Allied authorities. In those days we were all starved but we weren't bothered by difficulties. I had told these stories once too often even though I did vary the details, and Casorin and Moneta, who knew them by heart, started to chuckle, looking at me as though I were an aged applauder of the past.

"That's old rubbish!" said Moneta. "We've had empty stomachs too, and risked getting shot. . . . It's not a good reason to go on doing it now."

And Carosin: "That was a necessity but this is stinginess. We did what we had to do and now we think of it as something glorious that should never end. You'd like to go on enjoying glory, eh? With all this sentimentality we'll fall into ruin. And we're ruined already with your lovely sweetness of heart and your infernal presumption. Let's not discuss it, but let's change printing shops or better still, let's all go home."

They were both right in their own way. They stormed, shouted, protested, and exaggerated their contempt for work they were nevertheless doing with the greatest enthusiasm. They were determined to use with violence the right to criticize, and yet turned it first against themselves and the things they held closest and most beloved. While they seemed hostile and contemptuous, they were at the same time even too openhearted. They had outgrown the restrictions of youth and youthful servitude and, like all others in wartime, had learned confidence in men and also that logical companion of confidence, distrust. Their belief in people was so great that they felt they had to cover it with an involuntary blush and with a reticence they called irony and self-criticism.

It had been a time of meetings, of sudden revelations, when men were sniffing at each other like young animals to discover their friends. You judged one another by a single look. There really were no secrets left, so that Casorin and Moneta actually were ashamed, and almost wanted to defend themselves against it as though it were too indiscreet a blessing. Naturally they no longer looked at people's faces, as they had in the years of concealment, to find out whether or not they were spies (they remembered when they had wrongly judged a man just because he had a yellow face and thin lips — he afterward became their friend and their first teacher in the art of journalism), but nevertheless they pretended to mistrust, to want to look beneath the surface trying to discover concealed motives, to break down the facade or declared ideals and not to accept without discretion the exaggerated facility of a too-cordial world, a world returned to peace. Al topics lent themselves to their protests, quarrelsome protests on Casorin's part, gloomy and melancholy on Moneta's. They other editors imitated them. They echoed their protests with less energy. Only the youngest, the cub reporters who were scarcely more than children, didn't follow them, partly because they were timid, partly because they couldn't understand how people could joke about matters so infinitely serious and important. They worked silently and obstinately and didn't allow themselves to be distracted by Casorin's chatter. Nor did it amuse them. They even criticized it with a touch of slight and respectful indulgence. They were so happy to be part of a genuine, organic group, of a collective activity, that they gladly accepted everything, our miseries as well; the inferior printing shop, the walk home at night.

That evening I caught up with one of this young group as I was going downstairs to the press room, and we went down together. He was a boy with straight, light-blond hair and eyes like clear, pale-blue porcelain under a bulging forehead. His face was round, his nose and mouth small and graceful, between smooth cheeks with a delicate pink and white complexion. His skin was transparent, and one seemed to see his young blood flowing under its surface. He gave an impression of health and grace accentuated by a strong and well-proportioned body. Mario Dotti had been with the newspaper only a short time. He worked conscientiously. Slowly and accurately, in the handwriting of a child, he worked over the news files with careful precision. He had returned not long ago from Germany where he and his brother had been prisoners. His brother had come back with tuberculosis and had been sent to a sanitarium. Mario Dotti, as young as he was, was married and had a child. His brother had children also, and Mario provided for all of them.

"Here's the latest news," he said, showing me a sheaf of papers in his hand as we went down the stairs. (Among the editors we all used the familiar *tu* in addressing one another, but Dotti had not as yet used it with me.) "They're talking of an Orlando government. I went to the meeting. The Liberals and Communists were agreed. And there's something else I'd like to tell you —" He looked at me out of his childlike blue eyes and went on in the same serious and shy manner with which he had announced the news. "I went to the doctor's today and he found some lesions at the top of my lungs. It was caused by Buchenwald, like my brother's. The doctor said I ought to go to a sanitarium but I'd like to try to keep on working. I can't possibly leave, and then I'd be sorry, it's so interesting. Only I'd like to ask you if I could work a little more during the day at the *Consulta* or getting news, reducing my night shift at the printing shop a bit. The doctor says this air's bad for me."

We'd reached the make-up room at the bottom of the stairs and were received by cigarette smoke and loud shouting. Certainly that air, filled with lead, nicotine, and uproar, was poisonous for lungs gnawed by the germs of German camps. I told him that I excused him immediately from all night work, but he insisted on going on, only he'd leave a little earlier. He took off his hat, found a free spot in the confusion at the table, scowled, and bit his lips in an effort to concentrate and started to write with his devoted, precise slowness.

I went to my cubbyhole. That was filled with people too, like the other room. Besides the editors, there were friends, idlers, people who came to bring and to take away the latest news, or who had only come to gossip awhile. This evening the public was larger than usual. These days of crisis had called together in Rome friends from every part of Italy. If we'd had a palace everything would have been easy, but in these few square yards the crowd and the noise were enormous. Everybody smoked, sat on tables, walked up and down in groups between the linotype machines, talking together and obviously disturbing the operators. From time to time they were kicked out with loud shouts, and gathered in the passage under the stairs or sat on the steps holding their hands between their knees, but returning shortly after to our narrow rooms.

They had not come to laze around, like Martino, who was always there but appeared and disappeared suddenly. They didn't mean to hinder our work but to help it with advice, criticism, and discussion as well as with the warmth of their fellowship. Those among them who came from the provinces and from the cities in the North were especially convinced that something could be done, something, if only to use their fists again, or at least the influence of an explicit and energetic will. They stayed all evening at the newspaper, as though they were on guard, waiting for something that did not come, because newspapers in turbulent times are the natural places for meetings and guidance. They stayed late and, disappointed, could never make up their minds to go back to their little hotels or their friends' houses where they'd found a sofa or a mattress to spend the night on, many of them in one room in the fraternal custom of those days.

The speeches of the evening continued a long time later in the crowded rooms; resolutions for a political revival, for popular defense, hopeful desires for something new, the same that had sustained them only a few months earlier during long waits in some mountain cabin, when they sat around the flames of a green-wood fire that made their wet clothes steam, their eyes burn, and the barrels of their machine guns sparkle.

The atmosphere of Rome was incomprehensible to them. It was hateful and somewhat demoniacal. They moved about uneasily in it as though in clothes that were too long and tripped them at every step. They turned their eyes away from the ancient walls that, like the walls of China, seemed obstacles to anything living. There were four of them standing in front of my cubbyhole that evening when I arrived; four partisan chiefs, members of the National Council.

The first was a lawyer from Cuneo who for two years had protected the Valleys with his hands. He had brilliant black eyes and a dry and noble face in the style of the *Commentaries* in which he had written the chronicle of his own war.

The second man was a worker from Bergamo. He had escaped in a dramatic flight during the air raid as they were taking him out to shoot him. Pursued by bullets he ran across half the town. He was a tall, athletic man with a mild expression, a dark skin, apelike arms and elastic movements. He was an exact and colorful storyteller. His appealing tales were filled with charming folk imagery and common sense in spite of his stumbling and hesitant delivery.

The third was a judge from Novara who seemed twice as thin as he was since he had been very fat before the war. The war had sucked him dry and shrunk him, widening out the clothes he wore. He was as nearsighted as a mole, with enormous spectacles as thick as the bottom of a water glass. They didn't help him to see farther than the palm of his hand. His head was filled with rare juridical wisdom and candid honesty.

The fourth was an engineer from Udine, big, florid, and choleric beyond measure. He was in a continuous state of rage at the spectacle of injustice life displayed at every instant, which flushed his face, ruffled his sparse, blond hair, swelled up the nape of his neck like a bull about to charge into the arena. He was ready, like all men of ruddy countenance, to forget his rage when good food and old wine was put before him, but he would be enraged all over again, forgetful of food and wine, at the slightest offense to virtue and honor.

These four waited in front of my door. To fill the time they were talking as always about Rome.

"Here everything falls in the mire and loses shape," said the judge. "Or rather it takes on a rhetorical form and loses its own substance. That lovely theory of the continuity of the state could only pop up here, and now we're beginning to see its practical application. A continuity that means immobility or, worse, the way back. It's as if the state weren't everywhere, and we ourselves and the laws we've created in these years, although they're provisory and improvised, were not an integral part of it. If we followed their interpretation of the continuity of the state we'd still be in the Rome of the early days, before Tarquinius Superbus. This town is always the same, like stagnant water. The world changes, men change, even I lost sixty pounds in these years; but here we have continuity. It simply means that you can always sit in the same chair, now as in 1922. And people go right on being spellbound by words and the name of Rome. This town's all right for the Pope but we should have cleaned up the mess and moved the capital to Milan."

"That's what we all hoped, that we'd clean up the mess once and forever," said the worker from Bergamo. "Do you remember the times of the first air raids in '42 in Milan? At night, when work was over, half the city would leave on trains, in stock cars, to go sleep in some hole in the country. Sometimes when I found myself going back to Bergamo, standing up in the dark in one of those crowded cars, I could talk freely. If you spoke Italian nobody would answer you. In the darkness you might have been a spy. But in dialect you could say whatever you wished and they'd all answer you from the darkness, and not mincing words either. Actually, you couldn't see anything but the red points of cigarettes. And they were put out too when the air raid alarm caught us in the open country and the train stopped.

"'Here we are!' everybody said. . . . 'There they are! . . . Where will it be? This time it's for Genoa, or Brescia, or Turin. Perhaps they'll come back to Milan tonight. At any rate it'll be over soon.' They seemed happy about it. Nobody complained. They applauded the bombs that crashed into their houses. There was always someone who said, however: 'But what are they doing here? I know where they should go and it would be over once and for all!' And someone else, more explicitly, replied with everybody's approval, 'To Rome, it's to Rome they should go. Not here . . . and they shouldn't leave a stone untouched. That way they'd really liberate us. Rome is Italy's disaster.' Everyone applauded and laughed, happy as they pictured Rome's destruction, and they almost forgot that only a few miles away their own houses were going up in flames. They felt safer at the idea. They even started to light their cigarettes again."

"The same thing happened where we were," said the lawyer from Cuneo. "Every time they saw someone with a suspicious face go by they'd say, 'He must come from Rome.' The people in the Valleys aren't anarchists or revolutionaries. They're ordinary folk with common sense who like to see things done right and know how they're done, without too much talk and argument. They've all come up to live with us in the mountains away from the people of Rome because they didn't want to depend on Rome. They didn't want to wait any longer for Rome's permission to build a wooden bridge or put their cows to pasture, or to call their country by a name it's always had.

"They were fed up with greeting the first sparrow who came from Rome with an eagle on his head, who didn't come to bring them anything solid; nothing but slogans and passwords. People who say in Italian, or perhaps in Latin, '*Regere imperio populos*': that's what they have to say. We got along well together; but against them! We got along well with the French too. You know about the pacts we signed with the *Maquis* for working together with no boundaries even after the war. They too have their Quai d'Orsay. We never did have any use for the passwords of Rome, even when they came from men on our own side who knew nothing and spoiled everything.

"The Fascists sent us 'black brigades' and their forced enlistments. And all in the name of Rome, of the unity of Rome. Unity's all right, but the unity they make here's always wrong. It's theocratic or bureaucratic. This is sterile soil that bears no fruit. It takes from all sides but gives nothing. It's a country outside the world and outside of time. Rome's a receptacle of history but doesn't make history. All the beautiful paintings she has, who's made them? Berenson has something to say about it in his latest book. There's never been a Roman school of painting, or a painter born in Rome between Cavallini and Giulio Romano. There isn't a factory. We've built up the industries. There's no mass of workers, no peasants, only clerks, parasites. The only thing they know how to make is the wine of the *Castelli*."

"You call that wine, do you?" interrupted the irascible engineer from Udine. "That's not a wine, it's a poison. The fame of that yellow liquid's a sheer imposition. It swells you up, it's heavy, it weighs you down, it gives you a headache, it confuses you and puts you to sleep. Indeed it is a poison! After who knows how many generations of drinkers the Romans have got used to it. It doesn't hurt them anymore now, they've got it in their blood. It must be this hereditary habit that makes them so indifferent, lazy, and materialistic. But for foreigners it's a poison. You drink it because it seems pleasant and it makes you fall asleep. It's the secret weapon of the city of Rome. The man who comes here full of vitality and a desire for action, after he's been here awhile drinking that wine, loses his energy, finds a cool, sheltered corner, is content with an office job, falls into lethargy, and becomes a Roman. He's like a man who goes to the orient and gets the opium habit.

"In Rome they put a man to sleep with their Frascati and their chatter about high politics, and take advantage of him by offering him all their shipwrecked merchandise. And let's not mention the priests and the monks. But do you notice how many Fascist faces, as fresh as roses, you see walking around? They take it easy, and little by little every day they jump out again. Today they've overthrown the ministry, and nobody budges. Tomorrow they'll send our prefects away, the day after, if we don't watch out, they'll put on their uniforms. If I met one I knew, he wouldn't have an easy time of it. But that isn't enough. What we need is a general cleanup. We should come down here with our brigades. As for that wine of Castelli! I'll never drink a drop of it. I'll stay with my Valpolicella and Soave. That's the stuff for men."

This gossip reached me from the door as I was in my cubbyhole hastily going through news notes, articles, fillers, correcting a few proofs, and listening to the first draft of a polemic Moneta had written against a rival paper. They reached me like the last gusts on a windy day when it calms down at twilight. We'd heard those speeches, we had heard them all endless times, with a thousand intonations and variations, in all parts of Italy. This hatred of Rome was a sentimental feeling, more or less crude, the symbolic manifestation of one of the most lasting themes of our history. Now it reduced itself to the usual, to words. As Heine says:

Words, words, no deeds,
No dumplings in the soup.

However, for a while they had been able to motivate men and events. It had been, as Andrea had said, the art of the Luigini to transform these events into mere words, into harmless outbursts over the wine of Castelli. (It's really the Luigini, I thought, to whom my four friends at the door give the arbitrary name, "Rome.") They possess all the secrets of the ability to transform deeds into words and to subjugate words in order to change their meanings into anything they please.

How many words I had to listen to. They reached me from all sides; some lay written in front of me, others I would have to write myself before the evening was over. How many I had heard in one brief day! Words used in outbursts, to show off, to pretend, to cover up, to yell; complicated gyrations to hide what was there and simulate what wasn't there. Luiginian cunning is great indeed and even knows how to conceal itself among the noblest ruins. The four friends hated Rome because they thought by some mysterious choice of fate the ablest and most dangerous Luigini had found a hideout here. This was, to be sure, the common opinion among all Italians, not only as one would expect from those whom Andrea had named the Contadini but even because of envy among the infinite number of small Luigini in the provinces. It was not only the inborn and eternal hatred for those who supervise and command but also the rejection of a certain way of commanding and, indeed, a way of life that now seemed useless and intolerable. Rome signified all the negative aspects of a world that was false and had failed; its name stood for the centralization of power, inept and parasitic bureaucracy, nationalism, Fascism, the empire, the bourgeoisie,

the monarchy, clericalism, and all the common faults: the lack of
courage and initiative, cynicism, indifference and fanaticism, the
fear of freedom. All one's own ills and the ills of others were expressed in that name, and in hating it all men were brothers.

Yet at a certain period that hatred had stood for a positive value
and a genuine expression. For example, during the nine months
from the dramatic days of its liberation to the end of the war, the
entire city of Florence to the last artisan and boy had been united
in the name of freedom in a daily battle against Rome. They didn't
want to hear any more talk of those prefects, the ones they then
called "pro-consuls of Rome in the provinces," who were commis-
sioned, they said, to sabotage the rebuilding of the city that, since
it had defended itself and been liberated by its own forces, wanted
its own forces alone to govern and reconstruct itself. When the
prefect turned up in that glowing world, like an undertaker at a
wedding banquet, he was just an old Sicilian nobleman with a
hooked nose and bags under his eyes, broken in to every possible
regime and hostile to any emotion or enthusiasm. He tried not to
annoy anyone, to be as inconspicuous as possible, in fact to be un-
noticeable so that he could hold out, and in the end he was the
strongest and succeeded.

Meanwhile the walls filled up with scribbled inscriptions:
"Down with the prefect! Partisans! A new Enemy! Get out while
you've got the time! Go back to Rome!"

You could read these in coal, chalk, and varnish on the houses
of San Frediano and Cure, on the walls of the Quattrocento
palaces in the center of town, on the ruins of fallen towers, on the
parapets along the banks of the Arno — everywhere.

The prefect never left his house although no one was against
him personally but only against the institution he represented. All
parties agreed with the increasing popular ferment. Within the
walls of a city that felt itself rejuvenated as in the days when its
palaces were new and brilliant, no one dared defend the centralized state and its anachronistic instruments.

The local Committee of Liberation met, discussed and ap-
proved a moderate and reasonable plan to abolish all prefectures

or at least have them nominated by the local administration and not in Rome. They decided to go in full force, complete with all their members, to present their plan to the government for approval. They found automobiles and drove off down the smashed and unsafe roads where heavy military transport and tanks were still going by and where the thunder of cannon had only recently ceased. There were ten men, two from each party, all wanting to share in this errand. Each one carried their *cahier di doleances*, feeling charged with a kind of historical mission as though they were representatives of a new state that goes to treat with the final remains of an ancient regime, with the last ministers of a king to whom the least that could happen was guillotining on the Place de Greves. They represented a real power, a government that for better or worse was after all really governing its own city and was now going to impose its own will on a purely fictitious and formal power, on a minuscule government that only made believe that it governed to save appearances, knowing well that it was without strength and depended entirely for its own dubious legitimacy on foreign consent.

With this gay confidence and presumption, the ten men (I was one of them) climbed the stairs of the Viminale, carrying their heads high, wrapped in artless glory, and went into the chamber where the Council of Ministers had gathered to receive them. The ministers should have shared the opinions of the ten Florentines since they were the chiefs of the parties to which the ten belonged. It soon became clear however that things were not so simple, that there was something here we had not thought of, a different work, different interests, a different language that modified everything.

The president of the council was an old man with a goatee and a mustache that covered his mouth. He had a benevolent and cordial air and immediately spoke to the ten warriors, sounding like a little grandfather, a good-natured, indulgent little grandfather festively welcoming his grandchildren. In simple language he praised the noble zeal that had prompted them to undertake such an uncomfortable trip after so many heroic military trials. His praise had the understanding, indulgent tone he might have used to comment on a cute, childish prank. He told us that the document would be examined with the greatest interest, that we should leave it, and that as soon as they could find the time it would be studied with the care befitting anything of so much importance. We could trust them with that serious task. The Florentines had fulfilled their duty by presenting their demands. And he saluted us with a final eulogy as though he were dismissing us.

This method of burying our proposal was too simple and transparent. Various members of the delegation, from all parties, asked for an immediate discussion with such passionate energy that the grandfatherly old man could not refuse. They read the document and discussed it with heat, precision, and assured eloquence, requesting that each minister express his opinion. One after the other, each minister took up the argument. Only two said they were entirely in favor of it, yet in a vague and general manner. The others with great protestations of esteem, good fellowship, and agreement spoke at length to convey, in different ways and with different pretexts, that the problem was not ripe, that one should do nothing but wait for future developments; that they hoped that some day a constitutional assembly would be convened, would decide about everything, and that it was better now not to endanger anything by hasty decisions, and so on and so on.

The men who talked this way claimed to belong to the same parties as the men they were answering, but it was evident that theirs was another world and that the name "party" had an entirely different meaning in Rome than it had in Florence. In Florence a party was one phase of a common reality; parties in the old sense no longer existed, or did not yet exist. But in Rome parties continued to exist and were actually the sole reality and the only important element, something to which everything else had to be sacrificed. Nothing could be determined before the parties became so strong that they could determine everything. That was what these dilatory speeches meant. The party chiefs were not interested in the state's being reformed in any way (that would be bad for them in all ways) because what mattered to them was only the restoration of a structure, of a language, of a power that any reform might endanger. In this they were all naturally agreed, and joined together against their ten party companions whom they tried in a friendly manner to call back to order, to the secret luiginisian order. The important Luigini of Rome were stronger on their own ground than the Luigini of Florence, and they seemed to say:

"Companions of Tuscany, you are one with us. Why do you bother yourselves with things that don't concern you? What has driven you to espouse the absurd cause of the Contadini? You don't have enough experience and you let yourselves be forced by the sentiments and demands of the hour. But wait: everything will turn out well and everything will take care of itself. Just you wait."

That day the ten men boiled with indignation and started back for their city with souls ready for battle. But one of them made his way back to Rome and in a few months had joined the party chiefs, acquired increasing experience and power, and forgot completely all the youthful passion of the past. The others returned to their private lives and daily work and, like the four who talked at the door of my cubbyhole, they called their delusion and their disdain by the name of Rome.

This memory, this brief summary, came to my mind stimulated by the voices of the four friends whose black silhouettes obstructed the door. A fifth voice added itself to the others and in the colorful phrases and lively accent of Tuscany told them to stop their complaints and useless gossip, that listening to them was like talking to the honorable shade of nineteenth-century Massimo d'Azeglio, that their sentimental outlook was sterile, and that on that road they would do nothing but "get horns on themselves." He agreed in the fight against the traditional centralized state but it had nothing to do with Rome or no Rome, since it was in Rome that the battle must be fought. To free ourselves from old accumulated trash and parasitical habits we must not go back to municipal longings, but fight against the sovereignty of the state, of all states, work for European federation, and so forth.

The new arrival looked like an overgrown boy, mischievous and full of charm. He had gray whiskers and black eyes that shone with the honest candor of the impassioned idealist. The four answered him. Moneta mixed into the discussion. Martino came up muttering something about brothers and fathers, fratricide and patricide, the two diverse foundations of politics. The group in front of the door blocked the passage for the reporters and pressmen bringing proofs. Casorin was in a corner behind me filling sheets of paper with his illegible handwriting as he put down his angry, ironic, and romantic daily chronicle. But he interrupted his work to talk to Antonio, an old schoolmate of his we were trying out as an editor, an admirer of the great soccer players of the past. Soccer was one of Antonio's favorite topics. It delighted him and allowed him to forget everything else, as if the names of the players held an ineffable magic power.

"Zamora," he repeated, "Mateo, Hirzer 'the gazelle,' 'tissue-paper' Sindelar"; these names transported him like some eternal and poetic truth, far away from things of the present, from politics and the newspaper.

Looking through the door into the press room, I saw a man sitting on a stool between two linotype machines, holding a little girl between his knees. I waved to him from afar. He was an illustrious poet who was dear to us. He too had been brought to Rome by chance events and spent his days in sporadic happiness and fundamental anguish. I often published his limpid melancholy verses on the editorial page. Almost every evening he came to the printing shop to watch his poems being set up and to warm himself and smoke. He came, talked awhile, and left. He was tall, as strong as an oak, and still young. He had the air of an ancient sage, with flaming red hair and eyes as blue as fleurs-de-lis. He wore a cyclist's beret and had a big, curved pipe stuffed with rough stalks of tobacco that shot tongues of flame into the air, and he left a trail of ashes, fire, and burnt matches everywhere. He was talking with his daughter when I approached him. The little girl was as slender and as light as a butterfly or a cloud, with big, ecstatic blue eyes. She held a ball in her hand. I heard her ask her father:

"She was good, wasn't she? That woman? And there were a lot of cigarettes, weren't there? As many as ants. But there are more raindrops than ants, aren't there?"

Her father told me about it afterward. The little girl was talking about a woman they'd met shortly before on the Campo de' Fiori, where there's a little square closed off by a portico with a madonna in the corner. There's a tavern or a café there with little tables out on the street. When the customers leave there are always a lot of cigarette butts on the ground. An old woman, an old woman dressed in rags, gathered in the crop, as abundant as ants on an ant hill, but to bend down she had to turn her back to the image at the corner, and every time she straightened up and looked in front of her she crossed herself, murmuring a prayer and bending her knee. This way she alternated her reverences from the Madonna to the cigarette butts, between the good things of earth and those of heaven, as though she were asking for both pardon and approval. Each cigarette, a reverence, each cigarette, a sign of the cross. That scraping up of hers was like a rosary and the tobacco was certainly blessed. This strange act of devotion had impressed the little girl.

The father had come looking for news. After the afflictions of the past year, the atrocities, the fury, and the folly, he had hoped the time had come when one could breathe again. But now with the new crisis he feared that sad things lay ahead. He already envisioned men being burned at the stake on the square and black hoods dropped over men's eyes. I reassured him and stayed for a while beside him, enjoying as I did every evening his lyrical but sharp intelligence. I couldn't stay long, however, and soon I saw him go toward the stairs with the little girl who turned her head and her big blue eyes, wanting to stay a little longer in this marvelous place of mysterious things. She said farewell to me by waving the ball she held in her hand.

The linotype machines were buzzing and clicking. The huge American journalist with the red beard whom I had encountered at the Viminale meeting arrived like a gust of wind with great, cordial exclamations and cleared his way through the group that blocked the door. He brought me triumphantly a sheaf of telegrams in the name of the freedom of the press protesting against the minister who had spoken that afternoon. He had already sent them to the newspapers of his own country and was offering them to me to publish.

The telephone rang. It was the mother of a young reporter, a nervous woman, who just to calm her intolerable anxiety asked practically every hour of the evening if her son were still at the printer's.

Carmine and Andrea came limping down the stairs. Their smiling and cryptic faces wore the expression of men who have some news and betray the curiosity they are expecting to arouse in everyone else. A boy came running along bringing an official communication from party headquarters that we had expected for some time. It was a short, dry article by Roselli, written after who knows how many hours of discussion with Fede and others, that gave in a dispassionate manner some useless Machiavellian directives.

The confusion was extreme but, as on every evening, the work was proceeding in some fashion when suddenly the lights went out and we found ourselves in the thickest darkness. The sound of the machines was interrupted abruptly.

In the silence the voice of the foreman called out:

"Damn it! There we go —"

Here and there in the rooms matches were lit and the workers hurried to get the acetylene lamps ready. They put one in the composing room, another in the press room, another in my cubbyhole. The machines stood still, the printers started to smoke and chatter, and everybody moved around commenting and cursing. But we were used to this inconvenience that caused long delays in our work several times every evening. We waited a few minutes in the dim and spectral light hoping the current would return, but after the foreman telephoned for information he told us: "It's the same as usual. It'll take at least an hour."

An hour's interruption meant a much longer delay because the lead cools, and we'd have to wait for it to melt again even after the current came back.

"Let's go have a drink," said the workers. "You come with us, Director?"

Whenever the current failed we always went to a tavern across the way on the other side of the alley, and sat together around a table with a pizza and a glass of wine. As usual I couldn't resist the temptation. I still had to write my editorial. But the bad habit of waiting for the last possible minute is part of my nature. When my shoulders are against the wall and there's no way to escape, I start things.

There's an inertia in the world and a continuity of existing things that refuses to be changed by the arrival of anything new, whatever it may be. I happen to be a man who feels this inertia with all its infinite weight. The whole effort of creation seems to lie in this very capacity to move that weight. The first word on a page, the first brush stroke on a white canvas are decisive; they already contain the whole conception that can only then be executed with ease. But that initial moment, even with a small thing of no importance like a newspaper editorial, is a decision that changes the course of things and introduces a new element created right there. It is a birth full of labor compared to which the execution that follows is like a happy game. Any pretext is good for postponing that moment. I took the opportunity and climbed to the tavern with the printers. Casorin, Moneta, Antonio, Dotti, and some other editors and reporters stayed downstairs. They had to finish writing their pieces, to thin the news down to weak bran water or wait for the latest items from the hospitals and police stations. The other editors followed me, the friends stopped to gossip, saying they would come right away.

There was room for everyone around the table. Two candles stuck into the necks of bottles gave a trembling light. It was like being at an evening of gossip in the country when someone slowly puffs his pipe and starts telling stories.

—⟋ **2** ⟍—

They asked me to sit at one end of the table with the printers and editors grouped helter-skelter around me. All except two of the printers on our shift were Romans. They were almost equally divided between Communists and the old Republican party, which in substance was the popular party here in Rome and in the former papal states. This party difference was the usual subject of jokes, of friendly satire among them, and the names of Marx and Mazzini turned up often, like those of good-natured patron saints over which two groups of the faithful argue as to the one who has the most influence with God, and the greater capacity to work miracles.

Bitterer arguments, however, often broke out among the fans of the two local soccer teams. The two parties of the *Lazio* and the *Roma* did not parallel the political divisions at all. Republicans and Communists found themselves aligned in the polemics of sport. Roman and Lasio were saints too in their way, and each man claimed that his own, like Marx or Mazzini, was the most influential, miraculous, and unconquerable.

The two printers who were not Romans didn't take part in the contest. One was Matteo, born in Taranto, who wasn't interested in sport. The other one, Francesco, a Piedmontese, had every right to look on the futile rivalry of his Roman companions from the heights of the incontestable glory of his own teams, the *Torino* and the *Juventus*. Besides, he would never have confused sacred matters with profane, putting serious questions he considered the only reasons for life on the same level as a Sunday pastime. He, like Matteo, was an old militant. When he was little more than a boy he had taken part in "Red Week," and after the First World War in the "New Order" group. His comrades of those days were almost all functionaries of the party (except those who had died in prison in Spain, or in the war). For reasons of family and health Francesco had not been able to follow their career, but those now distant years of political experience remained the most important of his life. He had to leave his own countryside to escape arrest and had been in Rome for many years, but his heart had always stayed at the portals of his native city, among its factories where the debates of the Workers' Councils were carried on. And this inheritance, this education, this homesickness had given his manner a gentle seriousness, rough but almost affectionate.

His looks too kept the characteristics of a worker from Turin. He had a round head, a lean, dry, well-modeled face, definite cheekbones, and strong jaws. His gestures were easy and careful, and his bearing that of a mechanic, of a technical engineer who reflects in his own person something of the neatness of machines, and a confidence in the mysterious instruments that follow rules and a reasoned order.

Matteo was quite different, short and stocky, with a strong hairy chest, short arms, healthy complexion, cheeks with a dark stubble on them, lively, deep-set eyes under bushy, already gray eyebrows. He was an imaginative and rambling talker. He loved to tell of his travels. He's spent years in America where he worked at many things and ended up as a linotype operator, as he had been now for a long time here in Rome.

They brought wine and poured it in the glasses. They wanted to drink my health with the first toast. The second was to Cesare, a young proofreader, one of the Republicans of the group who was going to get married the following Sunday. They gave him their good wishes, clinked glasses, beat him on the shoulders, and re-peated the worn jokes about conjugal prisons, women, and the folly of voluntarily putting oneself in chains. Then, amid general applause, Tiro jumped up. His nickname was "Nero," although he was blond, plump, rosy, and mild.

Tiro, or "Nero," one of the Communist printers, wrote poems in dialect, Romanesque sonnets for all occasions, including saints' days. To be a poet is a fine and rare virtue and everyone looked at him with admiration. But "Nero" was modest and recited his verses in an apologetic manner. This time he read his sonnet of good wishes with a timid smile and acknowledged the applause gracefully. We returned to drinking and in the meantime my other friends had arrived and were sitting at the opposite end of the table. Among them the engineer from Udine and I asked him across the table if for once he wouldn't taste that poison. He parried the flow and although everyone insisted, covered his glass with his hand amid general disapproval.

"Barbera tastes better," said Francesco, "but this goes down too." Pouring me another glass, he winked at me with the complicity of a fellow native of Turin. "Our wine's more sincere."

He knew I would agree with him, that he could count on me.

"A glass of old Barbera during a bowling party on the Stura meadows; there's nothing better, my director, is there? And also how it warmed our hearts in bad times! I've never refused it. But that was long ago."

He was remembering the Turin of his youth and who knows what stories.

"Let's drink on it," he concluded. "What really counts is the struggle, the rest amounts to nothing. Here they don't know anything. They don't know what it means to live. They amuse themselves but they don't have any group spirit. Perhaps those days seemed ugly too, we did have our difficult moments when everything ended badly. But there it was more spirited than now. Our comrades meant more. Not that we wore long faces even then. We too liked to go up the hills with our sweethearts. But we were ready to make sacrifices for our ideal and we knew what we wanted. Now they only think of movies and they take everything easy and think everything's been taken care of. They don't realize that we're at the beginning and need organization. You could see they'd never been in a real factory where one learns how to live. And you too, Tiro." (Francesco was the only one who refused to call him Nero.)

"You're a good comrade and a fine poet and I've nothing against you. But why did you have to mention the Madonna in that poem of yours?" (Seduced by his rhyme scheme or by his memory of the poetry of others, Nero in his sonnet hadn't hesitated to compare Maria, Cesare's bride-to-be, with the Virgin.)

"One mustn't attack religion, but as far as Cesare's concerned, who's never once been in church in his whole life, he might as well leave the Madonna out of it. Or do you want to act like a parish priest too?"

These last words were spoken by Francesco with a very serious air. This was his way of being funny. Everyone started to laugh. Nero blushed, but since he was cleverer than one might think, he answered modestly:

"Religion has to be respected, even in those who have no belief."

"Especially in those who have no belief," said the voice of the judge from Novaro at the other end of the table; and another, perhaps the voice of the partisan from Cuneo, added viciously:

"And especially *by* those who have no belief."

"Bravo Nero!" said all the workers, laughing. Francesco also smiled and said:

"You employ good tactics. Tactics are necessary too. But remember what I said before. It's the struggle that counts. The rest means nothing."

We went on like this for some time at our end of the table, with jokes, glasses of wine, vague talk, and the warmth of solidarity. At the other end of the table a heavy discussion had started among Andrea, Carmine, Martino, the man from Tuscany, and the other four, but in the din their voices did not reach us. Our table was set against the wall at one side of the room. When we came in the place had been almost empty. Only an old man had been sitting at a little table in a dark corner, his face spotted by the white of a stubbly beard and marked by old scars. His eyes were mild and staring, he was wearing a black fur cap with a visor, and pants frayed at the bottoms, over a pair of old slippers. He was motionless and silent in front of a quart bottle of wine. While we had been talking other customers had come in without our noticing them and someone started to play an accordion. The sound came from a long table against the wall across from us where a large crowd had now gathered. I could see their long shadows in the dim light of the candles. The player was hidden from me by the other customers. He played some sad songs well, with rhythm and fire, and bit by bit without our realizing it our talk was falling into the tempo and sound of those notes.

An old woman dressed in black, her head wrapped in a handkerchief, came in from the street. She was leaning on a cane, and with short, ostentatiously labored and stumbling steps she came toward our table.

"Here's Granny," she said in a honeyed, pitiful sing-song voice. "Here's Granny. Who'll give something to Granny?"

I'd run into this old woman everywhere: on the streets, in the restaurants, in cafés, and I must confess I hated her. Every time I saw her she gave me an exaggerated and unreasonable sense of repulsion of which I was somewhat ashamed, but I still tried to avoid her whenever she stood in front of me with that sickly refrain and outstretched hand. I always tried not to notice her hand and avoided giving her alms. Now too I would have liked to have turned away my head so as not to see her round face, the fixed smile on her lips, her little, hypocritical eyes. She had the false manners of the old crones in the fairy tales who curse you if you don't give them alms, and change you into a snail or a toad. But the old woman bore down on me. Either she hadn't realized my antipathy or, as I believe, she had realized it and attacked me in revenge with increasingly sweet manners, as if I were a slightly dissolute grandson. She was almost on top of me with her big, round body swathed in black skirts, one hand on her cane, the other held out to receive.

"Bravo! Bravo! Do something for your old granny! It's started to rain and I'm just one big pain from my arthritis. I can't walk. I've come back to Italy to get cured but it's damp even here. Thank you and God bless you for the good you're doing your granny."

I was quiet because I couldn't wait for the minute she'd go off. But Francesco, who did not share my mad antipathy, asked her where she had been before she came back to Italy.

"In America for forty years," she answered.

"Where? And why did you come back?" asked Matteo with interest, who, as an old immigrant, looked on America as his second fatherland.

"I was most of the time in *Broccolino* — for many years. I had a lovely house with all comforts. I worked in factories as a dressmaker. I had all my papers to make an American out of me. Granny was well off over there; she earned, she always had a *giobba* and *dollari*. Then Granny fell and broke her leg. She got arthritis.

"They took me to the hospital and wanted to cut my leg off, so's not to pay the insurance. Do you know what I mean? They didn't say anything. But Granny knew they wanted to cut her leg off and she started to scream and wouldn't let them cut it off — that's why she left the hospital. They paid the insurance after two or three years, but the lawyers ate it all up.

"I was always having to look out so they wouldn't cut off that leg. So I said I wanted to go back to Italy to cure my arthritis. But they wouldn't let me go to Italy. I was American so they wouldn't let me go away. I wrote to the president, to Rosa Verde, so he'd let me go, but he didn't want to. That's easy to understand. How would Rosa Verde have looked if I'd come back to Italy in that state, when I couldn't even move my leg?

"When I'd come to America forty years before I'd been a flower, and if I do say it, straight and slender. And such a bosom everyone turned around to look. If they'd let me go back, what would they have said in Italy? That they'd taken bad care of me in America, which would be a disgrace for America and for Rosa Verde too. That's why they wouldn't give me my permission. But then Rosa Verde understood he couldn't keep me and he made me a passport so I'd never come back to America. Well, dearie, you like your old granny, don't you?"

They had wronged her. In the American paradise she had not had what was her due. They had not even known how to preserve her youth and beauty, this beauty that pleased Roosevelt–Rosa Verde so much on her arrival. Then, later, he had been properly embarrassed by her filthy old age. The American paradise had failed her, now it was our turn to compensate her for it.

"America, America, America . . ." played the accordion at the opposite table, and granny dragged herself toward it, bleating and smiling while a man in a dark corner started to sing harshly.

"America, America — you should sing that, Matteo," said the printers, elbowing their comrade. "That's for you." But Matteo drew away.

"I have no voice," he said. "Besides those aren't the songs we sang over there. We sang our own songs. The true songs. And even

oftener, their songs. Old union songs from Chicago and other
places. We learned them. To live over there one must first forget a
few things, also songs. It's a great country, everything's different.
You feel it's different, not because of the houses, the skyscrapers,
the subways, the elevated. It's different because they never turn to
look back, they don't have anything behind their shoulders.

"That's a fanatical old woman who knew what she wanted from
her Rosa Verde, and now she's come back to beg. Who knows
what she expected? But I came back too. There were so many
things here from which I couldn't escape. And then there were my
ideas. Over there ideas are different too. People speak in pictures.
Everybody's alike. It doesn't matter where you come from or who
you were before, they'll pick you out right away for some charac-
teristic they can feel or they can touch. As soon as I arrived they
called me 'Heavy,' That was because I was heavy. I was stronger
than those thin little men who worked with me in the factory. You
might just as well forget your real name, it doesn't count for anything. And it's the same in everything.

"You find yourself in the country or walking around the cities,
and you don't know their names, and also along the countryside
you don't know the names; there aren't any. Here in Italy every
tree, every stone in the street has a history, something's happened,
perhaps a thousand years ago, but there's always someone who remembers it or has heard about it and can tell you about it. Over
there a tree is a tree, a stone is a stone, and a man is nothing but a
man. They are honest and simple but you might feel that something's missing. We always have something over our shoulders: the
family, the country, the party, our own ideas, and what has happened before, but over there? — Nothing.

"You make the fire with your own wood. To be healthy, you
must forget everything, throw everything away and always start
from the beginning. You must plunge into the water. It's a difficult
step, a big sacrifice. It's like a revolution that burns up everything
that was there before. That's the only way to become American.
You have to enter the circle and run like all the rest, hurrying
faster and faster. America runs. It's not built like a house that

stands firm on its foundations the way we're made. It seems instead like a humming top or a huge gyroscope that rests on the ground at only one fine point and still stays steady because it's whirling, and the faster it whirls the steadier it is."

When Matteo started talking about America he'd never stop. It was his favorite topic, and whether he told anecdotes or stories of what had happened to him when he worked, shifting his jobs here and there in the States, or described the cities or the countryside, or like tonight tried to explain in his own way the character of that other world beyond the sea, it seemed to me from his speech and his images that he'd realized it only vaguely, that this mythological paradise of the emigrant was after all only a terrestrial place where man could live but the gods were not at home. It was a new civilization, tremendously powerful and of a strictly lay character.

The first colonists had left behind, with no will or chance to return, Europe with its worn parapets and its ancient gods and history. From this voluntary gesture of renunciation was born the new things that was America. This gesture with all it stood for was the American baptism. And that renunciation was required and always will be required from everyone, whether they were born in America or had arrived singing psalms on sailing ships, or had disembarked from third-class transatlantic liners with poor valises and swollen sacks across their shoulders. This individual renunciation is the American revolution and it is repeated every day by thousands of new men.

With this gesture they renounce the gods and also the possibility of creating or fabricating new ones. The local divinities that the redskins worshiped in the prairies were exterminated along with the faithful aborigines. Those massacres rendered the earth virgin again as at the beginning of the world. Without gods, either eternal, historic, or prehistoric, and without the gift of transforming words, objects, and actions into deity. There is no limit to this power.

It is natural that the atom bomb was born there, the fruit of that limitless abstract efficiency in a world completely rational and centered on man; detached from the root of things and with no ties with the land; where, as Matteo pictured it, the only contact with the land is at one invisible point; and continuous motion, abstract truth, and rationalization are substituted for it as the constant spinning accelerates faster and faster and never ends.

The accordion was silent to give the party a chance to drink and to eat the food they had with them in thick paper bags. They brought other candles and I could not distinguish faces. The musician took up his instrument again, played a few bars, and got up to sing. I saw him now standing against the wall. He was a blind man and his eyes were rolled back and completely white. His face was shapeless as though a sudden blow had disordered his features, throwing them into asymmetrical confusion. He sang with a visible effort and it flushed his face and swelled the cords of his neck. What I could see of his body, his shoulders and the upper part of his chest, was clothed in a greenish sweater and was exceedingly delicate. The instrument, attached to his body by crossed straps, seemed too great a weight for him. He played it very well, like a virtuoso, starting the first stanza of the song in a sharp, strained voice. Presently, as if to help him and spare him too great an effort, another voice similar to his but lower sang in his place for a while, until he took the song up again and finished by himself. It was the voice of a woman at his side, mistress, wife, or companion. She lit his cigarettes and put bread and a glass in his hands. She was middle-aged, thin, and dark, with a large pair of glasses and a big mop of gray crinkled hair that stood up on her head like a dusty woolen cloud.

The blind man and his companion were certainly professional musicians. I thought I'd seen them somewhere before, on a street corner or perhaps in Trastevere at the Velletrano, a sort of tavern with huge landscapes painted on the walls. Here one eats *pagliata*, a dish made of lamb and calves' tripe, sitting among passing teamsters, beggars, and shirtless young men with proud, highly colored faces, the last of an unmixed native strain. Half-naked children rolled about under the tables. They were dirty and happy and argued over bones with the mangy dogs as they were watched by the witchlike eyes of ancient grandmothers, twelfth-night familiars sitting there silently in the middle of the room. Watching over them too were the calm bovine looks of young mothers suckling their sleepy babies at their full, uncovered breasts.

Perhaps the musicians had come tonight not to work but to enjoy themselves. They were with friends, all of them probably from the neighborhood; no one yet wanted to be far away from home at night for fear of holdups. The proprietor must also have been a friend of theirs, certainly an admirer, because while the blind man sang, turning his white eyes up toward heaven, he came over and whispered to me:

"He's an artist. You should hear him singing opera. And he also sings songs he's composed himself. If he hadn't been blind we'd be hearing him in the best theaters with the best orchestras."

The proprietor, a strong young man with a red face and a long apron down to his feet, had a passion for music and told me he sang in the chorus. His voice was a fine baritone and, accompanied by the blind man, he began to sing a familiar romantic song by Tosti. Everyone applauded. A short, stocky little man sitting at a table by himself seemed to be the most enthusiastic. His face was round and of an indefinite age, lined by time and work, and his eyes dark and opaque like those of laborers from the South and, like a true laborer, his round hat was pulled way down on his head. He wore a black suit, a white shirt with a light-blue collar, and a flashy American tie. He must have drunk a lot already and was having fun as he listened. Every now and then at the most inopportune moments he would interrupt with applause. Then he would stand up, waving his arms to show his enthusiasm, and start to dance a kind of tarantella. As he waddled around he was in danger of falling down until someone grabbed him, pushed him back on his seat, and jokingly pulled his cap down over his face. His enthusiasm became most clamorous when the blind man, at the request of one of the printers, started to play the *Internationale*. He applauded, danced his tarantella, rolled wavering up to my chair and sang, clapping his hands:

We must build a world more just and sincere.

He made so much noise, dancing with his rustic awkwardness, that the blind man's friends, who seemed to know him well, threatened to throw him out.

Next to the blind man sat a tall, dark fellow with a high complexion. His eyes and hair were a brilliant black and he had shining gold teeth. His shirt was open over an athletic chest, his sleeves were rolled up showing a big tattoo on his forearm, his fingers were loaded with rings, his voice boomed, his gestures were wide and imperious. He seemed a kind of local bully, perhaps an ex-sailor or a peddler who had lately got rich on the black market. He was twice as big as the little peasant. He got up and went over to him, jammed his hat over his eyes, almost carried him to the door, acted as though he were going to throw him into the street, and then let him go. It must have been a usual performance with them, almost a game. The peasant didn't mind and came back to sit on his chair.

"All right, you Sardinian, it's your turn to sing," said the big tattooed fellow when the *Internationale* had ended amid applause. "Sing the Sardinian dialect song . . . how does it go? . . . 'Your kind . . .' 'Su re . . .'

Deu salvet su re
Salvet su regnu sardu
e gloria . . .

God save your king,
Save the Sardinian reign
And hail its glory . . .

"— Start singing!"
The mild little peasant in the round hat, with confused, wild gestures, tried to sing something incomprehensible in a drunken voice. It was lost in the general uproar and the protestation of the Republican printers. But the desire to sing possessed them all. They joined in a kind of singing contest, a frenzy of melodiousness.

The proprietor sang a piece of *Carmen* for the second time. The big tattooed fellow introduced himself with gestures, with varied and colorful tones and a great river of a voice, and sang a popular Roman ballad that told the story of a suicide for love. When he finished the Sardinian took his beringed hand and kissed it. The tattooed fellow wanted to sing again but was interrupted by an extremely dark, hairy man with a low forehead and cheeks bristling with beard. He had the look and costume of an artisan and was holding a sleeping child on his knees. He said:

"Let her sing now," and he indicated the woman at his side. The tattooed fellow, who knew his manners, bowed gallantly.

"Please sing for us, Signora,"

She had been sitting with her back to me in the dark and I hadn't noticed her before. I looked at her and saw splendid, rich, blond hair falling in a long wave and ending in a soft, heavy knot that followed the curve of her white, long, arched neck. It was as pliant as a swan's and moved with languid opulence, marked by gentle circles that accentuated its grace and force and supported, as a stem does a flower, the unimaginable face of a queen. She turned toward me ready to sing with a smile both obliging and haughty. Everything about her was unexpected, especially her presence here in this smoky tavern, in this rough company. She had delicate, transparent skin like a silk veil drawn over gold cloth. Her dark eyes were violet; you couldn't tell whether they were concentrated, ironic, or haughty. She had wide features, a thin, straight nose, and a large, sensual mouth with small white teeth. Her face was fairly young but her broad features were marked forever by a grace that lay not so much in shape or color as in an inner yet visible harmony and power. Even her most fugitive motions expressed nothing but unconscious beauty. She wore modest and simple clothes, a plain, knitted, gray-blue dress. She held in her arms a little four-year-old girl with long, blond braids who looked very much like her and was sleeping deeply, her fists clenched and her lids closed.

She took the child, whose arms hung at her sides, loose and heavy from sleep, and deposited her like some object next to the other sleeping child on the knees of the dark artisan. He must have been her husband, and he devoured her with eyes filled by a pride that asked everyone to admire her. She had freed herself of the weight so that she could sing. She stayed as she was, sitting on her chair with one arm resting along the back and the other dropped at her side, smiling before she started. She sang whatever they asked for, popular couplets full of double meanings and blunt words, in a delicate, clear, even voice, continuing to smile without shame or shyness but also without pleasure. There was a kind of gentle irony in it as though she were completely detached from the vulgarity of the couplets and lived in an inaccessible world of her own, yet was not too proud to descend to the levels of the others, as though it pleased her, as though she were performing a good deed.

Where did this woman come from? What was her story? How could she be the wife of that rough and dark artisan? How could a woman of such rare perfection spend her life in some black hovel working all her hours in such strange company?

Without changing her expression, except now and then to frown slightly in concentration, she finished singing with a pleasant nod and immediately took the sleeping little girl out of her father's arms.

Everyone had been silent as they listened, touched by that noble enchantment. But now the Sardinian got up again, staggered around clapping his hands, and the proprietor and the tattooed fellow advanced to be heard. The blind man, unaware of their rivalry, struck up a gay, noisy song and everyone joined in. Someone started to dance among the tables. They were all friends, close one to another. Time passed, the candles were half consumed. I saw at the end of the table that Andrea, Carmine, and the engineer from Udine had stopped arguing and were keeping time with their glasses on the marble table. The music was faster and all of us attacked the refrain: no one thought of anything but the rhythm and the noise of feet on the floor. Suddenly the lights came on. The interlude ceased. Dazzled by the return of light that made the candles seem dead and changed the looks on men's faces, everyone stopped short. Only the blind man went on with his out-of-tune accompaniment like the tag-end of a phonograph record that goes on turning emptily.

"It's over. Let's go," said the printers. "It's lasted long enough."

And they stood up, noisily pushing back their chairs to return to work. We waited to finish the last drink, say good-bye to the party, the proprietor, the tattooed fellow, the Sardinian, the artisan, and the woman, and followed on. By the door I saw Andrea smiling at me.

"Anything new?" I asked him. "What are our Luigini doing?"

"They're triumphant," he answered. "They've gone mad. They dream of all possible ministries. And they'll get them. They'll get what they deserve, and it's what we deserve."

It was raining heavily again with big drops that spattered on the shiny pavement; from near and far away the rain rustled, the spouts gurgled, small cascades burst from the gutters with the continuous noises of the shower. Puddles of yellow water shone along the sidewalks under the street lamps where the gratings were clogged up. From beyond the houses on the other side of the Corso came the swishing sound of skidding automobiles. The smell and the noise of the water enveloped us from all sides. We ran across the alley pulling our jackets over our heads, and flung ourselves, wet as we were, down the stairway of the printing shop where the lead had started to melt again under the blue light of the little flames.

3

The work lasted a long time that evening. The current failed many more times, but for shorter periods, long enough however to hold us up and make us all nervous. The tavern was closed now and we were eager to finish. We waited, swearing in the darkness, and the acetylene lamps were lit again. The paper was made up bit by bit in jerks and sobs like the speech of a stutterer. Fresh news arrived, including items from party headquarters that were considered "obligatory" and forced us to make last-minute changes in the paging.

Other visitors came and went, other faces, other speeches: a mountain of faces and words, side by side with the advancing night, the increasing smoke, cigarette butts, and the irritability of weariness.

The blond girl who had greeted me as I came out of the meeting at the Viminale happened along with three or four very young comrades. They were slender boys, handsome, with decisive movements, sure of themselves, and content with what was going on. They came to exchange news for their newspaper. They had no doubts and no problems. They said of everything: "That's important, isn't it? . . . It's very important."

But now we had no time to listen to them. I had insisted that Dotti go home. Casorin had finished writing and had fallen asleep on the bench. Perhaps while we'd been at the tavern he'd ordered some wine and had a little too much to drink.

Headlines were scattered here and there. The lead slugs began to fit into the pages like a mosaic with big gaps in it. Midnight had passed long before. Driven by necessity I had decided to write my editorial. I covered the sheets with words that I had no time to reread. Moneta snatched them one by one as soon as they were written and took them to the printers so they could put them in type without delay. By pushing me and hurrying me he was helping me to overcome the strong repulsion I had for the task of translating events, facts, and pictures into opinions, policies, and slogans; pretending to set men in motion by words.

When the last word was written, the last piece in type, and the group had finally thinned out as the friends had left us one by one, we started to lock up the pages on the table of the narrow room. The lead slugs fitted into that incomplete mosaic like dowel pins, the page took form and looked more and more like a picture. We had to cut lines here and there, twist around a news note, suppress another, substitute a shorter one. Rapid decisions, corrections without a chance for revision — the work of a painter in front of his canvas. We chose the type, decided how to arrange the headlines, avoided repetitions and tedious symmetry, tried to make clear pages whose appearance matched the content, and to reach this goal with the poor tools at our disposal.

Moneta had become a master at this art. The make-up men were experts. Surrounded by reporters Nero was calmly making up the second page. Paradisi, nervous and tense, his spectacles on his pointed nose, was bent over the first page. How easily they read the lines upside down to make the cuts and the corrections, how quickly they put in leads between the lines! What a pleasure it was when finally every piece of type was in its place, hammered carefully down with a wooden hammer so that all would be compact and firm! We tightened the bolts of the frame and there came Cesare with his inked roller to pull the proof. We looked at every proof marveling; but alas, they still revealed errors, wrong letters, lack of proportion, misplaced or miscalculated headlines. We made big, ugly marks on the wet paper with a special pencil and drew long arrows from the middle of the text to the margin. In a few minutes the corrections were made and off went the page on the trolleys to the furnace to be cast into semi-cylindrical plates. Our work was finished and we could have left. But it was so late now that we might just as well wait to have the pleasure of seeing the first copies come from the rotary press.

The reporters, editors, and Casorin hurried away while the printers of our shift washed their hands and took to their bicycles. Moneta stayed with me to smoke another cigarette as I was smoking my last *Toscano* stogie. That's the way it went almost every evening. This is partly because I have continuing habits, and while it's an effort to start things it's just as much of an effort to finish them, and it's hard for me to leave the place where I am and whatever I've started doing, or to leave anything behind. Besides, the hour of weariness and sleepiness had passed, the time that rises to its peak like a curve in a graph and then declines and disappears leaving a feeling of clarity and elation that removes all desire to go to bed. Then too we were not so hardened in our profession as not to be eager to see our finished work. Although we knew the limitations of our politics and ideas and were not satisfied with them, there was still something about a newspaper that had the quality of a work of art, changing each day with a value of its own. Something of the same surprise that lies in things you make with your own hands: houses, pictures, books.

In the small hours of the night when we saw the sheets come from the presses like white doves taking flight with a great beating of wings from their dovecotes, we felt as though we were assisting for the first time in the performance of a small, daily miracle.

Waiting that moment, Moneta and I walked up and down in the silent room. Then we went to warm ourselves beside the furnace, leaning against a file of old yellowed sheets of the newspapers of other days. The light failed and we had to wait again. When we finally went out with the first copies in our pockets it was almost morning. The time clock at the entrance said three o'-clock. We separated at the door as we went in opposite directions. It was raining slightly, a slow, gentle rain that carried with it the autumnal air and the silence of the northern lands. Walking carefully in the middle of the street to avoid the puddles and the dripping roofs, I went toward my new home.

The streets were deserted and my footsteps resounded among the echoes from the facades and courtyards like blows hitting a hollow body. I seemed to be walking in emptiness, as though I were walking inside the vast intricacies of a conch shell whose silent form had been washed up on a solitary pastoral bank of innumerable calms and storms, where an unknown river flowed and wild animals rustled over the deserted land. In the stone shell of old streets and alleys whose names I didn't know, I went like the heir of an immense feudal domain who circles it on his horse, astonished at what belongs to him. At every step a new vista opened before my eyes; the edge of a house, a dark doorway, a facade curved by history, an angel. Sudden squares opened wide, the shiny pavement wavered, a stone horse slaked its thirst beside a stone lion at a fountain, the columns on the facade of a palace seemed about to break and shatter at the impossible call of a stone trumpet, and an elephant carried an obelisk straight against the sky.

The innumerable wings of an empty theater opened out in a curve before me, ready for any kind of performance. The sound of my steps echoed in the theatrical and mysterious cavity. That sound came from me, from my own feet on the pavement (and I sometimes tried to step louder just to hear my own steps), but alone in the silence it made the silence deeper, more filled with expectation. I felt as if at any moment the houses might begin to creak like old furniture at night, or if I listened attentively I might hear the delicate grating of worms. Or I felt like a boy with my satchel of books over my shoulder, running to school in the winter through a big park, motionless from the cold, its bare trees white with frost in the soft, tense silence of the snow, awaiting with anxiety the faraway sound, like a scream, of a branch splitting from the frost.

Without meeting a soul I crossed the old part of Rome as if it were an abandoned countryside. I didn't worry for fear criminals were huddled in the shadows, although stories of them filled the news these months. To tell the truth I really didn't believe in them. People talked about it (they didn't talk about anything else), newspapers, including my own, described many holdups even in the center of town, but in the depths of my heart I didn't believe it. It seemed to me only a delusion or an exaggeration of fear that gave birth to these bloody and violent acts. Therefore I wasn't inclined to believe in them, perhaps because I wanted blood and violence to be over and instinctively refuted the evidence. In the same way I wouldn't believe when I was a boy that it was the wind that moved the branches of the trees, but imagined and believed the leaves moved spontaneously by a secret will of their own and that they stirred the air like green fans to create the wind. I spent hours and hours in my father's garden during the sultry August days watching my beloved plants, invoking their vegetable will, and waiting for the topmost leaf to move like a hand, signaling to all the others to bring a cooling wind and a storm.

I walked through Rome in the light rain as though through a calm and windless wood. And the silence of nature rested me after the noise and the words of the day. The alleys were like forest paths; slanting streaks of light revealed the wrinkles of the stone trunks and the green of moss. I came on a wide street like an opening in a forest. A flock of sheep moved toward me with its multitudinous tranquil step. They filled the entire space between two sidewalks. One could hear only a few low bleatings and the continuous padding of their hoofs like the nibbling of grass or the running of water. The shepherd walked slowly in front of the gray sheep carrying a newly born lamb around his neck like a scarf. Two white dogs ran at the end of the flock.

Perhaps they were coming down from the pastures of the Abruzzi now that winter was approaching, going their rustic way, the way followed without change for thousands of years. They had chosen this solitary night hour before dawn to cross the city in a measured course from one meadow to another, down the long, closed corridor between the cliffs of the houses worn by the usages of time and the passage of the seasons. I shrank back on the sidewalk surrounded by sheep, smelling their odor of grass, of wool and milk, watching them go by and be lost in the darkness of the street.

I had arrived at the doorway of my palace. I searched for a long while in the lock with my little key and went into the large, dark vestibule in the shadow of the old pillars.

5

The entrance was dark and full of black corners. An old lantern hung down from the middle of an arch. A faint red light shone from its dusty glass, filled with boredom and antiquity, like the light of a smoking torch in the wings of a theater that makes the darkness seem deeper. This octagonal light reflected the vague design of a star on the pavement. On the other side of the arch one felt an empty darkness opening out, the vast, mysterious space of the courtyard, its high walls confused with the opaque color of the sky and the night. A splash of water from the eaves along the roof mingled with the gurgling of the fountain and the light rustling of the rain. It seemed as if the entire palace were dripping from the ground to the attics and the highest turrets, dissolving in monotonous sadness the tedium of its long duration.

I followed along the arcade, cut by oblique shadows that prolonged the slanting lines of the pillars. I climbed the first steps and saw the whiteness of the statue of the dying Gaul, gigantic, confused, against the wall of the vestibule. The staircase rose in front of me in the faint light of some low-burning lamps like the slope of a mountain at twilight.

A noise filled the big cave of the staircase, a continuous roaring shout that seized the whole air and seemed to come rolling down on me. I couldn't make out what this noise was that reached me, shot off, multiplied, and reflected from a hundred niches, holes, hollows, and cavities of the staircase, every one of which was a howling mouth in the resounding confusion. I climbed the first flight in a hurry, surrounded by this cry, when of a sudden from the shadow a dog ran down rapidly and hurled himself toward me, his jaws wide open.

He was a medium-sized dog with short white hair on his back, ears, and muzzle. Two big black spots circled his eyes and hid them, giving him a ferocious look. He barked without interruption, with a powerful and tremendously violent bark as though he were raging and insane. The huge sounding-box of the staircase turned this mad howling into a deafening pandemonium.

I stopped to confront him. The dog stopped too, one stair above me, without interrupting his roaring, stiff on his legs, his fur rigid, ready to leap. I could see his wide-open jaws, his convulsed tongue, his teeth uncovered by his curled-back lips, his tail taut like a rope. I tried to calm him with words and a movement of my hand, but these blandishments had no effect. I then tried to threaten him, as if I were going to hit him or chase him away, but he didn't budge and only cried more loudly than before. I soon saw that although he confronted me so as to impede my way, he was at least not trying to bite me.

I know dogs. I have lived for a long time with my dog Barone, with his voice of bronze and his hobgoblin jumping, but I had never seen such savage fury or heard such a tremendous barking. I started to look fixedly into those black spots he had instead of eyes and, taking advantage of a second's respite, I climbed one step. The dog also moved backward, then started his infuriated cries all over again.

In the midst of this uproar I tried to listen for the sound of someone walking or a door being opened. It seemed strange to me that nobody in the entire palace had been wakened by a sound like the end of the world. But the heaviest silence, the deadliest calm surrounded that noise. We were alone. I found myself laughing at the absurdity of fate that had enclosed me so late at night in this cage of stone with this wild animal.

I continued to look at him fixedly and to climb slowly. I had to earn my way, stair by stair, with patience and caution, with long waits when the furor of the animal increased, and from stair to stair I always saw him in front of me.

I reached the first landing and the wide space stretched out behind me where a few hours before I had imagined I might find a Court of Miracles, a gathering place and refuge for the crippled and the poor. Perhaps someone was hidden behind the balustrade in the shadow of the great classic vase, or in the black corners? This place was distant and unknown to all men, part of a world totally unconcerned, that existed in an incomprehensible time of its own and into which I had fallen by some strange discard of fate, face to face with a mad dog.

How many stairs did I still have to climb? How much time would it take me to reach my door? How could I ever get there if the dog kept on trying to block me? I went on step-by-step, talking gently to the dog, as though gentleness could somehow soften his wild fury. I heard my own voice in that echoing tumult like something foreign and absurd. I felt as I had a few months before in the front seat of a light Martin bomber that had been converted into civilian service. I was alone between two motors that seemed to be flung for some immeasurable reason of their own into an inhuman world of clamor too strong for the senses to bear. In this mechanical fury I tried in vain to hear my own voice, to sing, to shout; I opened my mouth but I could hear nothing. With the dog too, as with the machine, it was a difficult dialogue.

We passed the gigantic marble finger, yellow against the wall. Perhaps it was a votive offering, offered to some divinity worshiped as a protector of hands. Farther up the Greek grammarian watched us go by from his stone seat with ironic condescension. Another flight and I'd finally reached the second landing in the shadow of the sphinxes. The worst was over. Now I only had to climb the narrower stairs that led to my door. And as I crossed the landing I started to laugh to myself, looking at the clamorous and inoffensive animal, imagining that he wasn't real but a kind of ghost, a symbolic apparition like a medieval she-wolf laden with our sins.

But when I had reached the bottom of the stairway where the flight became narrower, the dog stopped on his four feet, his cry became more lacerating, and whenever I attempted to go on he not only refused to retreat but tried to hurl himself against me. I attempted to cross the small space between him and the wall but he countered every move I made by blocking my passage, animated by an absolute and stubborn determination. Behind him the darkness was blacker. There were no lights on the last flight of stairs. They were extinguished or broken. The thought of entering the inky blackness in the company of that beast was not pleasant. The last faint lamp on the landing gave an oblique light cutting the first step in half, and behind this sharp line was obscurity.

An object lay on the floor, half in light and half in shadow as though it were cut in two. I looked closer. It was a man's gray felt hat turned upside down. I started to pick it up but the dog leaped forward to defend it. He stood on his step like a sentinel and it was impossible to move him.

I looked up the black stairway that I would have liked to climb, which separated me with its brief, impassable space from my bed and repose. Little by little my eyes became accustomed to the darkness and I began to make out something black. There was an object on the floor in the middle of the stairs, something dark and shapeless, and suddenly I realized that it was a man lying with his face toward me.

I lit a match. The man lay on his back on the stairs, with his head down near the last steps. Higher up his legs were lost in the darkness. He was motionless. His left arm hung down toward his head and the hand, grasping a cigarette lighter, was closed like a claw. His upside-down face seemed to look at me with motionless, distorted eyes. He had a sparse, reddish mustache, his mouth was half open and a cigarette butt stuck to his upper lip.

"He's dead," I thought. "Or perhaps he's fainted or only drunk."

I had to touch him. I lit another match and stepped forward with decision, but the dog leaped up with mad yelps and stopped me.

The man was certainly dead, not drunk, and the dog was his, crazed by terror and the sense of death. He defended the dead body. Nobody could have touched it. He defended it to the very last from death. I was sure that the man was dead. And yet I thought I might be mistaken, that I might still help him. In that darkness alone with that mad animal I couldn't do a thing.

The doors of the apartments a few feet away stayed closed in spite of the infernal noise. No light went on. I waited in a vain hope for company, then decided to call the porter, or some pedestrian from the street. It wasn't easy. The dog who wouldn't let me come close didn't want me to leave either. He didn't want to be left alone and couldn't resist the terror. He followed me with his howls, threw himself against my back, and caught hold of my jacket with his teeth. But I'd made up my mind now, and I went down slowly at first and then faster. The animal followed me, lamenting, to the first floor where he stopped, looked at me awhile, growling as though asking me to come back, and then went up the stairs again to watch over the fallen man.

I arrived in the courtyard and was about to ring the bell for the porter when I saw a night watchman coming toward me. He wore a dark uniform with a visored cap with silver braid on it. I told him about the man and the dog and he came with me immediately.

Together we were once more engulfed in that howling atmosphere. The dog up there would not stop for a second.

"A white and black mongrel? I know him," said the watchman. "He's a dangerous beast. I've come across him several times. I make the rounds three times every night. You'll find the man's just drunk. If he's the dog's master he often comes home late after he's been drinking."

I saw that the watchman had pulled his gun out of its holster and was holding it in his hand. The dog leaped at us. The watchman aimed at him. I told him we should take care of the man, and that the dog wasn't dangerous.

On the strength of my previous experience I climbed up in a hurry. On that wide stairway the dog couldn't hold more than one of us at bay at a time and meanwhile the other could gain ground. When we'd reached the bottom of the narrow stairway the dog again barred our way completely. But as we might have foreseen, his fury was now directed chiefly at the uniform of the watchman. I succeeded in slipping against the wall and furtively reached the outstretched body. I touched the forehead and hand. They were frozen and rigid. The watchman didn't have a flashlight. I told him to run to the police station and return as soon as possible and that I wouldn't move until he came back.

I waited with the dead man and the dog for about half an hour. The animal didn't stop his baying for a minute. He wasn't barking at me or at anyone. He was shouting his mad fear, growling his repulsion at an invisible presence. I waited and couldn't think of anything in that clamor. This funeral wake stretched out as though it would never end. To my relief I finally heard steps at the bottom of the stair. The watchman came back with a policeman. He had found only one, a young, dark fellow with a little mustache. Frightened by the dog he stayed ten steps below us and didn't want to come up. Besides, he too didn't have a flashlight and couldn't be of any assistance. We sent him away telling him to come back with others, with flashlights, and some means of carrying away the body. And we stayed to wait for him.

The night watchman asked me for something to smoke.

"He must be the bookbinder who lives in Number 13. Perhaps he didn't feel well. Or he got drunk and fell. He was lighting a cigarette. He still has it in his mouth."

The dead man looked at us with his hand outstretched. I had watched him so long that he seemed to me to breathe.

"He has a wife and children. They're over there . . ." And he pointed at a grated window above the landing. "They don't budge because they're used to his coming home drunk and then they don't open the door but let him wait outside. Even the neighbors don't bother. They can't help hearing the fracas. But you can't imagine the sort of people that live in this palace."

After another half-hour four policemen came with a lieutenant. They flashed their lights over the body. The dead man appeared to be about forty years old, thin, and dressed in a worn, dark-blue suit. The trousers, pushed up toward the knees, uncovered striped socks. His right arm was stretched rigidly against his body. Under the hair of his mustache one could see the cigarette and yellow teeth in his open mouth. I was tired of watching that motionless thing.

The lieutenant said one mustn't touch him until a doctor certified he was dead and turned him over to the coroner. He ordered the policeman to stay and watch over him.

The dog could not oppose so many men. He lay down beside the dead man and continued to howl without interruption, his whole body trembling with horror. From below the policemen lit up the flight of stairs with their flashlights. I went along the wall as silent as a murderer, climbed up, turned down the attic hall, opened my door, and was finally in my new home.

An unknown bed in which I had never slept was waiting for me. The dog's howls reached me, muffled and far away. Over the expanse of gray roofs the sky in the east began to grow white.

10

*I*T WAS VERY LATE WHEN I woke up. I didn't know what time it was and the little table with my watch on it wasn't beside the bed. The lamp with the opalescent shade stood on a projection of the wall that was painted in stippled white plaster. I'd forgotten to turn it off before I fell asleep and now it threw a sickly reflection through the room. The shape, direction, and size of these walls were new to me, as well as the arrangement of the furniture and those strange, round mirrors framed in white metal. The novelty of the place heightened the confusion of waking, that kind of rushed and disordered whirling, a residue of the images of yesterday that sleep has not completely abolished. They dissolve in the sunlight like the click of the tail end of a film in the projector and the flicker on the screen put to flight by new apparitions, things of the present, tangible and corporeal.

As I set my feet on the rug beside the bed, my dazed mind still held the words "spontaneity" and "cultural leadership" that were there, intact and undigested, from part of a discussion the evening before at the printing shop with the blond girl from the Viminale and her young comrades. These words were covered by shadows that had shrunk into vague monsters: the woman who sang, the rats, Marco, and many others in rapid succession. And above them lay something far more ancient, a Chinese landscape (I called it that because of a cedar of Lebanon and a pagoda-like roof that had become Chinese with the passing of time) that I used to see from my window as I woke up in the house where I lived as a boy; at the same time hearing the familiar sounds of voices in other rooms and a snatch from an opera whistled by my father while he was shaving.

All this became more transparent and empty from moment to moment, almost impalpable like a figure in smoke that vanishes in the air. My eyes rested on unknown things, faraway domes, trees of the Janiculum gardens black against the sky; a sound of bells was in my ears, my skin felt the chill of water, and I thought that those figures were like refuse or leftovers of thought that overcrowded in the same way the minds of all men, great or small, rich or poor, educated or uneducated. One finds them everywhere, the same in their formless and shifting inconsistency.

Since everyone recognizes himself in these figures, they have been mistaken in so many paintings and writings for the truest truth, the root itself of poetry and language, such an excessively vulgar language that it is in fact a dead language. These forms, these words common to all, are moreover incomprehensible to all because they have no meaning. They are the stagnant leavings of vanished things, or the pallid, futile larvae of things unborn, or the monsters and idols of unfinished things, faulty, uncompleted, and chaotic; the indeterminate tissue that like ballast fills absences and empty spaces, and within all of us is an indeterminate mass, amalgam, and nonexistence.

These pictures, these books, and such of our pictures and books as make use of this matter do not go farther and are complacent about it, are, yes, the art of the masses; the art of all, but they speak for no one.

These thoughts were in my mind as I was washing myself in the short little tub. I looked out across the rooftops with the

ringing of bells running over them like a wind. The sun was in
midsky in an expanse of gray clouds. Its rays came through the slits
in the clouds, descending obliquely like a transparent flight of
stairs over the hills and the houses. Beyond the yellowed tiles and
empty space of the palace courtyard, beyond other roofs, statues
and rooftop structures, between the violet wall of a tower and the
shell-like spiral of La Sapienza I could see part of a very high and
distant terrace. It was covered by a little corrugated tin roof held
up by thin iron pillars, like the ones jutting out from old-fashioned
railway stations, and was divided into narrow alleys by partitions of
wire netting.

Walking up and down in these alleys without pause were a
great many priests. I saw their black figures crossing one another
ceaselessly, like ants. Each one walked alone without speaking to
the others or looking at them. While they walked some of them
were reading the books they held in their hands. Others moved
slowly and thoughtfully with bent heads, still others were swinging
their arms keeping time with the quick pace of their feet. They
seemed prisoners in the obligatory corridors of a jail, out for their
hour of walking. I watched them for a long time, attracted by their
silent rhythm, asking myself who they might be. Were they perhaps the last of the morning's futile images of the potsherds and
useless fragments of fantasy? But these priests were real and my
eyes could see them. By this time I was completely awake, dressed,
washed, my beard shaved, ready to go out and start the day.

I heard graceless voices coming up from the room below along
with a noise of plates and chairs being moved around. These
sounds were real too and my ears could hear them, so different
and far away from those childhood images of my waking, from that
familiar and homely rhythm that gives something of calmness
even to shouts, that creates the warm unity of the nest. I looked
down from the pretentious Capri stairway that led into the studio
and saw near the window a small table set for three, with three

portions of steaming spaghetti dished out on the plates like little mountains. Jolanda and Giovanni sat at the table wrapped in their gorgeous dressing gowns. From the open kitchen door came the smell of frying and the sound of many voices, perhaps the girls, Jolanda's friends. As I came down the stairs the two at the table turned to me and Jolanda called out:

"Well, it's good to see you up. . . . And about time. . . . Don't you know it's long past noon? We thought of inviting you to lunch. . . . Hurry up or the spaghetti'll get cold!"

This unexpected invitation was certainly very thoughtful. But alas, it clearly showed a specific aim, the girl's attempt, now that she was free of her former masters, to take possession of the house herself, where I would assume the part of a tolerated and passive guest and have forced on me the presence of that dubious cousin of hers. Since the meal so courteously offered me had certainly been bought with the money I'd given her the day before to get some food for me, her intrigue seemed so palpable that it appeared bizarre, artless, and almost disarming.

"Come along, do come along, please have a seat," Giovanni said to me condescendingly, pointing to the chair. He smiled, showing his extremely white, little teeth under the dark glasses and silky mustache, and he carefully pulled both ends of his dressing gown over his knees as he sat down. "We've prepared the food in our own way. I don't know that it will please you."

The spaghetti was covered with a sauce of tomatoes and *pecorino* cheese.

"He helped me with the cooking," said Jolanda. "He's good at that as he is at everything." And she lifted her fork.

They both ate in a stately way, with exaggerated manners, holding the little finger gracefully apart and keeping their lips closed, as in a treatise on etiquette. They both seemed so thick-skinned in this situation they hoped I'd accept and so sure of themselves with the hypocrisy of their facial expressions, their manners and pretensions, that I realized the uselessness of any word or gesture unless it was a blunt rebuff. They might not even have understood that. Since I'd been taken so completely by surprise, I felt I couldn't do anything but play up to their game for the time being, and accept their counterfeit hospitality as genuine. Naturally, I'd find a way to clear it up as soon as possible. But I couldn't avoid a certain unpleasant embarrassment, nevertheless. The girl's highhandedness, however, had been sewn with a white thread and was therefore harmless and even amusing.

But what about that cousin of hers, that Signor Giovanni with his gold rings who wouldn't take off his dark glasses at the table? I watched him now tying his napkin around his neck with elaborate care. I'd been vaguely suspicious of him when I first saw him and now, like a disturbing question, this took a more precise form as he sat in front of me like this, in his dressing gown and slippers, looking like a man who never leaves the house.

I telephoned the newspaper. Moneta informed me of the morning's news. The crisis continued, they were continuing the meetings, the negotiations, and the proposals. Everything was undecided and in the air. I didn't have to go to the office. He would come to me himself after lunch, perhaps with Casorin. They wanted to see my house. They'd passed by yesterday but too early to find me (they were the ones, I thought, the chambermaid's two sadists). I asked them to send a boy with the newspapers and mail, and then I sat down at the table.

Jolanda told me in her own way the story of the dead man. She didn't know that I'd been the first to see him and I let her talk. It seemed they hadn't yet carried him away. They were waiting for the visit from the man of the law. The dog was still there but had no voice left. Naturally Jolanda talked of a possible crime, deploring the immoderate use of wine. She and her cousin were satisfied with just one glass at table. And his wife and the tenants? They hadn't come out. How bad people are! She too had heard the dog barking; she had such a delicate ear and she slept so lightly. From her room she heard everything that was said in the house. But she wasn't inquisitive, she wasn't like other women who always listened to gossip and repeated it to everyone. She herself didn't care about anyone and didn't mix into other people's business. Because she, as she could very well point out, although she came from a simple background, was a true lady. She came, it was true, from a peasant family and she'd had to become a factory worker and a chambermaid. Her brothers and sisters worked on the land, but she was different, she was a lady. Things would never happen to her as they had to her paternal grandfather who, after working the whole day long, was paid off at night with the heads from the fish served at his master's table. As for her, she knew how to make herself respected. She didn't look like her brothers. They were all blondish, while she had that hair, that hair, she said, that made everyone delirious. She had another skin, other emotions. She was of another blood.

I listened absentmindedly to her chatter, watching Signor Giovanni's tiny mustache, his tiny mouth in front of me, and his expressionless face concealed behind his glasses, framed by the napkin, and busy chewing. By nature I'm anything but suspicious and mistrusting. But this individual, like something twisted and contorted, made me uneasy.

It seemed to me I had encountered him before, who knows where or when. Certainly, judging from my instinctive repulsion, it had been in some painful place, time, and circumstance. The doubt that had entered my mind was now developing by itself and growing, piecing together different elements in the fantasy: the vulgarity of his looks; the obtuse and arrogant pretentiousness of his manners; the military fashion in which he had introduced himself to me (and that name of his, Colitto Giovanni, was it his real name?); his accent like someone used to giving commands, though in a subordinate and trivial milieu; his mustache and his seemingly peroxide hair contrasted with the black eyes I'd seen only for a moment in the kitchen; the sunglasses worn in this season and at home (one didn't know whether from affectation or cunning); the obvious idleness in which he spent his hours. All this was tying itself together for me. I suddenly realized that many people were still in hiding during these months, and all of them had grave things in their past they wished forgotten.

From that moment on, the man sitting in front of me was no longer as I had supposed from the start the usual figure of fiancé or lover, nor a pimp, the seducer of chambermaids, nor a petty thief or exploiter, but a far more dubious character. Still I kept telling myself, that expressionless and doll-like face displayed more vanity than violence. Or was he, perhaps, one of those weak people who had been dragged into adventures far graver than they could ever have foreseen, or one of those timid people who, over-frightened, drew back into their houses or under trap doors, waiting for more secure times or for the longed-for old days to return. But if this were true, why had Jolanda introduced me to him, why had she forced him on me with so much ostentation? And then, all of a sudden, I seemed to recognize him as though he came out like lightning from my memory, a figure glimpsed for a moment silhouetted against the sky, on a roof of the Piazza del Carmine in Florence. As agile as a ferocious monkey, shooting at some women who were standing in a line drawing water from a fountain, then dodging back and disappearing.

Meanwhile Jolanda, as one might have foreseen, started off telling me the probably imaginary story of her mysterious birth, the origin of her difference from her brothers, the mystical basis of her snobbery. Jolanda's mother, who had died when she was little, had been brought up by a market gardener at Roncole, near Parma.

"It's the birthplace of Giuseppe Verdi," the girl explained to me in a low voice as though she were confiding a glorious secret.

Her mother however was not, as everyone believed, the man's daughter. She had been born of the illicit loves of a beautiful Spanish princess. The birth had been kept secret and the child brought into the country and trusted to that peasant family. The true mother had never tried to see the little girl again, the most serious reasons had prevented her, and she must have been dead now for many years. But Jolanda had seen a photograph of her that showed her to be like Jolanda in every way. The same hair, that hair truly like a Spanish woman's, the same figure, the same grace, and that ladylike bearing.

She was the only one to take after the princely blood of her secret grandmother, everyone else in the family had remained plebeian. She had always felt different from all the others, even though she had carried heavy loads and eaten cornmeal mush as they had.

I don't know when this legend had been created for Jolanda, who was telling it to me now in order to appear noble in my eyes. Certainly that nobility of hers was the classical one of servants, all in the past and in the imagination and nothing in the present or in the actual. But it was enough to satisfy her. Although false, servile, and imaginary, it was nevertheless, in some way, an attempt at liberation. Having entered the superior world of the signori by this obscure route of heredity, Jolanda tried to sustain herself there by aping its customs. Her life had started off with an invention and was made of an imitation of invented and nonexistent things, of appearances without real support. She didn't know the world to which she pretended to belong except by having looked up at it topsy-turvy, or spying through keyholes, or judging it by the laundry she washed; intimacies, vices, baseness, seemed to her the summit of all human ambitions, the paradise of wealth. But these, when isolated and detached from any ultimate virtue or achievement, became grotesque caricatures. She had learned successfully from the signori coldness of heart, laziness, and greed, all hidden by a continuous and public display of virtue, unselfishness, and a disdain for money. Imitation had become her second nature, but it was clumsy, like the copy of a picture in a museum made by an inexpert child. Its fabric, full of blank spaces and holes, revealed crude and raw ignorance, even more stubborn and violent under the make-up of counterfeited manners.

She thought she must go on making conversation since she had freed the stream of her chatter. Now, following a presumed custom of those she imitated, she wanted to dwell on the subject of dreams. When we'd finished our spaghetti, big, fat Signora Violetta came from the kitchen stumbling over her long robe, bringing fried potatoes.

Then Jolanda started to recount some of her dreams. I didn't pay any attention to her boring talk. By now my fantasy had completed the image of the pseudo Giovanni whose plate Signora Violetta was filling, her eyes languid and admiring. I sat there considering the fate that had brought me to share involuntarily the same table with an absconder, perhaps a criminal, a torturer, or an assassin.

As for Jolanda's dreams, they were like all other dreams, the crude patrimony of symbols (if one thinks of them as such) that can be repeated over and over again because of their nature, empty receptacles that everyone can fill as he likes with his own feelings, images, and passions.

Hers were not at all commonplace, some of them developed in a rather dramatic and imaginative way. There were stormy skies, clouds like galloping horses, people transformed into statues, apparitions, and voices of the dead. Fortunately Jolanda hadn't the slightest notion of analytical interpretations. She only thought it was elegant to talk of them and to search for some hidden meaning. At the same time she was faithful to the popular belief in the efficacy of dreams for prophecies of the future, for picking lottery numbers, for warnings of good and ill fortune. The princess-grandmother, the mother, the market gardener–grandfather, and even poor Signora Graziosi had appeared to her. The Signora had been the maestro's wife, who'd been found dead in those days and about whom there'd been a lot of talk.

All of them were worried about Jolanda and gave her advice, and she ought to have followed their advice. When she spoke of the dead, Jolanda lowered her voice, donned a sorrowful look, and repeated their words in the foolish and dulcet tone of a prayer mumbled in a whisper. She was trying to show me her delicate sensibility, her reverent respect for those larvae beyond the tomb. But perhaps at the same time she was really a little afraid of them and actually believed in their agitated existence and in their arcane power.

"You're a good girl," the dead said in tremulous and affected voices, "no evil will come to you. We've suffered much in our lives but you're so honest and good you follow your own path, looking neither to right nor to left, and you deserve to be fortunate."

The dead were so touched by her goodness that was so rare and so exemplary that it raised the lids of their tombs and obliged them to weep with emotion. Perhaps I too would have been moved if I hadn't been distracted by the thought of that assassin who faced me, who, shamelessly sure of himself, was condescendingly inviting me to have another helping.

Mussolini also had appeared to her, Jolanda went on, almost whispering and with a contrite look.

"You should have seen him, pale, sad, with a suffering voice. He said they'd wronged him and betrayed him, but that up there where he was, the world was better, and that from up there he'd protect me, and especially Giovanni."

This high paradisiacal protection put an end to my last doubts. I turned to Signor Giovanni and asked him point-blank how he spent his time when he was outside my house, what his profession was and, indeed, who he was. I sat there anticipating his embarrassment, his reticence, and his prepared lies. If he were wrong in his impression of me and began confessing and appealed to my good fellowship it would be even worse. Instead Giovanni smiled, swelled out his chest, lifted his face, took off his glasses, happy at a chance to boast of his merits and describe his glories. He explained to me with so much precision and clarity, not devoid of arrogance, his duties and his work (if one could call it work) that I recognized the truth in his words. The whole castle of my fantasy crashed. He was not a collaborationist, an assassin, a Nazi, a torturer, a bandit, he was not in hiding nor was he an absconder; nor had he, according to the blandest hypothesis, been purged or suspended from his job to wait a judgment. He was only a government clerk, a functionary of the Ministry of Italo-African Affairs. An excellent functionary, from what he told me. He knew about the bananas in Somaliland and the navigability of the Upper Juba better than anyone else. Given his great competence, he naturally only went to his office when it was necessary, once a month. In addition to himself there were I don't know how many of his brothers, cousins, or other relatives, cronies, and fellow villagers working at the ministry. They were all as active, competent, and industrious as he was. Of course they helped one another. He, Giovanni, was the youngest. Others in the group were now far advanced in their careers and had splendid positions. He'd catch up with them himself, with patience, time, and their support. He never bothered about politics nor had he ever bothered about politics; he had too many other things in his head. He left politics to those who had nothing better to think about. He did a little business on the side, to be sure; after all one must get along and profit by good chances.

Outside his office, however, his interest was first and foremost in art. He loved it, indeed he loved it. If I would allow it, he would show me some of his works; he'd realized immediately that I was a connoisseur, a colleague. Jolanda interrupted, reaffirming these marvels and repeating the eulogy on his multiple capacities that I'd already heard the day before. There was nothing he couldn't do and in the very best way. As a functionary he was one of the most esteemed, but his true vocation was art. He spent all his hours at it. Besides, with that miserable stipend from the ministry it would be a pity to waste much time on the job. He was an artist: painter, musician, poet, writer, he could also make shoes, handbags, picture frames, furniture, and anything at all. He was also studying for a degree, and that would be useful in advancing his career. An artist!

The wind of those sincere boastings swept my doubts away like clouds and I felt happy and inclined to be patient. Giovanni left us to go down through the trap door in the kitchen to get some of his work. While he was gone Jolanda hastened to tell me, with the air of someone who's giving useful advice, that besides being her cousin he was also a little bit of a fiancé of hers, and insanely jealous. This was an unjustified jealousy of course, because her virtue lay beyond any suspicion, and then too she didn't like men. She had a cold temperament. Giovanni's jealousy was due only to his southern blood and to her own beauty that everyone turned to observe even though she was just walking down the street with a modest demeanor. Such things meant nothing to her. She really couldn't understand how one could lose one's head over them.

But he had a different opinion. He was really a man. At that point I had to listen to details that didn't at all rouse my curiosity. Jolanda divulged them in the awkward crudeness of terms she thought were sophisticated and that a lady of society would use. She spoke of her "physical integrity" and of what she termed honor, her own intact and infrangible and barbaric honor.

Meanwhile Giovanni had returned, his arms overloaded with small paintings on wood, pictures, and books, and he started to show me his creations with a little smile of false modesty.

What was a world of the signori for Jolanda was for Giovanni a world of art; something conjectured and not known to which he tried to belong, imitating from outside and at random its empty appearance. He showed me his paintings, little nudes with their arms behind their heads, mountain landscapes with trees, tiny houses, and cows in meadows, marines with sails mirrored in the azure waters, still lifes of fruit and flowers, copied from picture postcards with meticulous care. Nothing was missing from these objects that would make them seem real pictures. They were all framed in shining, polished gold frames. And carried at the bottom of the right-hand corner the big slanting signature *Colitto Giovanni*. This signature widened toward the border, large and flaming red, full of pride and ending in a glorious plume with a line that started to rise proudly from the last letter, redescended to underline energetically the entire name and lost itself in a hieroglyphic. These copies of the postcards you get by the dozen were true pictures to their creator, originals that properly carried his signature. No doubt grazed his mind. He had nailed and glued the frames, stretched the canvas and prepared it; the brush had coursed up and down depositing the colors, the signature had been written, a thick layer of brilliant varnish had not been forgotten; and finally the frame had completed the masterpiece. They were therefore pictures, the work of an artist.

His literary works were even more interesting. They consisted of various volumes nicely bound by Giovanni himself. There were the first white pages, the cases with printed lettering, written by hand but well imitated, giving the name of the author, the title, and the imprint of an imaginary publisher. The price was written on the back: 100 liras. Every volume had a jacket with a colored design, and a publicity band saying: "This is the latest work by the noted writer Colitto Giovanni," or "Read this book. It will keep you awake. It is the best novel by the great writer Colitto Giovanni."

The text pages were typewritten, but in very small type with an exact and uniform margin, so as to look as much like printing as possible. Each volume started with a page titled, "Opinions of the Critics." Collected here were eulogistic phrases and detailed appreciations that started and ended with asterisks to show that they were quoted from long reviews.

". . . Particularly lovely was page 13, where Colitto Giovanni unfolds his plot in dramatic and moving fashion . . ." and so on in the same tone. Every quotation was appropriately signed and dated with a precise notation of the newspaper where it had appeared: *Corriere della Sera, Giornale d'Italia, Avanti!, L'Unita, La Gazzetta del Mezzogiorno.*

Some of the dates were a few years back. That was quite natural since (as was hand printed on the cases) these volumes had already reached their fifth, eighth, or twelfth editions. Nor was an index lacking at the back of every book, and the last page carried the name of the printer. They were therefore perfect works, real books, complete in all their parts. They didn't have fantastic titles. They were titled according to their contents, divided into three literary genres. There was a volume of "Comedies," two of "Novels," one of "Short Stories," one of "Poetry," one of "Tragedies," one of "Narratives," an "Autobiography," a "Collection of Letters," and finally, the last of that *opera omnia,* "An Anthology of the Writings of Colitto Giovanni," in which the best parts, the most satisfying pages of all the preceding volumes had been copied.

While we waited for the coffee Jolanda and Violetta were preparing in the kitchen, I was leafing through them. Under the title "Comedies," I found with some astonishment serious, short prose narratives; there was also more prose in the book of "Poetry," and lyric verses filled the pages of "Tragedies." As for the "Novels," they were very brief. I read some of them rapidly. None of them

lasted more than seven or eight pages. In their own way they were
marvelous. Scenes heaped on top of one another, the dead were
countless, passions were consuming. Children lost and recovered,
twins exchanged, pistol shots, scenes of jealousy and espionage,
bisons on the mountains near Milan, betrayals revealed, corpses,
weddings, dark nights, moonlight, hidden crimes, and love. They
were unconscious masterpieces that utilized by ear, with an absurd and elementary imagination, all the conventional trappings
of pink romances, fairy tales, mystery stories, the comedy of errors,
and the illustrated serial. Not a word, an event, or an image had
the slightest meaning or referred to anything true, but they all followed the mechanical rule of a world he didn't know.

Here one encountered, deformed and approximated, all the
tricks and the resources of what is called "popular literature," because it offers itself as a fantastic escape to the man, and its bizarre
content and adulterated style are completely the opposite of the
natural language of the people that is spoken on the mouths of
peasants, in songs, in tales, and in stories; born from life and from
emotions and reflecting them.

This literature of the people is motionless in time, and has
been the same through hundreds and thousands of years. There is
labor in it, weariness, paradise, devils and saints, rich and poor,
resignation and patience, proverbs and seasons. There are also
women and love, but rarely passion and its bizarre frenzies. Above
all there are the eternal characteristics of man, that persist even
through changes of place and the variations of names and circumstance, on the edge of a field behind a church, in the thick of a
wood, on a mountain, among sheep in a pasture, or at a country
fair, a procession, or a wedding. And there is the crafty man with
thousands of expedients and clever frauds, the miser who loses his
life to accumulate useless heaps of gold; the jealous, the betrayed,
the wrathful, the tyrannical, the maiden ready for marriage, the
woman willing and restless for love and artful in getting herself
lovers, the old procuress, the witch, the priest, and the soldier.

And above all there is the simple one, the innocent whom
everybody cheats and who believes what he's told, the decoy of all

ingenious, cruel, and gay men and women, the subject of farces and jokes; the fool, the *minchiarillo,* that peasant simpleton, that Neapolitan jester who makes everyone laugh and who in a vein of good-natured and tender irony is at the roots the true hero of all these tales because in his defenseless weakness he is more the man than all the rest.

This art of the people is the same, with the same stories, characters and plots that came out of its woods and stables and entered books of the writers of the fourteenth century when men were eager to rediscover themselves. Then later it vanished like a subterranean river in the obscure countryside, in the custody of the peasants, without changing in any way or taking note of the shifting of times and fashions.

Giovanni's kind of popular literature, however, is completely fashion or the remnants of fashion. Here there is only passion, delirious love, strange and horrible killings, romantic emotions, and the roseate dreams of visionary ambition: false virtues, false vices, confused in the smoke of the balloons blown out by the characters of cartoons, an imitation of a nonexistent, earthly paradise where the signori take their tea, pronounce marvelous words, stroll in the shade of the trees like domesticated wild animals, and where everyone is welcome if he knows how to read.

The novels of Colitto Giovanni belonged to this category and were an involuntary caricature of it. A duke throws the little duchess, his daughter, out of the house. She'd been seduced by a stranger. But an English detective descends from an airplane. An officer whispers to the baroness to the strains of an Argentine tango during a party at the Grand Hotel, "I love you, you will be mine forever," and so forth and so forth. It's a grotesque review of ambitious and unobtainable desires like a regiment arrayed on the parade ground.

Nevertheless, reading these seven-page novels, I realized that they would certainly please women shut in their kitchens behind stoves, shelling beans and washing dishes every day of the year, and only a few yards away from the drawing rooms where such terrible and delightful things must happen. Printed as leaflets for a

few liras and carried into homes up the service stairway where the
errand boys, vegetable men, and milkmen go up and down, offered
through the door with a jocular word, a compliment, or even a
facile little madrigal, they would be grabbed by emotional hands,
tucked into white apron pockets, and would find a public of their
own, a public that would even appreciate the grammatical errors.

While we were sipping our coffee from three unmatched little
cups I hinted to the author that his writings might find readers,
and especially women readers. Giovanni was not astonished. He
knew he was an artist and, fundamentally, he and Jolanda were
both artists and in the same sense. He reflected on it a little, eyed
me with condescension, and made up his mind. With the unc-
tuous smile of an accomplice, as though he were about to offer a
bribe to a bureau chief at the ministry, he made me his proposi-
tion. If I'd do some prefaces to his writings and find a publisher
(easy for me to do), we could share the earnings equally between
us. This was certainly a splendid deal, but alas, it remained one of
the thousands of opportunities to get rich that as always, through
pure laziness, I let escape from my hand and get lost.

While Giovanni was insisting and magnifying the obvious generosity of his plan, the bell rang. It was Giorgio, the fat boy from
the editorial office. He arrived with his pimpled face, the limp and
greasy lock of hair down over his forehead, the honest, slightly
frightened eyes, flat feet, and ducklike walk. He was always hurried, tired, and faithful. He brought me, as I had ordered, the
bunch of morning newspapers, already checked and with mar-
ginal notes by Moneta. He brought letters, and also telegrams. Because of a touch of professional bias that I couldn't rid myself of in
spite of everything, I started to read the newspapers first. There
were those from Rome, and there were many of them: a daily
wave of words, of commonplaces, of exaggerated proposals, vulgarized opinions, incomplete one-sided truths, incomplete one-
sided falsehoods, that put alongside one another and compared
seemed to enclose the facts in a varicolored net, delicate 'but
strong enough to make them inaccessible. They disputed over the
facts, each one pulling toward his own side with ingenious crafti-

ness, showing their teeth like dogs around a bone. The meeting and the speeches of yesterday at the Viminale were reported and commented on in ten different and contrasting versions to influence the readers of the day for an hour and then to be left to the future historian.

As for the telegrams, they were addressed to "The Editor," and had already been opened by Moneta, except one with my name on it that was probably personal. Following an old habit of mine I laid that one aside without opening it, to look at later.

I always used to put off opening a telegram, sometimes for a few minutes, sometimes for many hours, perhaps to prepare myself better for unexpected news. Once I've opened them I start reading at the signature, rising bit by bit to the text, like players of games of chance who uncover small corners of their cards, one by one, slowly studying their value. I don't like these yellow announcers of good or bad fortune. Their style is aggressive, violent, indiscreet, truncated, and at the same time confused. Therefore I readily put off the moment of reading and as readily entrust it to others. If telegrams bring unimportant news they can wait without damage, if good the delay doesn't matter, and besides, news that's too good is saddening; and if bad, they bring it in the worst possible way, without explanations and without recourse, anonymous like the judgments of a tribunal, sentences for execution, refusals for pardon. Therefore I put the unopened telegram on the corner of the table Violetta had cleared.

Giorgio had been standing there waiting for orders and I sent him away. I asked Giovanni and Jolanda to leave me alone because I had to work, and dispatched that pair of apes to the kitchen, the trap door, and their friends.

I lit one of those twisted, nubbly, and vile-smelling cigars that had been made out of probably badly cured tobacco leaves and that Teresa palmed off on me as the true *Toscano* that you couldn't find anymore. I glanced at the open telegrams. They were the usual declarations of support for the fallen government from committees, councils, and commissions. I hastily read the few letters and, waiting for Moneta, I sat down to reread the newspapers and looked absentmindedly out the window. The birds were moving in low, rotating flights that spread out and loosened, then reassembled again, hurled through the air in a perpetual launching of circles without end. The black and silent priests walked under the rusty roofs. The sky was closing in, the clouds were pressing one against the other like shivering gray sheep, the slanting rays of the sun through the narrowing crevices thinned out, paled, were quenched, and immediately disappeared. The uniform ashgray of winter touched the roofs and the terraces, where laundry was hung and stirred in the interrupted gusts of a light wind, the announcer of rain. Far away, on the rung of a very high ladder leaned against the eaves of a roof, a workman was patiently fixing an electric wire.

~⟳ 2 ⟲~

Casorin and Moneta didn't keep me waiting long. They arrived full of exclamations about the beauties of my palace, of perplexity and horror at the corpse on the stairway, and of protest against the party leaders who, in their opinion, didn't understand anything at all. Fede had come into the editorial offices that morning and had criticized the slant of the paper and particularly the poetical notes and comments. In his opinion these were too controversial, bald, and explicit. Roselli and the other political experts agreed with him. They had decided, it seemed (but we were used to their being constantly changeable and didn't pay any attention to it), that it would be better to keep a detached, agnostic point of view, that one shouldn't take any position at all that would interfere with the secret and most important deals they were conducting. Casorin and Moneta were youthfully scandalized by these incomprehensible, wavering Machiavellianisms. It was clear that they had come to me only to be encouraged and supported. While we were talking, Moneta noticed the telegram on the table and apologized for not having opened it like the others because he thought it might be a private message.

Then I decided, finally, to open it. It was signed "Maria Vanni" and came from Naples. Maria Vanni was the name of an aged maid and housekeeper of my Uncle Luca. She was now a woman of some eighty years but she had come to my grandfather's from her native Garfagnana when she was still a child, long before I was born. She had become a family institution and had watched three generations of us pass under her eyes. At home everyone called her Mariona, an enlargement of her name that had perhaps been given her in those dim times when she was young and that body of hers was big and fat and abundant. When I was born she was already middle-aged, with a red face and a pointed nose and chin. And then, step by step, year by year, I saw her grow older, whiter, and thinner, but she always retained her dour and grumbling character that came, perhaps, from her origin among the peasant flock of Garfagnana, so difficult for its shepherds to lead, in that country of earthquakes inhabited by a mountain people, whose temperamental nature Ariosto knew and found troublesome when he governed them. With this original character of hers and her almost possessive fidelity, rustic and jealously affectionate, she had accompanied my grandparent to the tomb, and had helped to bring up interminable nephews, nieces, and grandchildren of whom I was one. Finally she had dedicated herself entirely to the service and company of my Uncle Luca, celebrated psychiatrist and biologist, who lived at Naples, alone with her and his studies.

A telegram from Mariona was absolutely unexpected and unusual, and there must be a serious reason for it. It must be bad news. The telegram read:

"Doctor grave. Come immediately."

The Doctor, my Uncle Luca, was still called "Uncle Doctor" by his nephews, nieces, and grandchildren. (This was an old-fashioned custom that is perhaps not in use anymore.) Uncle

Luca was much more to me than a close relative. He was really a friend. He'd been my teacher and almost a father to me. I hadn't seen him for some time, even before the eighth of September had put the war front between us. Actually, I'd seen him seldom for many years since he'd abandoned his chair at the university so that he would not have to swear allegiance to the Fascist government (an abandonment that wasn't much of a sacrifice for him, but even gave him pleasure since he despised in its totality the government and so-called "official science"). He had been forced to change his place of residence to avoid much police annoyance, and had left his native Turin for Naples, his wife's city, where she had an old house. After all, what did it matter to my uncle whether he was in one place or another? Everywhere there were men, and now that he was separated from all practical and personal care, he could encounter men everywhere and analyze their eternal nature. Everywhere, too, life unfolded so that he was able to discover its laws; in good and in evil, in health and in sickness, in the large and the microscopic; the Great Life that is present in all things, even in the subject that was first in his thoughts, insanity; and in evil men and madmen as well; what the poet Campanella calls "the half-tones and metaphors of his song."

My uncle was a man from another time, a medieval sage, intent on discovering the key of the world, whether it was silver or gold, and on gathering every kind of knowledge, wordly or ultra-worldly, magical, natural, or religious. He was aloof and oblivious to any circumstance, even one that concerned his own life if he thought it might distract him from the only truth. But he was of an inquiring mind and attempted to discover in all circumstances the eternal unity they all contained and that explains and justifies them.

His physical appearances seemed to carry a memory of distant places and centuries, perhaps a heritage from Arab physicians and Hebrew cabalists of the great Spain of the Middle Ages. He was tall and lean but he was strong. His thin, dark skin looked pale and transparent like parchment in contrast to his lively black hair. A huge mustache and a pointed beard framed his mouth and his thick, violet lips, which had a small wavy ridge of skin around them.

His forehead was high and narrow across the temples, falling straight to his nose that was large at the top and grew thinner toward the point like the beak of an owl. His eyes were terrible because of the power of their look, terrible even in their goodness. Were they black, gray, or blue? I don't remember and I will never know, but in the image I keep in my mind from long ago they are black, blacker than the blackest eyes because they looked into the depths of the soul. Perhaps it was this look, so penetrating yet at the same time so understanding, a mixture of love, intelligence, and good judgment that was in a way almost impossible to bear, that was the reason for his extraordinary capacity to cure; to calm the frenzied, to persuade those possessed of demons, to give orders to the delirious, and to untie the knots of obsessive ideas. Sometimes those eyes themselves became vague, as though a shadow was passing over them that was aware of all possible madness. Must not the physician, according to Hippocrates, have experienced all ills? Perhaps it was enough that he knew how to recognize them in himself.

This medieval sage happened to be born in the midst of the nineteenth century. Through a strange trick of destiny he had sucked in along with his mother's milk the myth of progress, German science, socialism, and Italian positivism. He had studied under Lombroso and came to consider biology as the sum of all science and the end of all philosophy. He had mastered and become impregnated with the interests and vocabulary of that time and of that school. If he had followed this course he would have become one of the illustrious teachers of positivist science, and this was considered a certainty from the promise of his early studies and early publications. But although the form of his thought and language was always marked by those first impressions, his natural genius drew him imperceptibly off on other ways.

One day he started to meditate on the problem of the sexuality of cells, perhaps not thinking he would go beyond a reasonable research into the facts, and facts in those days were idols. But in that purely material and objective study of male and female chromosomes, supposedly present in every cell of every organism, he saw the secret key of the biological world, a union of two principles, continuous yet continuously broken and then reconstituted, eternally disparate and eternally fused in an eternal unending circulation. Man and woman, both united and separate to the last fiber, to the last muscle, in the most microscopic and hidden nucleus. It was all very well for him to describe them in the vocabulary of the day as facts, matter, statistics, incontestable and visible objects. They were eternal principles, nevertheless, spirits of creation. They were the Yang and Yin of Chinese mythology that at the beginning of the world pursued one another in opposite directions around the tree.

He did not suspect at first where his meditation would lead him; but thought his work was over when he had made a new classification of mental illnesses quite different from the official and universally accepted one. This classification was a bipartite division, reducing them all to only two, hysteria and epilepsy, hysteria feminine, epilepsy masculine. But from there on he went from deduction to deduction, as if on an inclined plane, to an analogous classification of physical illnesses; and then little by little built an imposing and ever growing structure to which more and more new elements were added by means of this fundamental, bipartite division.

This structure, which he jokingly called "The Theory," became his dominating idea, his only continuing interest for which he abandoned every other concern, and it was enriched day by day and it followed him for the rest of his life. From then on he didn't publish one line, didn't make one speech, and disappeared from the world of science to everybody's consternation. He learned to look at things every day in the illumination of that light, whether it was true or false. And one by one he appropriated them for his own theory, losing himself in the contemplation of a universe made up of rhythm, pulsation, and the endless alternative between those two poles that coincided eternally in the good and separated only in error and sin.

Therefore he felt that the bipolarity of sex itself, of male and female, of nucleus and protoplasm, of nutrition and reproduction appeared again as if in a boundless structure of symbols, in working or sleeping, in the day or in the night, in justice or charity, in retentive or evocative memory, in mass and energy, and in asceticism and mysticism. A whole universe was born from this, bound together by infinite links that were reduced to one alone, always both alike and diverse where all things had one meaning and held themselves together like equivalent manifestations of one truth alone. He moved in this world discovering it in facts and daily gestures, in its every aspect in all fields: in religion, art, politics, in mythology and even in the hidden meanderings of language and in single words. They also were cells, monads in an infinite world of oscillating waves. This structure of his could never have an end because the world was too vast, and it seemed to him that new islands must always be discovered in this ocean without shores, and therefore he would never be able to chart, as he would have liked, a complete navigation map.

I had a vague notion of his thinking because he had talked of it with me many times, but I was uncertain as to whether or not this gigantic structure of his had a fundamental basis. From what I knew of it I could see all kinds of possible and easy criticisms. Was all this, perhaps, neither scientific theory nor philosophy but rather nothing but vision or mythology, or even, in part, splendid madness? But whether it was science or vision there was intensity in it, and infinite energy, the sincere life of a sincere man.

Of such was the man who was now sick, who was dying or perhaps was already dead. The telegram had been sent the day before. Many things could have happened since then. I mustn't lose time. I must leave immediately.

And then, as I said before, Luca was more to me than an uncle, friend, teacher, or father. He was these not only for what he was now, for his thinking and his way of life, for the council of my youth, for the affectionate care when I was sick, for introducing me to learning and to certain special interests, or for some right word spoken at the right moment; all this would have been enough to make him dear to me. But there was more besides. There was, I knew, beneath these latter reasons something older

and more profound, confused with the first signs of life and of con-
sciousness.

At the time of my earliest infancy my mother used to go every
day to visit her mother who was old and almost blind and lived
with her son Luca in the old house where she was born, and from
which, one by one, her children had departed. In all those great,
shadowed rooms were left only my grandmother, Luca and the
faithful Mariona. Sometimes during her daily visits my mother
would go out with my grandmother or on her own errands, leaving
me in the house under Mariona's care until she came back to get
me. It might only be a short while but to me it seemed to stretch
out for hours and hours, an infinity of time.

I was left to play by myself in a great, dark salon full of antique
furniture, hand-painted plates, strange objects, fragile knickknacks.
These rooms with their tapestries of dark materials were filled with
shadowy corners and frightening mysteries. They were also full of
awe and boredom, of respect and almost of anguish. I could play
and do anything I wanted to do as long as I didn't make any noise,
because Uncle Doctor was having callers in his study a few rooms
away. And I had to be careful not to break anything because there
was nothing in the room that wasn't mysteriously precious.

I looked at all these objects, so different from those at home that
I couldn't understand what they were used for. There was an infinity of them in that quiet twilight of shutters that were always
closed. Personages wrapped in great, colored cloaks gesticulated in
eighteenth-century paintings that hung on the walls in their
baroque frames. A half-naked man, his face dark and ferocious,
hurled himself with a knife in his hand to wound a young girl.
Solemn, bearded old men counted gold pieces with their fingers.
A Chinese statue sneered with a wicked grimace. An enormous os-
trich egg (that one mustn't touch because it might break) stood on
a console. The walls were covered with paintings, little pictures,
keepsakes, mirrors, plates, and fans. Lamps were everywhere, and
statuettes, shells, inkstands, and a porcelain coffee pot made like a
train, its smokestack and wheels ever so delicate. The furniture
gleamed in the twilight like the eyes of wild beasts, standing on

their four crooked legs ready to jump out at you from ambush. An inlaid chest of drawers was decorated with little amorous ivory figurines that seemed to be dancing naked around the handles and locks. A heavy cloth with extremely long fringes draped the table. There was something hostile, too, about the floor with its complicated repetition of inlays of different kinds of wood. The doors were closed and I never dared open them because at one side they led to the forbidden realm of Uncle Luca and on the other side to the rooms of grumbling Mariona, who for some unknown reason wouldn't let me come into the kitchen at any price. There was nothing in that salon to comfort me except a rocking chair of curved Viennese wood, the only friendly thing in that forbidden forest. I'd climb on the seat and start to rock, holding tightly to the arms, rocking faster and faster until I believe I cried out in joy and delight. But soon the pointed chin of Mariona would look in and she'd tell me to stop or I'd hurt myself. Then I was alone again, an annoyed and intimidated king in a realm of untouchable things. Here, one day in this room so richly decorated for daily torture, terrible events took place. As usual I was alone. Then Mariona brought me some sheets of paper and a box of pastels to play with. The box was new and unopened. Mariona had to break the seal.

"Be careful now," she told me, "the pastels belong to Uncle Doctor. He hasn't used them yet. I'm letting you have them on the sly. He must never find out. Watch out not to break them."

I believe I'd never seen any pastels before, that these were the first colors for designing and painting I'd ever had in my life. I was ravished as I looked at them and handled them, contemplating the green, red, and yellow tracks they left on the paper, as though they were the greatest miracle in the world. There came from my hands by enchantment lines, points, spots, intricate nets: I was truly in paradise. Up and down in all directions I covered the paper with fleeting masterpieces. But suddenly a green pastel I was holding in my hand and pressing with too much enthusiasm broke, and with it the enchantment of art was shattered and in its place was left the most terrible tragedy. I'd fallen so deeply in love with those pastels and they seemed to me so filled with a nameless, powerful magic that I felt the sin I had committed was inexpiable. Any punishment my uncle gave me would be just, but it would certainly be an enormous and frightening punishment. I couldn't have stood even a hard word from that man who was so huge with his pointed black beard and those terrifying eyes, who never spoke to me nor looked at me, and who lived within a cloud of supreme authority. But surely it would be much worse. He would throw me out, he would do and say horrid things as I deserved. And Mariona too was guilty because she'd given the pastels to me on the sly. But the guilt of others does not diminish our own, and I considered myself the only guilty one, entirely and completely sinful.

Surely I was still so small and lived so entirely in a world of absolute authority, a world of the Saturnian gods, that I might even with justice be devoured. I started to cry in anguish and desolation. I'd learned about painting, and already it was all finished. My mother wasn't there and didn't answer me when I called. Mariona didn't hear me either. I was alone in sin with those two malignant fragments of pastel that no human power could ever put together again.

The door opened and Uncle Luca appeared in all his terrible majesty. I felt myself die, and hastened to confess my crime, waiting for lightning to strike me with its unimaginable, anguished crash.

Uncle Luca looked at me and smiled. He smiled faintly; he did not laugh or shout. He smiled, caressed my hair, and said:

"You broke one? . . . Well, keep them all . . . they're yours." And still smiling he went back through the door and disappeared.

This was a true revelation. What does it matter that this story is nothing but a trifle? A small, childish trifle, an unimportant episode that Luca has surely forgotten, that nobody would remember?

At that moment the old gods of justice perished within me, driven away by a more human God. I had learned on that same day what painting was, and what goodness was, and that the inaccessible smiled on the one and on the other. Even a broken pastel can be the reason and the occasion for the world to open wide, and surely in that second it had opened. I moved in an instant from one epoch to another, I learned to make use of my hands, and to recognize a freedom made of love through which sin becomes nonexistent. I learned that art and moral conscience are not to be considered as distant and separate from one another, but friendly and united, born at the same time from the ruins of that terrifying omnipotence.

Thus, in one moment, I gained hundreds and thousands of centuries, if what my Uncle Luca told me many years later is true that *ontogenesis recapitulatio philogenesos,* or rather that all of history unfolds in every individual life. Of course this only happens when history does unfold, because it can also stop, or turn backward, or spin emptily on its own axis like a mechanical top.

I I

I MUST START OFF WITHOUT losing time; but it wasn't so easy. First of all, there was the newspaper, and I couldn't leave it in these days of crisis without giving careful instructions. And then, how could I get to Naples at this hour? There were practically no trains and they took a whole day to get there and were stopped at many points by the damage from the war — broken switches, ruined bridges, and uprooted rails. An incredible crowd of men and women jammed into a few cattle cars. They had sacks, suitcases, bundles, automobile tires, various kinds of boxes, packs, demijohns, tin cans for oil, and all kinds of containers. They climbed up and down at every station and at stops in the open countryside as well, actively trading goods. These were voyages in search of food and business. There was no place among them for a traveler in haste. Buses and little broken-down trucks made better time, but they left early in the morning and there was no use thinking of them.

Casorin told me that the only possibility was to take one of those private automobiles or taxis that carried passengers and left when all the seats were taken. Piazza San Giovanni was the place where they arrived and departed. I could go there. It was easier to find them in the morning up until noon, but if I didn't wait too long I could still find something.

I decided to do that. I succeeded in getting Roselli on the telephone after many vain attempts and loss of time. He promised to take care of things at the paper, to supply the news and watch the editorials. But he urged me to come back as soon as I could, if possible to return the next day. Canio too came to the telephone and gave me his rustic and affectionate good wishes. He said:

"Don't worry about leaving. If you take an automobile it'll cost you too much. Remember to haggle over the price. . . . Of course I do realize you're in haste. . . . You don't need to worry. I'm here."

Now I had to arrange with Moneta and Casorin about the work. I entrusted Moneta with supervising the paper and making up the pages. I made a bet with him that our bearded editor, who worked by day in a shoe shop and for many months had been writing daily editorials on the profound philosophy of history that I'd then daily thrown into the wastebasket, would profit by my absence and Moneta's distraction to print at least one of these incomprehensible masterpieces of his on the front page. I advised them both not to abuse my absence too shamelessly, packed my bag, and was ready to leave.

The dead man's body was still on the staircase where I'd left it the night before, with his head hanging down the steps. They hadn't touched him, but were still waiting for the police permit. They'd covered him with a sheet, and hidden thus he looked like a white package, smaller and thinner than a human being. At his sides they had placed two candlesticks with lighted candles in them. The candles were half consumed and burned lazy and yellow in the shadows. On top of the sheet the dog was stretched out prostrate over his body, his head between his paws, exhausted by fatigue and by terror. He had no voice left. As I passed he scarcely lifted his muzzle or opened his eyes. Perhaps he tried to bark but from his throat came only a hoarse growl. Then, tired by even this effort, he lowered his head and was silent. I hurried across the landing below the corpse where a woman and a little girl, their heads covered by black veils, were saying prayers, and two men, leaning against the wall with a bored air, silently watched the bundle illuminated by the candles.

Why does one conceal the dead, closing their eyes, wrapping them in shrouds, in sheets, in covers, covering them before they are hidden forever under the soil with an anguish that is called pity? Is it perhaps from a magic terror of their spent looks, of their power? This was the latest of the dead, but how many we had seen in those years stretched on the ground of both the city and the countryside!

At Ponte del Pino in the smoke and the dust of the rubble I had counted eighteen of the corpses lined up on the pavement. There had certainly been more, because here and there on the street lay pieces of other men. The first people to run up had covered them immediately. They had hidden whole bodies under fallen window shutters. Over the largest fragments they had put sackcloth or coats, whatever came first to hand; over the smallest they had put handkerchiefs. It looked like laundry put out on the ground to dry. Except that among the stones of the street and the rails of the trolleys shreds had been forgotten: clots of blood or of brains, a toe, an eye, a piece of skin with long blond hair on it, the hand of a child.

Frightened people running toward their houses turned around and looked at the remains and without stopping made the sign of the cross with pitying disgust. How many other dead, everywhere in incalculable numbers, had been left on the earth of Europe, uncovered and naked, in the sun and the frost, looking at the sky, until they were reduced to putrefied flesh, the prey of stray dogs and of the rain. Everyone had seen them, or it was as if they had seen them. People now hurried to forget in order to live, even though the air was still crowded with the presence of the dead.

We went down the stairs with faster pace than the solemn, princely staircase allowed. In the vestibule between the pillars, Teo, like a prehistoric stone, saw us hurrying by and hardly greeted us, nodding his frowning, marbled head almost imperceptibly, like the statue of the Commendatore at the passage of a Don Giovanni in flight, followed by two Leporellos.

We ran to the corner of the Piazza Venezia. I didn't want to lose anymore time. I was lucky. A little truck went by, and a boy sitting on the side leaned out and shouted: "San Giovanni!"

I said good-bye quickly to Casorin and Moneta, ran after the machine, grabbed the side and, helped by the occupants who pulled me up almost bodily, I jumped in.

This was an old, discarded truck like all the others that after years and years of service had run to hide itself during the German epoch in some ambush, under some shed or some stack of straw where it had ended up rusting and disintegrating. Later it had been adapted in a few hours for carrying people, equipped with wooden sides, iron frames that carried a canvas top for rainy days, two rough benches for passengers, tires that had been found at a bargain or stolen from the Allies. Bandaged and cured as well as possible, it had started to race the streets right after the liberation, to move people, to fill the road with noise and the stench of gasoline, cheerful, shoddy, and clamorous. Streetcars and buses were lacking; the trucks had taken their places; tattered, irregular, and disorderly, an army of sans-culottes in rags that held the traditional armies in check. They were ugly and uncomfortable, but still they were a free, popular invention of bad times, full of courage and initiative, and it was as if they knew this and demonstrated it in their sprightly, impulsive, and even enthusiastic gait. They were usually packed. Since they had no time schedule they stayed at their terminals until at last they were unbelievably jammed with passengers who waited patiently or cursed, with their knees fitted into their neighbors' like Nantes sardines in a tin can.

My truck, however, wasn't full. There were no empty seats, but by bending under the low, iron framework I could stand up back of the driver's box and from up there watch the street rushing along under the wheels. The wind blew in my face and through my hair. I felt as light as a bird. I didn't know yet whether I'd find a way to go to Naples, but I was already on my way, detached from things; from the town, from the people, filled with a delightful sudden sense of solitude. The world holds us with a thousand ties of habit, work, inertia, affections. It's difficult and painful to separate from them. But as soon as a foot rests on a train, airplane, or automobile that will carry us away, everything disappears, the past becomes remote and is buried, a new time crowded to the brim with unknown promises envelops us and, entirely free and anonymous, we look around searching for new companions.

I held the light weight of my briefcase under my arm. It was my only piece of luggage. That pleased me too. It had taken the war to teach us this readiness, a happy scorn of the most necessary things. How far away those days seemed, actually so near, when at every departure I'd youthfully weigh down my valise with unnecessary stuff from which I thought I couldn't possibly be separated. How could one leave one's letters at home, or manuscripts, or notes on work in progress, or the dearest of one's books, or all the other objects to which one was bound by affection? Things suffer when they're left alone, and when we leave them anything can happen: fire, earthquake, an invasion of rats or of the police. One had to take everything along to be prepared for everything. Only then could one feel safe. That's why a boy when he leaves home puts his knife in his pocket like a talisman, that jackknife with many blades, which can be used for anything, adapted to any circumstance, to cut bread or the branch of a tree, and especially as a defense against the enemy. I remember I'd seen at Martino's house an inventory, written by his grandfather at the beginning of the century, that listed all the indispensables to carry on a journey; objects the old man actually took along every time he happened to stir. It was an interminable list that covered eight written pages. It started with his linen, his suits, his shoes, and ended up with various kinds of nails, screws, clamps, hooks, hammers, pincers, wire, candles, and every kind of rope, cord, and string. We tried in those days to carry our lives along with our heavy baggage, but now we've learned to throw everything away without too much regret, and to start fresh every day.

From my lofty observatory I watched the asphalt run beneath the wheels. The houses fled, and the palaces, churches, ancient ruins, people on the sidewalk.

Farewell to Rome, to the time that is not time, and the place that is no place.

The Colosseum was already behind my back, and the poor little houses of a steep street, and the hospital, and the obelisk, and the Holy Stair that one ascends on one's knees. We had already come down into the square in front of the Basilica of San Giovanni, the place that is sacred to snails, to whistlers, to cloves of garlic brandished like bludgeons, to fireworks on the warm evenings of summer carnivals. Now a gray mist hung over it, from the open space in front of the facade of the basilica to the most distant houses. It was checkered by trees, sheds, stands, and by people posturing as if they were actors in a play. And the squalls of cold wind seemed to make the draped saints in the cornices shiver, and the street vendors blocked the way, crowding against the walls with their knickknacks on trays like shells encrusting a cliff. I made my way among them, going under the narrow arch of the bastion with its blackened tiles, and I looked out over the expanse beyond the walls where the basilica and the solemn ancient structures disappeared and a suburban part of town spread out, closed in by the geometric lines of tenement houses, squalid in their recent oldness, with their motion-picture houses and suburban taverns. And radiating out as far as one could see was a stretch of desolate streets.

Here, as I'd expected, a few automobiles were beside the elevated sidewalks, and others were cruising slowly, waiting for passengers. They had signs with their place of destination written on them, or else the drivers would call out now and then: "Anzio, Viterbo, Civitavecchia!"

They were all going to nearby towns. Those for longer runs had left before noon. But I was lucky this time too. I saw an old, black machine with its top covered by a shapeless mountain of valises and packages. The driver was tying it together with a rope as I approached. He was really going to Naples.

"Come along, come along," the man said to me. "It's the last that'll leave today. We usually leave earlier but we've had to wait to get a load. . . . Step in, we're leaving right away. There's just room for you . . . very comfortable . . . the tariff's one thousand lira. . . . Just look at this machine . . . in less than four hours we'll be there. . . . It takes off like a train. . . . The motor's like new . . . it's just been overhauled. . . . Rest easy . . . and the tires — all American. . . . We'll be in Naples before night. We leave right away."

As he said all this he opened the door of that broken-down wash tub of his, and I got in.

There was one folding seat free and I sat on it, with my briefcase on my knees. On the other folding seat sat a young man wrapped in a military overcoat. Three people were crowding the back seat, two women and a priest. They had already prepared themselves for the trip, swathed up to their necks in a thick blanket. The space between the seats was filled with sacks, packets, bags, handbags, and baskets. Next to the driver in the front sat another man. They were all silent. And I too kept still without turning around to stare at my companions. The man outside the car had finished his work on the roof, but we didn't leave.

A young man in mechanic's overalls arrived, carrying more bundles that were somehow shoved into that already jammed and crowded space. Then others came, with mysterious faces, and started to confabulate in low voices with the driver. Then an old man with a big mustache and a piece of paper and a pencil started going over endless calculations with him. Presently the chauffer went away with the old man. They walked under the archway, gesticulating wildly, and disappeared. It was getting late and they didn't come back. The priest and the women behind were mumbling to one another under their blanket. I was beginning to think we'd never leave when the driver appeared at the end of the square rolling along a big truck tire as if it were a boy's hoop. He tied it to the back of the machine on top of the heap of valises that already jutted out behind like an irregular tail.

A young man with a little bag in his hand arrived on the run. They put him at my left on a box between the two folding seats. And I could no longer move or even turn around. I knew it would be very tiring squeezed in like this for so many hours of the trip, but I'd acquired the necessary patience. While we were waiting with resignation it began to rain, a thin, slow rain that in a few moments made the asphalt shining and dark. We had difficulty extricating our arms to crank up the windows with their broken handles. The fellow in the mechanic's clothes came back, talked to the driver and gave him a small bundle of thousand-lira notes. The driver counted them carefully and put them in his big portfolio. When I'd lost all hope that these ceremonies and preparations would ever end, the chauffeur said suddenly: "We're ready." Then he sat down, started the motor, and we were off.

The folding seats had no backs. I adjusted myself to sitting rigidly, holding myself up straight. I couldn't move my feet because they were shoved into all that baggage on the floor. I made up my mind to endure this physical strain and that state of lethargy and voluntary torpor that brings with it a sort of laziness and artificial ennui. If one lets oneself go, it wins over the discomfort and almost changes it into a sort of slothful pleasure.

We had all become accustomed to exercise of this kind, to hard benches, to violent bumps, interminable stops, hours spent standing up, and the forced immobility that numbs the limbs. The whole of Italy rushed from one end of the country to the other in cattle cars and little trucks, in a continuous voyage that was a discovery, an adventure, a revelation to everyone. People who had never moved in their whole lives were traveling, and a completely new land, a different Italy, opened before their eyes. Some were escaping from the ruins of their old homes, some were searching for relatives and lost friends, some were returning after having been driven here and there by unexpected events, some came and went without any real necessity except a mania to be on the move, an exuberance of vitality, a vague hope of work and gain. The mainspring of all this was trading of one sort or another, the black market, large and small, the bargaining and the exchanging. Men went to the cities looking for jobs, young girls hurried from all directions like moths to Leghorn and other places where they could still find foreign troops. But most people were buying, selling, dragging bundles, exchanging merchandise. Everyone on his own and in a tacit agreement with everyone else was ready to circumvent the regulations, to overcome the obstacles, and to endure the fatigue. Italy's body, pounded by bombs and by armies, bloodless from war, was breathing once again. New and unforeseen blood was circulating in millions of corpuscles, carried everywhere in the most dubious and illicit ways, supplying the necessary oxygen.

People had never traveled as much when everything had been at peace and in order, rails intact, trains running and carrying people to their holidays and to political rallies, and when a strange miracle for so long had filled millions of hearts with a sweet feeling of glory, consoling them for graver evils — the miracle that the trains arrived on time. The new race of travelers, sprung by enchantment from all villages and all markets, had no timetables. They went like migrating birds, trusting themselves to wind and chance.

We had left the city behind after long stretches of suburbs, filled with holes and with scribblings on the walls, while none of the passengers had said a word. Everyone pursued his own thoughts accompanied by the roaring of the old, noisy motor. It was the first time since the war that I'd gone to the South. I was eager to see the landscape again that I'd almost forgotten after so many years. The rain striped the windowpanes. Through the veil of the glass the landscape looked gray, suddenly desolate and solitary at the gates of the city. The first ruins appeared, the hangars of an airfield twisted by the bombs. We continued to ride for a few miles in silence, without exchanging a glance in that monotonous expanse of naked fields. Puffing and sputtering, the machine started to climb a long, steep hill. Just as we reached the top and the road widened and turned into a curve, a sudden and violent explosion shook us. We stopped. One of the front tires had blown out.

"It's starting early," exclaimed one of the women from the corner behind me, who must have been used to trips of this kind and such adventures. "God knows when we'll get there."

In those days the tires were old and rotten and often of the wrong size and kind. The roads were bad and sown with nails. Blowouts were very frequent. Therefore it sometimes took days to cover a few hours' journey. One might even think that the tires were malignantly ready to delay those who were in a hurry. I remember two blowouts in rapid succession in the heat of a highway on a summer noon when I was driving many years before, in a taxicab with a young friend. We were accompanying a veteran political refugee, who was wanted by the police, to an appointment with smugglers who were going to take him across the border. We were late. The man was being forced to become an expatriate and was emotional about it and turned pale when he heard those explosions (that seemed to him like gunshots) and the machine swerved. Our gay jokes, tinged perhaps with thoughtless, youthful savageness, didn't comfort him, and he kept repeating, "We won't get there in time," as he sat waiting on the edge of the road for the car to be repaired, in the sun and the noise of the cicadas.

We got out of the automobile while the driver, helped by the man who'd been sitting beside him, fixed the jack to change the tire. The rain was light and didn't annoy us. In the distance at the bottom of the hill one could still see Rome and its vague domes. For a while we walked up and down to stretch our legs. I could get a better look now at my companions and exchange a few words with them, although they all seemed ill-humored and taciturn. The driver, who must have been the owner, was a dark-haired young man. He was short, had a little black mustache and long sideburns on a pointed little face. He wore a visored cap and high boots. While he was loosening the bolts he told me he'd brought some rubber cement that was very hard to find, and some tire patches, and also another spare tire. We could rest easy even if we had another blowout. He only hoped we wouldn't have another so we wouldn't have to drive too far in the dark. I looked at the vaunted American tires. Except for one front tire they were all ancient

Pirellis full of patches that could hardly stand up. The other travelers were also eyeing the pneumatics with doubt. The two women stood beside the machine. The younger one, wearing a lot of rings, was about forty, with big, swelling breasts covered by a dark silk dress. She had a short neck wrapped around by many loops of a necklace, and a red fox thrown over her wide shoulders. From this shining and hairy base emerged a huge face with painted lips, where two small black eyes were sunk in the fat under the shadow of a tuft of curly peroxide hair and the edge of a little felt hat trimmed with a very long, vertical feather. The other woman looked somewhat older, perhaps over fifty, with white hair, a long, thin, pale face, and bags under her eyes. Her manner was frightened and she looked demure in her simple black coat. She stood beside her companion in feminine solidarity, but it was evident they did not know one another.

The younger woman looked at a tiny watch, and one could see that they were thinking only of time passing and the perils of the road at night. The priest was ruminating on the same problems but in this casual gathering of strangers he didn't speak a word. He was advanced in years, big and fat, with gray hair, round, bulging eyes, flabby cheeks, and a highly colored face — the typical country priest. Everything about him, the worn and faded cassock, his corpulence, his thick shoes, his slow, kindly, ingratiating gestures, was tied by habit to a kind of professional manner, an expression at the same time inquisitive, humble, and greedy. All this corresponded so precisely to the traditional picture that it seemed almost an imitation. He'd lighted a cigarette and was smoking it in great clouds, holding it straight in the middle of his lips, pursing them at every puff like a suckling. As he smoked away like that he kept throwing preoccupied glances at his big, fiber suitcase on top of all the others at the back of the automobile. From the anxiety and fire of his looks, one might have supposed there was a treasure in it.

"It's well tied, your Reverence," the driver's companion shouted as though he were answering those looks. This was the man who had been sitting next to the driver when we left, and who had now finished winding up the baggage again in its complicated circles of rope after he had taken off the spare tire. I couldn't make out whether he was a second driver, an associate, or a friend of our chauffeur, or a passenger like the rest of us. Perhaps he was a steady customer who went back and forth every day to Naples in this machine to take care of business he probably shared with the owner. He was a strong-limbed fellow. His face was more animal than human; a low forehead, short, wiry hair under a visored oilcloth cap worn backward. His nose was fleshy, his features big and heavy, his jaw square, and he was ill-shaven, his skin was dark and burned by the sun in thousands of small wrinkles like old leather. He'd taken off his jacket in spite of the cold and now ran to busy himself around the wheels. He wasn't wearing a shirt but a thick American sweater, dyed dark blue. His sleeves were rolled up. His right arm was entirely covered with tattooing. He must have been a sailor or an ex-sailor. I was looking at the tattoos upside down. Right above his wrist was a kind of complicated and confused coat of arms. Higher up started out a huge design that covered the rest of his arm and lost itself under the sweater toward his shoulder. It was a man and woman embracing and dancing with their legs entwined. She was almost naked with a short skirt like a chambermaid's white apron. Their heads were hidden by the sleeve and I couldn't make out the design immediately. Seen this way only partially, it looked like an undecipherable arabesque but I could finally distinguish the two bodies, the four long legs of the dancers, male and female. Under their feet was a big inscription in blue block lettering, a little irregular because of the curve of the arm and the movement of the skin over the muscles. It looked like one of those inscriptions lovers on the Riviera cut in the leaves of aloes and that are deformed as the plant grows. I went over toward him and while he was testing the strength of the rope around the baggage, I managed to read it without his noticing. Was it an innocent title for the naive engraving on this skin, or was it a brazen declaration? It said: *Malavita Napolitana*.

The other two companions of the voyage, the young man with the military topcoat and the boy who'd been sitting on the box at my left, had gone farther off to the side of the road and were looking at the landscape. They hadn't yet found a way to talk to one another and stood silent and embarrassed. I walked toward them. The boy saw me smoking my cigar and asked me to let him light his American cigarette from it. He clumsily snapped open his big cigarette case and offered one to the other young man. And so we all started to talk together. The boy told me he was a Neapolitan student and had come to Rome to look for some relatives, but he had to get back home before evening. He was certainly no more than eighteen, perhaps younger. He was small, thin, and pale, with fuzz on his lip. He wore a black suit, simple and in style, the trousers a little too short, and he had a white silk scarf carefully wrapped around his neck. In spite of a certain affected nonchalance and the fact that his nasal voice was already deepening, one could see he was shy; the son of a petty bourgeois family who was well brought up, full of conventionality, ultra refinement, acquired opinions, courteous in his speech, and totally insignificant.

The other was a Calabrian peasant. There was a withdrawn and wary effect from his round, obstinate forehead, his little, deepset black eyes, and his face with its stubbly beard. Under his overcoat he was wearing worn military clothes and he had on scuffed-out boots. He reluctantly spoke a few clipped sentences in dialect. He'd been a prisoner of war in Germany and Poland, in those deserts of snow. He'd escaped and crossed Europe on foot. He'd arrived in Italy and was finally going to his own countryside in the mountains of Calabria, where his people perhaps thought him dead.

The repairs were finished, the wheel in place, and we rushed back into the automobile. Now it seemed even narrower than before. Crowded together and soggy, we drove off. We were in the *Castelli*, and one village followed another. Everywhere were ruins, disemboweled houses, perilous walls, in those lands whose names are famous for gaiety, feasting, and wine. In the midst of these ruins, a few inhabitants wandered about in an aimless manner. They took to the side of the road that was full of holes as the machine passed by splashing water from the puddles. Dogs came out suddenly from under the sheds and doorways where they'd been sheltered and sleeping, and flung themselves barking behind our wheels.

We were on a hill. Under us stretched a flat plain where the war had stagnated for endless months around a canal, a little ditch, and a farm. Beyond, the sea appeared gray and smooth under the clouds. Presently we took a side road. We had to make a long detour of many miles because the great bridge at Ariccia had been blown up. They had started to work on it, but it would take a few years to rebuild. The country was bare at this late autumn season. A few twisted olive trees rose in the abandoned fields, sown with cardboard signs warning in English against the presence of mines. Every now and then, like wreckage from ships drawn to shore by the waves, appeared gutted German tanks, overturned there where a bomb or cannon fire had hit them, carcasses of monstrous animals left to rot, exposed to the rigors of all weathers. It was the usual spectacle of all roads and all battlefields. Some of the tanks seemed intact, with swastikas and skulls painted on the sides, their identification numbers, their mysterious initials, and all the long guns of their turrets pointed toward the sky. Others were ripped and lacerated by lipless wounds in their multicolored iron carcasses.

There they stood, temporary monuments of war, in the gesture with which death had captured them, like the figures at Pompeii transfixed in ashes. But the peasants from the neighborhood came, and bit by bit, day after day, they dismantled those heroic machines. They carried off everything they could use to mend their tools: pieces of iron, motors, wheels, bolts, screws; reducing the tanks to naked skeletons, as termites undermine and devour the royal hut of some black king and the home of the pious missionary.

These cemeteries of armor were thinning out month by month and would be swallowed up by the grain. On the slopes at Radicofani, where I'd gone at various times, I'd watched the many dozens of vehicles that were posed there in the most dramatic attitudes when I'd first seen them shortly after the liberation. They were getting less and growing smaller, reduced to a few heaps of iron. One of them had remained intact and was perhaps still there. It brandished a long cannon that had been hit at the middle of the barrel and torn from side to side, opening an unnatural mouth like a wild beast with its throat slashed by the bite of another wild beast stronger than itself.

"We shouldn't spend the night here," the student whispered to me. "They tell me there have been three holdups already this week."

"Jesus, Mary, and God preserve us, what are you saying? . . . Three holdups!" cried the woman with the jewels. I looked at her out of the corner of my eye and I saw her hiding her face as if to protect herself under the blanket.

Finally we were back on the main road below Velletri. There we saw in front of the ruins of the railroad station the last of the tanks, pushed against an old, crooked billboard, with an arrow pointing the way through that desolate and muddy desert to the "Tavern of the Mathematician."

It was now warm in the automobile, behind the glass that divided us from the driver and the tattooed sailor. After a few more curves we entered the interminable straight length of the "Fettuccia" highway that runs directly across the Pontine Marshes. The rain had stopped. It was a hogback road, sticky and slippery, and stretched out of sight between monotonous fields.

The priest must have opened his little basket, as he offered bread and cheese to the women. I heard them slowly chewing for a while like animals in a stable. Then, when they had finished their snack, I realized from the regular sound of their slow, snuffled breathing that they had fallen asleep one by one.

The student also seemed to be drowsing. The Calabrian peasant sat upright watching the countryside with wide-open eyes and a blank, rigid face, as if he were absorbed in obscure, painful, hostile, unsociable thoughts. Beyond the glass the driver and the sailor smoked one cigarette after another, exchanging words I couldn't hear. The motor made a monotonous and deafening sound, although we were driving slowly to avoid skidding on the smooth macadam that was slippery from the rain.

On the right ran a canal swollen with greenish water. The fields around us all looked alike, vast expanses covered with water and reflecting the livid color of the sky. The breakdown of the power plants and suction pumps had brought back the old condition of the marshes; aquatic birds and malaria mosquitoes flew over them in swarms.

On the left rose bare, steely mountains, covered here and there on their crests by desolate villages, cyclopean walls, and shreds of gray fog driven before the wind. Nobody was visible at the thresholds of the broken-down huts in the midst of the flooded fields. Now and then on the road we met a frightened flock of sheep, the motionless shepherd looking at us and the dogs busy.

At the sides of the road were a great many automobiles, trucks, and *camions* that had crashed against tree trunks or against fragments of curbstones, or had turned over in the ditches or plunged headfirst into the canal.

This straight and slippery road was fatal for the convulsive traffic of these months because of defective machines, rusty steering gear, and rotted tires. How many times I had seen this same spectacle of broken and abandoned machines on the roads of Europe, which haste, anguish, and terror had overrun? I had seen the roads of France literally paved with the most undreamed of means of transportation; worn out, shattered, as if the machines themselves had sensitive nerves and could not bear the tension of those uncertain days of flight. I had crossed the whole country in a taxi, as I was now crossing the marshes, and I had found everywhere the same mechanical hecatomb. My first experience had been on the roads of gentle and orderly Touraine, with hills populated by miniature castles with graceful turrets and pointed slate roofs, the color of the soft and uncertain sky, and of the cool waters of the Loire. It was the first of September, the eve of the war, and the announcement was expected from hour to hour with varying courage and contradictory emotions. The machinery was in motion. Men and gestures no longer counted, except for custom and appearance, neither did heroic deeds that hadn't been accomplished, nor the feeble bellowings of the premier, "The Bull of

Vaucluse," nor the official pronouncements, nor the radio appeals. Fate had turned on its heavy hinges and everyone was alone in front of the dark mystery of that iron gate that was swinging open.

A wave of fear invaded France, like a tide that cannot be arrested. It was the "September Fear," the preventive fear, the first of those waves that later for years and years were to run here and there like insane bolts of lightning. Autumn had descended over Tours, over the cafés on the squares, over the ancient pavements and the little peaceful streets around the cathedral. A light, cold rain fell at intervals, with the first shivers of the wind (as it did now in the marshes), when one knew that the Germans had entered Poland, and voices spread the news that Paris would be evacuated and that in the next days the government and the Supreme Command would take refuge at Tours. These voices were more or less false like all the other thousands that were born at every moment, like lost fantasies of fear and hope. But the panic was real. One could see it like a factual presence on people's faces, in their movements and the sound of their voices.

The soldiers reported to the mobilization centers with faces like the dead, and with the disgusted mien of men who, contrary to all reason and with supreme boredom, are preparing to die, to die for nothing, to "die for Danzig."

At the monstrous and formless idea of war, everyone seemed to have been seized by a visceral nausea, like a man who is still on shore and already feels the seasickness of the future tempestuous voyage at sea. In Paris, crowds assaulted the stations to flee who knows where, to find refuge, and above all hide themselves from an obsession. Invalids, the dying on stretchers, young people, women, old people and children, entire families crowded for hours and hours under the roofs of the platforms. They trampled each other in the crush. The most agile got into the cars through the windows or climbed on the roofs, fighting savagely for a place in the lifeboats of that insensate flight. In this way terrified fantasy created for the first time, needlessly, what would become the forced reality of the coming months. The aged joints of society creaked. Everyone closed themselves up like hedgehogs, saddened and offended at the inevitable injustice. Only the functionaries resisted this pressure without fear, apparently insensible to collective terror. They were sustained and rewarded by the natural increase in authority, comforted by bureaucratic sadism and the roseate thoughts of its future triumph. The Luigini of France didn't let the opportunity escape them, they wouldn't miss one stamp, one signature, one paper, one residence permit. Posters appeared on the walls of the city with little crossed red, white, and blue flags and nicely printed letters that still had the smell of the Revolution about them. All strangers were ordered to leave the Department within twenty-four hours. All requests for delay and all protests were defeated by Military Necessity and Reasons of State. One could go wherever one wished in other zones. But there was no means of transportation, as the trains and buses were requisitioned for mobilization and forbidden to civilians. I met women with little children who had been thrown out of their houses by zealous landlords, who didn't know where to go and wandered sadly around in the rain.

Then I found a taxi, a big old shaky car like the one that was carrying me to the South today, and with women and babies we started for Brittany. This was one of the many journeys I made by chance means with unknown people on unknown roads. The countryside opened before us, green, feminine, and deserted, wrapped in the vague morning mist, not yet touched by the reveille of war, asleep in its soft curves in a warm bed in a dream of peace.

But in the sulky villages, lines of peasants in their blue shirts waited sadly in front of the municipal offices to get their kepis and guns, and even then at the sides of the wet roads we came on the first automobiles overturned in the ditches.

And I saw many more some months later when I fled in another car with other chance companions from Paris when the Germans arrived. It was an uninterrupted forest of scrap iron, as though we were in a river and were forced to follow its course, its rapids, and its eddies, prisoners of its waters. In front of us and behind us through the night, lost in the distance, a whole people was in flight on the road to Bordeaux by all possible means of transport: automobiles, bicycles, tandems, tricycles, wagons, carts, motor carts, vans, old cabs out of abandoned sheds, anything that would serve to leave home and the invader behind. Every break- down, every stop arrested the column for miles. We proceeded slowly, in jerks, with frequent pauses. People on foot or on bicy- cles, bent under their packs, got along faster slipping by obstacles or walking on the edge of the fields. The automobiles advanced overloaded, their roofs covered with thick layers of mattresses and of every kind of valises, pieces of furniture, bird cages, pots and pans, toys, and dogs.

For a while, in the midst of the forest, there was a funeral hearse in front of us. It was painted black, with torches, wreaths, and golden angels, and on the top a cross shaking with the pace of the horses. It came from Belgium and had traveled days and days. It had gone through Normandy among troops in flight, had crossed Paris, and was now on its way to Spain. A family of Flemish burghers were in it, pink and fat men, huge, blond, and full-blown women, and children holding balls, dolls, hoops, and rocking horses in their arms.

Perhaps this hearse with its angels, cross, and rocking horses would end up in a ditch at the side of some unknown crossroad. I left my chance companions at Bordeaux during a bombardment and never saw them again.

A few days later I looked out of the window at Arcachon where the gulf was planted with stakes like an underwater vineyard. Strange migrating birds were crossing the sky, airplanes of every kind in their flight toward the west, small tourist airplanes, big an- tiquated machines, and the last one with its stubby wings painted red, like a fish lost in the sky.

A friend called out to me from the street. "Come down at once," he said, "the Germans are entering the city. . . . We must leave. I've found a taxi and I've come to get you . . . there's no time to waste —"

In that confusion the only thing that stayed on its feet and tri- umphed was the police. We couldn't move without a permit. We'd have been stopped at the first roadblock. Fortunately this time the commissioner was a friend, and what counted even more, a man of good sense. He gave us a pass for the center of France, for Lot-et-Garonne, where we wanted to go to a friend's castle, as though we were two honest farmers "on farm business." It was summer. Cool brooks ran under the blaze of the sun, the thatched roofs shone, and the fields stretched out easeful and indifferent in their great, peaceful, noonday siesta. And from afar came the crowing of cocks, solitary and pathetic in the heat. The war seemed remote, nonexistent, a word in another world. But at the side of the road between the grass and the hedges there were from time to time the over-turned cars. And soon after, in this illusory Arcadia of sun, meadows, and shady woods, men dressed in black shot out like arrows on their black motorcycles across the road in front of us. They wore black helmets, black leggings, black gloves, and their skull-like faces were half concealed behind black masks; dreadful apparitions, the first heroic and monstrous heralds of the distant, advancing armies.

Those were the first journeys. But how many more had followed later on, in how many countries, and with what unknown companions.

The monotonous "Fettuccia" highway tied all these images together in a vague accumulation of names, countrysides, lands, and men — the vineyards of Carcassonne under the towers of the castle; the mirrors in the enormous cafés of Beziers, where one talked of bullfights; the lady who hid her jewels; the mustachioed mechanic who wanted to cross the demarcation line with false papers; a dawn among the baleful ruins of Leghorn; a storm after the carnage in the hills of Casentino; a kitchen fireside in a farmhouse near Arezzo where they had just slaughtered a hog; an automobile radiator smashed against the soft earth of a bank; a night at bombarded Foligno in the room of two sisters, simple peasant prostitutes, with the stove burning, their knitting, and the little oil lamp lit under the Madonna over the head of the iron bedstead. And the faces of all countries changed by destruction, disorder, and war, which appeared more foreign and newer because they had

once been familiar; and the inside of gutted houses open to the indiscreet sun; and chance meetings, and the natural friendliness of
strangers; and the people who walked in the midst of ruins on
paths in the wood, with valises, handbags and laundry baskets,
pails of water, bottles of milk, leading a child by the hand; and a
man who stops to look with a questioning face — infinite glimpses
of infinite destinies outside us and within us, without known limitations, except for a fragile image that escapes in the wind of the
journey's course.

Driving on, we had reached the end of the highway under a
high, gray mountain. Already we found ourselves on a wide,
straight street, with houses on either side that were most of them
bombed, running now and then into squares with crumbling
fountains and the fragments of statues of men without hands and
arms. We passed in front of a great building, perhaps a temple or a
theater, with a solemn portico of peeling columns and badly
chipped steps. At the end of the street we saw the sea. We were in
Terracina. On the single, long street there was nothing but ruins.
And yet in the midst of them moved a busy crowd. Men and boys
approached us at the entrance to the town, coming out from every
home and doorway, inverting their thumbs to make the sign that
showed they had gasoline to sell. At every door under the beams
broken off by the bombardment there were little repair shops.
Everywhere on the streets one saw mechanics straightening twisted
iron or stretched on the ground working under motors or inflating
tires with a foot pump. The street was filled with parked cars getting new supplies, heavy trucks with their high, closed cabs, and
drivers who rested, smoked cigarettes, and superintended the
loading. Crowds of people were standing in front of rooms that
had cracked walls and propped-up ceilings. They were cafés with
improvised counters piled with mountains of ham sandwiches,
machines for *espresso* coffee, and on wooden shelves nailed to the
wall, bottles of beer, liqueurs, whisky, gin, rum, all the precious
merchandise of the war years.

We stopped in front of one of these cafés and got out. Our
driver carried in a package and spoke to the bartender. Then he

came back and went off with the machine, saying he was going to fill it up and he'd be back in a few minutes. And the sailor with his bundles hurried on some business of his own. I entered the café that was full of people and noise. One wall was half covered by a big fragment of broken mirror. The others were full of cracks. On the floor, in the corner, and against the walls, were stacked valises, sacks, tire covers, and empty bottles. A numerous public jammed in front of the counter. The men were wearing boots, wind-breakers, and berets. There were truck drivers in overalls, mid-dlemen, youngsters in rags, old women wrapped in black shawls, and painted young girls with provocative smiles.

This was the place to stop and change halfway from Rome to Naples, the posting station of the great artery that had replaced the railroad, had grown behind the armies and, all by itself, still tied the North to the South. Everybody had something to sell or to barter, to transport; some deal to arrange, some affair to conclude. All was merchandise, the means of life, in an excited, active, myste-rious, and dubious atmosphere like that of some secret society with incomprehensible rites. Time passed rapidly and these opportuni-ties might not last. The town was almost destroyed but the automo-biles went through it like a river that deposits fertile mud on its banks.

The townspeople set themselves up as improvised mechanics and merchants, as if they were on a new frontier at the edge of the prairies. A few months before there had been nothing but rubble, ruins, and desolation. But there were the Emporiums of the Pio-neers, where one could find all the essentials, those elementary things whose value had been rediscovered: eating, drinking, women, money, and merchandise. In the cafés these ephemeral pioneers understood one another very well. One did not know where they came from. They arrived, left again. They labored at carrying their loads, with their minds full of calculations, obsti-nately pursuing their fortunes and their lives.

A bare-footed fisherman came in with a basket and offered me some freshly caught fish, but they were already sounding the klaxon outside and I was in a hurry. We jammed ourselves back into the machine and left the town. Then I noticed night was beginning to fall. In the gray twilight we drove along beside the almost invisible sea. The black outlines of the mountains were lost in the blackness of the sky. The road twisted in curves and bends as we approached the coast or went farther inland in that ancient borderland of the Kingdom of Naples. Every now and then some old houses appeared, abandoned outposts of customs guards and soldiers of the pope. Our headlights were on and the mountains disappeared in the shadows, and our eyes followed the holes in the road and the stones at the edges.

After the stop, my companions were wider awake. I heard the priest and the women murmuring something about where they would find lodgings in Naples. The student lit a cigarette and started asking me a few questions, the most futile and insignificant ones, like an inquisitive, ignorant, and bored boy who didn't know how to pass the time and didn't even realize the shame of his own foolishness. And I answered patiently.

He wanted to know how much my shoes cost and where I'd bought them, whether I preferred English or American tobacco, what kind of house I had, whether I found it more convenient to eat out or at home. I saw him little by little getting near the point where he'd be asking the question that the small village bourgeoisie ask each other by habit when they meet on the square, as I'd heard it so many times every day at Gagliano:

"What have you eaten today, Don Luigino?"

The boy was made from that same dough, from that same blood. And already the process of coagulation and dessication had started in his young brain, in which every idea is reduced to the conventional, to a cliché, an arid habit in a desolate desert of boredom and arrogant self-sufficiency. I therefore waited for the question about my supper, and I was already looking forward to enjoying it, like winning a bet, like the last brush stroke that would complete the portrait I was making of him, like the white lead highlight a genre painter puts on the shining nose of his beggar or his bibulous priest. Instead of that question he asked another that was nevertheless in a way its equivalent.

"You're a journalist," (I'd had to tell him that before), "directing a democratic newspaper, a newspaper of the Left," (a shadow of angry fear and obsequious disgust colored the words "democratic" and "Left"). "I wonder what you think of Guglielmo Giannini. I'm sure you hate and despise him and that you won't even want to talk about him, or who knows how many bad things you'll tell me about this enemy of yours. Do you know him? Have you ever seen him?"

I answered, naturally, that my ideas were very different from those of that sympathetic demagogue whose ephemeral star seemed to have risen to the crest of the firmament in these days. But that, although he was an adversary, I considered him a most deserving person; that I thought in spite of appearances and his obvious mistakes, he was performing a useful function in extracting the poison and virulence from his Fascist followers by means of his primitive liberalism and his good-natured and clownish anarchism; that I only knew him by sight and I therefore liked to believe that in private life he was most honorable and respectable.

My answer had an extraordinary and unexpected effect on the student, as though a bomb had suddenly exploded. He turned and looked at me stupefied. I saw that my moderate words had thrown all his preconceived ideas into the air, and also the rules to which he was accustomed. It had displaced something of his rigidity and crystallization and especially it had contradicted his need or mania or miserable delight in persecution that supported at the roots those rules and crystallizations. The student was still so young, so ingenuous and shy that he didn't try to hide his stupor, but rather let himself be invaded by it and expressed it openly.

"But . . . I didn't believe . . . I thought you were enemies and that you couldn't possibly talk of one another so kindly. . . . I thought the democrats, those on the left, were more fanatical, so to speak, that they didn't respect the others. . . . It's the first time I've ever heard anybody talk this way —"

Yes, a new idea, a gleam of truth had entered his mind. From that moment he looked at me with respect and regard as if I were a strange and somewhat mysterious being, and he stopped asking me questions.

It was now deep night. The landscape had become wild and solitary among the desolate black mountains with their irregular and disorderly outlines. The road wound upward in many curves in a rough and obscure gorge, bordered by uncultivated land with only a few twisted trees and naked rocks on it. We drove slowly; something in the motor wasn't functioning, and the sound was sputtering and irregular. On top of the hill, at the dark entrance of what seemed to be an abandoned village, a tire collapsed with a whistling lament. We were at Itri.

We had to wait here for a long while. There was no light in the village. An icy wind cut down from the ravine. The houses crowded near one another as though they were defending themselves against an invisible enemy. They looked like the inhospitable ruins of a fallen castle, or the nests of wild birds on a rock.

This wild and bombed-out hamlet was also, like Terracina, a posting station, a ring in the improvised chain that led to the South. But it was evening now and the day's traffic had ended. Only a few latecomers adventured on the street. The houses were almost all in ruins and their windows were barred. The driver and the sailor, knowing this place well, went to find a mechanic friend of theirs, and then came back with him and a lantern to begin working. I started to take a walk among the houses and climbed the slippery pavement of a steep alley between walls with loose and perilous stones. A reddish light from oil lamps filtered through some of the doors that were half open to let out the sharp smoke. Old women wrapped up in black rags were stirring kettles of thin soup. Black figures with black hair were huddled around the fires like gypsies around a camp. As I went by and stopped to look around out of curiosity, someone would come to the threshold and, without answering my greeting, eye me with a mistrustful and dark air. The empty sockets of the windows and the jagged profile of the ruins against the sky had the same hostile air. A bristling atmosphere seemed to hang over the village like a baleful spell. A dog barked angrily and others answered him from near and far in the shadows. Then, when silence had returned, a screech owl cried out in the sky. People say mistakenly that the chant of this bird, and of his elder brother, the marvelous gray owl, herald angels of the Last Judgment, is a prophecy of death. It has become familiar to me, and I had waited every evening for it to start over the jail of Mantellate. I looked for the birds from the window of the cell until I could see them, small and black, cloaked in the cold whiteness of the moon, perched in a row, three, four, five, on the dark wall of the roof, watching the prisoners from up there and launching in freedom their nocturnal call into the silent air.

For a long while, half an hour or longer, I walked through the ruins, until I heard the sound of the horn and hurried down to the automobile. The motor was working better. They had taken it apart, cleaned the carburetor and changed the spark plugs. One of the travelers must have complained of the slowness of the trip because the driver opened the glass that separated his cab from us and made a lengthy defense of his machine as he drove. It was the best on that route. Yes, we were late, but we'd left late, the road was wet, and it was better to drive carefully than to slide into a ditch. Two excellent tires had gone flat, but that was nothing on a highway full of stone, pieces of glass, holes, nails, and scrap. And besides, the worst was over and we were almost there. It was eight o'clock and we'd be in Naples by ten at the latest.

This speech calmed everyone and they started to doze off again. But now I became impatient. I imagined the fine, wise face of Uncle Luca on his pillow, and his old yellow dressing gown. I wanted him to be alive and to speak to me. And perhaps that was what he was wishing at this moment, while I was being delayed with these strangers on these slow, anguished four wheels. Still we were getting nearer, one yard after the other, climbing and descending on the road that never seemed to end, between bare fields and black, solitary villages.

I didn't want to think it was too late, that my voyage was useless. I imagined what Uncle Luca and I would talk about. Perhaps for the first time I might remind him of those childish pastels that he had certainly forgotten.

While I was building up these fantasies, I was absently watching the light rain falling on the dark disorder of the countryside. Wrapped in my overcoat, closed in by my thoughts, indifferent to the world outside, I let myself be carried on like a branch by the current of a river. I had scarcely noticed that at a point just before the fork at Sparanise there was a barrier closing the road. A bridge farther on had either not yet been repaired or had been carried away by the rain. We had to descend to our right by one of those rough, bumpy detours that had been hurriedly dug by the monstrous Caterpillar tractors behind the first advancing troops.

We went down slowly into a narrow glen with a grove of oaks on either side. We were moving almost at walking speed, shaken by the uneven ground, when something appeared in the beam of the headlights between the grass and the bushes. I don't know whether I saw him first or first heard the sound, but it was a man and he was shooting.

Everything happened in a second. He stood facing us behind a low bush. From there he had started firing at us, aiming directly at the people. Then he stepped forward out of the bushes and was now on my side of the car not more than two yards away.

The sound of the successive shots was very familiar to me. They were like a sudden, dry slap. I could see him clearly through the glass in the door. He was short, thickset, and powerful, with the round head of a peasant, a long, black unkempt beard on his cheeks. He wore an ugly, old, black hat with the brim pulled over his eyes, a black jacket, and short trousers. From the knees down his legs were wound with white cloth tied with a braided cord. He was a brigand, a true, classical brigand, with the body, the face, the costume and hat of a fairy-tale brigand, but nonetheless real, ferocious, present, with his weapon in his hand. That was the only thing I didn't have time to distinguish precisely. It was a long, dark object that he held to one shoulder and that spouted red flashes at every shot.

The image of peril, the strangeness of the adventure woke me suddenly from the fantasies to which I had abandoned myself. And immediately I felt myself invaded by that clear sense of coldness

and lucidity, the absolute lack of emotion that fortunately
for me comes over me whenever I find myself in a difficult
moment. It may be a paradox, a reversed form of fear, or a simple
and physical nervous reaction. And actually, what credit is it to me
that the heart continues to beat calmly, the hands don't tremble,
the eyesight becomes more acute, the senses tuned, the memory
entirely present and open, the thoughts clear as serene, winter
mornings, and everything becomes easy, instinctive, and calm,
with so unnatural a calm that I myself feel it with both hilarity and
disgust?

I saw the brigand shoot at two paces, as clearly as an apparition
in a dream, and in some sort of stagnant compartment of my
mind, I was astonished and laughed because he was in every way
the identical, childish, and popular picture of the brigand, with
the pointed hat, the black costume, the blunderbuss . . . but was it
a blunderbuss that he was shooting, or a machine gun, or a big
pistol? Who knows? I caught myself thinking in spite of myself
that this similarity had something miraculous about it, that the art
of the people is the repetition of a plot in which what seems to be
real coincides magically with what is real, that the brigand is a
brigand if he looks like one, and that you only have to know it to
be safe from him. But these absurd thoughts (that I confess here
with pretended shame) did not prevent me, on another level, from
feeling that my companions were all the prey of surprise and fear,
and that naturally, whether I wanted to or not, it was up to me to
act for them. I saw that the driver, terrified and uncertain, was
abandoning the wheel. I grabbed his shoulder through the
opening and shouted:

"Go on! Go on! Don't stop. Quick!"

At my order he pushed down the accelerator mechanically,
the machine jerked over the uneven ground and speeded ahead.
The brigand, left behind, continued to shoot, and was lost in the
darkness.

Now the road went up the other side of the narrow glen. I noticed that the glass of the door I was leaning against had been
pierced at the height of my shoulder and pieces of it were scat-

tered over my sleeve. We climbed the hill for two or three hundred yards and came out onto the big highway. We were safe. If there weren't any other bandits posted farther on, we had escaped the ambush. My companions were already shouting with relief (we hadn't gone more than some twenty yards up the road) when a flame leaped up from the motor. We stopped immediately and the headlights went out. The driver got down in a hurry, burning his fingers as he opened the hood, pulled off his raincoat and jacket and threw them over the motor to smother the flames and prevent an explosion. The red and blue light that was shooting up around him vanished, and we were in absolute darkness. The bullets had perforated the gasoline tank and the motor in many places. The tires were intact because the bandit had been aiming at the level of a man's head. What could we do? We opened the doors and got down on the road.

Then I noticed it was snowing. Small stinging flakes whirled in eddies in the wind and melted when they touched the ground. There was the smell of snow, gasoline, and scorched wool. My companions were all crowding in a dark group beside the machine. Nobody was hurt. It was so dark that one couldn't see two steps ahead. None of us were armed. If the brigands had reached us, we couldn't have defended ourselves. We had seen only one, only one had shot, but probably there were others with him in the underbrush. If they noticed the silence of the motor and found that we had stopped, they wouldn't hesitate to come and attack us. And whether they were many or few, or even only one who was well armed and, as we had seen, without scruple or regard, we couldn't escape. I told the others I thought we ought to get away from the machine without wasting time, taking along the baggage that didn't have to be untied, and, hiding in the fields, wait there protected by the darkness, then return to the automobile if the brigands didn't follow.

This was the most reasonable thing to do. But I gave it as advice, not as an order, and realized that they couldn't follow it easily. They were all still paralyzed by fear and, along with fear, by the terror of darkness and an irrational attachment to their possessions. The driver looked despairingly at his motor. He and the sailor were already figuring the cost of the damage. The priest had been fingering his valise that was tied behind the car, feeling with his hands in the darkness for the holes from the bullets that must have hit it.

"Your suitcase saved us from the last shots, Father," I said, but he wasn't consoled. The woman with the jewels complained like a child. At the idea of having to move she seemed about to faint into the arms of the priest. The other woman wept, the student kept walking around me in a daze. The only one who seemed calm was the Calabrian peasant. He was quiet, and it wasn't clear what he intended to do.

Since nobody moved, and I couldn't leave them there like that in confusion, I stayed with them. I sat on a curbstone at the side of the road and waited. Who could tell when we would arrive in Naples? We were now in the hands of fortune. I asked myself how late it was and realized with pleasure that I had no watch, and that the old paternal machine would not fall into the hands of brigands.

The minutes passed very slowly as we waited for something un-pleasant and disgusting to happen that we couldn't avoid any longer, when, from the direction of Naples, we saw headlights. We strung ourselves in a chain across the highway. A huge, white automobile with a round radiator and no running boards ap-proached at high speed and stopped in front of us. The driver, a young man with a red mustache, leaned out questioningly. We all circled around him, pointed at the burned machine and shouted: "The brigands! The brigands!"

It was as though he had heard the devil mentioned. As swift as lightning, and without answering, he threw his car into reverse and turned around, leaving us on the road, and retraced his route in flight, disappearing into the dark. We were left disconsolate, lis-tening to the sound of his motor growing fainter as he went farther like a fading hope, until complete silence returned.

More minutes that seemed extremely long passed. It was cold. The snowfall was thicker and started to settle, white on the ground, when, as gay as the light of dawn, we saw far away in the sky beyond the brigand's glen from the direction of Rome the glow of a line of headlights approaching. There must be many cars driving together for protection, as one often did in those days. Perhaps the bandits hadn't dared attack them. Here was the first one emerging safely from the road through the woods. But it didn't stop for our signals, and escaped at high speed. Then came the second, third, and fourth, almost together. They too grazed us without taking heed of us and went on. Behind them, slow and heavy, came an enormous red truck pulling a trailer. It sparkled with splendid round and triangular red lights. The truck stopped. Our driver took courage and showed his cunning. Winking his eyes and twisting his foxlike face, he asked us to keep quiet by moving his finger over his mustache, and whispered:

"Leave it to me! Don't you mention the brigands or he'll run off too. . . . Quiet now," and he stepped forward.

From the driver's cab of the truck appeared the wide good-natured face of a mechanic, one of those calm faces, sure of themselves, that you have confidence in the minute you see them. Then the door opened, he got out and stood in front of us. He was a giant, one of those enormous truck drivers you find in American films and on the highways of the North, a kind of solid cliff to which one can hold on. He came toward us, big and athletic in his overalls, and asked us briefly what had gone wrong. He was a Roman with an Olympian face and a lock of black hair over his forehead. The owner of our car was hanging around him with a thousand cajoleries like a little dog around a great Saint Bernard. I heard him explaining that our motor had caught fire, that we couldn't move, asking him at least to tow us to the next village. The truck driver gave one look at the machine and grumbled his assent.

"I'll take you right to Naples if you like. It's all the same to me. This is no place for you to stay. The roads aren't very safe."

Our foxy little driver winked at us to keep still, while the other one, calm and slow, was getting a rope and a hook out of his truck. The two of them attached the grapple to our bumper and I noticed the feverish movements of our driver's hands, who couldn't wait to leave, since the brigands might still arrive even now when we felt we were safe. He couldn't reveal his reasons to the other who was working deliberately to make the rope hold fast.

"That's all right, that's very good. We can leave now," insisted the little one while the big one was not convinced but would have liked to fasten the rope even more securely. At last, with God's blessing, the truck driver climbed up to his seat and we dashed to ours faster than soldiers called by an alarm. The truck roared, a cloud of smoke came out from under the wheels, the rope tightened and, dragged like a derelict, gently and happily we were off.

We were hardly in motion when the passengers, as though suddenly freed from an oppressive weight, relaxed with sighs of relief, in exclamations, shouts, and bursts of laughter. Their faces smoothed, they waved their hands around, they took deep breaths and, excited and hilarious, they all talked at the same time. The journey now became as gay as it was dreary before, and the company as sociable and loquacious as they had been somber and taciturn. They were happy and proud of themselves.

There had been an adventure, a great adventure, one of those stories one could often retell, rare, almost incredible. Since it had ended well they felt they were heroes, and congratulated themselves and their destiny. Then too they considered themselves subtle, tied together by a pleasant conspiracy in deceit, because they'd kept still to the truck driver about the existence of brigands. They decided they wouldn't say anything until they got to Naples; and that it might be better to keep quiet even there. Perhaps they felt particularly virtuous since they were manifestly protected by fortune.

"A miracle! A miracle! It was certainly a miracle, a miracle from heaven!" they said, wondering in loud voices how it could have happened. There surely had been a multitude of bandits and very ferocious ones. How was it possible they hadn't jumped on us and stolen everything we had? Nobody had even been wounded and the wheels were whole! If they'd punctured our tires we'd still be exposed to assault there on the road. Indeed we would have been stranded in the bottom of the glen and never have come out alive. Could they have believed we'd succeeded in escaping?

They must have noticed that we stopped. Perhaps they thought we were armed? Or perhaps they saw the headlights of the approaching machines before we did, and were disturbed in their terrible plans? The passengers went on discussing and analyzing until they lost their breath. The owner showed us a piece of iron from the motor pierced in two places, and we passed it around from hand to hand examining it as though it were a holy relic. What excited them even more was the hole in the glass beside my shoulder. It was as round and regular as a coin.

Moving around, turning, twisting in that narrow, crowded, dark space, lighting matches and clicking cigarette lighters, they searched under the seats and among the packages on the floor for the bullet. Judging from the hole, it should have drilled me from side to side. But to the general disappointment it was impossible to find it. Perhaps it had ricocheted out, or dodged into some inaccessible hiding place. The hole, the undiscovered and innocuous bullet, the crumbs of glass on my arm struck everyone as the most miraculous fact of all. This now gave them a pleasant shudder of fear and heroism. I confess that I, for one, would have liked to find the bullet. And I kept thinking about the strange fact that in all those past years of blood and civil war, death had never come so near to me, physically, and that I had never looked so closely into its face as now. Perhaps this time, in deference to fate and the absurd, death had chosen the shape of anarchistic revolt, like the magic mask of a savage warrior, the dark and serious face of a poor peasant brigand.

"It's been a miracle, a miracle of the Madonna," said the owner, turning his head around from the driver's seat. "I had the car blessed this morning, this very morning, with holy water, just a few hours before we left. This is the first trip after the blessing. And this morning I put a picture of the *Madonna del Divino Amore* up there too," and he pointed to the figure pinned over the windshield. "It's She who saved us."

Nobody doubted there had been a miracle, but opinions differed as to who had performed it, or at least as to who had interceded for it. The presence of the holy image should perhaps have

put an end to all doubts, and it certainly made a big impression on
all. But the woman with the jewels, fingering her necklaces and
bracelets to reassure herself of their presence, shouted in a stridu-
lent, throaty voice:

"It was Teresa who performed this miracle . . . I saw her myself
. . . St. Teresa of the Holy Child, my own little saint, the saint of
roses. . . . It's certain . . . when that black face jumped up, I saw
I was lost . . . I said, 'Mamma Mia, this is the last moment of my
life' . . . I closed my eyes and the saint appeared to me, smiling
in the midst of roses. . . . She's always protected me . . . she's my
saint. . . ." And here she set her big, painted lips in lines of ecstasy.

"She's granted me favors ever since I was a girl, before I married
my first husband, and she didn't allow me to be a widow for long—"
and here she started in to tell the story of her first husband who'd
been a *commendatore* and a holy man. She told us how he'd died
and how she'd married again, and now she was separated from her
second, but that she was very well off because, thank heaven, she
had money of her own and was handling her own affairs. She knew
how to live . . . the man was yet to be born who could cheat on her
or put her in a sack . . . and many other things that possibly concerned her private life rather than the little saint of the roses. But
where Teresa had intervened in the most explicit and indubitable
fashion was during an illness of hers a few years before, and she re-
counted at length its symptoms and course.

She'd had salpingitis. She'd had many attacks with fever, pains
in her belly, and complaints of all kinds. She'd had every sort of
cure: douches, injections, diathermy. She'd even gone to the waters of San Pellegrino. Finally she'd gotten into such a bad state,
only skin and bones, in danger of peritonitis, that everybody had
given her up. Then one night when she couldn't sleep and felt
like dying she remembered her patron saint, implored her protection, and by the next day the pains had stopped, the fever had
gone down, and a few days later she was so plump and rosy that,
she shouldn't say so, but that actually men turned around as they
passed her on the street. This time, too, there was no doubt at all,
it had been her saint.

"Perhaps in your case, Signora," said the owner. "I won't deny that . . . but for the machine and for the rest of us, let's not waste another word, it was the Madonna. What more could you want than having been blessed shortly before and having her image along with us. I can't wait until I get back to Rome to commission a fine picture or a solid silver statuette, and carry it as a votive offering to the *Madonna del Divino Amore.*"

The sailor agreed with his associate. He too believed the Madonna had saved us. As to the saints? They were all good. And he had nothing against Teresa who was certainly most powerful and who had perhaps protected the signora from the final shots that had been aimed at them from behind and had perhaps lodged in the reverend's valise or in the other baggage. But without any question the most powerful of all was St. Nicholas. He had tested him in a thousand storms at sea where all seemed lost. Even that time when his oil tanker had been torpedoed and the naphtha caught fire on the water, and a great many of his companions had been burned or drowned, while he himself clung to a board for twelve hours between Tunis and Sicily before they came to rescue him. St. Nicholas, there was a saint for you!

The sailor faced us and lifting up his sweater from his chest he showed us, in the light of a match held by the student, a picture of the saint on the dark, hairy expanse between his stomach and his navel, tattooed in blue and bestowing a blessing. On both sides of the saint were boats with big, unfurled flags, and the inscription "Royal Navy." Farther up, halfway between the nipples, almost hidden in the shady forest of black hair, the Madonna sat upon a cloud, and over her crown and halo was a band with the inscription, *"Ave Maris Stella."*

"Fine piece of work. It was done by an artist. This is the Virgin of the Sea," said the sailor, touching her with a finger. "And this is St. Nicholas, the first of all saints. . . . Don't you agree, Father?"

The priest, questioned thus, got out of the theological dispute with diplomacy. He didn't mention miracles, avoided comparing the power of saints, and said that Divine Providence had surely wanted to protect us after having first put us through such a hard test. What seemed to be more deeply on his mind were the bullets in his valise. He asked us if we really thought the valise had protected us and whether or not it had been hit. It was a pity he couldn't get out and have a look. He feared a disaster might have occurred since it contained a little flour . . . just a little bit . . . and then there were some little cans of oil in it . . . if the oil has leaked into the flour, you know what that would mean! Well, there was nothing to be done, one could only have patience and trust, and he hoped that since we'd all been so providentially saved, his poor valise wouldn't be the only thing to suffer from our terrible adventure.

While we went on talking and arguing during this slow ride, undisturbed by the sound of the motor, the truck that was towing us slowed down and stopped. It was a road block at the entrance to a village. We were surrounded by *carabinieri* who came from all sides out of the black depths of the night, with their white belts and shoulder straps, guns over their shoulders and flashlights in their hands. I've never been able to find out what these road blocks were good for, whether to hinder smuggling that was after all indispensable and necessary, or to make it more profitable to smuggle, by adding a touch of danger to it. These were the days when the bandit Giuliano, an unknown peasant, carried a sack of wheat on a bicycle into an isolated village in Sicily, and killed among the prickly pear trees the first guard who tried to confiscate it. At the same time immense mountains of all kinds of merchandise were being calmly transported hither and yon on the big highways in spite of laws and controls.

This new encounter provoked in my companions, if not the mad terror of the other one, a minor but plainly visible discomfort and agitation. Evidently the machine carried not only the priest's flour and oil. The travelers became dumb, with preoccupied faces. They made themselves seem small, to avoid attracting attention, so as not to be scrutinized and searched. I thought that the Calabrian and I were the only ones who weren't carrying anything illicit and could sit there with a peaceful conscience, were it possible not to feel somehow guilty faced by those representatives of the state, by their warlike disguise, their firearms, their divinely in-expressive faces, and their ritual of blame.

The guards were examining the truck driver's papers. A few snowflakes fell in the icy air. I signaled one of the *carabinieri* to come closer and told him about the attack, so that they might save other travelers from the same experience. He wasn't astonished by my story and said there had been various attacks in the preceding days, and he called the sergeant who came up and asked me to re-peat the details and describe the scene. Then he said with a pre-occupied air that he'd report it and do all he could but that they had too much work and couldn't be everywhere, and he went off into the dark calling his soldiers and ordering us to be on our way. In this fashion, thanks to the brigand, we avoided opening the valises, and once more Divine Providence had protected us, and this second ugly encounter had also resolved in the best of ways. But what anxieties are necessary to save life and possessions, and that little bit of hard-earned wealth!

As we drove slowly down the road, our spirits were relieved and gay, freed at last from worry and fear. After my companions in various ways and with various exclamations had congratulated one another on escaping from danger, the conversation turned back to saints and their miraculous power and to the private lives of each traveler. After what had happened they all now felt united. They had no more secrets and they were fired with the desire to tell the most intimate things. The sailor, who came from Apulia, told of his voyages to distant lands; the woman with the jewels informed us that she was born in Forli, but had lived in Rome ever since her first marriage to the *commendatore*, and that she was obliged to make frequent trips for business reasons. She had a house in Rome and one in Naples, but the nature and purpose of these houses remained obscure; the fate of her second husband also re-mained a mystery although she talked of it for a long time. He had disappeared suddenly, but it wasn't quite clear to us whether he had fled for love, for business, or for some small reckoning with justice. Over these mysteries fluttered her protectress, the saint to whom she never ceased proclaiming her devotion as she kept adjusting her red fox around her neck. It was she who presently started to question the woman who shared her seat, calling on her as a witness to the virtues of Teresa.

I then heard, for the first time since we had left, the voice of the other woman and I was amazed because its violent and youthful tone did not at all correspond to her sad and old appearance. It was the voice, inflection, and pronunciation of a *vasciarola,* of a washerwoman of the slums of Naples, used to standing on her threshold and shouting constantly to the neighbors and children in the tumult of the street. It was one of those voices that starts out from the first syllable at top pitch and full power, and maintains itself on the same level of inflection, dropping only at the very end, as though every word were a shout calling out to someone very far away, from one end of a deserted valley to the other.

"St. Teresa of the Child Jesus," shouted the woman, "if she would only help me too. I've made a vow to St. Rita, St. Rita, so that she'd help me find my son again, that poor boy. I've covered Italy and I can't find him. I've been to Leghorn, Florence, Bologna, and Milan; I've been everywhere. Now I'm going to Padula, to the internment camp. They say I may find him there. It would have been better if I'd never borne him.

She had been so silent before, so mute, wrapped in her own secret, jealous of it and hiding it, that she now unburdened herself with greater freedom, abandoned herself more completely in this speech that was like a shrill, monotonous lament for the dead, a desperate and visceral cry.

"I'm telling you the truth," she said. "I've never spoken about these things to anybody but you're like brothers to me. I talk to you as though I were talking to my brothers. This son of mine, Antonio, is my eldest. I made him when I was just fifteen years old. He's a fisherman and a sailor, as lovely as a flower. When the Germans came he was in the submarines. The bad kind got hold of him, they took him along to the North with the Tenth MAS.

Torpedo boats, with those bad people and Commander Borghese. Everybody said the commander was like the devil, he was worse than the devil, he killed the poor things, gouged out their eyes, and didn't even respect the priests.

"But not Antonio. He wouldn't have hurt anyone, he's a good boy, he's his mother's son, the son of my bowels. . . . And he can't be found anymore. Look here, just look how lovely he is, my poor son —" And she took out a photograph of a young sailor in uniform from the canvas bag she held on her lap, and also another picture where that same Antonio was dressed like a fisherman standing in the middle of six other boys and girls from five to fifteen years old. They were all brothers, her seven children, she said, as I looked at the picture in the light of a match. She also wanted me to see her identity card and her marriage book where the names of her seven children and the dates of their births were entered.

"Look here, won't you have a look?" she went on, holding the book open as though it were a precious text. "Everything's in order — legitimate. . . . What difference does it make if I'm the daughter of 'Unknown,' that I haven't an education, that they didn't even teach me how to sign my own name? . . . I brought them up myself, those seven children. . . . I took the bread out of my own mouth . . . and he, the first one, so lovely and big, was already helping me, and those bad people have taken him away."

I saw from the book, to my astonishment, that the woman, Grazia Jannilli, born Butrito, wasn't yet forty years old. She was of Sicilian origin, she told me. She'd been born in a village of the interior, in the region of the sulfur mines. She didn't know who her father was. She'd been brought up by an aunt at Torre del Greco, and had become Neapolitan that way.

"When I was twelve I was already a woman. At fourteen everybody wanted me. But I was childish and only wanted to play and to laugh. I said no to everyone, even a sergeant of the *carabinieri* who wanted to marry me, and another one too, a gentleman, who had wanted me absolutely and who went away because of his disappointment. I didn't want to get married because I still wanted to play. Then the one came along who was later my husband and I said yes right away. To my misfortune I said yes without thinking for a moment, who knows why? I was convinced, my head was full of him, and a lover's spell is worse than a witch's.

"He was the best-looking boy in Torre del Greco. When we got engaged, the girls and the old gossips were so angry that they made the sign of the cross upside down. Then he started to make me babies, one a year. . . . Look, the little book says so. . . . Seven are alive and two died when they were small. He shipped off to sea, traveled, came back home, and I made another baby, then after a while he started to get tired of it, and was furious and said I was making too many, and he beat me and stopped sending me money. And yet he was earning a lot, he was a waiter on board. Finally he didn't come back to Torre del Greco, he had set himself up with another woman but I didn't know. I went to look for him in Genoa and he took me to her house where he was living, saying he lived there because it was cheaper. And she received me in her house and started to give me a song, but she had it all mixed up. She said love changes but you've got to let him fly away. Then I understood the whole business and I told her in Naples we say it different. And I gave it to her right, that song: that if love changes, the one who's unfaithful's got to die. . . . And I should've done it, but I didn't. My husband gave me a thousand oaths and kept me from it, and so I went back to Torre del Greco by myself. Later, during the war, he died at sea, and I had to keep my seven children from going hungry all by myself. I can make nets and help the fishermen. We live all in one room, but nevertheless there's never been a day without its piece of bread. And now, if he's alive, I must find Antonio, and the saints ought to help me."

"My name's Antonio too," said the Calabrian, as though Grazia's story had touched his heart with the sound of something recognized and familiar, and had waked him from that sort of hostile, painful, and diffident daze in which he'd been plunged before. "I also am called Antonio and I've returned. Also your son will return. Also I can't write, the same as you. I'm young, but I don't know whether Regina, my fiancée, has waited for me. . . . I don't know a thing. . . . They think I'm dead. . . . I don't know whether there's any work at my village or whether I'll find my sheep. I'm a shepherd and I've had a hard life but never like in these years. There's things you can't tell. I've been in accursed places where the Lord never passed. Your son couldn't have been in worse places, nor with worse people than those who commanded me. It was really bad . . . they made the blood come out of our eyes . . . they made us eat the garbage like pigs and do labor like mules and tortured us like Christ on the Cross. The people died like mad dogs, they had no bodies left, only skin and bones, not even a voice to complain with. You can't say those things . . . your son can't have seen worse ones. . . . And yet, as you see, I'm here and I'm on my way home. You can see that my saint, my St. Antuono, held his hand over me while I was in the middle of those devils. . . . Also your son, if he hasn't harmed himself by offending the Christians, St. Antuono will bring him back.

So it was that, undefended and unprovided for, armed only with the name and the very certain but supernatural power of the saints, men and women went about on the streets of the world, driven into a time that was not their own.

Besides, St. Antuono, the St. Anthony of the peasants, is more than a saint. He is an ancient divinity of the earth, full of a powerful and ambiguous mystery. He is the tiller and herdsman of Christ. It was St. Antuono who first cultivated the earth and domesticated the animals, and taught for the first time those unchanging arts. He was also the inventor of fire, a saintly Prometheus that no eagle can wound on the rock. One day there was no fire for Christ's supper and Jesus told him to look for some. Antuono went down into hell and stole a firebrand from the devil, brought it to earth, and the supper was cooked. From that time forward fires were lit each day under the kettles in the houses, and in memory of this thing that happened at the beginning of the world, on his saint's day big bonfires rise on all the peaks of the mountains and in the village squares.

He also invented the packsaddle for the asses. One day he went into the forest to bring wood to his Master, Jesus. But how could he carry it home when there was so much of it? He had with him an ass, who until then could do nothing but bray and kick out. Antuono slipped two green branches of a tree under the skin of his sides and they were immediately transformed into a packsaddle, the first that had ever been seen. In this way he carried the wood to Jesus.

He domesticated, protected, and healed the animals. He himself, one can say, was half man and half cow. He remained for a time in the shape of a cow so that his fiercest enemies, the devils, would not recognize him. Once he was carrying images of Christ and the Madonna, and the devils with a thousand cunning wiles wanted to steal them from him. Antuono, disguised as a cow, went out into the countryside carrying the images with him. He went into a cave and hid them at the bottom. As soon as he came out, his friend, the spider, wove a gate with his thread and closed the mouth of the cavern. The devils who were looking everywhere passed by and saw the gate that was shining with the silver of the dew and thought that nobody had gone within. Only a cow, and one could see the tracks, had stopped there shortly before to browse in the grass. Thus they did not enter the grotto, they were fooled, and the images were saved and are still there.

Every year, on his feast day that falls on the seventeenth of January, the peasants too, as the shepherd told us, disguise themselves as cows. They put on white undershirts and long, white drawers, cover their faces with white veils, hang a tail on behind, and ribbons of all colors. Only one is dressed in black and he is the bull. They all gather in the square, mooing. Each of them carries around the neck or in his hand a huge bronze bell. Ringing their bells and mooing, the flock of peasant-cows, followed by children, the sucking calves, climb to the chapel of the saint on the mountain and make the round of the sanctuary three times to be blessed. Then they descend into the village and for a whole day one hears the mooing and the sound of bells and firecrackers, until night comes, and the flames on the mountains, and fireworks in the winter sky. So true a saint does not abandon his peasant flock.

One cannot count the wearied mules and lame horses that Antuono heals every year. One cannot count his miracles.

"A neighbor of mine, a boy who was called Nicola," said the shepherd, "had gone to gather wood. The weather was bad. A big rain came and thunders and lightnings. To be quick and get home Nicola didn't go in the big woods. He made his faggots in a little woods around the chapel in a hurry, and down he comes with his load on his right shoulder. He got home, wet everywhere, threw the faggots on the floor by the fire. And right then he couldn't move his neck anymore. It stayed twisted like his bundle of faggots was still against it. His mother was frightened. She asked him: 'Nicola, what's the matter? Where did you get that wood?' Nicola said he'd taken it, because of bad weather, from the little woods of the chapel. 'That's the saint's,' said the mother. 'Take it back right now.' She picked up the wood, put it back on his neck, and pushed him outside, and it was the time when even the wolves are so cold they come out of their holes and nobody trusted himself on the roads. It was luck that did this, that Nicola climbed to the sanctuary, left the wood on the ground in front of the chapel, and hadn't even put it down when his neck turned straight and well. And if he hadn't done it, he'd have been twisted all his life."

While we were talking we drove quietly over the road at the slow, even pace of the truck. We'd already passed Formia and its lugubrious ruins, and the distant lights of Gaeta, crossed a temporary wooden bridge over the flat banks of the Garigliano, that had been so fiercely contended, and climbed up and down through a vague stretch of country among grape vines and olive trees toward the Volturno. It had stopped snowing and the north wind was blowing and drying the road. One could see a star through a rift in the sky, and of a sudden, between the clouds, veiled by shifting brightness, the timid moon.

Perhaps at this same hour the poor brigand of Sparanise was hiding from the pale light that sifted through the branches like a human glance as he squatted in the shadow of a bush in some thicket, or some cave in the rocks, all one with the trees and the animals, strained to listen for rustlings and the voices of wild animals, breathing the smell of wet earth and grass. He must be concealing in some lonely convolution of his mind the desperate rage and anguish of a life that was decadent in our time but that perhaps in another time and among other men would have been a powerful and yet equivocal nature. Was it the same nature as that of the earth spirits, of the peasant saints and devils, the same as that of St. Antuono? In such a nature, is there any distinction between man and animal, between man and plant; where the sun, the rain, the forest, conception and death, the entire world that surrounds us are one with the man who lives like a tree, plants his roots in the soil, flowers, bears fruit, and, in his own time, withers away? Good and evil abrogate one another and mingle alternating in the vicissitudes of day and night, in endless seasons and ineffable presences.

One day at Matera many years ago I met an old man at the threshold of one of those cave dwellings dug in the clay of the Sasso Carveosa. He was a visionary, tall and upright for his eighty years, with a big, white mustache and a long, black cloak. He rose at dawn and looked fixedly at the sun, and in that sphere of fire he saw the future.

"The Deluge will come," he told me. "It will come very soon, for everyone, for the whole earth. . . . Within me, it has already commenced." He added that not everyone would die, some would save themselves, and that after the Deluge many things would return that now seemed lost, and that outlandish people, evildoers, and brigands, would appear in the heavens, like angels.

"Because," he said, "everything is double. All the saints are demons."

We crossed the Volturno in the light of a moon that appeared and disappeared behind the clouds, and we drove through a ghostly countryside full of high trees and shadows. The plants and the leaves looked as though they were coming toward us, like slender human beings twisted and bent forward, hoping to reach the level plain. Naples was nearing us and we already felt its presence, and the thoughts of my companions turned to their arrival, to what they would find when they got there, the business deals, the miseries, the necessities, the weariness. They started to talk of life in the city, of the thousands of ways the poor devise in order to exist; of the thievery, the black market, and the daily cunning.

The student, the woman with jewels, the sailor, started to tell anecdotes that everyone had heard before, but were nonetheless true. The stories of drunken colored soldiers whose bodies the Neapolitan street boys passed from hand to hand, selling them like any other kind of merchandise; the tales of ships that had been unloaded right in the bay without anyone's knowing how, or that had actually disappeared; or about the life that went on after the war in the deep caverns that had been used as shelters; of the pimps, the prostitutes, the resourcefulness of pickpockets, and the markets for the most unbelievable objects. The woman with the jewels mentioned thefts and warned me to be careful because I wasn't familiar with Naples. They stole everything right under your eyes. They leaped on moving automobiles and made their getaways, carrying off baggage and spare tires. It was enough just to set a package or a valise on the ground for a second, and it had already disappeared, heaven knows how. It seemed, she said, that they used containers with double bottoms. They knew all kinds of ingenious tricks. They'd come by with a little bag of fleas and throw them on your jacket. Then they'd tell you that you've got bugs on your neck, and while you turned around to catch the bugs they'd make off with your watch or your wallet. They even succeeded in stealing the hats from people's heads without getting nabbed. A young man comes by with a basket on his head. Inside it a little boy is hidden who quickly snatches the hats.

"They even know how to steal the shoes from your feet," said the student. "One of them says, 'Would you like to have a fine pair of American boots? Just exactly like the ones that soldier is wearing? . . . Two thousand only . . . it's a deal . . . want them? . . . Wait here and I'll let you have them right away. . . .' If you say yes, the boy will approach the soldier and offer him, *sotto voce*, a young girl, a dark-haired, fourteen-year-old girl as lovely as a flower. 'Come with me and I'll bring you to her.' They go into a house,

and when they're on the stairs the boy points to a door and says,
'She's in there. Her name's Concetta. But you mustn't make any
noise because her father and mother are there too. Take off your
shoes and walk on the tips of your toes. Then knock at the door.
Concetta expects you and will open it. Go on, I'll wait here for
you.' And he's off, taking the boots to his customer."

They told these stories and many others of the same kind, with
gratification and a trace of pride. They were part of the now classic
and established legend of the ingenious and quick-witted poor of
Naples, the penny epic of a subterranean world that was daring,
fanciful, without illusions, miserable, and yet full of resources in
the daily fight against hunger. This shifting rabble was cautious,
active, and shabby. These people in rags, these good-for-nothings,
street urchins, and picaresque beggars had not only a legend of
their own but a king, a true king, the King of Poggioreale. It was
the sailor, who knew him and perhaps had done some business
with him, who told us his story.

The King of Poggioreale was not a mythological figure. He really existed. I'd heard about him and seen pictures of him in the
newspapers. He was a rather stout, pale man with yellowish flabby
cheeks, lively, fanatical eyes, filled by a black fire of cunning and a
strong will. He was above all a king. His house at Poggioreale was
a palace with a throne room and a real gold throne, where he sat
when he gave audiences to his subjects and the dignitaries of his
realm. The walls of the salon were decorated with great portraits of
Victor Emmanuel II, of Umberto I, of Victor Emmanuel III, and
of his son Umberto, now a mere Lieutenant of the Realm, and of
himself, Giuseppe I, the real king. His wife was the queen, and his
sons the princes. He had a court and his ministers, which he, as a
monarch by divine right, named according to his own indisputable caprice, and revoked at will. When he was receiving he always wore a crown on his head. And always, morning and evening
and perhaps even at night, he wore a kind of vest with the cross of
Savoy in a royal coat of arms embroidered on it.

He was as rich as the sea. In a few months he had earned bil-
lions. He had bought land with this money and rented it at a low

price to laborers who were out of work. He also bought palaces in town where he let the families of his poorest subjects live for a modest rent. He had also acquired splendid automobiles with gold handles. He ordered his royal doctor to attend the beggars who were sick, and the old, the ailing, the feeble. Then he made them get into his open automobiles with their golden doors and drove them to the Via Caracciolo, to the Riviera di Chiaia, and Posillipo, so that they could benefit from the pure sea air, away from the usual stuffiness of their alleys and basements.

Giuseppe had become king by his wits and not by birth. He'd been a very poor junkman and had a rag shop in an alley behind Toledo where he lived miserably. His name was Giuseppe Biscaglia, the same as the owner of the great Biscaglia department store that everyone in Naples knew, but he wasn't a close or distant relative of theirs. He was the son of poor folk and lived alone, hardly earning a living. One day, many years ago, he met a lovely, dark-haired girl at the market. She was buying linen at the counter, and as soon as he saw her he fell in love with her. He took off his hat and asked her why she was buying tablecloths and sheets.

"I'm the right age," said the girl, "and I'm preparing my trousseau."

"And have you found a husband yet?"

"No, but I'll find one," she replied.

"You have already. Tomorrow I'll come and wait on your father."

The girl's parents were rich merchants of Bagnoli. Giuseppe borrowed a black suit and a carriage and presented himself to his future in-laws as the son of his namesake Biscaglia, the department store owner. Of course he was received with open arms and the two old people agreed that they would go the next day to settle everything with his father. They came to Naples and while they were hesitating in front of the big department store, an elegant young man came up to them and asked them what they wanted. When he heard they were going to visit Signor Biscaglia, the young man obligingly pointed at the windows of the apartment over the store, and added in a confidential manner that he wasn't sure they'd be received, since the signor was beside himself with fury, having had a frightful scene with his son all night long because the boy seemed to have fallen in love with a middle-class Bagnoli girl, while his father wanted him to marry a very rich princess. The husband and wife looked at one another, thanked the young man for his courtesy, and decided it was wise to put off their visit to another day. In the meantime, Giuseppe, with his black suit and his equipage, was back in Bagnoli while his in-laws were still standing in front of the store. And he abducted the girl on the pretext that he was taking her to his angry father, but when he had climbed into the carriage he carried her to his basement full of rags. Then he said:

"I'm not the son of Biscaglia. Everything I have is these rags. But if you'll stay with me I promise you that you will become a queen." The woman stayed, and Giuseppe kept his promise.

The war came. Don Giuseppe started in to trade, first in a small way, then larger and larger. He found work for everyone: the poor, beggars, gangsters, fencers, pimps, prostitutes, stevedores, pickpockets, people without skill or profession, those who'd been bombed out of their homes, the resourceful, and the miserable, all those human beings who needed a living and had no one to help them. They worked honorably with soldiers, merchants, and speculators. They worked in the squares, the markets, the streets, and the port, by night and by day. The town was half destroyed, the factories closed, but they got on.

Don Giuseppe became king and his wife queen. He was beloved by his people and had an immense power. In Naples nothing was done against his will. It was he who arranged the election of the mayor, his own creature, and of the other functionaries as well.

"Of course," said the sailor, "that's the official city government. As for his own, he puts it together the way he wants it. He has a Minister of the Navy, who is charged with reporting the ships that come into port and what's good about their cargo, you understand what I mean. The Minister of the Interior keeps up his relations with the police, and aids the subjects who have gotten into trouble. The Minister of Industry and Commerce keeps track of the market for tobacco, canned goods, watches, and all such, including the women and everything else too.

"Sometimes he's quixotic about his nominations. He's capable of making ministers, or at least undersecretaries, out of poor devils who don't know a thing, that are perhaps even a little bit touched in the head. There's one, they tell me, who's really a fool. But the king says he's a good boy and a devoted subject and protects him. He's also got him a special privilege such as you couldn't imagine, because Don Giuseppe's human and kind-hearted and knows you have to take care of the helpless. Two months ago they changed the Commissioner of Police in Poggioreale. The old one was wise to the situation but the new one was a stranger and nobody knew what was in his head. The commissioner arrived at his house the first day with a wife and a beautiful new automobile. He left it outside and the five tires vanished, the four on the car and the spare. The commissioner gets in a fury, goes to the king and says:

"'Your Majesty, hand over those tires, and quick!" The king started to laugh. 'What do I know about your tires? Aren't you the commissioner? . . . Go find them yourself. It's a big world . . . you'll have to go a long way to find them.'

"The commissioner realized he'd used the wrong approach, and changed his tone, asked for the king's help in getting them back and that he'd show his gratitude.

"'Favor for favor,' said the king. 'I don't know a thing about your tires. But if you're to find them home again, you must consent to something. It's a just thing and will cost you nothing.'

"'I'm at your service,' said the commissioner, and shook hands on the bargain.

"'Look at that subject of mine,' said the king, pointing out his feeble-minded protégé. 'He's a good boy, but he's not too bright. I even tried naming him Undersecretary of War, but he isn't even good at that. He's really out of luck. He tries, but what can you expect? He's not fast enough . . . he hasn't any agility. He tries a few jobs, but they catch him, and he spends more time inside than outside. Now he's got to live, don't you think? Now Your Honor must consent to let him work on a trolley or on the street twice a month, only twice, not more. Two small jobs, of course, watches or wallets, things of little value, enough to live and to keep his hand in. . . . Do you agree to it?' The commissioner gave him his word, went home, and found the five tires waiting for him at his door."

But the greatest undertaking of the monarch of Poggioreale, the sailor went on to tell us, had touched the heart of the whole city a few months before, and could only have been accomplished by him. It was his by right. Wasn't he perhaps the most commoner-king, the foremost worshiper of the most commoner-saint, the one whose saintly blood boils twice a year as a sign of good luck, the one whom the old women address with the affectionate *tu*, and curse out of love?

The treasure of San Gennaro, an incalculable amount of gold, was taken to Rome during the war to save it from bombing or plundering. And it had remained there. Nobody would bring it back. The government wouldn't undertake it. The roads were much too unsafe and full of brigands. There weren't enough soldiers to escort such a precious load. But what brigands would dare to touch or interfere with Giuseppe Biscaglia, that human and transient king of the beggars? Supplied with the necessary formal papers, the sovereign left for Rome in his automobile of the golden doors, covered by flowers. The treasure was consigned to him and, secure and fearless, he crossed the countryside sown with bandits, bringing the gold untouched to his people, to Naples in triumph. "I was there to witness it," concluded the tattooed sailor. "Feats like that won't be seen again."

In the legendary shadow of kings, saints, brigands, and beggars, the last stretch of the road before we entered the city flew past. We drove down a long, straight, tree-lined road and crossed the streetcar tracks, then coasting along the big wall of the royal palace of Capodimonte, we plunged into the descent between high houses into streets that at this late hour were almost empty. The woman with the jewels looked about anxiously, turning around to the rear window as though she feared some winged street urchins would descend in the night from the sky to steal her valises tied on the roof. We turned into long, half-dark streets and came into a wide, shadowy square surrounded by ruined houses. Here the truck stopped in front of a garage that was closed by an iron lift gate. We had arrived.

The truck driver got out and, as he leaned against the side of the automobile, he noticed the hole in the glass of the window. The owner then told him about the brigand of Sparanise and the attack. The truck driver put his finger through the hole, examined the door with the look of an expert, shook his head, and said one word:

"Miracle."

While the garage was being opened, the student left us in a hurry in search of a late streetcar to take him home, and the Calabrian shepherd went with him. The others stayed in the machine to wait at ease while their valises and packages were being assembled inside the garage. I remained alone on the sidewalk, my briefcase in my hand. The stone slabs were loose and shining, full of puddles from the recent rain. The sky was overcast, and a wind with a hint of snow in it was blowing. I didn't know in what part of town I'd landed. In a side street I saw the lights of a restaurant, its shutters half closed. I walked toward it and was received by the bow of an obliging and tired waiter who was piling the chairs on the tables. And I went into the deserted place.

12

THE RESTAURANT WAS ABOUT to close but the waiter nevertheless hurried to invite me in and offered me some supper. The first thing I did was to ask for the telephone and I called Uncle Luca's house, my mind in suspense for fear there might be bad news. Mariona's voice, as she answered at once, fortunately sounded aggressive and gay.

"At this hour?" she said, chiding me. "Couldn't you have come earlier? . . . The professor's doing well. . . . I was frightened yesterday, but the crisis is over. He's not asleep yet, but I'm sure he'll be able to rest tonight. Don't worry. I'll give him to you now."

I sighed, cheered and reassured, and told her I'd come to see him tomorrow morning, since fortunately there was no reason for urgency. I knew that their house was very far away at the outskirts of town, that there wasn't a guest room, and if I'd gone immediately Mariona would have given me her own bed and Luca would have lost hours of sleep to stay up with me. And now here was his voice on the phone, ever so slightly more deliberate than usual, with the shadow of a gasp between his words, but as always sonorous, penetrating, and deep. He greeted me with a father's tenderness and solicitude, he asked me about my journey, my work, and my health, as if he were the strong one and I the invalid. It distressed him, he said, that I'd been inconvenienced, that I'd come from Rome to see him and must have left some very important business. He'd be happy to see me and to talk to me, but all the while he never stopped apologizing.

"Old Mariona telegraphed you without asking me. I'd never have given her permission, and now she's brought you on a useless journey. She's a good woman, but as you know she's an hysteric and wants to do everything her own way. One must be patient with her, but I'm sorry you've been inconvenienced. I've had a heart attack, my blood pressure's a bit high, the arteries are hardening a little, but I'm perfectly well. Apparently it's not yet time to carry me off to the devil."

Luca used this jesting tone and these familiar expressions to reassure me because he was concerned about me and my peace of mind, since he was always the wise doctor who cures the ills of others; and he had also the natural, deep, and instinctive reticence that goes only with genuine things, with genuine emotions, that puts them beyond reach, protecting them with a veil, both delicate and strong, like the tender kernel within the shell of a nut. I realized how sick he must have been from the affectionate care he took to hide it from me. I imagined those moments when one feels the heart beating with an anxious and interrupted rhythm in the most remote parts of the body, as though that rhythm, outside its own confines, had invaded one entirely, hastening with the anguish of unexpressible pain toward black silence; like a watch whose mainspring is about to break and that races, unregulated and insane, marking with violent speed the last seconds of a nonexistent time; and then, of a sudden, stopping.

Luca reassured me again about his health and asked me to come to see him in the morning.

"I'll annoy you with a little chatter," he said, "if you have time to listen. I'd like to discuss many ideas with you that you don't know about, and that I've been thinking in these years when we haven't seen each other. 'The Theory' has enlarged and has become enriched by experience. One might say, if one can talk of completeness in these matters, that it is concluded. Day by day I have written down a thousand detailed observations, but I would like to arrive at a series of systematic formulae, to arrive at a law. Perhaps, if you want to, you could help me with that."

Luca interrupted himself a moment, perhaps because talking was tiring him. But he went on:

"You can' know, because you are young, how beautiful life becomes as one approaches death little by little; how it increases and is illuminated in each of its smallest details with truth and with reason. At a certain moment when death is at one's back, one seems to be walking through a world made up on every side of infinite truth. To an analytical mind these truths are really infinite, having no end, and one labors in vain to search for them all, one after another. They are like a varicolored crowd of people whose common language and common nature one does not know. Even so, however, with only a disconnected and partial vision, how beautiful and filled with life every object and human being seems! But as we approach death we learn to distinguish the common nature of man in superimposed layers of time and in the tangled thicket of the world; and the great circle that binds and circumscribes the infinite individual destinies, the infinite phenomena. Thought is no longer bound fast to one point, to a single object, but departs from that object and expands in waves without limits. It is like climbing a mountain when the horizon widens beneath us at every step. It may well be that when we arrive at the top the horizon will be so vast and so distant that it will merge completely with the sky, and that will perhaps be death.

"If this be so, we live in order to die. The Christians say the opposite, that we die in order to live; but isn't it perhaps the same thing? Good-bye, my dear, come tomorrow. Good night, my dearest."

I hurriedly ate what the waiter had brought me, and asked him where I could find a room in the neighborhood to spend the night. "Leave it to me," he said. We were near the railroad station where there were many hotels, but it was difficult to find a room. He telephoned in vain to many of them, then he offered to accompany me because we would find something only if we looked ourselves. We went out into the night together and made the rounds of five or six hotels. Everywhere there were signs in both Italian and English reading NO ROOMS. We were told there was nothing free, not even a bathroom or a cubbyhole under the stairs. I started to wonder if I'd have to spend the night walking the streets. The waiter, who was following me half a step behind like a puppy, said to me:

"It's difficult to find a place in these big hotels. Most of them have been bombed and almost all the others have been requisitioned by the Allies who've forced themselves in everywhere and only left us basements and tumble-down shacks and eyes to weep with. The few hotels left are always crowded, they're filled to bursting. But if, Excellency, you'd be contented with something more modest I'll take you to a clean hotel where they know me and they'll make a place for you. For one night you might put up with it. Perhaps in the company of some other traveler, some fine gentleman. Their customers are all men of honor. It's only a few steps from here."

This proposal didn't please me too much. But I was tired and I'd even have slept on a chair. Besides, how many times in these years I'd had to share a room with chance companions who left early in the morning before I woke up! I followed my guide, driven by necessity and also a little by the desire to oblige him. We turned down a narrow street beside the station and went into the doorway of a big house that looked like a tenement. There was no sign on it to show that it was a hotel. We crossed a dark entry, with only an empty porter's cage in it where a little lamp burned under a crucifix, and we came to a small courtyard crowded with pushcarts. It looked like the bottom of a well, surrounded by four very high walls, like huge, filled-in arches, studded with windows. At the rear of the courtyard was a staircase, faintly illuminated by lights under some holy images. One of these was above the door, a shadowed print whose details I couldn't make out. It was crowned with a wreath of leaves. We felt our way up in the half darkness. On the landing at the second floor, in a glass-covered niche, was a Madonna, a great, painted, papier-mâché doll almost as tall as a human being, smiling with her little teeth, her transparent blue eyes. She was wearing a lovely brocaded gown covered with gold and a mantle that was held up by four little naked angels at her feet. The Madonna was strangely motionless as she raised her hand in benediction, and in the light of a small oil lamp the niche around her was filled with flowers, with white and yellow artificial roses, with silver hearts. Beside her there was a half-open door, and on the frosted glass was written ROYAL HOTEL. This was our hotel.

I found myself in a vast, bare anteroom with peeling whitewashed walls from which I could see through a green curtain the beginning of a dark corridor. The greater part of the room was occupied by a table set diagonally across it. Four old men were crouched on the floor around a metal brazier that still held a few almost burned out briquets. They did not lift their heads or move when we came in. Two more old men sat at the side of the table. One of them was asleep with his head leaning on his arms, the other, looking off with a sad expression, slowly shifted here and there sheets of paper that covered the table. The old men didn't seem to have noticed our arrival. They all had something monstrous or deformed about them: blind or crossed eyes, rolled up eyelids, humps, tumorous growths, or shaking legs or hands.

The waiter announced loudly that there was a gentleman who wanted a room for the night, and one of the old men around the brazier lifted his head, got to his feet, and came toward me. He was of medium height, strong-limbed, wearing a dark-blue wool sweater and a long jacket with raveled edges. In place of a face he had something shapeless. Under his low forehead, between his sunken eyes, a deep, vertical scar like a ravine ran all the way to his mouth and divided his nose in two parts. Each one of these two noses completely occupied a cheek and almost reached to his ears. The noses were composed of an intricate series of little valleys, cavities, and protuberances, like a mixture of varicose veins and bowels, or rather, of the convolutions of the brain. It was really as though the brain, divided in its two hemispheres, had run down through his nostrils and had been stuck like a mask over his face, but instead of being gray, this double brain was pinkish, violet, brown, blackish, and, in certain spots, even green. While he was getting up I'd asked him if there was a place for me, and then as soon as I saw him I regretted having spoken. But the old man with the two noses was already answering me, asking me to wait a minute, that he'd go see how he could best accommodate me, and pushing the curtain aside, he disappeared in the corridor. While I was perplexedly waiting for his return I watched the slow-moving hands of the old man sitting at the table. A cold draft that came in from the cracks in the windows moved the thin sheets of paper that filled the table toward which his melancholy looks were directed. I looked at them more closely. They were all receipts for lottery tickets. The paper was almost as light as tissue paper, and of various colors. Numbers were written in ink on them, and they lay in many piles. There were certainly hundreds of them.

The man with the two noses came and frightened me with the announcement that there was a place for me. I'd be quite comfortable, since the bed was large, and the two customers already sleeping in it were both thin, took up little space, and were clean. I answered, with a certain embarrassment, that when I'd asked for a place, I'd meant a room, or at least an entire bed.

"You want a room by yourself?" replied the old man, shaking his head in a silent gesture of negation. "We don't have any. But wait . . . perhaps one flight up at the Hotel Imperial there may be one. A Polish officer left tonight. Come with me —" And he kindly made way for me.

On the third floor, in another niche full of paper flowers, a big Holy Heart of Jesus illuminated the stairs and the door of the

Hotel Imperial. A middle-aged man came to open the door. He had a little round belly, and long black sideburns on his yellow cheeks. He was without shoes and in his shirt sleeves, with suspenders hanging down from his pants pockets. As we came in he was slipping into a black jacket, as though we had waked him from his first sleep. He hesitated to answer my question about the room. He spoke privately to the old man and the waiter, and finally made up his mind, telling me I was fortunate, that by chance he had a free room, the best room in the hotel. When we were alone he gave me a police registration to fill out, and stood there watching me with a very strange face, half sardonic, half fawning, like something between a barber and a pimp, as though he were waiting for me to voice some special desire. But alas! I didn't say a thing. When he saw I'd written on the form: "Profession, journalist," his yellow face opened in a smile.

"Journalist?" he said. "Then you must know Giannini. What a man he is! He made a speech in Naples last Sunday. You should have heard him. He puts them all in his pocket — ministers and politicians. There's a man who knows what he's doing."

Without waiting for an answer he started volubly to talk about the Polish officer and his woman, who, luckily for me, had left an hour before. He took my bag and went ahead of me. We crossed a twisted corridor full of "Liberty" style consoles with vases of artificial flowers, and conch shells with historical pictures carved on them. A mixture of noises of all kinds came through the doors of the rooms. They were joined and drowned out by the continuous bass of snoring in different keys and various parts. We reached my door. He invited me in and said:

"This is the Pole's room. It's a jewel. There's nothing missing. . . . There's a jug of water. . . . It's a real jewel." And he left me.

I was in an exceedingly small, narrow, and high room, with no space for anything but a bed and a jug and basin on an iron tripod in a corner. And that's all there was. The ceiling lost itself in an immense distance toward the sky. Perhaps it seemed higher because of the smallness of the room. But that unexpected lack of proportion gave me the impression that it was tipped to one side, putting the ceiling and the floor where the walls should have been, like a wrecked ship floating on one side in the water.

The measurements of the bed were also reversed from the normal. It was short and very wide, so short that I had the impression that one's feet would stick out, and so wide that three or four people could have slept in it comfortably without touching one another. The lack of proportion was so strange that I started to measure to make sure. It was less than nine hand lengths long, and nearly fourteen wide. This deformed bed occupied almost the entire space, leaving only a narrow passage to the walls on three sides. There were no chairs or clothes hooks. Only, set squarely across a corner, there was a wooden shelf with an old toothbrush and a broken comb on it. Above the shelf was a colored and framed print of St. Vincent, hanging obliquely on a nail.

It seemed to me as though I had been poured into a topsy-turvy world that had confused its measurements. But I was tired. I put my bag on the floor, threw my clothes on the opposite side of the bed, buried myself in the sheets with my head flat because there was no pillow, and I plunged suddenly into sleep.

2

I got up early the next morning, awakened by nearby piercing voices and noises that came through the walls of the hotel rooms. And like a musical lament over the varied and distant hum of the city, arose at intervals the drawn-out street cry of a wandering peddler. I hurried to leave the capsized wreck of a room that was even more squalid and strange in the daylight, and passing the feeble lights of the Madonna, I went down to the street.

Coming out of the shadowy doorway I was suddenly enveloped in a penetrating atmosphere of light and motion, unexpected and extremely clear, so that for a moment I had to close my eyes to the brightness. The sun shone serene and splendid; its rays seemed to permeate the most hidden places, even the transparent shadows, and to penetrate the whole air, giving it lightness, mobility, and delicacy. Nothing was still in this limpid tissue of light, but all things interlaced and crossed in a manifold, infinite whirl, like thousands of stars rotating in their orbits and throwing out in harmonic disorder their own colors from within.

The air was cold, stirred by an exhilarating breeze that moved the sheets hanging like white banners on ropes between the windows, and carried along with the sound of voices a fresh smell of lemons, grass, and the sea. Streetcars, carriages, and pushcarts passed by, and a numberless crowd walked or paused on the sidewalks and around the kiosks, talking and gesticulating, as though moved by some common excitement that was measured and melancholy. They were dressed in rags, and enveloped in light as in the clear water of a brook. Over this harmonious whirl, this flutter of festive rags, this colorful and murmuring movement, stretched a high, cloudless sky of the lightest blue, slightly softened by gray, like a great, wide-open and fantastic eye.

I walked along the streetcar tracks on the disrupted stones of the pavement, between tall, simple houses with painted blinds waving in the windows. I felt the pungent air filling my lungs like bitter, sparkling wine, exciting and crystalline. I knew vaguely the direction of Luca's house on a climbing street over Mergellina. I could have taken some kind of transportation but I decided to walk at least part of the way, seduced by the buoyant air that carried me along like a balloon escaped from a child's hand and tossed by the quixotic games of the wind.

Following the current, I crossed a wide space where carriages with plumed horses were standing. I went down a crowded street among small cafés and street vendors and suddenly came out into a large, irregular square. It was enclosed by a varied succession of buildings: houses, ruins, walls of different heights with edges jutting out to form shaded recesses, the cylindrical bulk of towers set between broken-down shacks, and the solemn side of a great church. At the back was a monumental gate that opened its arch between two dark, gigantic towers rounded out in stone. I had arrived at Porta Capuana.

The sky opened wide over this great expanse that lay with its jagged edges like a green leaf; the light fell down over it, running freely and scattering like the water of a cascade broken into a thousand jets. At this early morning hour, in the sparkling cold of the wind, the square was already alive with people and merchandise, swarming with variety, with activity and the transactions of trade. Pushcarts stood everywhere, and stands had been set up and covered with simple wares. Here a man was spinning sugar, and the little colored candy sticks were on display; over there someone was roasting peanuts in a kettle that looked like a railroad train, and that every now and then emitted a lamenting whistle and puffs of steam. Here and there rose kiosks with festoons of green and yellow lemons that spread a wave of wintry and pungent perfume in the air, and on display were all kinds of iced mineral waters, including the sulfuric *Telese*.

On one stand I found the common peppered *taralli* rings, on others white rolls and the old-fashioned hard cookies, familiar from childhood, covered with pink and blue icing and cut in the shape of flowers, tiny roses, or a star. Farther on they were selling simple toys and balloons, and silver hearts for votive offerings. Heaps of tobacco were on display, separated for color and quality, cigarettes, cigarette stubs, and cans of peas and of meat from America. Some stands carried hardly anything, a couple of onions, toothpaste, a package of chewing gum, with a man standing behind, silent and intent.

Stands were lined up too all along the other side of the square. Here marvelous fish with glittering scales opened their mouths and widened their round eyes. White and violet polyps tangled themselves in webs; baskets with black mussels and gray clams shone in contrast to the yellow of the lemons and the shiny green of the seaweed; mullets reddened like flowers. A marine perfume of brine and waves rolled over these trophies, still lifes from the seventeenth century, where the pale, flesh color of bellies gleamed among the blues and quivering silvers, and the gray, flat bulk of the sting rays dominated a dazzling cohort of whitefish, mountains of red fish, of rock fish with monstrous cheeks, winged plumes, and crowned with thorns. The fisherwomen called me while I stopped to look, asking me to buy some of that glowing, reddish freshness. But farther on in another basket, heaps of golden fishes and the serpentine tangle of yellow and black marine eels tempted my eye, and farther still, vegetables, fruit, and herbs shone richly in the sun.

High-wheeled carts rolled through the center of the square, with their shafts painted red, and as the horses walked they shook the bows, feathers, ribbons, and bells like peasants' brides on a feast day. Children dressed in rags, their feet naked in the cold, ran here and there picking up cigarette butts, or were curled up behind shoe-shine boxes. Men and women went by continuously, carrying bundles on their shoulders and under their arms in a concentrated, isolated activity, without interfering in any way with one another. Others bought and sold, discussed and gesticulated, throwing their words and shouts into the air, that were collected and fused in a continuous hum that seemed to be a silence peopled by ghosts. In the distance someone blew a bugle, and every now and then one heard the sing-song street cries of a man with a sack who announced that he was buying human hair. An old man with eyeglasses sat at a little table and offered lottery tickets. Behind a row of empty stands, I thought for a moment I saw a man dressed all in white, leaping, singing, playing the fool.

All these faces, bodies, motions were vivacious, active, and full of life and airiness like moving particles of light that filtered through everything and spread white and delicate over the scene; and they had an ancient beauty like statues, refined by time, that seemed to have come out of paintings and encaustics hidden for centuries under the earth, with their clear-cut profiles and big black eyes. The ovals of the women's faces, at the same time classical and familiar, under their locks of untended hair, had the proud naturalness of goddesses, covered by the modest naturalness of the poor, and were veiled like a marble image. The children bending down to shine shoes, or pursuing the passersby asking for liras, moved their half-naked limbs, stiff from the cold, and their faces of little men with the spontaneous grace of a breed that had always been civilized. And the old men and women too carried the signs of their age like vagabond gods, hiding under this trembling and feeble disguise so they would not be recognized.

Everyone went swiftly on his own way, and seemed attentive and impassioned at this work, charged with bright energy and measured liveliness. But what spread this pallor on all their faces and added a febrile fire to their eyes? What gave a disconsolate gravity to their faces and gestures, a melancholy sense of awareness, like someone who knows and has tried everything and who still lives his life with the courage of a passion without hope? It was as if behind each one of these men and women, these children, vendors, artisans, and old people, as if behind this whole airy crowd shifting and easeful, there was another world that had already lived out its time in its own eternal and unchangeable law of simple sorrow, and that in that ancient and sorrowful world, people considered themselves nothing but an ephemeral ornament, a transient expression, and yet were putting all their good will into adorning it with passion and with grace, contemplating their own swift passage through it without illusion, like the splendid and tender light of dawn.

At one side of the square, between a pushcart of prickly pears and a stand with time-passing salted pumpkin seeds on it, was a small shrine with glass walls, and under a tabernacle inside, a great cross painted on a wooden panel. A papier-mâché Madonna knelt at its feet, dressed sumptuously in brocade like a queen. A Latin inscription explained that this shrine had been removed at the orders of the plunderers of the Fascist regime and had recently been returned to its old place by the interest and financial generosity of a devout woman, now deceased, and by the good offices of her nephew as well. Paper flowers and fresh flowers shone at the foot of the cross, and there hung from all sides of it silver arms and legs, silver infants, and tiny silver men dressed in the latest fashion. A little farther on between the crucifix and a church door, was the canvas of a street fair. Two caravan wagons stood close to the church wall, and in front of them some women were cooking on little rustic stoves. A small crowd of poor people and youngsters were watching a tent entirely covered by paintings of half-naked women, lions leaping through flaming hoops, and ballerinas balanced on running horses. On the platform in front of the tent, between wooden stairs on each side, before a drawn curtain that hid the interior, a barker was talking.

He was fairly young, slender, with the face of a bird, dressed in a simple gray suit, with a huge white handkerchief knotted around his neck. At his left was an old man with a red visored cap, a big red jacket with gold frogs, and old frayed pants. He held a trombone in his hand and every now and then, when the barker signaled him, he abruptly blew a few notes. On the other side was a young woman standing straight up, covered to her feet by a blue mantle studded with stars. On her head was a veil that fell over her face. The barker lifted the veil, and the pale face of a brunette with red lips and frightened eyes appeared. He pulled open her mantle for a moment, and one could see a plump body in pink tights that made her look naked, with a belt around her waist and her breasts bound in brilliant silver with blue sequins. She was shivering with the cold. The barker smiled as though apologizing for that terrestrial weakness, and let the mantle fall.

"Do you see this maiden?" he said. "Do you see her? So well built, so young, so rounded — roseate like a flower? . . . Have you looked at her? Does she not seem like a star, and smell like a bouquet? . . . Does she lack anything? Have you looked at her well? . . . Observe her once more. . . ."

He slipped the mantle from her shoulders, and made her turn around as she shivered all over, while the old man blew the trombone.

"Have you looked at her from the front, from the sides, from behind? Have you looked at her breasts, her back, her arms, her legs? Have you seen it all? . . . Does she please you? . . . Is she well built, this creature of God? . . . Very well, then! . . . This young woman you now see before you, this maiden, this virgin, will in a few instants be sawn in half, separated in two detached pieces. A saw will pass, signori, without shedding a drop of blood, through her graceful, living body, precisely at her waistline, and will saw her from one side to the other, so that the upper part will be on

one side and the bottom part on the other . . . and you can pass
your hands in between. . . . But have no fear, signori, this is not a
bloody deed, not a ferocious crime at which you will assist. . . .
The two parts will be reunited and the lovely maiden will make a
curtsy before you for your delight when she is whole again and of
one piece.

"This is not a tragedy, nor a crime, nor an evil deed, it's a
marvel. Or even better, signori, it's a miracle. . . . Yes, it *is* a miracle. . . . But not a miracle of religion, such as the saints perform,
and the madonnas, and the most holy Jesus. . . . It is a more
human miracle. The miracles of religion heal the sick, make the
lame walk, open the eyes of the blind, and raise the dead. . . . But
our miracle, which you will witness, does something else, something different, and perhaps more important. . . . It will make you
daydream. . . . Do come in. . . . This is not a miracle of religion, it
is a miracle of art. Do you want to indulge in fantasies?"

A few of the attentive and curious crowd of poor people and
youngsters climbed the stairs and went through the curtain.

"Do you want to daydream?"

I too would have liked to go in with those children, those
women, and those beggars. But time was running out.

I moved away and, passing between the two princely Aragon
towers that bore the names "Honor" and "Virtue," I entered the
city through the great gate.

In the glaring sunlight, with my hands in my pockets from the
cold, I walked slowly up a wide street with high castle walls on one
side and a church and a police station on the other. I was carried
along, almost pushed, by an excited crowd: men in dark clothes
with briefcases under their arms, and peasant men and women
dressed for a feast day who carried little bundles and the knotted

ends of napkins with gifts in them for some patron. They were all going in the same direction. Along with the crowd at the end of a short climb I found myself before the gate of the castle. It was built like a square tower, with a great clock in it, and memorial tablets of marble, and an eagle between double columns with the inscription *Plus Ultra*. This was the Tribunal of La Vicaria.

Unconsciously following that invitation to go farther, and the movements of the people, I took a few steps toward the courtyard and was immediately enveloped in a tumult of voices, shouts, calls, altercations, and weeping. Men and women pursued beadles and lawyers, brandishing registration forms, discussing, quarreling. Young attorneys squeezed through the crowd, their coattails pulled by imploring hands. A numerous group of relatives, children and women, followed the litigants with shouts, lamentations, interjections, and loud speeches, trying perhaps to awaken Justice with their uproar, and to gain her favor. Witnesses and idlers were breathlessly looking for the audience chambers, and children ran up and down. The big courtyard seemed like a coop full of squawking chickens.

I left in annoyance. I had already reached the entrance when a carriage stopped on the street and a corpulent little old man got out. He was dressed in gray, with a pearl stuck in his silk tie. His good-natured face ended in a well-tended, pointed beard. He had scarcely put his foot on the ground when the crowd surrounded him. Some dropped to their knees, others bent to kiss his hand, and they all cried:

"The Savior. Don Luigino! Our Savior!"

The great criminal lawyer allowed them to kiss his hands, to touch him, weeping as though he were a holy relic, while he advanced, solemn and slow, all a great smile, greeting and benediction. Amid applause, tears, and kisses, he made an entrance, with tiny steps, into the tribunal.

I came out and turned into a long street opening in front of me that ran straight to the center of the city. It was narrow and crowded. Between the ancient little shops with poor displays, where old women wrapped in shawls looked up from back of their braziers, there were little lottery booths, hospitals, churches, holy images. On the other side were the high facades of houses full of windows: the people walked fast and close to one another like bees flying busily in a beehive, which paused at the threshold only long enough to explore with their feelers. Although there was less light and less brilliance in the swarming air because of the narrowness of the place, they seemed to be the very same people, in their constant variety, that I had seen whirling around at Porta Capuana; men who had gone out at dawn for the uncertain and providential adventure of the day. With their intent faces they seemed to be living this one day, this morning, as though it were the last, the only day of their lives. They lived it according to the varying misery of each in a varied, yet impassioned and perfect way. They were rich in nothing but themselves, free and diligent in the unpredictable present that is as fugitive as a voice in the air, a voice welcomed as new today, but nevertheless identical with all the other infinite voices that, with the same tone of will, love, and desperation, have been heard through immutable time.

A tall gaunt man stood at the corner of an alley, with his long arms against his body. His pale face with its big black eyes under his discolored eyelids was slightly turned to one side. He wore five or six varicolored overcoats over a lightweight suit full of holes, patches, and rents. The overcoats were equally worn and frayed; he hadn't put his arms through the sleeves and they hung down one over the other loosely from his shoulders like the cloaks of the Cavaliers. The man stood still under that weight like a clothes hanger, and he looked straight ahead. He was absolutely immobile with the indifferent immobility of the dead, and his dark face with its sunken cheeks and black-ringed eyes would also have been that of the dead had it not been for the steady way he looked at things as though he were appraising them without being touched by them.

I stood watching him for a while. He did not move a hand or a muscle, but remained impassive and rigid in his overcoats, under the flowers and the lights of the Madonna di Montevergine, by the corner of the house at the entrance of the alley. It was a dead-end

street, narrow between high houses. The sunlight never penetrated here, but filtered through a crack between the walls,
through the innumerable rags hanging between the windows, and
reached the ground grayish and green, like impalpable mold.
Doors opened into that nocturnal corridor; it was like the gloomy
floor of the sea, full of stagnant, green water, covered with mud
and the decayed remains of seaweed. No sound came from it. In
the distance there were children, small and black against that
spectral background, moving in silence like fish in dead water.

I passed the motionless Cavalier and went into the alley. The
pavement was slimy and green from the humidity and the refuse.
Through the wide-open, low doors one could see images of saints
and big, unmade beds inside. In some of them old men or invalids
were still lying between the untidy covers. Women stood in the
doorways and followed me with their looks. In a corner children
had lit small fires on the floor with dry sticks and were warming
themselves over the pale, smoky flame. I walked to the end of the
valley that became increasingly darker, blacker, and more humid. A
slovenly old woman held a little girl between her knees and was
combing her hair. She saw me stop and asked, perhaps aggressively,
perhaps simply with resignation, "What are you looking for?"
Without answering, I retraced my steps and went back to the street.

On a small square with a baroque obelisk like a candle in
stone, some very small children were playing and seriously trying
to turn a rude carousel around, pushing it with their feet. Then I
saw the sides of churches and the doors of pawnshops, and faces of
women at windows, beds made of wooden slats, and old women
playing *tombola* marking the numbers on their boards with dried
beans. Children were selling their wares among pushcarts, baskets, and heaps of useless leftovers of war materials. They were
shouting incomprehensible words in the continuous movement of
the changing crowd. On both sides of the street, on stands or in
shop windows hung quartered animals on display: sheep, calves,
goats. Their bodies were split and opened wide, with entrails of all
kinds: hearts, lungs, livers, brains. There were fish, polyps, and
shells also, but mostly tripe of every variety. The tripe was lined up

on the shelves of the pushcarts, or hung up in front of the shops, white as snow or yellowish, gray, or brown, shaped like a roll, a book, a knot, a braid, a curl. Some of the pieces were like large sheets of paper with holes punched in them, others were cut in long bands like ropes: gizzards, intestines, stomachs, bowels. And along with them lay pieces of head meat and the flattened out muzzles of animals. Water was sprinkling over these entrail displays, lemons refreshed them with their perfumed light, and the whole street was covered and papered with them.

I seemed to be walking inside an enormous animal, that the street was a gigantic, fleshy bowel, the stomach of a huge fish, ready to dive down to the roots of the mountains, and I, for three days and three nights, like the ancient prophet, would stay in the fish's belly, and traverse it and follow it in its voyage to the abyss.

I thought, however, that had I been Jonah I would not have asked the Lord to release me, to be spewed out on the dry land, and that still less would I have complained, as in the biblical story, if the city and the thousands upon thousands of men who could not distinguish the right hand from the left, and the flocks that belonged to them, had not been destroyed. The men I was now meeting between these intestinal walls *did* know how to distinguish, and they had already been (who knows how often) destroyed and resurrected. I felt that I was in a true place, in one of the true places of the world.

Walking thus as in a great fish, turning into alleys and streets, I found myself suddenly in front of a house that I recognized because I had been there before. It was an ancient palace of simple architecture with a both solemn and abandoned appearance. Here the philosopher Vico had once taught a noble boy, and walked on these stone steps and on the stone floors of the great, bare rooms. Here, through the wisdom of chance, lived the master of our sages, the keen old philosopher who had appeared in my dream presiding over the imaginary tribunal. I was urged on by curiosity and respect. I could go up to greet him, to see him again among his daughters, like that time so many years ago in my timid, early youth. But what would I say to him now? Uncertain, I climbed the large staircase with its whitewashed walls, and stopped in front of his door. On the wall next to the entrance there was an ornament, a bas-relief, whether an original or a plaster copy I don't know. It was a round medallion with the effigy of a naked man on it, whose whole body was covered with hair and fish scales. This was Cola Pesce, the mythical sailor who lives at the bottom of the sea with the sea monsters, scaly too like a fish, a male siren who calls the other sailors into the abysses and devours them. Perhaps it was not without reason that the master of the house kept him on the door instead of a name plate, he who with so suave a chant knew how to seduce the young men who ventured forth on the sea of dialectics, he who sank ships covered with the sails of pseudoconcepts in the whirlpools of precise distinctions, and seized with his scaly hands rash sailors, captains, and cabin boys to devour them.

I was about to ring the bell, but while I was staring at Cola Pesce I became suddenly restless. If I stopped I would be late, and my uncle was waiting for me. I went down the stairs, driven by a kind of mania that forced me to hurry, and I didn't stop to watch a little puppet show that was performing in front of the door of the house. I looked for a streetcar and presently I was walking up the steep street toward Luca's house.

It was a modest little nineteenth-century villa with only one floor, surrounded by a small, untidy garden where a few orange trees stood dark green and somber among the bushes and weeds. The gate was open and the old dog, Dim, did not bark at my arrival, as I walked over the crunching gravel of the pathway. The door of the house was also half open. Without knocking or ringing the bell, I pushed it wide and stopped in the vestibule. From another room Mariona appeared. Before she even spoke I could see from her expression that Uncle Luca was dead.

"He was so happy last night," she said. "He seemed really well. His breathing was regular and he was in good spirits. He wrote awhile as he always did, and then fell quietly to sleep. At three o'-clock he had a very bad attack. I gave him some digitalis, but I was alarmed and wanted to call the doctor who lives in the next house. You know your uncle never wanted to consult doctors, but this one was a friend. He came immediately and stayed a good while before he went away again. The attack was over, and it really seemed as if there were no more danger and that he had completely recovered. I stayed to talk with him for a while, waiting for him to fall asleep, and suddenly, while I was straightening his pillow, it must have been about five o'clock in the morning, he passed away. Come and see him."

It is customary, perhaps for the comfort of the survivors, to speak of the beauty of the dead, to say that all of their features acquire a fulfillment, repose, and perfection never reached in life. Very rarely, I believe, does that really happen. How often have I seen the absurdity of that casual rigidity, of that extinguished serenity, like an irreparable lie, that pallid and hostile silence that is not beauty, but terrifying dreadfulness.

But Luca's face, so full of communicative power in life, was really beautiful. Deprived now of the intolerable light of his glance, and also of every mark of suffering, of every momentary reflection of things of the present, he rested on his pillow among the flowers, outside of time, as affecting as a statue. Characteristics of his youth that I had never seen in him touched his features, and family resemblances, and other more distant things, very ancient and archaic, as if all ages had united, as though he had really made that last step when everything becomes true and heaven and earth are one.

I stayed a long while to look at him, and searched for my face in his face. I thought of the death of my father far away from me, and the bitter sense of freedom that came over me when I heard about it, a freedom made of things lost, of ties cut off, of solitude, when one has nothing left behind one's back, and nothing comes from outside.

The house was full of people, friends, relatives, pupils devoted to Luca. Later his sons arrived, whom Mariona had called when she called me, but who had made a longer journey.

Mariona took me aside and said: "Last night, after the attack, when he seemed to have recovered, your uncle saw I was agitated and wanted to comfort me and reassure me. He said: 'Mariona, why are you making such an ugly face? You're really an hysterical old woman (you know how he used to talk to me); I'm very well, and we'll live together until I'm a hundred. Tomorrow I want to say many things to my nephew. We're going to have a fine discussion.'

"Then laughing, because he didn't want to frighten me, he added:

"'But if I should die, one never knows, tell him that I entrust him with my writings, and he should see if there's anything that can be used.'

"Now I want to show them to you."

And she opened in front of me a huge closet that contained hundreds and hundreds of notebooks. I took out a few at random. I knew that large, clear handwriting in which, day by day, from the beginning of the century, he had described the world, expressed his thoughts, and searched for truth. It was an immense collection of observations, of ideas, of comments on incomprehensible and now forgotten events, and on eternal things, different in style and character, from the most narrow positivism in the first notebooks to a free broadness of thought in the last. They were often confused, fragmentary, incomplete, but all were pervaded by that subterranean stream of happiness that revealed the presence of things that are alive.

When would I ever have the time and the method of reading these millions of words, patiently put down, one by one, throughout an entire life, or to discover (and by what criteria?) the parts that seemed true to me, and to make them my own, to communicate them to others? While I was reading with sad and impassioned curiosity here and there in those writings, Mariona came back and said:

"And there's something else your uncle asked me to do last night. He said: 'If I die, I would like you to give him my watch as a remembrance.'

"Now I'll get it for you." And she brought it in.

It was a gold watch, a doctor's watch, with a hand that counts the seconds, a splendid old Omega, in every way like the one my father had given me.

"Cherish it dearly," Mariona said, as I held it in my hand and looked at it. "Your uncle had it ever since he was a young man. I've always seen him with it, and it has never lost a second."

Someone had gone to inquire if it was possible to take the body to Turin to the family tomb. I heard that the sons had decided not to have a funeral but to arrange for the immediate transport to the North. I stayed for a while with them and then I left Luca's room and went out into the street.

The afternoon sun shone resplendently in the crisp sky; the cold, morning breeze had fallen, a late-summer warmth brought back the fragrance of the flowers, citrus fruits, and grasses, rousing into flight the last big, golden flies. The bay was bright with tender blues and silvery whites; fabulous islands lost themselves in a violet haze; Vesuvius was plumed by straight, lazy smoke; people had become more daring in the warmth, and ran lightly to bargains, quarrels, loves, amusements, gains. And aloof from all these things, I walked through the city, wrapped and closed in by my own thoughts.

I had nothing more to do here and didn't want to spend another night. I might as well go to the railroad station or near it, where all kinds of little trucks collected, to see if there was still some way to reach Rome by evening, in time to work at the paper as I had promised Roselli.

I walked on slowly and a little bit at random in that direction when, as I was passing the door of a house in an unfamiliar street, I heard someone call my name. It was Nardelli, an ultradiscriminating art critic. I hadn't seen him for many years. He was of a tall and elegant build, his incompletely sketched features suffering, bitter and worn by the strain of his dilettante fanaticism. He worked for a left-wing daily newspaper, and when he heard my story, he told me I was lucky, since Cabinet Minister Tempesti was in Naples and was going to leave for Rome by automobile before evening, and would most certainly take me along. I could wait for him right upstairs in the editorial offices. He'd be arriving at any moment.

I had to wait a long time among busy and nervous people in the editorial offices, a line of great, bare rooms. The lights over the desks were already lit when Tempesti arrived. He was short, stout, tough; all muscle, obstinacy, and energy, charged like a machine.

"You come along with me," he said abruptly, in an affable and imperious manner. "We'll have a lovely trip. I wanted to leave earlier but the party conference took a long time. Now let's go for a few minutes to the festival at the Floridiana, and then we'll leave. They're expecting me, I can't fail them, but we'll just stop a minute."

He stayed more than an hour at the newspaper where he had to give some important instructions. We arrived at the Floridiana late at night.

In this lovely garden, the abode of nymphs, fireflies, nursemaids, and lovers, the people's festival, organized by the party, was being held, and they had waited for the cabinet minister for some time, since it was he who must open the dance. When he got out of the automobile, he was received with applause. Everybody surrounded him, greeted him, called him by name, and pulled at his coat. He advanced with short, energetic, and resolute steps, smiling with friendliness and authority, responding to the applause, the shouts, the greetings, bestowing little brotherly pats on the back of one, giving clipped and indisputable answers to another's questions, turning and pirouetting tirelessly, like a wound-up spinning top, talking without being bored; efficient, ingratiating, and mechanical.

"Wait for me here," he said hurriedly. "We'll leave in two minutes." And he disappeared in the crowd.

There were festoons of Venetian lanterns, an orchestra in uniform, a buffet, a place to win a lottery, and one danced in a ballroom of the villa or outside under the trees. I sat on a bench waiting for Tempesti.

The festival was orderly, serious, and homelike. Everyone amused themselves, with the satisfaction at the same time of doing their duty. While they danced they felt they were contributing to something important. The girls wore high-heeled shoes and party dresses; the young men their most conservative ties, their whitest shirts, their shiniest brilliantine. Their gestures were contained, their gaiety dignified, as though they were engaged in pleasant labor.

Time passed, and Tempesti did not finish distributing advice, smiles, and instructions. I looked down at the city swarming with infinite lights through the whole basin, and other lights on the sea, and the sky reddening over Vesuvius like a nocturnal sunset behind the black branches of the pines.

Tempesti came to tell me that Colombi, another cabinet minister, had telephoned asking to come to Rome with us, and that as soon as he arrived we'd leave.

"I couldn't refuse him," he said. "It will be a tight squeeze, we're all three fat, but we'll get him gossiping."

Half an hour later Colombi arrived. They both belonged to the resigning government. But Colombi represented the Right, and Tempesti the Left. He was older than Tempesti, with a strong physique and a pointed nose and chin. His eyes were hidden under heavy lids, his skin was thick and wrinkled like the skin of a prehistoric lizard. He had also a lizard's mouth, thin and extremely wide, and a lizard's neck with the skin lying in folds. A strange, toneless voice came from his throat, tremulous as though it were always about to break, hoarse, and at times almost soundless, but his words were measured, carefully chosen and appropriate. I had seen him, as I'd also seen Tempesti, at yesterday's meeting at the Viminale. Both were old acquaintances of mine, and both of them, although in different ways and confronting different dangers, had been fighting for many years for freedom. When Tempesti had finally finished his audiences, his instructions and greetings, and had climbed into the automobile amid the applause, he said:

"Now we'll stop just one moment at police headquarters, and then we'll leave. . . . I've given instructions for us to have an escort. The roads aren't safe yet." In spite of last night's encounter about which I'd told him, it would have seemed more comfortable and less strange had I again trusted in the saints.

In front of police headquarters a jeep was waiting for us, full of armed men who were to accompany us. I don't know whether they were policemen or *carabinieri*. It was difficult to make out their uniforms, half Italian and half American. There were many of them and they were heavily armed, with machine guns strapped on their shoulders, pouches full of hand grenades, and steel helmets on their heads, as though they were off to war. Their leader, a sergeant with an enormous black mustache that stretched across his whole face, introduced himself to his excellency.

Everything was in order, the machinery of the state was functioning like a watch. Preceded by this armed escort, we finally departed.

I sat in the middle between the two cabinet ministers; we were really squeezed in. They immediately started to talk. Colombi had come to Naples to preside over a financial meeting, questions of the port administration, the banks, credit, and loans. Tempesti had come to take part in a popular demonstration and the festival of the party. They talked about everything: the economic recovery of the South, reclamation, agrarian reforms, local questions, eternal formulae, eternal speeches. The crisis in the government did not worry either of them, it was as if they both knew perfectly well how it would be resolved. As long as the alliance of the two great mass parties continued, a thing they never doubted, everything would be resolved in the best of ways. Basically there was only one problem, and they were completely agreed about it: to restore the authority of the state. One had to free oneself of certain anachronistic holdovers from the Resistance movement, to suppress everything that no longer fell in with the international situation, to preserve unity at all costs, in order to accomplish that necessary Restoration.

They were ready to make every concession for this, although in different degrees. Colombi talked in a lukewarm fashion of reforms. Tempesti, when it was his turn, wholeheartedly professed a reverence for the religious beliefs of his colleague. The crisis might prove useful, a good step along the road to normalcy. It didn't matter, although it was obvious, that to each it meant something different. The expression was the same and all that really mattered was that it should seem identical. Both were optimists, even about what would happen later when the power of the state was restored and normalcy attained, because each thought without saying so that he was the stronger. Their words betrayed this like conviction, categorical and openly declared by Tempesti, more hidden, hesitant, and embarrassed by Colombi, who nevertheless knew that in this game he had all the winning cards in his hand, and had a tranquil spirit, so tranquil, so candid and amused that at one point he dropped the conversation, sighed sweetly, and fell asleep.

We were driving rapidly through the night. Our jeep escort was stunting, shooting way ahead of us, and then back to trail us. In the glare of the headlights I could see their guns, their helmets, their belts, their mustaches on the Broad Highway.

Tempesti started to tell me about months he had spent in a death cell, about the hunger he had suffered in a foreign country when he had no papers, money, ration cards and no link with his comrades. These were heroic things, but now nothing but memories. Tempesti was a tough man, efficient, a machine that could not become rusted by sentimentality. He explained to me how he had nourished himself for months on seaweed and sour milk, and what was the best technique for using them, and how he had discovered a way of cooking seaweed on a stove and transforming it into croquettes.

We drove along the same road I'd covered the evening before in the opposite direction, and at a slow speed behind the truck. We had crossed the Volturno and the Garigliano, the ruins of Formia, and were approaching the fork in the road at Sparanise. I would like to

have seen the brigand's thicket again, but when we arrived at the fork
for some reason we turned onto the road that passes by Frosinone.

Tempesti knew everything, had read everything, and talked
about everything. But his passion was folk songs. He knew thousands of them by heart. He was perhaps the greatest expert on this
subject, and furthermore, since there was no language he
didn't speak perfectly, he started to sing me some very beautiful
songs of the most distant countries, in their original language.
Colombia slept, and Tempesti sang Uzbek, Tartar, Brazilian,
Afghan, Neapolitan, and Kirghiz songs, when suddenly the automobile stopped in front of an old house with its lights lit at the side
of the road. We were in the midst of a plain littered with rubble,
piles of stone, tangles of barbed wire, pieces of wood, tumble-
down signs, heaps of mines gathered from the fields, bomb craters,
holes and crosses, like an abandoned cemetery. Here and there a
few wooden shacks stood in this disorder. In the background
against the starry light of the sky stood out the rough profile of a
mountain covered with strange rocks, fissures, clefts, rents,
wounds like a beehive perforated by malignant wasps, or a huge
pile of unburied bones. We were in Cassino.

We had to put water in our radiator, and we took the chance to
get out. Colombi, waking for a moment, preferred to remain
seated and snuggled back into his corner. In the shack there was a
café and a kind of shop for gasoline and odd merchandise. In the
light of an acetylene lamp a few women were standing, wrapped
in black shawls, with frightened faces, and some mechanics in
overalls and workmen watched with mistrust the arrival of our
armed escort.

Tempesti wanted some wine, and calling the sergeant, he gen-
erously bought drinks for all the soldiers. They must have been
half frozen in the uncovered jeep. While they were drinking, the
cabinet minister quickly looked around the circle of that shapeless
land that was no longer even a countryside but a poisoned funereal expanse, where even the trees seemed dead, and he assured
me that even though nothing much had been done about it yet,
the reconstruction would soon be proceeding according to plan.

When we were back in the machine, and our warriors, now perhaps a bit warmed up, were shooting forward and backward like arrows, I asked Tempesti to sing again. He sang some Czechoslovak, Basque, Sicilian, and Hungarian songs, but I noticed that his voice was weakening little by little. He was a man of steel, and never slept; but this time he was caught by sleep, stopped singing, and dropped off suddenly, with his fists closed, like a child.

While our two machines continued their course, regular and swift, the two cabinet ministers slept, Colombi at my right, Tempesti on my left. The bumps on the road shook them like two sacks, pushing them inch by inch toward me from both sides; we had passed Frosinone, we had passed Ferentino; first the one man and then the other gently rested his head on my shoulder. The two cabinet ministers slept with deep and infantile breathing; full of peace, perhaps they were dreaming too, because every now and then they mumbled incomprehensible words.

Squeezed between them, holding their weight and their abandoned heads, I didn't dare to move, nor to disturb their rest, and I wasn't able to sleep.

The undulating landscape stretched out under the lazy smoke of light mists, in the motionless enchantment of the moon. Except for that absurd heap of armed men in front of me, rigid on their seats like insects, night was everywhere around me, profound silence, and sleep. The air was still, without a feather of wind, and not a leaf on the olive trees moved, nor a blade of grass in the fields. The black farmhouses scattered over the countryside merged with the ancient and modern ruins. The darkened villages seemed uninhabited except for the green light of a cat's eye that fixed on us for an instant and then disappeared in the shadow as we passed. The solitude spread mutely to the farthest edge of the horizon, beyond the distant profile of the hills, lying on their backs like immense human beings under the impassible sky, and even farther, as far as thought could reach, to the forests of brigands, the populous cities, the sealed hearts of men.

A mortal drowsiness seemed to descend over the whole earth from the tenuous, silver threads of the delicate, round moon, making the fields seem alien, the streets, paths, and homes desolate; the woods, meadows, rocks, and mountain brooks wild, and the bizarre shadows foreign; it silenced voices at the lips and transformed thoughts into confused webs or the gathering fog.

In this infinite expanse, unfeeling and forgetful, in this motionless mysterious land, concealed in sleep or in death, I seemed to be the only one to keep vigil, the only one moving and remembering. I strangely imagined that this drive would never be finished, but that it would continue forever and ever without end, that no day would follow this night, but that through the infinite, immutable unrolling of time I would be carried along this road, climbing and descending, squeezed between the cordial and tranquil weight of these overconfident men, escorted by that clumsy war machine shining with guns, driving swiftly and alone under the cold look of the moon. It seemed to me that the entire world, people and things, had disappeared forever in that sleep and that I alone was preserving their existence, and holding them in my memory. Everything was sunk in that motionless shadow, all I had left behind me, and all I would never find ahead of me again: the still face of Luca, the volcanic light of Porta Capuana, the maiden who was sawed in two and reunited again by a miracle of art, the overturned room, the beggars and their king, the brigand hidden in the grass like a serpent, the protecting saints, the solitary Premier, the Luigini, the Contadini, the newspaper, Fede and Roselli, Casorin and Moneta, and the rats of La Garbatella, and Marco, Giacinto, and Teresa; the dead man of the stairway with his dog; the shining of the sun and the slow fall of the rains; the secret interrelations of things, and love, and the courage of living, on the face of men.

But the night already opened to the lights in the first streets, to familiar places, the twisted hangars of Centocelle, and the sky was illuminated by the reflections of the approaching city. I remembered the watch in my pocket and looked at the time. It was almost three in the morning, too late for the newspaper. Presently I saw the first houses of Tor Pignattara, the black arches of the aqueducts, the long streets of the suburbs. At Porta Maggiore I woke the two cabinet ministers. They rubbed their eyes with childish motions.

"We've arrived," they exclaimed. "What a lovely trip, without any troubles."

Following the natural precedence of their authority, we first took Tempesti home to the end of the Via Nomentana; then, speeding crazily through the deserted streets, we took Colombi to the Parioli quarter. Here I stayed alone in the machine to be taken home. I didn't know what orders the guards had received, but the jeep had continued to follow us like an impassable shadow through the whole city, and it still followed me now as though it were attached with a rope, ten feet behind, without losing a yard, with the refulgent machine guns and hand grenades, from street to street into the center of Rome, like an obsession. When we finally came to a halt, the mustachioed sergeant presented himself and gave me a military salute. I thanked him in relief and told him he could go back to his barracks.

I was left alone, holding my briefcase in my hand, on the square in front of my palace. The huge city moon, high in the heaven, was bending like a mother over the architecture. The pavement shone clearly in this light, spread with silver. On one side, the oblique shadow of the church threw the baroque profile of the saints on the ground. A night watchman dressed in black went along the white sidewalk like a beetle. The facade of the palace was invested by the moon that revealed each cornice, each wrinkle, each stone. Under the balcony the angel-woman looked down through her lowered lids from her hiding place of bats.

I crossed the threshold through the columns, went through the vestibule, and slowly climbed the great stairway in the midst of the statues. I came to the top and went into my home.

From the window I heard the striking of the hours from a distant bell tower. I looked out. The city was spread below me, and was living, and breathing in the vagueness of the moon with the indistinct murmur of a forest of ancient trees, hardly stirred by the light breath of the wind. I stopped to listen, bending over intently, to that faintly murmuring silence, and I heard from the distance — was it from the streets or from the depths of memory? — the mysterious sound of the night, the roaring of lions, like the echo of the sea in an abandoned shell.

ABOUT THE BOOK

The text for this book was composed by Steerforth Press using a digital version of Electra, a typeface designed in 1935 by William Addison Dwiggins. Electra has been a standard book typeface since its release because of its evenness of design and high legibility. All Steerforth books are printed on acid free papers and this book was bound by BookCrafters of Chelsea, Michigan.

Other Steerforth Italia Books

OPEN CITY
Seven Writers in Postwar Rome
Edited by William Weaver

THE WOMAN OF ROME
by Alberto Moravia

A WEAKNESS FOR ALMOST EVERYTHING:
Notes on Life, Gastronomy and Travel
by Aldo Buzzi (AVAILABLE FALL, 1999)

JOURNEY TO THE LAND OF THE FLIES:
And Other Travels
by Aldo Buzzi (AVAILABLE FALL, 1999)

THE CONFORMIST
by Alberto Moravia (AVAILABLE FALL, 1999)

LIFE OF MORAVIA
by Alberto Moravia and Alain Elkann (AVAILABLE WINTER, 2000)

TWO WOMEN
by Alberto Moravia (AVAILABLE WINTER, 2000)

ROME AND A VILLA
by Eleanor Clark (AVAILABLE WINTER, 2000)

LITTLE NOVELS OF SICILY
by Giovanni Verga (AVAILABLE WINTER, 2000)

THE TIME OF INDIFFERENCE
by Alberto Moravia (AVAILABLE SPRING, 2000)